JAMIE HOLLAND was born in Salisbury in 1970. He studied history at Durham University, and has subsequently worked for several London publishing houses. He is married and lives in London.

By the same author

One Thing Leads to Another

Jamie Holland

AN ALMOST
PERFECT MOON

HarperCollins*Publishers*

HarperCollins*Publishers*
77–85 Fulham Palace Road,
Hammersmith, London W6 8JB

www.**fire** and**water**.com

This paperback original published by
HarperCollins*Publishers* 2001

1 3 5 7 9 8 6 4 2

This novel is entirely a work of fiction. The names,
characters and incidents portrayed in it are the work
of the author's imagination. Any resemblance to actual
persons, living or dead, events or localities
is entirely coincidental.

A catalogue record for this book
is available from the British Library

ISBN 0 00 651416 2

Typeset in Minion by Palimpsest Book Production Limited,
Polmont, Stirlingshire

Printed in Great Britain by
Omnia Books Limited, Glasgow

Acknowledgements

I would like to thank Susan Watt, Patrick Walsh, Peta Nightingale and Harrie Evans for all their help and good advice; Katie Espiner, Tilly Ware, Lee Motley, Fiona McIntosh and the Sales Team, and everyone else at HarperCollins who has worked on or helped with the book; Peter Bell and Charlie Bryant for talking me through Ben's job; and Stu and Bella Mills for allowing me to use their house and village in Northumberland as the basis for Flin and Tiffany's new home. But I owe the greatest debt of thanks to Rachel, for her constant support, patience and good ideas.

For Pip

The indefatigable pursuit of an unattainable Perfection, even though it consist in nothing more than the pounding of an old piano, alone gives a meaning to our life on this unavailing star.

Logan Pearsall Smith, *Afterthoughts*

contents

part one – *spring*

CHAPTER ONE

Sunday and raining

Outside the rain continued, putting paid to the planned walk on Wandsworth Common. Lucie had delivered the kind of high-class lunch her husband and close friends had come to expect. All the same, at seven-and-a-half months pregnant, she had warned all of them this was going to be the last she would be cooking at her and Ben's house for quite some time. In the short-term future, if anyone was expecting to be fed on a Sunday, Ben would have to be the cook. Her husband had shrugged and the others had agreed that in that case, they should definitely make the most of the spread before them.

Now, having eaten and drunk too much, the small party slumped in front of the television, the fire gently flickering in its even, gas-infused way. They were watching *Rebecca*.

'Oh my God, it's burning,' Tiffany exclaimed as Maxim de Winter hurtled down the drive towards Manderley. Flin was half reading the paper, and Harry seemed mildly distracted, but the other three were content to watch the final events of the film unfolding on the screen.

Ben was the first to pass judgement, as the final image – a single R surrounded by flames – melted from the screen.

'I'm sorry, darling, but that was bollocks.' He stretched his arms above him and yawned.

'It's a great film,' sighed Lucie. 'Don't be such a bloody heathen. Didn't have enough guns for you, I suppose.' She slapped him lightly on his shoulder and dug one of her legs into him. Since cooking the lunch, she'd refused to lift another finger; it was her prerogative to sit down and gently soothe her swollen, semi-spherical belly.

'Well, I thought it was great. Really romantic,' put in Tiffany.

'Although I have to admit,' added Lucie, 'theirs was a totally unconvincing relationship. Never would have worked. There's too much stacked against them. He's dominating and dismissive and she's wet. Not to mention the manslaughter bit. Because that's what it was, even if she *was* dying and he was driven to it. It's so sordid.'

Ben leant over and kissed her very delicately on the cheek. 'Then we're obviously doomed, darling: you're dominating and I'm meek.'

'Oh, be quiet,' retorted Lucie, prodding him in the ribs.

'See? I rest my case,' he grinned.

But Tiffany, who hadn't yet married Flin, said, 'Okay, so what do *you* think makes a good marriage then? You guys always seem so great together. What's the secret?'

'An adoring husband,' said Ben.

Ignoring him, and deciding to take the question seriously, Lucie replied, 'I don't know really – I suppose you've got to be best of pals. Shared interests. You've got to like each other's friends. That's important.' She looked thoughtfully in the direction of the bookcase. 'Fancy each other, of course.'

'No problem there,' said Ben, 'I've always fancied the pants off Luce.'

Finally giving her husband a hint of a smirk, Lucie added, 'You've just got to *know* you're right together. Deep down. But you guys might as well be married. You live together just like we do. What's the secret for you? Much the same I expect.'

4

'I don't know, honey, what's the secret?' asked Tiffany, craning round to look at Flin.

'What you have to realize,' said Flin, half-heartedly covering Tiffany's ears, 'is that as well as being a gorgeous Aussie babe, Tiff is one of the most laid-back, easy-going people I know.'

'And I like pubs a lot,' added Tiffany, 'which is important to you, isn't it, honey?'

'And you like pubs.'

'And beer,' said Lucie, 'which considering you're so tiny, I've always found extraordinary.'

Tiffany shrugged, then laughed. Flin looked at her, blonde hair dishevelled, and outsize woollen jumper stretched over knees tucked under her chin. He probably loved her more now than ever. He was a lucky man.

Ben decided to provoke Lucie. 'Still,' he began, glancing conspiratorially at Flin, 'I think you might be wrong about Laurence Olivier and Joan Fontaine. I reckon they'd have worked out. After all she's marrying pots of cash and he's got a young wife to have great sex with. Anyway, I want to know what the film expert thinks,' said Ben. 'Come on, Flin.'

'Oh, I'm with you all the way,' agreed Flin. 'Great sex and loads of money can overcome all sorts of other problems, I'm sure.'

'I know what you're doing, you two, and it isn't going to work.' Lucie folded her arms adamantly.

Tiffany laughed. 'If only you were rich, Flin.'

'If only I were,' said Flin, stretching, 'but I'm not sure I really see the point of getting married. And if Tiff ever does insist on it, I think we should go and do it on a beach in Barbados or something. I've seen so many people get hitched and everyone, without exception, seems to become totally over-stressed and argumentative over it. Seems a lot more hassle than it's worth.'

'That's why it's good for any long-lasting relationship,' said Lucie. 'It's a test. If you still want to be married after an engagement full of wedding organization and arguments with future in-laws, you know you're definitely made for each other.'

'Fair comment,' admitted Flin.

'I quite like the sound of Barbados,' said Tiffany, turning round to see Flin's reaction.

'OK, let's go next week,' he grinned. 'Can everyone here make it?'

'Great. I'm up for it,' said Ben, holding up his hand, classroom-style. But Lucie hadn't finished on the important matter of the de Winters' future.

'I still think Laurence and Joan wouldn't work. It would develop into a miserable loveless marriage. Really, they're two completely different people – different ages, different classes, which was important then, and for most of the film he treats her more like a daughter. He was certainly old enough to be her dad. And he never once called her by her name. By the end of the film you still don't know what her bloody name is! I mean, what kind of a marriage is that?'

'What about "opposites attract"?' suggested Ben. 'And "darling", he did call her "darling".'

'Yes, but in a patronizing way. He was *always* patronizing her. I'd have slugged him one, personally, but she was so bloody feeble and infatuated she put up with it.'

There was slight pause after Lucie finished her speech, and she interpreted this as confirmation of an argument won.

'Well, if that's how you feel,' said Ben, yawning again, 'at least there's no chance of anyone accusing *you* of being wet, hey baby?'

'Lucie, were you always this strident, or is it a side-effect of being pregnant?' asked Flin, not looking up from his paper.

Lucie threw a cushion at him, grinned sheepishly, and then said, 'Well, what do you think, Harry? I'm right, aren't I?'

Harry, miles away, had only been half listening. Sitting on the wing-backed armchair (his favourite spot whenever he came over), a leg dangling over one of the arms, he was staring up at the bookcases, filled with Lucie's creased-arched paperbacks.

'I'm afraid I'm with Luce on this one,' he said at length, 'they didn't seem to have a lot in common.'

'Thank you, Harry,' said Lucie triumphantly.

'Yes, but come on, Harry, look at Julia. She's absolutely gorgeous. You can't say that doesn't help.'

'Sure it does, but is it enough?'

'Looking at those breasts and amazing legs of hers, I'd have thought so, yes.'

'Ben!' Lucie glared at him.

'Darling, that's nothing against you: I think you're perfect, but from Harry's point of view, Julia is a very attractive proposition.'

'And she's pretty well-off, isn't she, Harry?' added Flin.

Harry nodded wistfully.

'So what's the problem?' asked Ben.

'There isn't one, I suppose. I don't know. It's just ... well, I mean, you lot – you're all so happy with each other. Ben and Lucie, you're married; Flin and Tiffany, you might as well be. But I can't see myself ever marrying Julia somehow.'

'Why not?' asked Ben. 'You get on really well. She makes you laugh – you said so; she's stunning; for some reason she seems to adore you. Sounds to me like you've got it made. Anyway, I thought it was all going well and that you were really keen. Has something happened?'

'No, no, nothing. Nothing at all. Forget it.'

'Harry, I do think you're jumping the gun a bit,' put in Lucie. 'I mean, you've only been going out a couple of months. Stop comparing yourself with other people and see how it goes.'

'Yeah, you're right.' He force-smiled at them: Ben and Lucie, looking so *comfortable* on the sofa, despite Lucie's pregnant awkwardness; and Flin and Tiffany, Flin's hand loosely draped over Tiffany's shoulder while he read the paper, she sipping more red wine, the very picture of contented togetherness. It had been a mistake to mention his doubts about Julia. It was obvious what they would all say.

Ben, eyeing his friend, decided on this occasion to let it go. He'd call him up, arrange to go for a drink after football on Tuesday, and get to the bottom of it then.

Flin meanwhile had gone back to his paper and was leafing through the previous day's property section, when something caught his eye.

'Tiff, look at this,' he said, slapping the paper down in front of her.

'What?' asked Ben.

'A house,' Flin told him. 'A bloody big house – four bedrooms, a couple of old outbuildings and seven acres of land. Jesus, I must be mad.'

'And?'

'And look at the price. It's worth less than our flat.'

Tiffany passed the advert to Ben.

'I mean, when I see that,' Flin continued, 'I'm just *so* glad I live in a tiny two-bedroom flat on a seedy street in the arse-end of Hammersmith. Jesus. Makes me feel really quite ill. What the hell are we all doing here, for God's sake?'

'Yeah, but, Flin, who the hell wants to live in Northumberland?' said Ben, passing the paper round to Lucie and then Harry. 'I mean, it's so *bleak*. And nothing to do unless you've a bit of a thing for sheep.'

'I wouldn't mind,' said Tiffany. 'I think it looks nice.'

'You like sheep, do you?' asked Harry, handing the folded paper back to Flin. 'It's cheap for a reason.'

Flin looked at it again. The house seemed to be nestled in a small valley, although behind it, to emphasize the land that came with it, could be seen the empty Northumbrian uplands. Beautiful, but Ben was right – not exactly practical.

'You're right,' he said at last, 'but to think I *could* own that when I live in a glorified shoe-box still makes me feel a bit depressed.

I mean, just look at all that space. The fresh air, no traffic jams, no graffiti, and yes, just the melodic sound of contented sheep bleating from the upper pastures. Maybe that's the way forward. Get out of the madness of London and wind down for a while. Lead the simple life. Destress. It'd be great, wouldn't it? I'd get out of bed and be greeted by a vista of uninterrupted fields, instead of a mirror image of my own flat on the other side of the road. No Underground to scrabble through. No feeling grimy and soiled as soon as I got to work. Just clean, wholesome living.'

'Wholesome but piss-boring,' added Ben.

Flin looked at the picture once more. 'Yeah, maybe,' he said. 'It was just a thought.'

As Harry left Ben and Lucie's that afternoon, he was pleasantly surprised to note how the March days were slowly lengthening. He looked up to see a suggestion of clear blue above the Common. The ground was wet underfoot, but the air felt dry and bracing after an afternoon spent surfeiting on food, drink and warmth. Feeling bloated, Harry decided to walk home. Anyway, he could never be bothered to wait for buses. Much better to be on the go.

The walk back to Brixton took half an hour. Across the quiet, wide-open stretch of Clapham Common, then an amble down the genteel calmness of Abbeville Road. The boundary between Clapham and Brixton was unmistakable. As he turned onto Acre Lane, he was greeted with immediate bustle and noise. Not far away, sirens cut across the evening air; then a shiny four-by-four with blacked-out windows thudded past him, vibrating music pulsing tremors along the road.

As Harry arrived outside his flat, he made his normal inspection of his beloved old Citroën, but, as usual, it was fine, not a blemish to be seen. His fellow Brixtonians seemed to respect rather than resent it. He sighed, feeling uncharacteristically low. On the cusp of thirty and a life that felt suddenly empty.

He stomped up the stairs. In his kitchen, a faint odour of cleansing fluid still lingered around the sink and surfaces. His answerphone, neatly attached to the wall by the door, was flashing the message light. Underneath, lying equally neatly on top of each other, were two bills, two more final warnings. Harry cursed himself. He'd intended to pay those first thing on Saturday morning but had forgotten. That meant he'd have to phone the following morning and explain that he would pay them that day, as he was bound to have already exceeded his seven days' grace. This was the trouble with being a self-employed artist: irregular pay which encouraged irregular payment of bills. Still, nothing he could do about it on a Sunday night. He pressed the answer machine.

'Oh, Harry, it's your father here. Need to come down to town this week and was hoping to bunk up at your place. How about tomorrow? Bye.' His father often did that, always 'bunking up' or 'bunking down', armed with his old leather overnight bag and battered briefcase. Harry smiled; he loved the fact his father felt he could. The second was from Julia, her smooth Galaxy bar tones filtering their way through the distortions of the machine.

'Hi, Harry. It's Julia. Just wondering when I'm going to see you next. I loved last night. Call me.'

He would, but later. In his bathroom he undressed and ran a bath. Pausing in front of the mirror, he realized how tired he looked. It wasn't surprising. There were just a few grey hairs in the otherwise light, soft mop that shaggily covered his head, and the beginning of a wrinkle at one side of his mouth; curiously the other remained unblemished. Nearly thirty and yet his life still felt utterly directionless. His other friends seemed to be leaving him behind. Most were now married or living with their partners. Ben and Lucie were about to have a child. His parents had been about his present age when he'd been born, but there still seemed an enormous gulf between his present situation and settling down.

He wished he could; he felt ready to in his heart, but he just didn't seem able to find the right person to do it with.

What *was* the matter with him? Was he so obsessed with finding his one true love that, like Mrs Danvers, he would slowly go mad, eventually setting fire to his flat and himself? He plodded out of the bathroom, his towel wrapped around him, put on some cheering music, and sighed once more, this time a little more heavily. At least he had his flat. That was something. Just his and no one else's. He could be as selfish as he wanted without it affecting anyone. Slumping down on the sofa, he looked about him. His taste, his choice; the television positioned in the corner, or the painting by his mother next to the door, simply because he wanted them there. There was no one to compromise with over what video to watch or when to have a bath. No one to stop him farting if he felt like farting. He could eat what he wanted to eat, and not be chided for putting too much butter on his toast like Lucie did with Ben. And no matter how envious he might feel of his friend's advanced situation in life, once the baby was born, Ben's life would not be the same. Being an artist also meant he was his own man, with no one telling him what to do. Unlike Julia, or his other friends, he wasn't a slave to some higher being. Really, he had a lot to be thankful for.

The rain had finally given way to a half-clear sky as the blanket of cloud slowly disappeared. But as they left Ben and Lucie's, Flin barely noticed the upturn in the weather; his mind was preoccupied with a different matter entirely.

'You know what, Tiff? Perhaps we should leave London,' he suggested, in what he hoped was an offhand, easy-come, easy-go kind of manner.

'OK,' said Tiffany, as the bus pulled up on St John's Road.

'Well, perhaps we should,' said Flin again, his excitement level rising.

'When?' said Tiffany casually as she stepped up to the driver. 'Two to Hammersmith, please.'

She took the tickets and they squeezed themselves into one of the seats, which was far too small for Flin's six-foot-something frame. His knees were wedged against the carpet-backed seat in front, and even Tiffany, who was tiny, looked cramped.

'Are you serious?' said Flin.

'I don't know. Are you?'

'I'm not sure. Am I?'

Tiffany laughed. 'You're so funny. Flin, baby, I don't know. I mean, what would we do?'

'I'm sure we could find work. There must be PR companies worth working for outside London.'

'Well, if we can both find something to do, then we could think about it. I wouldn't mind moving out to the country. Don't forget, hon, I'm a country girl. I'd never been anywhere a quarter of the size of London before I came here.'

'It would be good though, wouldn't it?' continued Flin. 'We could get a dog, have long walks, it'd be really quiet. We'd probably become regulars in some flagstoned local boozer. And just think – no more of this: taking hours to get anywhere. If we wanted to go to the beach, we could just go; we wouldn't have to fight our way through one traffic jam after another, and walk past endless amounts of litter and graffiti.'

She looked up at him and grinned. 'Darling, I'll go anywhere with you. You know that.'

'Be serious,' said Flin, prodding her.

'I am! Ouch! Get off me!'

'No, you're not.'

'Honestly, honey, I think it's great that you see a house for sale in the newspaper and then decide we should throw in our jobs and move out.' Flin saw she was trying to keep a straight face. 'I mean, I think we should put our flat on the market straight away. Nothing like acting on a whim. Probably best just to be spontaneous. In fact, first thing tomorrow, let's put an offer in on that house in Northumberland.'

'That's not funny,' said Flin.

'I think it's hilarious.'

Both began giggling.

'Tiff,' he said, gasping, 'share my vision.'

At which she started laughing again so hard, she could no longer speak. Eventually, she recovered. 'Look, stop making me laugh. Everyone's staring at us.'

'I still think we should think about it though,' said Flin.

Tiffany rested her head against his shoulder. 'But seriously, Flin, you're always having these plans. Don't you remember last year you were dead set on us moving to France?'

'It was a great idea at the time.'

'Except that neither of us speaks French and we wouldn't be able to get any work. And then you wanted to buy a houseboat.'

'But that would have been great too.'

'Yes, but you couldn't talk about anything else for two weeks, then you realized it was actually going to cost a fortune and that was the last I heard of it. Then there was the time when we were going to take out loans and learn to fly. And then that was shelved and the money was going to fund us for a year of travelling the world. I love your enthusiasm for things, darling, but I can't take this latest "vision" seriously because it'll probably be dead in the water by next Thursday.'

'But it's only ever been lack of money that's prevented us doing this stuff. If we can get jobs and so on, it might really be possible. And you have to admit, it would be good to have a little bit of land, wouldn't it?'

Tiffany said nothing.

Flin continued. 'That house we saw had a couple of fields, didn't it? Just think, we could have a few sheep, get some geese and chickens and grow things. We could eat lots of really fresh, wholesome food. It'd be brilliant, wouldn't it?' Flin kissed the top of her head.

'Brilliant,' she said, and closed her eyes.

But Tiffany was probably right. Did he mean it? He simply wasn't sure. In theory, the idea of moving out and pursuing the pastoral dream definitely fired him. But in practice ... well, it *was* a big, big step.

'You know what?' Flin said to Tiffany a while later. The telly was on and she was snuggled up against him on the sofa.

'What?' said Tiffany, absent-mindedly tickling his arm.

'I think I've just eradicated all the arguments I used to use for staying in London.'

'Still on this one then. And what are those?'

'Well,' said Flin, counting them off on his fingers, 'firstly I always used to say all my friends were here. But they're not really. Not any more. Jessica's in New York, Geordie's in Wiltshire, Josh is in Sydney. That's three really good mates who've left me behind. Secondly, I know film PR is fun and glamorous, but I have always said it was a young person's job, and not for life.' He paused. 'Perhaps I *should* leave now. Sort of quit while I'm ahead.'

'You do love your job, darling, you know you do.'

'Well, yes and no, actually. I mean, having to deal with all those egos gets a bit wearing. And after all, it's just promoting a product really. I'm sure there're other equally interesting products to promote outside London.'

Tiffany put her arms around him and gave him a quick squeeze.

'And,' he continued, 'I'm thirty now. If I'm ever going to take a risk in life, now's the time to do it. No more of this complacency. It's time we showed a bit of *carpe diem*, or whatever.' Tiffany continued watching the TV.

'You'd be able to get work in TV research outside of town, wouldn't you?' he continued.

'Well, maybe. There's the BBC in Bristol, and there are other production companies in all the major cities. I suppose, in theory, it might be possible.'

'Exactly, it would be a doddle. And I'm sure with my experience I could get another job in PR without too much problem.'

'Well, honey, there's only one way to find out.'

'Exactly.' He knew he was really preaching to himself, not her. Excitement lit up his face. 'Come on, Tiff, let's just do it. Bloody well take the plunge and live a little. Really, what have we got to lose? We're still young, no kids – who cares if it all goes pear-shaped?'

'Whatever, honey.'

'I know what you're thinking, but it would be great – a new life.' He kissed her.

Tiffany turned back to the television.

'OK,' said Flin, wanting to seem as though he were compromising, 'but look at this place.' He waved a hand around their little sitting room. 'It's great and everything, and all ours, I know, but it *is* a shoe-box. In the country we could have something probably four times the size.' He looked about him. With their two sofas, laundry-box coffee table and bookshelves, the room did look particularly narrow. 'Just think of all that space. It'd be so great. A proper, grown-up house.'

'Where's that?' asked Tiffany, pointing to the TV. Jerome Flynn was gallivanting around the countryside in a four-wheel drive saving an otter.

'Northumberland,' said Flin.

'Wasn't that house you were looking at earlier in Northumberland?'

It was true, it was. Perhaps someone was trying to tell him something. He hadn't thought about that part of the world for ages, then suddenly two pointers in one afternoon. But the north-east did hold some unique possibilities. He knew Newcastle from his university days nearby at Durham, and he liked it too, from what he remembered. A big urban centre –

lots of shops, cinemas and nice places to eat, so they wouldn't feel too cut off. And surely they had PR companies up there? There was certainly television. Then there was Northumbria itself: the long beaches with the castles of Bamburgh and Dunstanburgh, romantic cliff-top outposts that he remembered captivated him so much when he'd holidayed there as a child. There was Hadrian's Wall and dry-stone walls and sheep and lots and lots of space. How could he possibly get stuck in a traffic jam up there? Most importantly, it was cheap. Or, at least, cheap compared to Wiltshire: he'd love to go back there, to be near his family and his oldest friend, Geordie. It would be wonderful to live the rest of his days in the countryside where he'd grown up and been so happy. But what could he do there? Salisbury was hardly a heaving urban epicentre. It was also pricey – he always looked at the property prices in the *Salisbury Journal* and it never failed to dishearten him. No, if he wanted space, *real* space, a house with a bit of land, heading up north was the better option.

They went to bed quite early that night. Flin was already propped up rereading *The Darling Buds of May* when Tiffany joined him from the bathroom. Seeing her petite frame never ceased to thrill him. Nimbly tucking herself into bed, she put her arm over him and he felt her breasts, face and hair nestling on his chest, and one of her legs wrapping itself around his.

'Thank you,' he said to her.

'For what?'

But he didn't answer, just kissed her instead. He and Tiffany just felt so *right*. He knew what Lucie had meant when she'd said that about her and Ben. He and Tiff'd been together four years now. He remembered when he realized she fancied him, and how surprised and delighted he'd been. She had been working for him, temping on her first job since arriving in London. On her last day, he'd overheard her talking about him to one of the other girls in

16

the office. That night, after work, they'd gone to the pub, drunk too much and ended up in bed together. Since then, they'd hardly spent a day apart. No one understood him better, or made him laugh more. He knew he had a tendency to complicate his life; she was the most patient and uncomplicated person he knew. He was certain she would be prepared to move to the country; maybe it was her Australian blood, but she loved the outdoors. When they'd first started going out, it was she as much as he who'd suggested they go off camping at weekends and backpacking for their summer holidays.

Flin had always thought he'd move to the country someday, but it had been something one did when one was older, much older, so that he'd carried on living and working in London without really pausing to consider whether the rural idyll was actually a possibility. But now that time had arrived, sudden and unexpected – prompted by the mere reading of a news-paper! – and, really, there was nothing to stop them. He'd been subconsciously using his fears and the potential risks of the Big Move as a reason for staying put; but by playing safe he would become increasingly ensnared by the London tentacles: he'd never be able to leave his job because, before he knew it, he'd be past his sell-by date for anything else. No one else would want him. A sobering thought. Clearly, he *had* to take the plunge now, break free from the rope that was pulling him ever more firmly towards a lifetime in the city. Be bold, make the move while they were still young, and the pastoral dream could be theirs. He felt excited – and nervous – but determined to see it through. At least, he hoped he'd still feel the same way in a week's time.

Apart from trips to the loo, Lucie remained true to her word, and didn't lift another finger that day. Harry and Ben had done most of the clearing up earlier, but once everyone had left, Ben finished the job and then brought his wife more tea.

'How are you feeling, my love?' he asked her, running his hands through her short, thick hair.

'Fine. I think. Tired. You can carry on doing that though.'

'All right, but my arm's beginning to ache.'

'A bit longer. I'm definitely highly emotional and need lots of care and attention.'

Ben sat down again on the sofa, resuming his earlier position with Lucie's legs straddled across him. He was very happy with their house. Three bedrooms, reasonable-sized kitchen at the back and a bit of a garden, half grass, half paved. Lucie, who had an eye for style, had decorated it beautifully – everyone said so, including Harry, whose opinion as an artist they valued. They'd filled it with some old pieces of furniture stolen from her mother, but newer stuff too – such as the large Indian table and dresser, and the kind of sofa that encouraged deep-seated comfort. There was an abundance of cushions. It was the home of a young couple whose tastes had merged and who were doing well in the world.

He glanced at Lucie. He felt so proud of her. She was such a marvel, so wonderfully pretty and funny. And brave to be bearing the pregnancy with such calmness. He worried for her though. She always said she wasn't pushing herself too hard, but he never quite believed her. It was all very well Harry accusing him of being a control freak, but he just wanted to make sure nothing went wrong. He wanted his baby, his family and the family to come, to be perfect. Sometimes he worried something terrible would happen and Lucie might be torn from him. It didn't bear thinking about, he loved her so much. And the thought of having to put up with what his father had had to: four boys to rear almost entirely on his own – well, it would be awful, terrible, unbearable. His father, just past retirement age but still forced to work, had looked so old last time Ben had paid him a visit. He'd always looked older than he was, the strain of looking after his sons and working long hours having taken its toll at an early stage, but even so ... It wasn't surprising his dad had never remarried: he'd never had the time to meet anyone else.

Lucie too had lost a parent: her father had been killed when she was just two. It had been a bond between them from the outset. But her father died flying a helicopter and Lucie was able to grow up proud of the handsome, heroic figure in the photo frame. Ben kept no picture of his mother. After she'd left them, she was simply never mentioned again. Sometimes it was as though she'd never existed at all.

Ben had never understood her desertion. What had they done to deserve such an unnatural act? Aunts and family friends were no substitute. Ben was brought up hearing his father yell at his older brothers Stephen, Matthew and Andrew as they found themselves in one sort of trouble after another. Gradually, they wore him down: by the time Andrew had dropped out of school, his father had long since given up trying to control them.

Ben was different. From an early age he'd recognized that the way to escape this oppressive family life was to keep his nose to the ground and work hard. His brothers helped with this. All of them were big; nobody messed with the Armstrong boys, so their little brother evaded the normal bullying meted out to swots. It was the one thing for which he would always owe them. By the time they'd all left school he was big enough to look after himself. At fifteen he was six feet tall and shaving every day, and no one touched him. He was left to study as hard as he liked, and it soon paid off. The first of the brothers to get any O-levels, he stunned the rest of the family by managing ten straight As. From then on university was just a formality. None the less, the day he'd won a place at Cambridge to read economics had been the best of his life. His ticket to freedom.

'I wonder if the little thing will have any hair to start off with,' said Lucie, suddenly opening her eyes.

'I don't know. At least we know what colour it'll be.'

'Worried I've been with the postman?'

Ben laughed. 'If it's not very dark indeed, you'll be in big trouble.' He rubbed her tummy gently. This was what he'd been looking forward to ever since they'd married: a son or daughter, so he'd have his own proper family. Just six weeks to go. He couldn't wait. This was what he worked so hard for. He wasn't going to make the same mistakes his father had. He would always be able to provide for his family. Lucie would be effectively retiring in a few weeks' time – he now earned enough for her to extend her maternity leave indefinitely if she so wished, and still put money aside for the future. Their child would always have a parent at home. Ben glanced around the room. Life was pretty good. Upstairs he'd carefully decorated the nursery – yellow, because he felt it was good for boys and girls, and he'd also lined the room with a frieze and a mobile of wooden parrots. It was the only yellow Lucie had allowed in the house – elsewhere, she'd firmly banned it as being 'too early nineties'.

'But I like yellow,' Ben told her, 'it's cheerful.'

'But, darling, everyone has yellow. It's so *faux.*' Ben bowed to her better judgement. After all, she knew much more about style and current trends than he did – as she should, the number of magazines she subscribed to.

Later, as they lay in bed, Ben said to her, 'So what d'you think is Harry's problem with Julia?'

Lucie put down her magazine, paused and then turned to him. 'Harry's a romantic, darling. But I also think he's terrified of committing to anyone other than his mythical perfect person. And I'm not sure she exists.'

'Maybe.'

'Perhaps he's right, and Julia isn't the one for him, but all I'm hearing is how wonderful she is. I don't really understand his problem. And anyway, I thought all men liked big tits.'

'Not at all. We don't all adhere to men's magazine ideology. And anyway, I love you and yours aren't exactly huge, are they?'

'Ben, I feel *so* flattered.' She laughed. 'But I do think Harry should give Julia a bit of a chance. He wants too much – no couple are going to be in perfect unison all the time, but he just won't accept that.'

'It's his mum and dad,' Ben told her. 'Perhaps we're at an advantage – we've got no standards to judge marriage by, but he's got his brilliant parents, still happy together after thirty-five years. Harry says they even still sleep together, and his dad's now seventy.'

'Well, I wouldn't worry too much about Harry. We're going to have more than enough to think about in a few weeks – I want you to concentrate your energies on us.' She kissed him, and turned off the light.

CHAPTER TWO

Harry faces a conundrum

The following morning Harry started up his Citroën and headed back towards Wandsworth. That was the good thing about this particular job: it was fairly close by and there were no parking restrictions on the road outside. To avoid using the Underground, with its cattle trucks of commuters and dilapidated escalators, Harry drove wherever possible.

He was enjoying this current project, a mural for a middle-aged couple's kitchen. As usual he rang on the bell, got no answer, and then let himself in. Ian and Anna both left for work long before Harry even thought about opening his paints, and usually he finished long (he suspected) before they returned. Little notes would be left for him, words of encouragement, or a sudden change of heart, and would he mind terribly, if it was not too much of a pain, just adding another bit to the scene? On two occasions they had left him photos of buildings or sights they wanted incorporated. Harry didn't mind. After all, he was there to paint what they wanted. That was the whole point of his murals: to realize his clients' dreams. He would make suggestions, talk through ideas, and provide sketches, helping the clients crystallize whatever it was they had in mind. In this case, Ian and Anna had been quite certain they wanted a river scene running all the way round the kitchen between work-surface and overhead cupboards, with images of their favourite parts of the countryside as background. Since he had been a comparatively young child, Harry had nursed a love for and fascination with architecture. From the Suffolk churches and grand houses in and around the area where he grew up, to the medieval castles discovered with glee on family holidays, Harry's taste had always been broad and varied. But as he grew older, read, learnt and saw more, so he developed a love of classicism. William Kent, Capability Brown, and Vanbrugh were his heroes; Fragonard, Watteau and Boucher his artistic inspiration. Much of his work reflected this, his skills honed by a year at art college. After leaving Cambridge he'd shelved any ideas he might have had for becoming an architect, and instead, spurred on by his mother, he'd enrolled at St Martin's. Although this had crippled him financially at the time, the gamble had paid off: ever since, he'd been able to maintain a career doing what he loved most. As always, he'd sketched the whole thing first on paper, then lightly onto the wall, so they could begin to see how the finished painting might look. Did they want people, birds and animals added along the way? Quite definitely, Anna had nodded emphatically. And what about a few more ruins? Or a folly on a hill in the distance, perhaps? Yes, they'd agreed, that might be fun.

He walked downstairs into the basement kitchen, with its large, square central space and thick terracotta tiles, put down his kit, and made a brief examination of his work. Over halfway through now. He should be finished in a couple of weeks. Luckily he had another big job to go to in a restaurant, plus a very small cupboard decoration in another private kitchen. He often found juggling the work difficult, so that sometimes he would take on more than he could really cope with, and on other occasions he might be unemployed for several weeks. Still, he'd never been out of work for long, and he certainly saw no point in worrying about it. So far, between bouts of feeling very cash rich and extremely short, he had survived very happily. The restaurant might take as long as a couple of months, though. Perhaps he could paint the cupboard while he was at the preliminary sketches stage of the other. Marcus, the restaurant owner, need never know. He would just have to work into the evening for a few days. But then there was the bathroom in Chelsea to do. He'd forgotten that. Damn. Perhaps he could do the prelims for Marcus, but postpone actually working on the walls for a week or two. He'd already postponed the Chelsea job once. He would just have to work a bit harder and longer over the next few weeks, Harry thought to himself as he boiled the chrome kettle in Anna and Ian's kitchen.

His mobile rang. Below ground reception wasn't great, but he could still hear Julia's voice.

'What are you doing now?'

'Working incredibly hard. Making myself coffee.'

'God, you have it easy.' She laughed. 'And do you have plans tonight? Why don't you come over?'

'I tell you what, why don't you come over to me? Come straight from work and I'll cook you supper.'

'OK. That would be great. I feel I've hardly seen you.'

Harry paused. 'Come whenever you can. Bye.'

He put the phone back down on the work-surface and blew onto the top of his coffee. How could she say she'd hardly seen him? They were together all Saturday. And he'd spent the previous Wednesday night at her flat too.

Ben was right though, he should be thanking his lucky stars. Perhaps he was being too choosy, too particular. From the outset, he had found Julia easy to talk to, down to earth and lacking pretension. And she was stunning, no question about it. Ben, though, had a vested interest in their relationship. It was he who had introduced them in the first place. Initially, Harry had felt his normal wariness of City workers. They were all (with the exception of Ben, of course) over-worked, materialistic machines, fit only for sneering at. Anyway, he was sure she wouldn't think much of him. He didn't even know how to read the FT share prices. But Ben had refused to listen to his attempts to wriggle out of the evening, and so eventually he'd given in and gone along. To his surprise, but as his friend had promised, Julia was broad-minded, self-deprecating and, despite being an extremely proficient investment banker (Ben had told him so), reluctant to discuss her own work for fear it would sound too dull. At the end of the evening, they'd exchanged numbers, met up a couple of evenings later, and gone to bed with each other two dates after that.

Harry slurped his coffee, in between peering intently at the mural and laying out his paints. It had certainly been an unusual first night. They'd met up in Soho, and she'd suggested they go to a Chinese restaurant she knew on Wardour Street.

'It's a really fun place. The waiters are always extremely rude, but the food's great,' she'd told him. Harry had been further surprised by her restaurant choice, having prepared himself for a ludicrously expensive meal in one of the top restaurants in town. Glazed brown ducks had hung by their necks in the windows, their heads pathetically limp. Harry shuddered and followed Julia in, hoping he wouldn't be forced to look at them throughout dinner. He needn't have worried. No sooner had they entered the slightly steamy atmosphere than a waiter bluntly told them to 'get upstairs'.

'See?' said Julia. 'I told you they were rude.'

'Other people seem to like it too,' said Harry as they were frog-marched through the crowded first floor to a table.

Harry found himself liking Julia more and more. As she talked, he attentively held her gaze, absorbing the details of her face. A slender jaw-line, straight nose and pale blue eyes; bobbed blonde hair and distractingly perfect white teeth beneath her narrow lips. Her skin, protected by a light brushing of foundation, looked pale and perfect, almost translucent. He imagined her playing a *femme fatale* in an old film; she would look even more beautiful in black and white.

After the Chinese, they managed to hail a taxi surprisingly quickly and, getting in, Julia said without conferring, 'Cottesmore Gardens, please.' Following her, Harry had no intention of avoiding what was inevitably going to ensue. He felt more attracted to her than to anyone else he'd met in the past few years. As the taxi trundled off, Julia turned to him seductively, her lips shining with a renewed gloss of lipstick, her long legs folded towards him.

'Great Chinese,' said Harry. 'What do you think happens if you're rude back? Do they poison you? *Has* anyone ever been poisoned?'

Julia laughed, then said, 'I've had a lovely evening, thank you. It's been *such* fun.'

'Good, I'm glad you've enjoyed it,' he grinned. She was looking at him intently. Clearly, the time had come. Leaning over, he kissed her, catching a deep infusion of her scent as he did so.

Once in her flat, Julia led him to the sofa, then disappeared only to reappear a few moments later with a bottle of champagne and two glasses. The place reeked of refined elegance: thick curtains hung luxuriously over the twin french windows facing out onto the street. Antique furniture – a beautiful dining table at one end of the room and two small console tables – stood beneath original artwork and a huge gilt mirror. Harry had never known anyone his age live in such style.

'Cheers.' She carefully chinked his glass and sat down next to him on the big sofa. He was conscious that the scene unfolding was perhaps just a bit contrived, the seductive champagne maybe a bit too planned. Quite flattering though. Carefully putting down his glass, he kissed her once more. Moments later, they lay full stretch, each grappling with the other's belt and buttons. Harry marvelled at her wonderfully sleek and well-proportioned body. It felt good to be back in the fray at long last. As he kissed her all over, she murmured gently, her legs contentedly stretching out beneath him. As he moved his arms behind her, she raised herself slightly, enabling him to neatly unclip her white lacy bra. With his hands and lips caressing her breasts, she began digging her fingers digging into his back. Suddenly, she pushed him up and, smiling mischievously, said, 'Let's go next door.' Only her knickers lay between her and complete nakedness.

'Now, where were we?' She smiled once more, calmly pulling down his trousers and boxer shorts. 'Ah, yes. You were about to fuck me, I think.'

Harry was slightly taken aback by her choice of words, especially as he'd never once heard her swear before, but was none the less happy enough to oblige. He hadn't made love to anyone for over two years and, feeling incredibly aroused, was worried he might ruin everything by firing off in under thirty seconds. Desperately trying to think of anything non-sexual, he found the task slightly easier when Julia started repeating, 'Fuck me, Harry, fuck me, Harry,' quicker and quicker. What did she think he was doing? he thought, pummelling in and out of her.

'Fuck HARDER,' she yelled, and Harry, obeying her demands and pounding as hard as he could, tried desperately not to laugh. Still, he thought, if that was her kick, who was he to start objecting?

'I hope you didn't mind me shouting like that,' Julia said afterwards. 'I can't help talking like that whenever I have sex.'

Harry shrugged and smiled. He couldn't really think of an appropriate answer.

But it wasn't the kinky sex talk that bothered Harry. It was something he couldn't quite put his finger on. He supposed he'd been worrying slightly about where he and Julia were heading, but this concern had taken a different turn over the past two days, ever since he'd seen Jenny at the theatre. Or at least, he was pretty sure it had been Jenny. During the interval, Julia and he had been chatting about the play, wedged in one corner of the bar with their pre-ordered drinks, when, over her shoulder, Harry had spotted two girls talking animatedly on the far side. Something about the back of the chestnut-haired one looked strangely familiar, and then she turned. She was quite a long way away, but he was certain it was Jenny. The way she smiled and brushed her hair from her face as she laughed was just *so* Jenny, it had to be her. When Julia asked him what the matter was, he said, nothing, just someone he thought he recognized; but when he looked up again she'd gone. Vanished into the ether, as though she'd never been there at all.

He began sketching the outline of the Palladian bridge Anna had requested, between a lawn on one side and a row of poplars stretching away on the other. Perhaps Jenny hadn't been there the other night. Perhaps he'd just seen a ghost of her. Every time he thought of her, a pang of regret came over him. Jenny had been lovely. Still, it had been a long time ago. He'd been eighteen then. They'd met, briefly, in Africa, where both had been spending six months before going on to university. But they would probably never have seen each other again had it not been for the fact that their parents lived quite close to each other in Suffolk. As they sat outside their tents watching the sun set over the Ngorongoro Crater, the world had never seemed bigger; discovering they lived barely fifteen miles apart back home struck them as a particularly strange piece of serendipity. On his return, he bravely called her up. Her father was in the RAF and they'd only been posted there a couple of years before, while Harry had lived in the same house in Polstead all his life. He was able to take her places she'd never been before – the best pubs, the prettiest spots. The relationship moved fast. Most of his other friends were still away, so he and Jenny spent almost all of the final couple of months before university together, totally wrapped up in their own little microcosm into which no one else was allowed or required to enter. They would meet up in the evenings and drive to a pub, or go to see a film. At weekends they took themselves off camping, walking for miles and miles and talking incessantly, so that in a short time Harry felt he knew more about Jenny than just about anyone he'd ever met. They even took a week off to go to Paris together, holding hands as they idled around Montmartre, gazing into each other's eyes across café tables. Making love by night. Harry remembered feeling quite heady with the romance of it.

He felt he'd come of age during his time with her. What were his previous relationships compared with what he had with Jenny? Nothing. Merely insignificant teenage fumblings. Everything was different with her. They were just so right together, they laughed so much, had so much fun, and the summer days seemed so particularly summery: long, light and warm. Youth tasting the cup of adulthood without the weights of responsibility. When he wasn't with her, he thought about her: the smell of her dark flowing hair; the long eyelashes that protected her hazel eyes. He would think of the delicate curve of her neck and the outline of her collar bone, so sensuous, feminine and alluring. Harry felt an intensity to his love, his feelings given added confidence by Jenny's incredible love for him.

So how had he allowed her to melt away from his life? Everything had changed once he got to Cambridge. He was there, and Jenny was in London, beginning four years of teacher training at Roehampton. They were no longer half an hour apart and it was no longer summer. For a brief, blissful while, they had been flowing in the same wind, but with the flick of a switch, their lives were suddenly set on totally different courses. All around him at Cambridge, his fellow students were getting drunk, debating the meaning of life and sleeping with one another. Jenny sounded distant on the phone and hurt when he didn't ring when he said he would. He began to feel resentful that she seemed to depend on him so much; the balance of their relationship had somehow shifted. When she came to visit him, early on in the term, he felt embarrassed: young freshers weren't supposed to be involved in serious – and hence boring – relationships; they were meant to be young bucks, carefree, unshackled and irresponsible. By the Sunday afternoon, Harry was snapping at her irritably and she was looking at him with disbelieving pain. They went for a walk across the water meadows, but it was no good. The magic of the summer had gone. Then she asked him whether he'd slept with anyone else, and he admitted he had. He'd got drunk, ended up in some girl's bed, screwing her while someone else was sick in the corridor outside. It hadn't meant a thing and he hadn't seen or spoken to her since. Jenny looked desolate. Without saying another word, she drove off in her cluttered Peugeot. It was the last time he saw her.

From rather enjoying thinking about the fun they'd had that summer, Harry now felt rather depressed. To make matters worse, he'd never really gone out with anyone else at Cambridge. All those pathetic plans to sleep around and be a 'free agent' – what a sham. He'd kissed quite a lot of people, slept with some of them, and then started seeing a girl called Katrina in his last two terms. Looking back on it now, he realized he had been fairly horrible to her too. He rarely saw her during the day, creeping round to her rooms last thing, spending the night with her, then drifting off the following morning. Once they'd left Cambridge, their relationship, if it could be called that, ground to a halt. They liked each other, but not enough to make an effort any more.

Who came next? A year of being single and jealous of friends who had settled relationships, and then Jo, an old Cambridge friend. She had been single for a while too, so it became a pairing of convenience. They carried on being friends, only they slept together. Harry wondered whether he might feel more for her once he knew every inch of her body. But he didn't. Then she found someone to fall in love with properly and that was that. They were still friends though, which was more than he could say for Jenny or Katrina. And Jo got married to the man she'd fallen in love with. Harry and he became friends too, and when they asked him to design the service sheet, he felt only too happy to help out. He liked doing that kind of work. It was something slightly different, didn't take long, and all the compliments at the wedding gave him a smug sense of satisfaction.

Harry switched on the radio, hoping for some old classics on Radio Two or Heart FM, but didn't recognize anything they were playing, so switched to Classic FM instead. It was never long before they played something he knew, and the stuff he'd never heard before was always bearable as background noise. Soon after Jo, he'd started seeing a New Zealander called Tanya. She was almost very beautiful, but something about the end of her nose and her slightly crooked teeth spoilt things. And he also had a suspicion that her eyes were just slightly too wide apart. He kept hoping that somehow these minor flaws would iron themselves out as he grew more and more fond of her. It was Ben who put him straight. Tanya's flaws weren't her nose or teeth. It was simply that they weren't really suited. Harry knew his friend was right, but carried on going out with her until, fortunately, she decided to go back to New Zealand. As he waved her off at Heathrow, Harry felt an enormous sense of relief and liberation sweep over him.

There was only one other person he'd slept with before Julia. Christ, he couldn't even remember her name. That was terrible. He stopped painting and stood back, rubbing his chin. A man's name, shortened for a girl. Sam, or Marty. Toni? What was it? Clary. That was it. Not a man's name at all. She'd been voracious though, pulling off his clothes the moment they were in her room, then leading him to the shower and getting straight down to business. He remembered thinking her sexual confidence must stem from experience, and then becoming terrified she might give him some dreadful sexually transmitted disease. Still, she was feisty and attractive, and Harry was slightly drunk and his fears quickly subsided. But after making love for a second time back in her room, she pulled out a cigarette and started to smoke. He hadn't touched a cigarette himself for a couple of years and the smell, at that time in the early hours of the morning, seemed particularly repugnant. The lights were off, but the room was still suffused by a faint orange glow from the streetlights outside, and Harry watched in horror as the burning red tip glowed brighter every time she inhaled. Then, her fix of nicotine complete, she leant across him, her left nipple brushing against his chest, and stubbed it out on a plate on the bedside cabinet.

'Hmm,' she breathed over him, and thrust her tongue in his mouth once more. The taste was vile, like kissing an ash-tray, and completely unerotic. The next morning he left as soon as he could, appalled at his own cheapness.

That had been nearly two years ago. Until Julia, he'd forsaken casual sex and any relationship vowing that unless he met someone he could fall in love with, he would rather stay both single and chaste. Harry smiled to himself. He hadn't thought about his former girlfriends for ages. But it was sad that, with the exception of Jenny, he'd slept with five people and only really liked one of them. That was Jo, and she'd been a friend anyway. If he'd known what he knew now, he wondered, would he have discarded Jenny so casually? But at the time, in his youthful imagination, he'd pictured a future full of wild love affairs and nights of passion with a string of beautiful women, until someone swept him off his feet so completely he'd never want for anything again. He stopped painting again, and went upstairs and out onto the road, clutching his phone.

'Ben, hi, it's me,' he said into the phone.

'Oh, Harry, hi. Listen, I can't speak now. I'll call you later, OK?'

'Yeah, yeah, all right.'

He tried Flin, but got his voicemail. He nearly left a message, but decided against it. Perhaps Lucie was around. She wasn't, only her assistant, who said she was terribly sorry, but Lucie was in a meeting. Could she help at all? No, thought Harry, no one can. He didn't really want to talk to any of his other friends. There was a simpler remedy: stop thinking about what might have been with

Jenny. Things had worked out differently. Now he had Julia, and if he wasn't in love with her just at that moment, then perhaps he would be in time. She was certainly more fun and better looking than anyone in between. And he *was* very fond of her. Or maybe he was in *love* with her, but just didn't realize it. Maybe memory was preserving his relationship with Jenny in a rosetinted frame, and it had never been half as good as he remembered.

Stomping back downstairs, he heard the hourly news. More misery in Chechnya. Mass killings in Sierra Leone. Harry picked up his brush, humbled. It was easy to distance oneself from horrors in a far-off land, to feel sorry for the people involved, but then to shrug and put them to one side. But really, if all he had to worry about was whether he was in love or not, he couldn't be doing too badly. And at least he didn't have to go to meetings. *He* didn't have to call back later because someone was hovering over him. *He* could do what he liked, and, at the end of the day, if he so wished, he could go back to his flat and do whatever he wished there too, without anyone to get in his way.

But when he arrived back home later that evening, he padded upstairs and, in a move that had been secretly premeditated since before lunch, dug out his photo albums. He soon found the picture he was after, his favourite photo of her, the one he'd once kept in a frame by his bed. The colours were fading, but every line and curve of her face still looked, even after eleven years, heart-breakingly familiar.

CHAPTER THREE

Flin receives a shock

When Harry asked Tiffany about Flin's great plans to move out, she admitted they had come to very little.

Harry laughed. 'I had a feeling they wouldn't.'

'I've worked out a very simple way of dealing with Flin's sudden impulses and new crazes,' Tiffany told him. 'I go along with it initially, then throw in a word of caution and wait for his enthusiasm to trail off.'

'And that always works?'

'So far,' she grinned.

Flin returned with more drinks. 'What are you lot laughing about?' he asked suspiciously.

'Nothing,' said Harry. 'So when are you moving out to the country then?' Sniggers from around the table.

'You may laugh,' Flin told them, 'but it *will* happen.'

'You've only mentioned it twice this week though, honey. That's an eighty per cent drop on last week. And that was a fifty per cent drop on the week before,' said Tiffany.

'The Flin enthusiasm barometer is definitely dropping,' added Harry.

Flin looked sheepish. Perhaps the sense of urgency had waned somewhat, but, as he pointed out to them, the idea had far from gone away. He did still think about all the wonderful things they would do once they moved to the country; and he did still gaze wistfully at passing Land-Rovers. He'd even reread all his H. E. Bates novels and bought *Country Living*.

'But you haven't actually *done* anything about it though, have you, baby?' said Tiffany. Well, no, that was true. But he would, and soon.

Privately though, Flin found there always seemed to be something holding him back. It was a very busy time of year at work. There were big films coming out, with PR he was already committed to. Furthermore, his assistant had left too and he considered it a bit churlish to leave before he'd found a new person and helped him or her settle in. Then there were the big summer blockbusters to prepare for, as well as all the normal day-to-day work to be done. And anyway, moving out wasn't something they needed to rush. Waiting a few months for everything to quieten down at work wouldn't make any difference in the long run.

Then one evening something happened to Flin which was to change this attitude irrevocably.

The day started brightly, with clear early April skies and the promise of warm, mild weather to come, and Flin set off for work cheerful and fairly content with his life. There was nothing especially exciting happening that day, although he'd arranged to meet Ben for lunch and was going to a screening of a new film in the evening. It meant he would be home late, but that didn't bother him; it was a film he wanted to see and an aspect of his work he'd always enjoyed.

In fact, lunch with Ben took nearly an hour and a half out of his day, but he returned to the office thinking more positively about his job than he had in ages. Really, when he thought about Ben, he considered himself very lucky. There was no one watching his every move. The working hours could be very intense and busy at

35

times, but on the whole were fairly relaxed – compared to Ben's at any rate; he met interesting people, even if egos sometimes got in the way, and he could wear whatever he liked. *And* he was paid to watch films he would have handed over to go and see anyway.

That afternoon he managed to secure a weekend magazine front cover for one of the films he was working on, spoke to Tiffany four times and made plans to visit Geordie in Wiltshire the following weekend. The film in the evening was even better than he'd hoped and, after loitering at the end for a few drinks with some journalists, he set off for home feeling even more cheerful and sanguine than he had that morning.

He jumped on a bus at Piccadilly. Usually he cycled to work. He enjoyed cycling, although there was a more practical advantage to it too: it was the only way he felt he could get around London without being constantly late; but if it was going to be a long day, or if the weather looked ominous, he was perfectly happy to allow a bit more time and take the bus. That way he avoided the Underground and could still see the streets of London as he travelled to work. Furthermore, the bus he took was one of the old-fashioned variety: an open step-on at the back, and seats facing each other towards the rear. This was important to Flin. He was tall and it meant he could sit there without feeling cramped, and see the faces of the people opposite, which he liked.

By the time he reached Olympia, the weather had changed dramatically. Rain poured down, and he wasn't wearing a coat. Cursing, he shoved his hands into his pockets, hunched up his shoulders and set off. The road between the exhibition halls and the railway was always well lit, but behind it, the way suddenly darkened. This had never bothered Flin. Ever since he'd moved to London, no one had so much as shouted at him. He'd never seen a mugging, a fight, or even a traffic accident. Nor had he ever been burgled. If that was just good luck on his part, he'd never bothered to think about it. Instead, a confidence in his own security steadily grew, so that he thought nothing of walking down dark ill-lit streets late at night or chaining his bicycle with nothing but a cursory shackle between frame and railing.

He'd seen the four youths sheltering under a delivery bay to the rear of the halls, but had barely given them a thought. Had he been more alert to the possible dangers, he might have thought it odd that four people should be hanging about in such a place at such an hour on such a night, and briskly walked to the other side of the road. Or even run. But he didn't. It wasn't until he'd already passed them that he realized one of them had given a nod to another. And by then it was too late.

Hands grabbed him from behind, while someone rushed to his front and punched him hard in the face and then the stomach. He heard the sound of his nose breaking, felt the blood pour in a warm stream over his lip and chin, and tasted the thick sweet-metallic taste on his mouth. It happened so quickly. A youth, spotty and with tufts of stubble on his chin, pulled a knife from his pocket and held it to Flin's neck, the point breaking the soft and vulnerable skin.

Flin gurgled and gasped as another knife slashed off his bag and hands rifled through his pockets. Then another punch, this time from behind: hard, swift, and unbearably painful into his kidney. He crumpled to the ground. Grazed skin on his face and hands stung as he hit the wet roadside. For a split second he wondered whether they would kill him. An enormous wallop hit him in the ribs, a kick at full strength, blasting the last bit of air from him. Then footsteps running off into the night. The attack had lasted no more than half a minute.

For a few moments, Flin lay there, the rain spattering his back, and the cold, dirty water from the pavement seeping through his jacket and shirt, cloying against his skin. He could only just see, his vision blurred by the rain and his rapidly swelling eyes. His nose hurt like hell, while his ribs and back throbbed, and tiny specks of grit stuck to the sides of his grazed hands. Blood continued to stream down the side of his face. Still in shock, and in extreme pain, he put his hands out flat on the hard wet concrete and pushed himself up onto his knees, and then falteringly to his feet.

Leaning against a wall, he felt for his handkerchief, his raw hands stinging as they met the edges of his pockets. Holding it out to the rain, he dabbed at his eyes as they swelled further with each passing moment. He groaned with a humiliation keener than the pain. He'd been fleeced by four youths, probably nearly half his age, and left sprawled out on a rain-soaked roadside. What had he been to them? Nothing. Just something to rob, a walking cash opportunity.

He made it home, staggering, although he was nearly run over as he crossed the road to his own street. A car turned a corner and he never saw it, never even heard it. The attack had dulled all his senses. At his front door, he pressed the buzzer; his own keys had been in his bag.

'Tiff, it's me. Can you let me in?' His voice felt strange, not his own, as though his tongue had been stung repeatedly.

'Oh my God, Flin, what happened?' cried Tiffany as she opened the door. His jacket was torn, and, soaked, bloodied and squinting, he was barely able to stand.

'Mugged,' he stammered, 'punched. I think they broke my nose. Oh, Tiff, it was horrible. So frightening.'

Tiffany grabbed his arm and led him to the bathroom. There she gently undressed him and washed his wounds.

'I'm going to take you to hospital,' she told him. 'You need someone to look at you.'

'I'm fine,' said Flin. But he knew he wasn't. He gently massaged his neck, unable to forget the sensation of a knife-point digging into him. His body began to shake all over, uncontrollably, as Tiffany dabbed at his wounded face. She insisted they go to Casualty, and Flin felt unable to resist. So, an hour later, he sat in a hospital cubicle, exposed and humiliated for the second time that night, as a doctor began to stitch up his broken face.

'You'll be fine,' the doctor told him matter-of-factly. 'Wear dark glasses for a couple of days and you should soon be OK. The swelling will go down and, although it might hurt for a bit, I think your nose will look its old self soon enough.'

Flin also had a broken rib, although there was nothing to be done about that. He would just have to be patient, not exert himself and wait for it to mend.

He said nothing as Tiffany drove him back to their tiny flat, just gazed distractedly out of the window. He wanted to be in bed, safe and warm, holding his beloved Tiffany, far away from a world of dark menace and violence.

As the doctor predicted, Flin made a swift physical recovery. His side was sore for quite some time, but after his face had turned a myriad of different colours, the swelling and bruising gradually diminished. After a couple of weeks, only a scar across the bridge of his nose remained as physical evidence of his attack. But his confidence in London as a fun and vibrant place to live altered dramatically. The plan to move out suddenly returned as an urgent priority.

'Do you mind, Tiff?' asked Flin as they drove off for another weekend in the country. He drummed his fingers on the steering wheel. 'I can't stay here now. Those youths were obviously sent to give me a kick up the arse. Must have been. You know, Tiff, I don't want to live in this kind of world any more. I don't want to feel crowded, obsessed with work, and constantly worn down by the stress of living in a city of eleven million people. I just want to be with you, on our own in some rural haven. I want to live in a place where we can shut everything else out if we want, batten down the hatches and create our own little existence untroubled by modern life. The real world's too dark, too sinister. I don't want our kids growing up in a place where they could be set upon at any moment. They should have open fields to run about in, and woods for making dens, where they're not threatened by a constant stream of cars and lorries hurtling past them. And nor do I want to live solely on tasteless packaged food, being conned by supermarkets and eating chickens full of chemicals. Let's grow our own, Tiff. Vegetables, animals. The Good Life. Wouldn't it be great? We really could be like the Larkins if we wanted. We've just got to take the plunge. This isn't just a passing fad any more. This is something I think we should do, now, right away.'

'Have you finished?' said Tiffany calmly.

'Yes.'

'Good because, Flin darling, if we're going to do this, let's do it. I'm fed up of hearing you talk about it, then never getting off your arse and actually making plans. We're doing something about it now, or not at all.'

'OK.'

'And I think we should also think about going to Australia.'

'What?'

'Australia. Perhaps we should go out there for a bit. It's the perfect place to get away from it all. You could meet my family properly.'

'I don't know, Tiff. When I meant move out, I meant within England really.'

'Can you at least think about it?'

Flin paused. 'OK. I'll think about it.'

Over the next few days, he thought of little else. He'd never imagined living there before. Moving to the north of England was one thing – they might be a long way from their friends and family there, but being on the other side of the world was quite a different matter altogether. In Australia, he really would *never* see them. And with the exception of Tiffany, he wasn't sure how much he really liked Australians. They always won at cricket and were so damn hearty about everything. He suspected that might grate after a short while. Then there was the climate. Great for some people, but wouldn't he find it too hot? And there were sharks, and dangerous snakes, and crocodiles. In England there was nothing but the odd midge and an adder if you were very unlucky.

But the idea was out in the open now, and he could tell it was rapidly growing on Tiffany. He never wanted to do anything to lose her, but to emigrate, and leave behind the country he loved, and all his family and friends completely . . . well, that would be a terrible, terrible wrench.

For a week, they barely mentioned moving again. Tiffany left books on Australia in strategic positions about the flat, while Flin did the same with *Country Life*, and made a great play of laughing out loud when he read *Cold Comfort Farm* in bed. But the issue had to be confronted, however unwilling Flin might have been to do this. As each day passed, the silence between them over the matter became louder.

'So,' he said as they sat down to supper one night. He'd bought some fresh flowers and cooked lamb shanks and mashed potato, a favourite of hers. 'The Big Move. I've been thinking.' He poured her a glass of wine, and took a deep breath. 'Give me this summer to find a job and somewhere for us to live in England, and if that doesn't work out, we go to Australia. What do you say?'

Tiffany put down her knife and fork and, eyeing him carefully, finished chewing her mouthful of lamb before speaking.

'It's a deal,' she said eventually. 'But you know, Flin, really I just want to know where we're heading. I can't relax while everything's so up in the air. You're always talking about these great romantic plans, then doing nothing about them, so that I don't know whether you really mean it, or whether it's just hot air. I don't particularly mind if you want to stay here, but I just want to make a decision, then stick to it for a change. I know you're upset about the attack. It was horrible and gave us both a terrible shock, but is it really a reason for moving? Has it really changed what you feel about London, or is it just a short-term reaction? And you know my current contract at the Beeb is about to end

– I need to know whether I should be looking for something else in London or not.'

'No, I really do want to move, Tiff, I really do. I promise. No more dallying about. Let's go to the country, and as soon as we possibly can.'

'If you're sure. It's not going to be all sweetness and roses, you know. There'll be times when you may regret it, and you'll think you've made the most terrible mistake. Are you prepared for that? I am. I've been thinking about this a lot too, and this time, it is something I really want to do too. But I'll tell you now, I'm not turning round and coming back again after six months.' She took his hand, softening. 'Sorry, I don't meant to sound stern, but it's not all pie in the sky, OK?'

'Tiff, you have my word. I want to make a success of this.'

'Then let's do it. Let's begin our new life.'

part two – *summer*

CHAPTER FOUR

the first whole day of Thomas Armstrong

Everyone told Ben first babies were usually late, and despite Lucie's desire for a slightly premature birth, he hoped they were right. A delay of two weeks would probably mean the Prospero deal would be signed, done and dusted by the time the baby arrived. Before that, and life could become very tricky indeed.

He'd only been working for Farman Gore for just over six months. They worked him hard – very hard – but he knew he could never regret having made the move. Although he'd enjoyed his time at Landsberg Warner, he'd been unable to resist the offer being made by this American company just setting up in London. Carl and Jon had been sent over by the New York office to get things up and running and approached Ben as one of their first recruits. It was an exciting opportunity: a good name the other side of the Atlantic, a dedicated team being brought together in the new office, including Ben's old work colleague Steve, and the prospect of working on some really good deals. Carl and Jon had been big players in the States, and Ben felt sure there was much he could learn from them.

One of the first major deals he'd been working on was the takeover of News Associated, a national newspaper and magazine company, by a regional conglomerate called Prospero Limited.

The deal had looked as if it had completely collapsed at the beginning of the year, but had recently suddenly resurfaced. It was back on with a vengeance, and Ben was in the thick of it.

By Lucie's official due date, there was still no indication that the baby was about to budge. At six-forty-five in the morning, Ben had kissed his sleeping wife and headed off to Clapham Junction to catch the train to work, his mind swimming with details of the deal, rather than the forthcoming arrival of his first child.

Just after seven-thirty he and Steve met in Carl's office for a de-brief. Steve had been drafted in to cover Ben in case the baby did suddenly arrive. Even so, Steve's presence would hardly let Ben off the hook.

'So where are we at then, Ben?' Carl asked, as immaculate and fresh as ever, as though he'd already been up and about for hours.

'It's basically a question of going through the merger model.'

'Early thoughts?'

'OK. So far, I think it should be a straightforward enough job persuading NA.'

'Good. What about the press release?'

'First draft end of the day, maybe tomorrow morning.'

'Excellent. We've got to get the underwriting agreement sorted by the end of next week. This deal *has* to go live a week Monday.'

Ben was still number-crunching on the Excel charts on his computer when the phone rang just after ten o'clock.

'It's your wife on the line,' Tara, his secretary told him, emotion absent from her voice.

'Great, quick, put her through,' Ben snapped back. A moment later, Lucie was connected.

'Ben? Ben, my waters have broken,' gabbled Lucie. 'It's disgusting, I was just walking into the kitchen and then whoosh.'

'Oh my God.'

'Anyway, it's about bloody time. I've been feeling more than bursting for days now.'

46

Ben felt stunned. Somehow, he hadn't ever pictured this moment arriving. It just seemed an event too enormous to contemplate, and now it had happened he didn't really know what to say or do.

'Brilliant,' he told her; it was the first word that came into his mouth. 'Have you called the midwife?'

'Yes, darling.'

'And a taxi? You need to be in hospital right away.'

'Ben, calm down. I'm fine – I can certainly wait for you to come home.'

'Luce, please. You know what the midwife said: as soon as your waters break, you should go straight to hospital in case of infection.'

'Ben – darling – calm down. I'm fine, honestly. Just come home, and then we'll go in. An extra half-hour won't make any difference.'

'Jesus,' said Ben. 'All right, if you insist, but I'm coming back right now, OK?'

'I'm fine, I promise.' His heart-rate had quadrupled and his palms were sweating. 'I'll be back right away.' He ran his hands through his hair. This was it. This was bloody it. He was about to become a bloody father.

Tara put her head round the door. 'Everything OK?'

'Yes, no, look, I've got to go. It's beginning.'

'Deep breaths,' Tara told him coolly.

Ben smiled at her sarcastically, then rushed over to Carl's office.

'Carl, look, terrible timing, I know, but the baby's on its way,' Ben told him.

'Right. So are you saying you're going now?'

'Yes.'

'OK, but you're going to have to keep closely in touch with Steve, and I still want you going through that press release when it arrives.'

'Sure,' said Ben, as Steve joined them.

'Steve, you continue the work on the merger model, and e-mail the press release to Ben as soon as it comes in. Ben, let everyone know you're out of the office and keep in touch with me and Steve. Yes?'

'Fine,' said Ben.

'And Ben – congratulations. Tell your wife her timing's terrible.'

For eight months, since they'd first found out Lucie was pregnant, they'd been building towards this moment. Ben had read books on the subject, dutifully dragged Lucie to the ante-natal classes, watched *Look Who's Talking*, and mentally prepared himself. But sitting in the back of the taxi, anxiously clicking his fingers, he realized he knew nothing. He didn't know what he should be doing, what they would do when the baby was actually born, or how he could help Lucie. He'd tried to persuade her it might be a good idea to get a maternity nurse – just for a couple of weeks – but Lucie had scoffed at the idea. 'How hard can it be?' she'd riposted. 'I don't need some total stranger hanging around my house telling me what to do.' Still, with things as they were at work now, he wondered about raising the matter again. Outside, the traffic slowly crawled along the Embankment, and he cursed repeatedly. It was nearly eleven in the morning, what the hell were they all doing? Hadn't they realized rush hour was supposed to be over? He leant forward and tapped his feet, wondering whether there was any time in this stupid city when there wasn't a traffic jam.

'Jesus *Christ*,' he said out loud, throwing himself back in his seat and clasping his head. His heart still pounded, only now even faster and more heavily. He felt sick with worry and nerves. Panic, that was what he felt, sheer panic.

The same could not be said of Lucie.

'Hi, darling, you're back,' she said as he rushed into the sitting room. She was walking up and down, eating a yoghurt and looking calm and quite contented, unfazed by the ordeal ahead of her. Ben could only sit down and marvel at his wife's serenity. She'd been this laid-back all the way through the pregnancy. 'Do we *have* to go to the ante-natal classes?' she'd pleaded. 'They're all so bloody earnest. I don't see why we can't just read about it instead.' But Ben had insisted, anxiously taking notes while Lucie's attention wandered. Really, she'd been amazing, as she was with everything. No morning sickness, nor any signs of excessive tiredness. In fact, it was only really recently that she'd grumbled about the back-ache and discomfort when trying to sleep. They'd still gone out, still seen their friends; and where Ben constantly worried about the baby's health and lived in fear of it developing some terrible deformity, Lucie seemed more concerned that it should have enough outfits, costumes and the right kind of three-wheeled buggy. 'I'm not going to look like some awful washed-up old hag,' Lucie told him categorically, 'I want to be a glamorous mother with a glamorous child.'

'But aren't you worried about it all being OK?' Ben had asked her one time as they scoured Baby Gap.

'Not really,' she told him, picking up a little pink outfit with 'Cool' written on it, 'you do all the worrying for me. No point in us both getting het up.'

All the same, Ben had still insisted they have an ordinary pram too. At the ante-natal class, they'd been quite emphatic about that: for the first three months, it was important for the baby to lie flat, and he was going to play it by the book, even if Lucie wasn't.

'Come *on*, Luce,' said Ben. He was standing in the hallway, clutching Lucie's overnight bag just as the phone rang again. But she had already picked up the receiver. He'd only been back a few minutes and yet in that time Lucie's sister Susie, and Vanessa, her mother, had both rung. Then Steve had called his mobile, the jarring cacophony of ringing phones adding to his increasing stress.

It was Vanessa again.

'Mum, I'm fine, honestly – I've got Ben here . . . he's being brilliant actually, so there really isn't . . . no . . . no . . . we'll call you later . . . NO, MUM, I don't want you watching me give birth. Bye.' She put the phone back.

'Luce, *please*,' urged Ben.

Lucie ambled through to the hallway. 'Jesus, she is just impossible sometimes.' Then putting on a shrill voice she mimicked, '"But darling, it's not natural being without your mother, and Ben's a man and he's bound to be hopeless." What bollocks – Oh, yow!' she cried again, grimacing and clutching her stomach. 'Can't be too long now.' She looked up, giving him a reassuring smile. With a protective arm around her, Ben ushered her out of the front door.

But there was still a little way to go yet. At the hospital, Lucie was quickly put to bed, but there was still no sign of the baby. Afternoon dragged on to evening, and Ben started to feel increasingly helpless, alternately pacing up and down antiseptic corridors and clutching Lucie's hand at her bedside. The last few hours were torturous. Lucie's pain became increasingly apparent, but he was powerless to do anything about it. This was a full-on attack against all his natural instincts to be gallant and protective towards her. It shocked him to see someone normally so composed and pragmatic about everything yell and clench her teeth, sweat pouring down her face. And somehow so undignified: legs straddled, and people gaping at her ever-widening vagina. Thank God he was born a man, and saved from all the shoving and prodding that went on. Strange thoughts circulated his mind. He suddenly remembered how once he'd had to drop his pants for a doctor when he was about twelve: it had been the most embarrassing moment of his life. But such concerns were clearly the last thing on Lucie's mind as she grimaced and shrieked and puffed. He hated to think of her suffering so much, but what could he do? There was a limit to how often he could say, 'I'm right here, darling, you can do it,' in sympathetic yet determined tones.

But the baby finally emerged just after midnight, red, angry, but complete with a shock of dark hair. Lucie started laughing then crying, then doing both at the same time. Ben just gawped open-mouthed. His son! A brand-new human being, alive and perfectly formed. He stared, unable to comprehend the magnitude of what they had achieved.

'Look, he's got a little willy,' Lucie managed to say between sniffs and sobs and giggles and Ben found himself suddenly laughing too, marvelling at the tiny, eight-and-a-half-pound baby cradled in her arms. A son. He had a son. Truly, unbelievably amazing.

'And to think you thought he would be a girl,' said Lucie.

'He's perfect. Just perfect. You're so clever, Luce, so, so clever. I can't believe it. I just can't believe it.'

Lucie looked at him, laughing again despite her tear-stained face, then kissed the baby's head. 'Thomas,' she said, 'just Thomas.'

'He's bloody perfect!' said Ben again. He couldn't understand what he was feeling; it was all too overwhelming. Shock, relief, happiness, fear, deep love. As the three of them lay there on the birthing bed, he knew this was the most intense emotion he had ever experienced.

Vanessa came over in the morning, with Terence (her 'boyfriend' who, at forty-six, was eight years younger than Lucie's mother) hovering uncertainly in the background. She brought with her a huge bouquet of flowers and clucked ecstatically over her first grandson. But Ben could tell Lucie was exhausted, and after the initial elation of the previous night, saw her start to become a bit riled and scratchy. A couple of hours after the birth, she'd been moved from the birthing room to the maternity ward, but there other newborns were wailing and she found it hard to sleep. Then, just as she dropped off, the paediatrician came round to check on her, followed by the midwife, who immediately started asking her about her sex life and advising her not to have sexual intercourse for at least six weeks. Ben watched as Lucie's expression turned from one of extreme exhaustion to that of utter disgust.

'Couldn't think of anything worse, quite frankly,' Lucie told her sharply, adding, 'Anyway, my fanny feels so huge I think Ben would get lost in it if he tried.'

Then they were left to it. No one else really bothered with them, although either side the constant pitch of crying babies became almost unbearable. Thomas soon started screaming too, his tiny head screwing itself into a deep red contortion of anger.

'What the fuck am I supposed to do?' Lucie asked Ben, just a hint of panic in her voice.

'I don't know – feed him, I suppose,' suggested Ben.

'This is so embarrassing. I mean, I just feel really self-conscious,' Lucie told him in hushed tones as she unbuttoned her nightdress. It was miraculous, Ben thought to himself, that Thomas knew precisely what to do, latching onto Lucie's breast hungrily.

'How is it?' asked Ben gingerly.

'Fucking painful, just like everything else to do with birth,' said Lucie, gazing down at the little bundle sucking noisily. Ben watched, intrigued at this new use for Lucie's breast.

Then he said, 'Look, darling, what about this maternity nurse? What with this deal and everything, won't you reconsider?'

'Darling, I know you worry, but I really don't want anyone telling me what to do every five minutes. I've said I'll manage. Anyway, could you get me a cup of tea? I suddenly feel very dry.' He noticed her pull the sheets up, limiting further the amount of flesh on public view.

'Course. Sure you'll be all right?'

Lucie just smiled at him weakly, so he kissed her, then kissed

Thomas, and wandered off towards the canteen, a place he'd discovered early on the previous afternoon.

But on his return, he discovered both his wife and son fast asleep, Lucie's arm gently supporting Thomas. He watched them for a moment. It was hardly surprising she was exhausted; he felt exhausted himself, physically and mentally. Placing her tea on the grape- and flower-table by her bed, he looked at his mobile, thought about ringing the office, then put it away again. Just for a few hours, he could be forgiven for not thinking about work, and for concentrating on his wife and son instead.

With contented thoughts swimming around his mind, he decided to quickly wander outside and get some fresh air. The sanitized constant warmth seemed suddenly cloying, almost stultifying, and he started walking increasingly briskly to escape. Endless squeaky corridors of shiny linoleum led into one another, but eventually he found the exit and walked out, blinking in the bright morning sunshine. To his left flowed the river and opposite, the great Gothic minarets and towers of the Houses of Parliament. Images from the future filled his mind: his son clinging onto his hand as they walked down to the playground, or at the beach building sandcastles together; then later playing football in the park. Thomas would love him unconditionally, depend upon him, think him the best dad in the whole wide world. They were good thoughts. His family was going to be different – they were going to be happy, carefree and close, and he was always going to look after them.

As he sat on a bench, looking out across the river, relief surged through him. Lucie was fine. Thomas was fine. Nothing had gone wrong. Their child was perfect. Throughout the pregnancy, he'd feared that Thomas would be handicapped or deformed in some way, and worried about how they'd cope. Worse was the worry that Lucie would die in childbirth. He knew this was ridiculous and that he was indulging in Brontëesque melodrama, but he couldn't help himself. As the birth drew closer, these fears and his desire to protect her constantly increased dramatically. The previous evening, there had been times when Lucie appeared to be in so much pain he felt stabs of panic that she was about to leave him, one final gasp before life slipped away for ever. It didn't bear thinking about; he'd be lost without her. She was the only person who made him feel safe, secure and, most importantly, deeply loved. How lucky he was. So, so bloody lucky.

A deep wave of emotion engulfed him. It rose from the pit of his stomach, up his throat, bursting to express itself, and he knew he was about to cry. Desperately trying to repress it, he felt the water welling up at the edges of his eyes, making it hard to focus. Then he could take it no more. Relief, intense happiness, and gratitude for the twin gifts of his wife and son, overwhelmed him so completely that he began to cry. A couple walked by, but Ben looked at them without apology, making no attempt to halt the flow. He stood up and clutched the railings, but as his breathing juddered and he struggled to control himself, he realized he was no longer crying, but laughing instead.

Twenty-four hours after first going in to hospital, they were back at home, surrounded by flowers. Ben insisted Lucie sit down on the sofa with Thomas and do nothing, while he took the flowers and fetched anything she required. But despite this activity on his part, all the tension of the previous weeks had oozed out of him; he felt soft-limbed, his heartbeat back to normal.

Pausing to sit with Lucie, and admiring his son's perfection for a while more, Ben wondered whether fatherhood would always be this good.

'Don't you think we should start ringing a few people?' asked Lucie sleepily.

'Probably should really.' Ben grabbed the phone and began tapping in a number.

'Who are you calling?'

'Steve.'

'Steve? Can't you forget about work just for today?'

'Darling, you know I can't. I haven't spoken to him once yet today.' He'd felt even Carl wouldn't have expected him to work that morning, but now they were back at home, it was his duty to call in. If only the deal could have happened two weeks before. He put the phone to his ear. 'Oh hi, Steve. What's the latest? Is the press release in yet? . . . It is. OK . . . A boy. Thomas . . . Fine . . . Sure . . . Bye.'

He looked at his wife. 'Sorry, darling, but you know I'm only doing it for us. And now we have Thomas there's even more reason to work hard. There's someone else to think about now.'

'I know,' said Lucie gently, leaning her head against him.

Ben punched in another number.

'Who now?' asked Lucie.

'Harry.'

'What about your brothers though, darling?'

'They can wait. Harry?'

'Ben! How're you feeling?'

'Unbelievably content. Bit weird.'

'How's Lucie?'

'Couldn't be better. More tired than me,' Ben told him.

'Get him to come over,' Lucie whispered loudly.

'What, now?' Ben replied, moving the handset away from his head.

'Yes. Well, later. I feel I need to see someone normal and I want to show off our creation.'

Ben put the phone back to his head. 'Why don't you come over after work? Bring Julia if you like.'

'I'd love to, mate, but I don't want to get in your way. I mean, don't you want to be on your own?'

'Not at all – we need to show off Thomas. As long as you're not expecting supper.'

'Tell you what, I'll bring it. Some Chinese or something.'

'Harry, you just don't know how good that sounds. Thank you.'

'And Ben? I can't wait to see Thomas. You must feel fantastic.'

'Yeah, it's brilliant – but very strange. Amazing though, really, really amazing. More than amazing. And it makes you unable to talk properly.'

Harry laughed. 'I'll see you later.' He rang off.

The house soon looked even more like a hothouse. But despite the arrival of yet more flowers and their deep happiness, Ben and Lucie felt strangely alone and vulnerable that afternoon. They simply didn't know what to do. Lucie had tried to change a nappy, with Ben watching.

'Bloody hell,' he said, 'how could so much poo come out of such a small bottom?'

'God knows,' replied Lucie, trying to keep her face well away, 'but the pong and *mess* of it is revolting. Makes me feel quite nauseated. I also feel *really* uncomfortable. I think I'd like my old body back now.'

'I'm sure it won't take long,' said Ben.

'It'd better not. I can hardly walk and I've got a flabby, over-stretched stomach. You don't know how lucky you are,' she told him.

'You'll feel better once you've slept properly,' suggested Ben. Thomas chose that moment to start crying again, prompting Lucie to pick him up hurriedly and try to calm him down.

'Well, you're very beautiful even if your mummy's gross and unattractive, aren't you, darling?' she said, gently kissing her son's puce little head.

'I think you're both beautiful,' said Ben.

'Creep. Isn't Daddy a great fat liar? Here,' she said, lifting Thomas, 'you take him.'

Carefully, Ben cradled his son in his arms. So tiny. Tiny but perfect.

'He looks even smaller in your great big arms,' said Lucie.

'He does, doesn't he? But I meant what I said, darling. I don't think you look gross at all.'

Having settled back down in her bed, Lucie reached out for Thomas once more. Rocking him gently, she stared pensively ahead, while Ben wondered whether he should say something sympathetic or begin phoning again. He was just reaching for the phone when Lucie said, 'Do you think I'm going to be a natural mother?'

'Course you will. What a funny thing to say,' said Ben immediately.

She paused again, then added, 'I hope so. I just feel so . . .'

'What?'

'I don't know.'

'Try.'

'No, honestly. I'm being silly. I suppose I just don't feel ready for this. I wasn't prepared for the birth, really. It was horrible. You know, I couldn't get out of that place soon enough.'

'Well, you're safe now. You did it, you know. You should feel bloody proud. I do.'

'Hm,' said Lucie, and closed her eyes.

Thomas had calmed down and, like his mother, seemed to be sleeping. Ben had to admit he did look rather tiny and fragile. And it did feel odd and slightly unnatural when he held him and tried to soothe him. His head seemed so floppy, his body so weak: Ben wasn't sure if he was hurting the little fellow by clasping him too tight. But they'd be all right, he was sure. It was only natural that parenthood should seem a bit strange to begin with, just like anything new. Lucie was going to be a perfect mother. How could she not be? Leaving his wife and son asleep, he quietly opened his lap-top and began poring over the first draft of the press release.

It was blatantly obvious Julia had a natural affinity with babies. While Harry kept hugging both Lucie and Ben and telling them he felt emotional, Julia immediately dropped into baby talk and Thomas stopped crying instantly. Then from her bag she produced a present, a gift-wrapped Tiffany's silver rattle.

'Oh Julia, how brilliant of you!' exclaimed Lucie, 'Tiffany & Co – my favourite!'

'However did you find the time to get there?' asked Ben incredulously.

'Ah ha!' Julia winked, then confessed, 'I bought it last weekend actually.'

Ben kissed her again on the cheek. 'That's very thoughtful of you – and really appreciated.'

'Mine's coming,' Harry told them, his flowers already swamped by the florist shop emerging from the living room.

There was a slightly nervous pause as they all regarded Thomas, who, miraculously, was still not crying.

'He's gorgeous,' Julia told them.

'Perfect,' agreed Ben.

Lucie looked proudly down at him. 'Yes, he is, and all curled up, bless him, wishing he was still inside. It must be such a shock arriving in the outside world. Would you like to hold him?'

'I'd love to – if you're sure you don't mind?' Julia replied, leaning over carefully and unleashing a waft of scent despite the abundance of flowers.

'You're a natural,' said Ben, full of admiration as Julia, elegant as ever, bobbed Thomas up and down to an accompaniment of soothing superlatives.

Lucie turned to Harry. 'Would you like to hold him too?'

'Me? Oh no, it's fine – I'd probably only go and make him blub.'

As Julia handed Thomas back, he screwed up his tiny face before slowly turning red, and beginning to cry once more.

'He wants some dinner, don't you, darling?' cooed Julia.

'I think you might be right,' said Lucie, looking about uncertainly.

'Are you OK, darling?' asked Ben.

'I'm embarrassed – I think I should go into another room.' Lucie made to lift herself up from the sofa.

'Don't be ridiculous, it's only us. Anyway, you've got to get used to it,' Ben told her.

'Yes, don't mind me,' added Julia.

'OK, but no sniggering,' agreed Lucie, gingerly lifting her shirt as discreetly as she could.

Ben could see Harry looking at Lucie quite mesmerized, and then she noticed too.

'Harry, stop staring,' said Lucie sharply.

'Sorry, I can't help it. I've never seen anyone do that before.'

'Well, what do you think happens? You know, Harry, this is painful enough as it is without you gawping.'

'OK, OK, sorry, but it's fascinating – seeing breasts used for something other than sex.'

'Harry, honestly,' chided Julia.

'It is. I mean, look at the way he just *knows* what to do. But I'll turn my back if it bothers you.'

'It did this morning – in the hospital, with everyone there – but Ben's right, I'm going to have to get used to it. He's needs a lot of feeding so I'll have to overcome my embarrassment and whip my tits out whenever. You see how my standards are already slipping.'

'Come on, Luce, you've just given birth, for God's sake. What do you expect?' Ben put an arm round her.

'Anyway, we should probably let you get on with it,' said Julia.

'Yes, leave the new family to their first night together,' added Harry, standing up and clapping his hands together.

'No, it's OK, stay a bit longer,' said Lucie quickly.

'Yes, why don't you?' put in Ben. 'You've only just got here. We could maybe watch a video or something. And anyway, aren't you staying for supper?'

Harry looked expectantly at Julia.

'No,' she said firmly, 'the Chinese is for you two. Honestly, you should be on your own. With Thomas.' She smiled at Thomas again. 'You'll be fine,' she added to Ben and Lucie.

They smiled weakly. Ahead lay the daunting prospect of parenthood, and their first night with Thomas under their roof.

CHAPTER FIVE

Gloucester sojourn

The weekend after Thomas was born, Harry had agreed to drive up to Gloucestershire with Julia to meet her father for the first time. He'd already met her mother, Bobby, a trim soft-spoken lady of fifty-two. She'd been divorced from Julia's father for ten years now, and on doing so had moved back to town, taking up residence in what used to be their town house on the King's Road. Harry had crossed that hurdle without too much fuss as Bobby was friendly, welcoming and clearly so much a part of Julia's everyday life. But her father, Charles, was quite a different proposition. He lived on a huge estate south of Stow-on-the-Wold, had married for a second time to a woman only eight years older than Julia, and now had another son, Dominic, to add to his other two by Bobby. Julia was clearly slightly scared of him, and did little to assuage Harry's growing apprehension.

'Do you mind terribly?' said Julia, as they headed out of town.

'No, no, I'm sure it'll be fine,' Harry lied. 'Anyway, I'm intrigued.' They had taken his Citroën. Julia insisted they should, saying it would give him something to talk about, as her father loved cars.

'He's got lots of them,' she told him.

'Really?' said Harry, interested. 'What kinds?'

'Oh, I'm not sure. Some quite old ones I think – including a James Bond type – but none as smart as this.'

Harry laughed. 'Of course not.'

'They're not. I much prefer this to anything he's got.'

'OK, if you say so.' With the sun breaking through, the clouds above were mirrored on the long black bonnet; the mounted headlights, bulbous and twinkling, pointed the way as they surged down the M40. Harry thought his car had rarely looked shinier.

'I mean, this car really is *so* stylish,' said Julia, turning to smile at Harry. 'So much more fun than mine.'

Did she really mean that? he wondered. He'd been in her car, a fast, luxurious BMW, with a CD player and an impressive array of additional gadgetry. His, by contrast, was slow, stark, and had no mod cons, least of all a stereo. Sometimes he couldn't tell whether she said things because she thought it was what he wanted to hear, rather than because it was what she really felt.

'I hope he isn't too gruff with you,' Julia said as they crossed the border into Gloucestershire, 'only he can seem a bit grumpy and stern at times. But he's harmless really.'

'Honestly, Julia, stop worrying. I'm sure it'll be fine.'

'And you know Dominic will be there, don't you?'

'Absolutely. He's six and a brat, but I mustn't let him make me play with him.'

'Exactly,' said Julia, biting her bottom lip.

'And Stella's a bit thick and after his cash, but otherwise quite harmless.' He turned to her and gave her a reassuring grin.

'Sorry, you must think I'm ridiculous. It's just, well, I adore Daddy obviously, but things haven't been the same since the divorce. It's weird going back home to find him with a completely different family. You know?'

'I can imagine. Please don't worry, though. I won't disgrace myself, I promise.' It was strange seeing Julia like this. Normally she was so confident, controlled and charming. But now, seated beside him, she was so edgy she'd even started biting her beautifully manicured nails.

'But I can't wait for you to see the house. I know you'll love it,' she added, rubbing his thigh.

Harry had to admit it to himself. The house was one of the main reasons he had agreed to come. Julia had told him about it in great detail, how the main part was built in the 1760s onto the remains of a ruined abbey. The owner had made the abbey habitable, so that the house was in part solidly medieval, and part Georgian refinement.

'I absolutely adore it,' Julia had told him. 'One minute it's all Gothic arches and the next you're looking out of delicate sash windows.' What a place to grow up, Harry had suggested. Of course it was, but now that her father had remarried and started another family, she no longer felt it was her home. 'But I love that place more than anywhere in the world,' she'd sighed wistfully.

'I'll show you the folly when we get there,' said Julia as they turned off towards Oxford.

'There's a folly?' said Harry incredulously. 'You never said anything about a folly.'

'Didn't I? I'm sure I must have done.'

'Believe me, I wouldn't have forgotten.'

'I suppose it's more of an obelisk really. Quite pointless, but rather fun. I told you the owner back then was mad.'

'How brilliant. I can't wait,' Harry grinned.

'Daddy'll know who the designer was. Quite famous in his day, I think.'

'You know, I just feel certain I'm going to love this place.'

'I think it is rather up your street. You'll have to incorporate bits of it into one of your murals.'

Julia had always shown a great interest in his work, which he appreciated. 'You're creative, I just push figures about,' she'd once said. Harry had pointed out that at least she made lots of money doing that. 'Doesn't make it very stimulating though,' she'd countered. He remembered playing a game once in the pub with some friends, including Ben and Flin. You had to pick someone else and say what they did during a normal working day. Everyone got it hilariously wrong. They simply didn't have a clue. Recounting amusing incidents at the office, or talking about plans to become the biggest entrepreneur since Richard Branson, or boasting how their company car was due to be upgraded, were regular features of the banter Harry enjoyed with his friends; but no one actually discussed what they *did* to earn the BMW upgrade, because, in truth, no one else cared. Harry didn't really know how Julia spent her day either.

As they turned into the drive, Harry saw her visibly tensen. He'd seen the effect a broken family had had on Ben, but until now had never known how wounded Julia had been by her parents' divorce. It made him realize just how lucky he was to have a family he adored, and parents he could still greatly depend on. Now that both had retired, they led even more active lives, always keen to try something new, whether it be travel, food, drink or anything else. His parents had given him a wonderful upbringing and even now, in his thirtieth year and long gone from the nest, he still felt as close to them as he always had. He knew his was an exceptional case, but how terrible it must be not to have that rock, that support. He didn't know how he'd feel if his father decided to start another family in the old house where he'd been brought up. It was unthinkable.

As Julia had promised, the house was amazing: one end ordered, graceful and refined, the other a mismatch of passageways, thick walls and sudden open spaces. And the view was spectacular. To one side of the house the lawn led away towards a ha-ha, and then beyond lay a snaking valley, banked on either side by a sylvan curtain of lush green trees. Overlooking the whole scene, imperious in its splendour, stood the obelisk, testament to an eighteenth-century landowner's vivid imagination and excessive wealth.

Much to Harry's relief, Charles wasn't around.

'So sorry, Julia, but he's huffing about sorting out a problem with the wild boar,' explained Stella with a roll of her eyes. Slim, tall, but rather plain, Harry thought she seemed friendly enough. Dominic, effectively an only child and clearly used to getting his own way, marched up to Harry and said, 'Who are you?' in an indignant tone of voice.

'He's Harry, a friend of Julia's, darling.'

'Do you want to marry her?' he asked.

'Dominic! Really, that's not polite,' scolded Stella.

Harry, feeling himself pinking, looked at Julia and Stella and, laughing feebly, said, 'Well now, that would be telling, wouldn't it? Ha, ha.' He knew he sounded faintly avuncular, as though he should be handing out a shiny sixpence and then cuffing Dominic gently around the ear.

'Well, do you want to see my train set?' Dominic asked next. 'I bet it's bigger than any you've ever had.'

'And there you'd be right,' said Harry, 'as I've never had a train set.'

'Honestly, Dominic, you really shouldn't say things like that. It's rude to brag,' Stella told him, dropping to her knees and looking him square in the face.

Dominic shrugged and turned back to Harry. 'Do you want to see it though?' he persisted.

'Not now, OK?' said Julia testily. 'Later maybe. Poor Harry's only just got here.'

Dominic grinned inanely, twisted round on his toes and then ran out of the hall.

'I'm going to show Harry his room and take him for a tour if that's OK,' Julia told Stella.

'Sure, be my guest. We're having supper at eight but I think your father will be back much before then.'

'I am your guest,' muttered Julia once Stella had headed back towards the kitchen.

Harry was put in the abbey part, the room dominated by a huge four-poster. Unlatching the leaded window, he peered out and above him saw a weather-beaten gargoyle, its mouth a conduit for the guttering that led towards it.

'You like?' asked Julia.

'Very,' grinned Harry, 'it's amazing.'

Her tour led all round the house and then out to the garden. It was a warm day, although there was a cooling breeze. Large white cumuli spattered the deep blue sky. The lawns had just been cut and grass clippings scented the air. Wood pigeons cooed from the trees, their low, soothing song floating out across the gardens. As they paused at a bench by the rose beds, Harry closed his eyes and felt the sun on his lids, his head warm on Julia's lap.

'Ah, this is the life,' he sighed. 'What a place.'

'It's certainly peaceful at the moment,' agreed Julia. She was thoughtful a moment, then said, 'I hope I can live here one day, and not that brat Dominic.'

'What about your brothers?' asked Harry. Mark, four years younger than Julia, had dropped out and was travelling somewhere in South America, while Toby, still only eighteen, was in his last year at school.

'I don't think Mark would want it. One of the reasons he's buggered off is to escape our family. And Toby is in line to inherit my uncle's place in Yorkshire. But he might drop out too, I suppose.'

'I thought you had high hopes for him?'

'No, you're right. I'm sure he'll be fine. He's not as sensitive as Mark. More like Daddy.'

They walked on, over the ha-ha, and then skirted round the valley, until eventually they reached the obelisk. Despite the moss and lichen at its square base, the column looked strong and solid, proudly extending some seventy feet into the air.

'What a wonderful spot,' said Harry, taking in the view. 'I bet you can see this for miles and miles around.'

'You can. It's rather fun, isn't it?'

From their vantage point, they looked towards the house, its full scale and layout clearly mapped out. They spied a Range Rover pull into the drive and then stop in front of the main entrance.

'That's Daddy back,' said Julia dismissively. Harry regretted Charles's return. Somehow it spoilt everything. They'd been quite content, just the two of them, ambling round the garden and fields surrounding the house. It had been so effortless, but Harry feared being with Charles would be an enormous test of good behaviour and concentration. If Julia was scared of him – and she hadn't got to where she was by being intimidated – her father was bound to be a handful.

'Harry?' said Julia at length.

'Hmm?'

'Do you ever wonder whether you'll get married?'

'I've never really thought about it,' lied Harry.

'I hope I do,' continued Julia, 'and have children . . . but I don't think I could bear getting divorced. I'd have to marry someone who was really going to look after me, you know?'

Harry smiled weakly. Just where was this heading? There was another pause, then Julia said, 'I mean, do you think we've got a future together? Have we got what it takes?'

Harry didn't want this conversation. He desperately wanted to be falling madly in love with Julia, and hoped it might still happen, but he didn't feel that way yet. Julia and he had been having fun though, and although he had recognized the significance of meeting her father at the old family home, he liked the way things were progressing slowly. He didn't want to be rushed or pushed into a corner in any way.

'Harry?'

'I don't know, Julia,' he told her, 'I hope so. Don't tempt fate yet though, hey?'

She smiled at him, revealing a vulnerability he'd never noticed before. The sun lit up one side of her face and blonde wisps of hair gently blew across her cheek. Without her normal armament of eye and lip make-up, she looked softer, more naturally beautiful.

'I think I've fallen in love with you,' she told him. Then she looked away, as though embarrassed by her confession.

Harry's mind raced. What should he say back? What she wanted to hear, or what he really felt? Sitting by her at that moment, with her looking as lovely as she did, he felt he should be in love with her too. But could he say it and really mean it?

Suddenly their relationship, previously so easy and relaxed, had taken on a whole new meaning. Julia, without consulting Harry, was moving them on a stage, and he felt panicked.

'I love you too,' he said.

She smiled, then laughed bashfully, and Harry could see her eyes glistening. Shit, shit, shit! he thought. It was all wrong – he was being forced into a situation he didn't want.

'I've never said that to anyone before,' she told him, kissing him and then standing up.

'Oh, I used to all the time when I was younger,' said Harry, as cheerfully as he could, 'but I never meant it.'

'But you do now?' said Julia playfully.

'Of course,' Harry replied as they headed back to the house, conscious he'd lied twice in as many minutes.

Harry finally met Charles at the pre-dinner drinks. He was quite short, with a widening girth, white wispy hair and a garrulous, ruddy complexion.

'Nice to see you,' he grunted, cracking into the champagne. 'Sorry not to be here when you arrived. Problem with the bloody boar. Let me tell you now, don't ever have a stock of boar. More bloody effort than they're worth. Dangerous beasts too – can easily break your leg if they run at you. Even worse if you get gored by the bastards. Still, make good sausages and no one else is doing it for miles around. Our sausages are eaten all over the world in fact. Places you probably never even knew existed.'

He continued in this vein until they sat down to dinner, telling Harry everything about the farm, how successful it was while everyone else was struggling ('Small scale's a waste of time. No wonder the smaller farmers are having problems – they need to think bigger'). He barely paused for breath and yet somehow he'd still managed to finish off several glasses of Krug.

Then Dominic ran into the room, dressed in his pyjamas.

'Dominic, you should be in bed,' growled Charles.

'He just wants to say goodnight to everyone, don't you, darling?' chipped in Stella.

'Yes,' said Dominic, standing firmly in front of his mother, 'and have a drink like everyone else.'

'Here, pass him this, would you?' said Charles, handing Harry a glass of water.

Harry passed it to Dominic, felt him grip the glass and then let go. Immediately, it crashed to the floor, splinters of glass flying everywhere.

'Dominic! For God's sake,' muttered Charles.

'Sorry, I thought he'd taken it,' said Harry helplessly as Dominic burst into tears.

'Don't worry, it's not your fault,' Julia told him reassuringly.

'You're over-tired, darling, that's all,' Stella told her wailing son.

'He didn't give it to me, it was *his* fault,' bawled Dominic, pointing an accusing finger at Harry.

'Come on, bed,' said Stella decisively, grabbing his hand and leading him from the room.

'The sooner he's packed off to prep school, the better,' muttered Charles, bending down awkwardly and picking up the larger pieces of broken glass. Harry squatted too, and hunted for scattered shards, aware of Charles's suspicious glances. Julia, too, looked embarrassed, but Stella soon returned and did her best to diffuse the situation.

'Don't worry,' she said to Harry, 'he was just tired. You know how children can get.'

'That your Citroën outside?' Charles eventually asked him as they began to eat.

'Yes, it is,' Harry replied, elbows in and gingerly cutting his gravadlax.

'Bloody good everyday cars in their time. They were very modern when they first came out. First mass-produced monocoque car. That's why they're called *traction avant* – it's Frog for front-wheel drive.'

Harry, who'd been obsessed by these cars since childhood and knew intricate details about paint codes and production numbers, didn't need to be told this.

'Well, mine's one of the later models – he began, but was cut off.

'A Light Fifteen, that's what they call your type.' Now he was being incorrect too – couldn't this fat git tell the difference between a French and a British model?

'Actually, it's an *onze légère*, Daddy,' said Julia, adding, 'it's a French one.'

'Yes, I know that, Julia,' snapped Charles testily, 'but in English, they're called Light Fifteen.'

'Does it really matter what it's called?' Stella smiled. 'It's still a jolly nice old car.'

Harry winced slightly and tried a question of his own. 'I hear you've got a few cars yourself.'

'Yes. Half-decent motors too. A couple of XKs, a Phantom II and an old DB5.'

'I thought you had a Jaguar,' put in Julia.

'I've got two, Julia, those are the XKs.' He rolled his eyes knowingly at Harry.

'And which one's the James Bond car?' she persisted.

'The Aston Martin DB5,' Charles told her wearily. Clearly, this was men's stuff.

'Very nice,' said Harry appreciatively, conscious Charles hadn't offered to show them to him.

There was slight lull between courses, and then Julia said, 'Harry's an artist, Daddy.'

'Oh yes?' said Charles sceptically. 'Not that modern crap, I hope. If you ask me, it's a bloody joke.'

'Well, I'm not a modernist actually. Murals is what I do mostly, but I'm a big fan of neo-classicism and the rococo.'

Charles grunted a begrudging approval.

'But this place is magnificent.' Harry tried a change of tack. 'Do tell me more about it.' He thought he might be very rude any moment, and hoped this would change the rapidly developing *impasse*. It did: Charles launched into a detailed history of the place, his family and more anecdotes about the first owner, barely pausing for breath until fetching the port and lighting himself an enormous cigar.

'Well done, Harry,' said Julia, once Charles had announced he was ready for 'Bedfordshire'. Stella, having cleared away most of the table things with the help of Harry and Julia, had disappeared long before.

'She hardly said a word all night,' whispered Harry.

'I think she's quite shy, but it's not helped by Daddy playing the dominant male.'

Harry stretched and yawned, suddenly tired. His single room now appeared an even more attractive proposition; he didn't feel up to satisfying Julia's voracious sexual appetite into the early hours. He just wanted the night off so he could have a really good long night's sleep. Charles had more than lived up to his expectations; he didn't know how anyone could put up with such a cantankerous, misogynistic, bullying old bore. No wonder Julia had been so apprehensive. Still, what a house, and a fantastic place to be if only her father could be avoided. Having seen Julia to her room, he stumbled back down the weaving corridors towards his own at the abbey end. Had he not been so exhausted, he might have found the dark, aged walls quite spooky, but as it was, the moment his head hit the pillow, he fell fast asleep, his concerns about Julia temporarily put on hold.

He awoke as Julia slipped into bed beside him.

'Julia, what are you doing here?' he mumbled, still full of sleep.

'I suddenly felt bad leaving you all on your own down here. Anyway, Daddy's fast asleep now – I could hear him snoring.'

'Why should he care anyway?' said Harry, sitting up in bed.

'We're Catholic. I'm lapsed obviously, but he's against sex before marriage. Or so he says. Although I can't believe he hadn't slept with Stella before they married.'

Harry always slept with the curtains at least half open as he liked waking in summer to see what the day was like outside. This night, an almost full moon shone through the lead-latticed windows, giving the whole room a luminous glow. Harry was just wondering whether he had the strength to perform when Julia peeled off her silk pyjamas and started kissing him hungrily. Her smooth body, with just a hint of goose-bumps, looked creamy pale in the moonlight, which emphasized its every curve. Thrusting her sex towards Harry's face, she began to moan.

'Lick me, Harry, suck my fanny!' she exclaimed loudly.

'Shh, darling,' said Harry in hushed tones, 'I really don't want to be shot by your father.'

'Oh don't worry about him – these walls are so thick he won't be able to hear a thing,' she breathed heavily into his ear. 'Oh yes, please, Harry,' she continued to moan.

Then she was straddling him, pumping up and down on his over-used penis, the four-poster rocking and banging against the wall with each rhythmic thrust.

'Oh yes, yes, hurt me, harder, ow, ow, OWWW!'

The door swung back and crashed into the wall.

'What the bloody hell – Julia?'

'Daddy! What are you doing here?' screeched Julia.

'Thought you were being bloody raped!' Charles stood in the doorway, his pyjamas and dressing gown loosely covering his bulky frame. And he *was* carrying a shotgun. Julia vainly clutched the sheet to her breasts, while Harry turned his head in abject horror, burying it in the pillow with a loud groan. Charles, lingering by the door, was clearly shocked.

'Get back to bed now – and as for you, young man, we have rules in this house. Julia, you should know better. You both disgust me.' He spat out the words, wild, angry eyes homed in on his naked daughter. 'I want the pair of you out of here first thing.'

'Daddy, please!' wailed Julia, embarrassment, humiliation and anger evident in her beseeching.

'You're in no position to argue,' barked Charles.

'I can't believe you're doing this,' hissed Julia, her rage winning through. 'You fuck up all our lives and even now, when I'm nearly thirty, you're still trying to ruin everything for me.' She began crying, deep convulsions interrupting her words, and then, ineffectively clutching her pyjamas, she sprang from the bed and ran out of the room, her sobs echoing down the corridor.

Charles paused a moment, then calmly said, 'I don't ever want to see you here again.'

Harry, frozen with horror, heard the door slam, then started laughing manically. Julia and her fucking pillow talk was going to be the ruin of her. Christ! How embarrassing had that just been?

But at least with Julia banished he could now go back to sleep. Slowly, he sank back under the covers and closed his eyes. But after the shock of Charles's interruption had worn off, he lay awake thinking he would never be able to marry Julia while Charles was alive, or at least not without eloping. Even then, Charles would probably track them down and shoot him with his shotgun. That was what people like Charles did to filthy curs like him.

He didn't want this. He wanted everything to be uncomplicated, and to have a normal, happy, utterly contented relationship, with his ideal partner, he adoring her, and she adoring him; no hang-ups, no trauma. Just – *perfect.* He'd played his hand badly – dishonourably, even. Ben and Lucie had got it right: happily married and welcoming their beautiful baby into the world. So had his parents. Turning over, he tried to find a cool patch of pillow. He was so far behind them, such a long way from finding his dream.

CHAPTER SIX

paternity leave

While Harry's Gloucestershire weekend was descending into surreal farce, Ben and Lucie were beginning to appreciate what an overwhelming amount of attention a baby required. Added to this was the steady stream of visitors and telephone calls that seemed to litter the day, and the fact that although Ben was officially on leave, he was still expected to put the work in on the Prospero deal from home. Lucie's mother, Vanessa, usually with Terrence in tow, came round at least once a day; her sister Susie and her boyfriend Bill came up from Bristol on the Saturday, and a steady stream of friends – Flin and Tiffany included – also dropped by to see Ben and Lucie's miracle.

Finally Ben's brother Stephen phoned to say he was bringing Tessa, the two kids and their dad Tony up from Brighton to see the new baby on Sunday afternoon.

'Fantastic, that's all we need,' said Ben once he put the phone down.

'And you can make more of an effort than you usually do,' added Lucie sharply. 'I'm not going to do all the hosting this time, OK?'

'Perhaps I should tell them I've got too much work on.'

'Ben, you can't. Just be nice to them. It'll all be over soon enough.'

Ben dreaded his family coming to town. His father always looked so bloody meek and miserable all the time, while his brothers made snide remarks about his comparative success. And it always left him feeling guilty. Guilty that he had his own comfortable middle-class life, and guilty that he couldn't wait for them to leave. They were his family, his flesh and blood, and he'd virtually disowned them.

They arrived accompanied by the usual awkwardness. Ben never knew how to greet his father – whether to give him a hug or shake his hand, and so did neither. That then set a precedent, and so he didn't greet Stephen or any of the others with anything more than a hand held up and a terse, 'Hi, you made it then.'

Lucie was better. She always gave them all a brief kiss on the cheek, although it made Ben wince when his father, as ever, appeared slightly startled by this spontaneous act of tactility.

'Come on in. Come on in,' said Ben, ushering them into the sitting room. His nephews, Ashley and Luke, with their spiky shorn hair, looked sulky and disinterested. Clearly this was a mind-blowingly boring day for them: a car ride followed by adults cooing over a stupid baby.

'He's got the look of his father,' said Tony, awkwardly perched on the edge of the sofa designed for deep-seated comfort.

'No, he looks much more like Lucie,' countered Stephen. His brother was growing fat, Ben noticed. He still had a thick dark thatch of hair, but his gut now sat tight against his rugby shirt. A big man, Ben thought. Thomas lay peacefully on a baby-rug on the floor, for once not crying.

Ben, hovering by the door, offered drinks. It was early afternoon and as he felt tea would be a bit premature, he went to the sideboard in the dining half of the room to fix beers and gins, leaving Lucie to handle the conversation.

'Mum, can I put the telly on?' asked Ashley. At eight years old, he already wore a Manchester United shirt.

'No, of course you can't. Why don't you play with your Gameboy instead?'

'It's boring.'

'Well, just sit still for a moment, all right? Sorry, Lucie, you were saying?'

'Nothing really,' said Lucie, 'just that it seems very odd to think this time last week he was still inside and now . . .' She left the sentence unfinished, as Ben started handing round the drinks. Tessa looked exhausted, Ben thought. He knew she must be only about thirty-five, but she seemed older. And she never bothered about her appearance – no make-up, no jewellery, just faded black leggings, a large checked shirt and a shapeless haircut. He couldn't imagine Lucie ever going to pot like that, even after two kids.

'Why's Ben's house bigger than ours when there's more of us?' asked Luke suddenly, who was six and draping himself across his mother's legs.

'Because he makes lots more money than Dad,' Tessa told him, adding, 'You've got a really lovely place here, haven't you, Lucie?'

'We're really very lucky,' said Lucie, 'although we bought this with some of my dad's inheritance, so you know it's not really to do with Ben's job.'

'But I bet you take home a tidy sum all the same, don't you, Ben?' said Stephen, finally entering into the conversation.

Ben smiled, his irritation already rising. 'But they take away my soul, the amount of hours I have to work.'

'Yeah, and you'll probably regret that when the baby's a bit older and wanting to play football with you.'

'Probably, yes.' There was no point in rising to Stephen's challenges. Instead Ben turned to his father, who sat silently gazing at his gin and tonic. 'So how're things with you, Dad?'

'Fine, yes. You know.'

'And Brighton?'

'Much the same. They're thinking of rebuilding the West Pier.'

'Some hot-shot developer,' added Stephen. 'Waste of time if you ask me.'

Ben noticed Ashley whispering to his mother about the television.

'You can watch it upstairs in our room if you like,' he said to him.

Ashley smiled disingenuously, pretending to be embarrassed, said, 'Thanks, Uncle Ben,' then, with Luke in tow, thundered up the stairs. Thomas started crying.

'Sorry Ben, they're complete terrors, I know,' said Tessa as Lucie rushed to comfort her son.

Stephen, who refused to sit down, preferring to pace about instead, caused further anxiety by lighting a cigarette.

'Stephen,' said Ben quickly, catching Lucie's look of horror, 'let me show you what I'm hoping to do outside.'

'You great oaf,' said Tessa, 'what about the baby?'

'Really, it's not a problem,' added Ben hastily, 'but let's go into the garden, just while Thomas is around.'

Stephen shrugged, took a deep drag and followed Ben through the french windows.

'You're doing well, really well,' Stephen told him outside, 'but how you can put up with London, I don't know.'

'You get used to it – all the cars and everything. I quite like it actually. And the park's just round the corner. I miss the sea, but otherwise ... You know, we've got quite a few friends here.'

'Playing much football these days?' asked Stephen.

'Try to – every Tuesday night with a few mates, you know, just for a laugh and a bit of a kick-around.'

'Just you wait – a couple of kids and it won't be so easy,' Stephen told him, stubbing out his cigarette on the terracotta stone patio. 'I haven't done much sport for a long while now. Not enough fucking time.' It showed too, thought Ben.

Ben offered a second round of drinks. Tea this time, with cake and biscuits, which he made sure took plenty of time to organize. After watching hot mugs scald the waxed table and crumbs being ground into the rug, Ben whisked away the tray and plates, and clattered about the kitchen clearing up and wasting more time.

'He's a lovely-looking baby.' Ben hadn't noticed his father standing by the door, and he turned with a start.

'Do you think so?' Ben smiled.

'Of course. How are you finding it? Parenthood, that is?'

'Fine. Exciting. You know.'

'Ben,' his father began, 'I wish, that is, it would be good, if . . .' Tony looked down, momentarily shifting feet. 'Well . . . you know you're always welcome at home. Don't feel you have to stay up here all the time. Or if you want any help with Thomas. A weekend off . . .'

'Sure, thanks. I'd love to come down more, but you know, for the moment, we should probably stay in London most weekends. Especially when Thomas is so small. But soon. Lucie and I'll come down soon.'

His father looked around the room and shrugged. 'Of course. Well, just thought I'd mention it.' He smiled sadly, then turned and went back to the others.

They left soon after. As they shuffled out, Ben, clutching Thomas, followed and waved them off, conscious his farewells were considerably more heartfelt than his welcome.

'Your dad was as chatty as ever,' said Lucie once Ben had returned and sprawled on the sofa. 'I swear he says less every time I see him.'

'He's got nothing *to* say,' said Ben, sighing audibly. 'I feel sorry for him, I really do. He's so used to having a terrible time, he's completely forgotten how to enjoy himself. He asked us to come down more. Said he'd look after Thomas if we wanted a weekend off.'

'Oh, Ben, it's so sad. I wish you could get on better. Maybe we should get him up for a few days on his own – take him out, see a show, you know, force him to do something interesting.'

'Maybe,' said Ben. Seeing his family reinforced his belief that he'd been right to escape. This was why he'd worked his arse off: so that he wouldn't end up like them. Was this snobbery? Maybe, but it was more than that. Seeing them always reminded him of those dark days. His father had been hard up and complacent, and his mother had left. He wouldn't make the same mistake.

For the new parents, Monday came too soon, and Ben's paternity leave was almost over. He desperately wished he could have an extension, and that Thomas had been born during a quieter period at work, but such was life. He'd been lucky to have the best part of four days off. Carl wanted to announce the deal in a week's time, and there was still much to be done. The press release needed further ironing out and the week ahead was going to be full of endless meetings with the various parties concerned to confirm the equity financing and underwriting agreement. Steve had nobly carried the can, working through the weekend, but now it was up to Ben to take up the reins once more. It would be a manic seven days. There was no way round that, and he knew it. If you worked for a high-powered investment bank you had to show total commitment at all times, and this could mean working virtually around the clock when a deal was going live. It was the price to be paid for a good salary and few worries financially. Still, he didn't have to like it, and he hated the thought of leaving Lucie on her own. Even more, he resented having to spend all day away from Thomas. It was going to be a terrible wrench.

'Are you sure you'll be all right?' he asked Lucie on Sunday night. Thomas was asleep, and they were lying in bed.

'Of course I will. I've got to get used to it, so the sooner the better,' she told him.

'I'm afraid I'm not going to be able to get back early at all this week. You know that, don't you?' Ben told her.

'I do, darling.' She kissed him. 'But if you didn't work that hard I wouldn't be able to give up work and we couldn't afford the life we live.'

'And you're sure you don't want to hire a maternity nurse? We can afford it, you know.'

'I know, but, darling, I want to try to do this on my own. I just don't want some stranger living in our house. So no more talk of that, OK?'

'As long as you're sure. Ring me any time?'

'Of course.'

'And at least your mum's near to hand.' Vanessa lived in Barnes, a mere stone's throw away.

'I want to try to keep Mum out of it actually, darling.'

'Well, whatever you think best,' Ben said as he stroked her hair.

'It's just that she's already starting to get on my nerves. Somehow I always seem to be doing everything wrong. I'm changing a nappy or trying to rock Thomas to sleep, and suddenly I'm aware of her hovering nearby, just *itching* to point out the mistakes I'm making. I try not to react or respond in any way, and then she can't resist it any longer. She honestly can't help herself. "If I were you, I'd try it like this." It's fucking annoying, especially as she's inevitably proved right. Then, *then*, and this is the bit that really bugs me, she gives this kind of patronizing glance as if to say, "Of course I'm right, but your mistakes are entirely natural." It's totally infuriating. I mean, I've got to find out myself, haven't I?'

'Well, I did notice she was being a bit superior, but I didn't like to say anything. Couldn't you tell her how irritating it is?'

'I did this morning. I finally snapped and told her not to keep telling me how to do everything. She looked hurt, of course, but couldn't help a stinging riposte.'

'Why, what did she say?'

Lucie mimicked her mother's high-pitched voice, '"All right, darling, but I'm only trying to help, and one day you'll thank me for being here for you. Just try doing it on your own like I had to in Germany – a foreign country."'

Ben kissed her. 'You'll be just fine.'

'Do you think so?' Ben had rarely seen her look so worried. 'Maybe with you at work,' she added, 'I'll be forced to come to grips with motherhood. But it does seem so hard. I'm nervous. I don't feel in control, and I'm not used to it.'

'You'll be fine,' Ben said again, 'really, darling, please don't worry.'

Lucie smiled at him uncertainly. 'I'll try not to,' she said.

It was dark by the time Ben eventually made it home the next day. As he slammed the door behind him, there was a momentary pause before the crying began again.

'Oh dear, woken the little fellow,' he said heartily, heading for the stairs. 'Coming, Thomas,' he called up cheerfully, adding more loudly, 'Any supper left? I'm famished.'

He hadn't really noticed Lucie standing in the sitting room, not even given her a kiss. Eventually bounding downstairs again, he found his wife crumpled on the sofa sobbing and sobbing. This shocked him.

'Darling? What's the matter?' he said, rushing over to her and lifting her red, tear-stained face.

'There isn't any supper,' she choked, 'I'm a failure, a total failure.'

'What are you talking about?' said Ben, incredulous.

'I can't do it, Ben, can't you see? I'm hopeless.'

'Luce, what is it? What do you mean?' He had never, ever seen her in such a state.

'Thomas hasn't stopped crying all day, apart from when the midwife was here to sort him out. What does she do that I don't? It's so humiliating. And no one's phoned, apart from you – and that was just the once. I really hoped you might surprise me and be home early. It's chaos here, absolute fucking mayhem, and I feel out of control, incapable, incompetent.'

'Luce, it'll just take time,' said Ben, feeling her hot little head gulping into his chest.

'Oh, Ben,' she sobbed, 'why didn't anyone prepare me for this?'

He held her tightly. The flowers everyone had bought had begun to look tired too: drooping sadly, yellowing petals falling onto the floor below. The euphoria was over.

CHAPTER SEVEN

Flin's quest to become a modern-day Pop Larkin takes a step in the right direction

True to his promise to Tiffany, Flin had immediately taken the initiative and put calls out to several PR recruitment firms. He had eight years in film public relations under his belt, and was able to make his CV look impressive, but even so, he worried he was good for nothing but work in the same field. But, to his relief, the recruitment consultant he saw a week later seemed confident he wouldn't have much difficulty finding PR work of a slightly different kind.

'You've worked with high-profile people and you know high-profile people. That counts for a lot,' she told him, whilst making it abundantly clear she thought he was mad to want to swap the glamour and excitement of working on major films for the quiet mundanity of a regional publicist's job. Flin, recognizing this, began to explain.

'I don't want to live in London any more,' he told her simply.

'Why don't you commute?' It was a reasonable question.

'Couldn't do that – I want to be really in the country, not some commuter-belt village with pavements and neon. Anyway,

I want to be away from London completely. I'm through with this place.'

'Wouldn't you miss working in film?'

'Don't think so. There're a lot of egos, you know. All very exciting to start with, but I assure you it does wear thin.'

The consultant, who, Flin noticed, had a George Clooney calendar on the side of her desk, looked unconvinced.

'Well, there *is* a job going in Newcastle, which might be good for you. I'll certainly put you forward for that,' she told him, the doubt still present in her tone.

It was obviously fate, Flin told himself. It had to be: first job on offer in his preferred location. Scarlet Media Relations were an offshoot of the parent advertising agency, and their client list seemed to Flin pretty impressive. He'd assumed the work would largely be for the council and local industry, but Scarlet had accounts with all the sports, television and arts in the area, suggesting the work might well be more interesting than he'd initially supposed.

Tiffany was quick to add a note of caution. 'But are you sure that's where you want us to go, Flin?' she asked him later, as they sat at their tiny two-man table in the kitchen, a bottle of wine open in front of them.

'I don't know. I think so – I mean, it has lots going for us, doesn't it?'

'But it *is* quite a long way north. Not for an Aussie, of course, but for a southern Pom, Northumberland must seem a million miles away. What if one day we have a kid? Won't you want your parents nearby for that?'

Flin ruffled his short mop of hair, then looked at Tiffany searchingly. 'Of course I would *ideally*,' he said, 'but we can't have everything. It's much cheaper up north, and my parents can always come and stay whenever they want, can't they? And so can our friends. Just think – the weekends will be brilliant.'

Tiffany reached across to him and gently put her hand on his cheek. 'Well, that's fine then. I just want you to be sure.'

'I am,' said Flin decisively. 'And we *will* be fine. We'll love it up there. Anyway, I've got to get the job first.'

The interview proved to be an informal affair; more like a chat really. Doug was the man in charge of the Media Relations part of the company, with a team of twenty underneath him. He needed a number two, as his present second-in-command was moving abroad with her husband. It was a shame, he told Flin, as Anna had been a great asset to Scarlet over the years and had helped forge a great little team. But, he added, some London experience, especially from someone with such obviously good contacts, could give the company a great lift.

With mounting excitement, Flin realized that Doug was desperate to like him and to be able to offer him the job. Amazing really, Flin thought, hoping Doug wouldn't ruin things by asking tricky questions about promoting tourism along Hadrian's Wall, or some other north-eastern feature. But the grilling never came. Instead, Flin sat in Doug's neat bare-brick-walled office, with its views across the river and the famous Tyne bridge, and listened eagerly as his supposed interviewer talked about the format of the company, the links with the advertising team on the floor below, and how Scarlet Media was simply 'a great environment in which to work'. He then showed Flin a selection of framed photos of himself with famous footballers and dignitaries, before leading him on a tour of the building.

'We've only been here a couple of years,' Doug explained in his bland, distinctly southern accent. 'The whole of the river front has been really revitalized during the past decade. This used to be an old warehouse, but the developers got hold of it and converted it into offices.'

'I'll bet you're rather glad they did, aren't you?' said Flin, looking out through the huge windows between the blasted brick walls.

'You bet – it's a great place to work. Very New York.'

Flin grinned delightedly. It was certainly more aesthetically pleasing than his office in Soho, with its chaos and stale-looking carpets. Quite *slick*, in fact.

Flin really took to Doug. With a very short ring of hair around the sides and back of his head, he looked forty or so, although Flin knew bald men were often younger than they appeared. He was much shorter than Flin too, but, as he gesticulated freely in his media-black suit and grey shirt (no tie), Doug gave the impression of enthusiasm tempered with neat self-control. He too had started his career – and life – in London, but he reassured Flin that he found his work for Scarlet incomparably more rewarding than anything he'd ever done down south. Flin found the sales pitch this man seemed to be doing on him hugely gratifying. He just desperately hoped he hadn't misread the signals.

But later, on the train heading back to London, Flin gazed out of the window, ruminating on what they would be letting themselves in for. It was a hell of a long way north, no matter how quick the train links were. Perhaps Tiffany was right. And perhaps he would miss his friends too much. As he sipped a plastic cup of tea, the train jerked slightly, scalding his mouth and spilling hot sugary liquid down the front of his suit.

'Damn,' he cursed to himself. Why did the train always jolt just as he put the cup to his mouth? The child sitting opposite him started laughing and this prompted a wave of extreme irritation to sweep over Flin. Why did life have to be so complicated? Why couldn't he be like Geordie and able to live pretty much where he wanted? He'd always had it in mind that one day he would return to Wiltshire, to the gently rolling chalk landscape of his childhood. Now, as the train rushed through the featureless middle-England countryside on its way south, he realized this was unlikely. If they moved to the north-east, it would be very hard ever to come back down south again – the regional differences in property prices were simply too great. And what of Tiffany's point about kids? Wouldn't they lose out being so far away from their grandparents? Then again, perhaps it was better to start afresh, and put his sentimental attachment to south Wiltshire behind him. With sudden clarity, Flin understood he was fast approaching a defining moment in his life. His twenties had essentially been a continuation of his late teens: spending time with girlfriends and surrounded by friends, going to bars, taking weekends away. Now he had just turned thirty and the time had come to establish a grown-up, adult life complete with a house in the country, and far removed from the world in which he had existed for the past decade. Time to say goodbye to his old life, and swap it for an existence far more like that of his parents. This was natural enough; and at thirty, he was the age his mother and father were when he'd been born. Quite a sobering thought. Scary too.

Three days later Doug phoned offering the job. Having excised all his doubts, Flin had returned to his earlier stance of pro-Northumberland enthusiasm and so accepted immediately. A letter, offering to match his present salary, 'plus benefits of company car, pension and membership of the Waterfront Health Club', followed a day later.

'So, you're going to accept?' Tiffany asked.

'Yes, as long as it's what you want too.'

Tiffany clapped her hands together excitedly, then said, 'Fantastic!'

Later that evening, and barely able to contain their excitement, they went out to celebrate the new life that lay before them. Flin's current job's notice period would give them plenty of time to rent their flat out, find somewhere to live, and for Tiffany to look for work too.

Sitting by the window of their local Pizza Express, they clinked their glasses happily.

'A new life darling. Cheers,' said Flin, grinning.

'Cheers, honey. This is just *so* exciting.'

'We could be up there in a matter of weeks. Just think.'

'But what happens if I can't find anything to do?' said Tiffany.

'Well, we might be a bit hard up, but I reckon we could survive off my salary for a bit. It's much cheaper up there, you know. I honestly reckon we blow half our monthly spending money just to compensate for living in London – all that travel, those over-priced sandwiches and coffees and all the eating and drinking out we do – it's hideously expensive. Geordie says he hardly spends a thing now he's moved to Wiltshire.'

'Yes, but, hon, I know Geordie's your oldest friend and everything, and please don't take this the wrong way, but he is minted and we're not. I think your and Geordie's idea of "not spending a thing" are slightly different.'

'Yes, well, maybe, but even so, Tiff, it's got to be cheaper than living in London, hey?'

'OK, I'm sure your basic point is right. Anyway, I don't mind being a bit broke for a while. But you must remember not to take it personally if Ben or Geordie still seem to go on flash holidays and we don't.'

'I promise.' He knew Tiffany found this slight competitive tendency annoying. He'd always compared himself materially with his friends and had always felt he came second best. Totally ridiculous, but luckily, he had Tiffany to put the brake on his less attractive traits. It was one of the many reasons Tiffany was so perfect for him.

'And anyway,' she continued, 'I might find a really good job up there; the BBC and Tyne Tees Television are based in Newcastle for starters. Something'll turn up.'

And so it proved, largely owing to a couple of pieces of serendipity.

A few days later, Flin was in his office when Tiffany rang. 'Guess what?' She sounded excited.

'Well? Have you done it?'

'Sure have, and David's been brilliant. He said he was sorry I'd be leaving, but could completely understand, and then to call his old mate Iain who makes documentaries for – and you'll never believe this – Yorkshire Television and Tyne Tees!'

'No!' This *was* good news.

'Yeah! I promise. Isn't that wild? And it gets better. Apparently he's just been commissioned to make a documentary about the Battle of Britain, and is looking for another researcher. David's going to phone him. It's so exciting. I just knew this was all going to work out.'

Flin rang off. Perhaps the mugging, in some perverse way, had been a good thing. If it hadn't happened, it was all too likely they would never have taken the plunge. Everything was going so smoothly, so perfectly according to plan. He only wondered why he hadn't done it sooner.

By the time Flin arrived home that night, Tiffany already lay stretched out on the sofa reading a newly bought paperback about the Battle of Britain.

'He rang,' said Tiffany delightedly, 'David's friend Iain. He's coming down to town next week and I'm meeting him for a drink. I feel so excited about it, but you know, kind of apprehensive too. This is just too much of a freaky coincidence to screw up.'

'You won't, Tiff, you'll be fine.'

Iain did offer her the job. Later she told Flin how it had been the most informal interview of her life.

'He even bought me a pint,' she told him as they wandered down the road to the pub. David, she explained, had warned her not to dress up and just to be herself, as Iain was apparently notoriously down-at-heel. Anyway, since they were meeting in a pub, she knew it was hardly going to be a formal interview. Having got there first with plenty of time to spare, she spotted him as soon as he walked through the door a short while later: tall and slightly gaunt, wearing a battered Barbour and smoking a pipe. She felt glad she'd taken David at his word and worn her jeans.

'And did you like him?' asked Flin, putting his arm around her.

'Yeah, he was great. Funny, and really friendly. We just chatted away, and then a few of your granddad's yarns later, he said, "Well, the job's yours if you want it," and I said, "Too right I want it," and we chinked our pints and that was that.'

'Brilliant. Just brilliant. See, I told you this was meant to be.'

'Contract's only nine months though, I'm afraid, but something else is bound to turn up. And of course the pay's not quite so good, but even so.'

Outside the Bird in Hand, Flin paused and held her hand, listening to the noises of the city. Sirens cut across the air and music throbbed from a nearby open window. Artificial noises; no birdsong. All that was about to change, he reflected happily.

Finding a house proved to be far more of a problem. They became close personal friends with a small number of Northumbrian letting agents and spent several weekends looking around properties in a large triangle stretching away from Newcastle along Hadrian's Wall and as far north as Alnwick on the coast. But they could find nothing that was quite right, and began to despair. They both agreed they wanted a little bit of land – geese, the odd sheep, and a bit of space for growing things were very much a part of the rural dream they'd painted for themselves. And obviously the house needed to be old, a 'character' property. Unfortunately though, most of the places on offer were either renovated with modern, shiny interiors, or out of date and run down. This depressed them, and also slightly embarrassed Flin; having completely succumbed to the friendly charm of the letting agents, he hated having to repeatedly turn down everything they offered.

Just three weeks before they were due to head up north, Flin and Tiffany sat in the Atlas having a drink with Harry and Julia, initially talking not of houses, but of Ben and Lucie. They were all a bit worried about them.

'I'm amazed, to be honest,' said Harry, moving his chair closer to the table in a conspiratorial fashion, 'I mean, I really thought Lucie – the most competent no-nonsense woman I have ever met – would take to motherhood like a duck to water.'

'It's not like running a business though,' said Tiffany. 'Your body changes shape, your hormones go haywire and a baby doesn't respond in a way that adults in a board meeting do. I don't think anyone can tell how they're going to react to being a mother until it happens.'

'Poor old Ben,' said Flin, standing up to buy more drinks.

'Poor Ben?' said Julia accusingly. 'Poor Lucie, more like. It's not as if he's had to go through what she has.'

'No, I didn't mean that. I meant it must be a shock to him. He had this image of coming home to a smiling wife and fresh-faced bouncing baby boy, supper on the table and the house looking immaculate. And obviously the reality is a wailing kid, a fraught mother and the house looking a tip.'

Harry sighed. 'I remember thinking marriage seemed such a big deal a few years ago, and of course it is, but really, nothing changes things like kids coming along. Your whole life is altered irrevocably. I haven't been for a drink with Ben in ages. He's not even coming to Tuesday night football at the moment. Honestly, why do people do it? I think I'm too selfish to have kids. I like being in control of my life.'

Julia shot him a hard look, not missed by Flin.

Tiffany laughed. 'You just resent not being able to go round to their house whenever you feel like it as you used to do.'

'That's true. I do miss them,' he admitted.

'Well, both you and Flin are godfathers. Why don't you try to help out a bit more? Take Thomas off Lucie's hands once in a while. That way you might discover the appeal of young kids *and* you could see more of Lucie and Ben.'

'Hadn't thought of that,' said Harry, rubbing his chin thoughtfully. The prospect of looking after a crying baby and feeling completely helpless didn't hugely appeal, but perhaps he should try to overcome such fears. And Tiffany was right: it would mean seeing more of his friends. Maybe they would appreciate a helping hand from someone who wasn't a mother or family member. He knew Ben was certainly tiring of Lucie's mother.

'But I'm sure Lucie'll pull through,' said Tiffany, 'it's just getting used to the huge change, that's all.'

As Flin returned with more drinks, Julia said, 'So, how's the house-hunting going?'

'Not so good actually,' admitted Flin, sitting down again. He explained how they'd scoured half of Northumberland with no success.

'Maybe we're being too picky,' said Tiffany, 'but you know how it is. You have a mental image of how your house should look, and so far nothing has even come close.'

'Can't wait to come up and visit though,' said Harry.

'If we ever get there,' muttered Flin.

'You know, I might be able to help you out with this,' said Julia casually, as a big waft of cigar smoke from the next-door table enveloped Flin.

'Really?' he said brightening, and trying to flap the smoke away.

'A cousin of mine lives up there. Has loads of houses on the estate. Why don't I ask him if he's got anything suitable?'

Flin glanced excitedly at Tiffany. 'That'd be great, if you're sure you don't mind. Where does this cousin of yours live then?'

'Near Corbridge. It's rather lovely actually.'

'Between them Julia's family must own half the country,' put in Harry. 'I've never met anyone with more cousins, uncles and

93

great-aunts in my entire life.' He grinned at Julia, who lit a cigarette but said nothing.

'So your cousin is near Corbridge, then?' said Flin politely, after a short pause.

'Yes. Willie's a sweetie. And I'll ring him for you later, I promise.' She looked tense.

Once Julia had gone to buy more cigarettes, Harry turned to Flin and Tiffany. 'Nightmare family,' he whispered, 'a bit like Ben's except loaded, landed and ten times worse.'

'Is she screwed up by it?' asked Flin.

'Parents divorced at the wrong time – and sounds as though the father was pretty mean to her mother. Makes you realize how lucky you are.'

'I guess you're right,' said Flin.

'So, stability is not something Julia knows much about, although if she can help you find a house there's obviously something to be said for huge, mad aristocratic families,' said Harry, as Julia slunk her way back towards their table.

As promised, Julia phoned her cousin, and then rang Flin and Tiffany. It seemed they might be in luck. Willie was renovating a house on the edge of the estate and it was almost ready. They should ring the estate office and have a chat about it, which Flin did, the very next morning. There were no particulars but as soon as the estate manager said 'castellated roof' and mentioned an 'ancient standing stone' outside the front door, Flin instinctively knew they'd struck gold.

'Well, would you like to come up and have a chat with Sir William then?' suggested the manager. 'He likes to meet prospective tenants, obviously.'

'Yes, please,' said Flin immediately.

Which was why, almost precisely three months after Flin had picked up the property section of the Saturday *Telegraph* at Ben and Lucie's house, both he and Tiffany came to be waiting in the estate office for an interview with Sir William Powlett, baronet of Rydale. Tiffany, anxiously sitting beside him and twiddling her hair, looked just about as smart as he'd ever seen her. The baggy trousers and outsize jumpers that normally covered her tiny frame had been put aside, replaced, for this important occasion only, by a neat dark blue skirt and jacket. Flin glanced at her apprehensively. She even wore pearls, gently resting against the delicately freckled skin above her jacket.

Flin nudged her. 'D'you know, you look gorgeous in those pearls.'

'Shh,' she said, trying not to smile.

'I'm worried though. What with getting the jobs so easily, it's bound to be the house that lets us down,' said Flin, another wave of nerves jangling in his stomach.

'No, I've got a good feeling about this one.'

'I hope you're right. We're cutting it a bit fine otherwise. What will we do if it's awful?'

Tiffany sighed. 'Look, stop worrying about something that hasn't happened, OK?'

'*OK*. I'll try.'

From everything they'd heard, both Flin and Tiffany had expected Sir William to be middle-aged, rosy-cheeked and up to his neck in tweed. So when a youngish man with light sandy hair wearing jeans and an open-necked shirt came by and introduced himself as Willie, it took them both a moment to realize he was in fact their prospective landlord.

He beamed. 'Gosh, I hope you didn't dress up on my account.'

'Um, well, we did rather,' admitted Tiffany.

'I'm touched. Sorry I look such a bloody disgrace myself.'

'Not at all,' mumbled Flin, noticing Willie elongated his vowels just like Julia.

'I hope you like it. We've almost finished up there, and to be honest, I think it's going to be a *really* super little house. Shall we go straight on over and have a look? That's probably the best thing, isn't it?'

He took them out to the yard and whistled. Suddenly a brown Labrador appeared and bounded over to them.

'In you get, Roger,' Willie said, opening the Land-Rover door.

'Sorry, it's Flin actually,' said Flin.

Willie threw his head back and roared with laughter. 'Oh sorry, Flin,' he said, recovering his composure, 'Roger's the Lab!'

'Oh,' said Flin, feeling himself redden, 'how stupid of me.'

'Not at all,' said Willie, still chuckling, 'that's an *absolute* classic. Love it.'

As Flin got into the car, Roger jumped over the back seat and onto his lap.

'Roger, get back there,' shouted Willie, but it was too late: Flin's suit was already covered in paw-prints and brown hair.

'Christ, look, sorry about that,' said Willie as they headed off.

'Don't worry – it'll brush off.'

'Course it will,' added Tiffany.

'Yes, well, anyway, I called him Roger because it always seems *such* a shame that dogs can't be given human names. And I rather think it suits him. I've also got a Springer called Pete.'

Flin nodded. He couldn't think of any other response.

'So you're mates with Julia then?' continued Willie.

'Yes, down in London,' said Tiffany.

'Great lass. Bloody fit too. Got a lot of time for Julia. Mad father though. Totally bloody tonto, but that's another story. Ah, here we are,' he said, turning off the road and pulling into a yard between some outbuildings and a house. As soon as they stopped, Roger leapt back over the seat again, across Flin and out into the yard.

'Bloody dog, no respect,' remarked Willie smiling, politely opening the passenger door for Tiffany.

*   *   *

The house was everything Flin had hoped for. Open fireplaces for big fires in winter marked two of the downstairs rooms, and sash windows with window seats and internal wooden shutters gave the house a light, warm feel. The hall stretched the depth of the house, and the kitchen, complete with Aga, looked bigger than all the rooms in their London flat together. Upstairs there were four bedrooms, the largest of which had an en-suite bathroom, already fitted with an antique roll-top bath, and views stretching uninterrupted across the fields.

Flin could barely speak. It was perfect, exactly the place he'd been dreaming of. Outside, on the other side of the road, stood the standing stone, as firm and resolute as it had been for the previous three millennia. And then there was nothing – just gently undulating fields and trees.

Willie walked them round the back, to an old yard, with a ramshackle barn and what appeared to be a row of sties. Flin's mind raced. A new vision of their future was opening up before him, refuelling his ideas for their pursuit of the rural idyll.

'You like?' asked Willie, gently kicking one of the old sty doors. 'I mean I think it's *really* rather sweet. There're a few bits and pieces still to do, but you could probably move in tomorrow if you absolutely had to.'

'It's just amazing,' said Tiffany, and for a moment Flin thought she might burst into tears of happiness.

'I love it. I just love it,' he told Willie. 'It's perfect.'

'Well, then it's yours for eight hundred quid a month. Sound fair?'

'Brilliant. Absolutely brilliant,' said Flin, quickly realizing he was going to get more a month for their two-bed flat in Hammersmith.

'And when did you say you want to move up?' asked Willie, pointing to the corner of one of the garages. 'Oil tank goes in there on Monday.'

'In a couple of weeks, ideally. Beginning of July. We've struggled to find anything suitable up until now, so it's all a bit rushed,' Flin explained.

'Ideal,' grinned Willie, 'after all the place is empty and ready to go. Anyway, might see a bit more of Julia now.'

While Willie was talking to Tiffany about what the nearby village of Cotherwick had to offer and the best local pubs, Flin wandered back round to the front of the house and leant on the gate by the standing stone, looking out across the empty meadow. He breathed in deeply the fresh, uncorrupted air. Despite it being a warm, bright summer's day, a cooling breeze fluttered across the field, gently ruffling the hay. So everything had worked out, Flin thought to himself. Now they had the house, their dream was about to be realized. They even had a yard for geese and chickens, a field where they could look after sheep and sties for pigs, if they wanted. And enough of a garden stretching down to the woods at the back to grow some vegetables. Maybe they could live an old-fashioned Pop Larkin type of lifestyle after all. And so quiet. Nothing had passed along the road in the twenty minutes or so since they'd arrived there. Twenty whole minutes! What bliss. He smiled contentedly. This was what they needed. A place where they could really, truly escape. A home where they could do their own thing, untroubled by the frightening city-world of commercialism, supermarkets and millions of people. Escapism, that's what he dreamt of, and this was where it could be achieved. He and Tiffany were going to be really happy here, really, *really* happy. Of that he was certain.

Initially, Flin's talk of sheep and chickens had been something he had absolutely no intention of seeing through. In fact, he was rather doubtful about whether they'd even manage to grow a few of their own vegetables: it was all well and good when discussed in the safe confines of a Hammersmith pub, but unrealistic and rather impractical in actuality.

His mugging though, had caused him to think differently. It had, he came to realize, been his very own Road to Damascus experience, and from then on he determined his life should become far more intimate with the natural. What could possibly be more rewarding than living off fresh produce planted and nurtured on one's own land? How much more wholesome and tastier would lamb be if eaten straight from the field? And just think about all the things one could do with a pig! Bacon, hams (boiled and cured), pork, sausages, salamis. And all tasting wonderfully rich and delicious. This, he felt sure, was the way forward, rather than festering in cities, obsessed with careers, politics, traffic and arguing about the London Underground, and feeling competitive with all his friends. He had come to see city life, especially in London, as ill conceived and unhealthy.

'When we're in the country,' he announced one morning to Tiffany, 'I think we should reject supermarkets altogether.'

'We might need them for the odd thing, though, hon,' she countered.

'All right then – condiments and household goods only. Everything else we should try to grow ourselves or buy locally. What do you think?'

'OK. What about things like Ribena? And sugar?'

'Well, all right, some things may have to come from supermarkets too, but basically we should reject them in every other way.'

'And Nutella. I don't think you'd last very long up there without Nutella.'

'All right, yes, that too. But just the bare minimum.'

'Fine,' agreed Tiffany (although later she confided to Ben and Lucie that she was worried Flin had become slightly depressed since his attack and wondered whether this new rural evangelism of his was a side-effect or just another of his fads. Lucie told her she thought it was probably just a fad).

Initially, he kept his growing smallholding desires to himself, conscious he might otherwise overplay his hand, but gradually he began making indirect references to the beauty of 'growing one's own vegetables' and the virtues of a 'freshly laid egg'. He bought books on horticulture and flora and fungi, and even began subscribing to *Farmers Weekly* and *Country Smallholding Monthly* and leaving copies lying around their flat. Tiffany responded with equally indirect enthusiasm, leaving him still groping to find an opportunity to confront her with his plans head on.

With just a week to go until their move, his enthusiasm reached new heights with the arrival into his life of *The Complete Guide to Self Sufficiency* by John Seymour. Harry gave it to him after discovering it in a second-hand bookshop near his parents' house. It soon became Flin's bible, his mantra for their new life, filled as it was with useful titbits of information for the wannabe smallholder. As he read through the inspiring pages and pored eagerly over the illustrations of how to slaughter a bullock and skin a rabbit, all pretences of subtlety were abandoned.

'John Seymour says pigs are fantastically sensible animals to keep,' Flin told Tiffany another morning over their tea and toast.

Finally Tiffany responded. 'Flin, baby, I've got the message. I'm really up for this self-sufficiency stuff, but I think it should be your job, OK? And don't you think getting a pig might be taking things a little far? I mean, what if we become friends with it? We'll never be able to eat it then.'

'We'll just have to be very strict with ourselves. Not call it a name and keep referring to it as "It". That way it'll be non-personal and no different to any other bacon you eat at the weekend.'

'Not convinced, I'm afraid. Wouldn't it be more sensible to stick to chickens and vegetables to begin with?'

'Baby, bear with me a moment. Pigs are very cost effective: they live off your kitchen waste, plough up the soil with their foraging instincts and fertilize it while they're about it. What could be more sensible than that?'

'But, hon, we'll both be at work all day. Who's going to look after it?'

'That's the beauty of it. According to this book, pigs don't need constant tending. You don't see a farmer perpetually wandering his fields keeping them company, do you?'

'I suppose not.'

'Exactly. We'll feed it twice a day, keep an eye on it, and the rest of the time it can amuse itself. Really, if you're thinking in terms of chickens and geese we may as well go that little bit further and have a pig as well.'

With such thoughts swimming about in his mind Flin finally came to bid adieu to London. He felt a little strange as he left his office for the last time. His boss had organized a small drinks party, said a few words and then handed him a carefully wrapped-up spade as a leaving present from them all. The gathering fell silent, all eyes on him as he tore off the paper and opened his card with pink-faced bashfulness. Soon after, everyone drifted away to get on with their weekends, leaving Flin suddenly alone in his office, silently packing away the last of his things. Then down the lifts for the last time, and out through the streamlined Soho foyer.

'Night, sir,' said the night-porter, as though it was just another Friday evening and not a leap into the great unknown.

'Night,' said Flin, hoisting his bag onto his shoulder and walking out into the crowded street.

Ben and Harry had also organized a party for them, in the upstairs room at the Atlas. It was the obvious place for it. This had been his local during his house-sharing days with Geordie and Jessica; it was where he and Tiffany had been for their first date, several years before; and it was a place his friends continued to use as a meeting point, even now. The amount of time they'd spent here that year he'd lived with Geordie and Jessica! Good times, on the whole. Then Geordie had moved back down to Wiltshire, the first one to take the plunge and leave town. Last year, so had Jessica, when she took a job in New York. Now it was his turn too.

By nine o'clock the place was humming. Even Lucie, who had barely been seen in public since Thomas had been born, managed to come along for a short while, having persuaded her mother to babysit. Old friends from university he hardly ever saw had made it; former work colleagues; an Australian delegation; a few faces from Salisbury days who, like everyone else, had followed the great caravan trail that led to London. A flattering number, Flin kept thinking to himself.

'Quiet please, everyone,' said Ben, soon after.

'Sshhh!' shouted Harry, standing next to him.

'I just thought it was right that someone should say a few words,' Ben continued, prompting heckles from the floor. 'Another two bite the dust. Flin and Tiffany are leaving behind friends, the best pub in town' – cheer – 'and the most exciting and fun city in the world so they can live in *Northumberland*.' (Laughter.) 'Now, I'm sure most of you will agree with me that this is an odd decision – to say the least – for a variety of reasons. One, it's a very long way north; two, it's bloody freezing up there; and three, there's sod all to do, except watch the rain and scrape sheep-shit off your shoes.' (More laughter.) 'But,' he continued, 'but . . . that's their choice, and I must – we all must – respect them for that. And, Flin, I want you to know, if this *is* just a passing phase, you can come back with your head held high, and the assurance that I, for one, will not make you suffer for it. At least, not much. And now, to help you on your way' – Harry passed a package to Ben – 'we have this for you both.' Everyone clapped and cheered again as Flin and Tiffany walked up to the bar where Ben and Harry were standing. Tiffany unwrapped first paper, then layers of plastic bubble-wrap, Flin feeling the spotlight bear down on him for the second time that night.

'Thank you so much,' said Tiffany, kissing them both, then Lucie and anyone else in the immediate vacinity.

'We thought an old map of London might remind you we're still here,' said Harry.

After thanking everyone again, and assuring them Northumberland wasn't really that far away, and certainly not, as Ben seemed to be suggesting, a satellite state of Lapland, Flin paused to look around. He wondered how many of the faces in front of him he'd still see in a year's time. Even now, he saw most of them only at weddings or thirtieth-birthday parties. Or leaving parties. Perhaps this would be the final severance with his old life. Maybe, from now on, he could only be friends with a carefully chosen few. It was the inevitable pattern of changing friendships that happened through life, like the seeds of a dandelion: once clustered together, then blown and scattered to distant corners. He lifted his pint glass, his mind deaf to the noise and clamour around him. He had arrived at a defining moment in his life.

Harry slapped him on the back and the momentary reverie was broken.

'So – no regrets?'

'No,' said Flin, 'none whatsoever.'

CHAPTER EIGHT

fate throws a cat amongst the pigeons

Having dropped Julia at her flat, Harry drove his Citroën back through London, heading for his Brixton home. It was the day after Flin and Tiffany had left for Northumberland and big swirling stormclouds darkened the morning sky, appropriately mirroring his mood. The day before, he had accompanied her to a wedding of another of her cousins. He'd accepted the invitation weeks before, and since the bride came from Julia's mother's side, he'd felt it was still safe to go, even after the débâcle in Gloucestershire. Also he did feel sorry for Julia, aware that the whole episode had been of far greater embarrassment to her than him. She'd raged for days afterwards, swearing she was never going to see her father again, that this time he'd gone too far, and promising Harry it was something he would never, ever have to experience again. Well, she was right about that, Harry had thought, almost finishing their relationship there and then. But did he really want to add to her all-too-evident misery? He still felt very fond of her, and still found her attractive. So he'd thought he would leave it a few weeks – let her get over the humiliation at the hands of her father, and be at her side for her cousin's wedding.

But it had been a dreadful experience. Julia, of course, had looked stunning, but he'd hardly known a person there – he'd never even seen the bride or groom before. The afternoon had bored him beyond belief. Worst had been the knowing looks from Julia's numerous relations. At one point an aunt had said, 'I suppose you two will be next.' He'd laughed disingenuously, but felt a suffocating sense of entrapment, and that, by encouraging Julia to believe in a future that wasn't there, he was being unscrupulously caddish. He hadn't wanted to snap at her, or lose his temper in any way, but nor had he felt at all amorous, and when Julia started to kiss and stroke him later that night he had had to turn over and feign drunkenness to avoid having sex. This sudden desire not to betray himself sexually had felt so strong, he'd been quite angered and shamed by it.

Large raindrops started to appear on his windscreen, but the wipers were ill equipped to deal with them. They tried hard, eagerly swishing the glass with an unco-ordinated lack of synchronicity, but as the drops quickly developed into a downpour, it became harder and harder to see clearly ahead. Having resolutely kept his cool all weekend, he was overwhelmed by a sense of annoyance and frustration.

'Oh, shitting HELL!' he yelled, narrowly avoiding crashing into the car in front at the lights. This was not how it was supposed to be. He'd avoided going out with people precisely so he could prevent the terrible sort of mess he'd got himself into with Julia. Yet he had been so bored with being single, and frustrated that he'd been unable to find his lifetime partner in the way so many of his friends had.

Cars lined the road outside his flat, forcing him to park some way further down the road. By the time he finished his fifty-yard dash to the front door, he was soaked. Still muttering and cursing to himself, he stomped up the stairs and stripping, headed into the shower.

He still had several hours to kill before he was due to meet up with Marcus at the new restaurant. The refitting was now almost done, with Harry's murals the only thing to be completed before reopening. Marcus wanted to make a few last-minute suggestions, and so he suggested they both stand in front of it and work it out together. Having dressed and made a coffee, Harry sunk into his sofa and glanced at the TV pages, hoping for an old black-and-white, or a classic war film to distract him for a couple of hours. But there was nothing that fitted the bill. He supposed he should work, but wasn't really in the mood. Glancing up above through the skylight he saw it had stopped raining. The storm had passed. Harry stretched, finished his coffee, then squinted up again at the sky. Perhaps he would go to a gallery. The National, maybe. Try to feel inspired before the meeting.

Just over an hour later, Harry sat in a café on St Martin's Lane, reading the paper and contemplating whether to order some lunch. The place wasn't too busy and he had a table to himself. The door opened and closed occasionally, but with both elbows on the table and his head in his hands, intently reading the paper spread out before him, he wasn't paying much attention to the various comings and goings. A larger group came in, chatting noisily, and Harry half heard them settle around two tables beyond the bar.

'Is anyone using this chair?'

He looked up. There in front of him stood a girl of reasonable height, not obviously beautiful, but pretty in an open sort of way.

'Oh my God – Harry!' she said.

'Jenny. Wow! God – how are you ? What are you doing here?' He too hurriedly got to his feet, knocking the chair back to the ground awkwardly. 'Whoops,' he said, cursing himself silently as the blood rushed to his face.

'I'm over here on a hen weekend.' She looked back at the party, waving a hand vaguely in their direction. 'We're all feeling a bit rough.' She laughed nervously, eyes straying up and down him.

'Great. Great. So. How've you been?' He didn't know what

to do with his hands, so hopelessly clutched at the rim of the table.

'Fine. Good. You know. God, sorry, Harry, I'm just so, well, you've caught me off guard, you know. It's been a long time and now, well, to see you suddenly here of all places, like this. It's . . . just a little weird, I suppose, and . . .' She waved a hand around, as though hoping this would help her formulate better words.

Harry nodded. She looked lovely. Tired, but lovely. Same chestnut hair, same grey-green eyes and tiny freckles on her nose.

'It would be lovely to catch up properly,' he told her. 'Plan it, so neither of us can feel surprised when we turn up.'

Jenny laughed. 'Yes. That would be nice. I'd like that very much.'

'You live in London?'

'No, well, not at the moment. Do you?'

'Yes, yes, I do,' Harry told her, then, feeling about his pockets, pulled out a pen. 'Here,' he said, writing on the corner of the paper, then tearing off a strip and handing it to her. 'My home number. Call me sometime.'

'OK, Harry, I will. I'd give you mine too, but I'm between places just at the moment. But I'll call you, I promise.' She glanced back at her friends, then paused a moment, looking at Harry, searching his face.

'I'd better let you get back to your friends,' said Harry.

'Yes. Bye then.' She shrugged, turned, then wandered back to the group.

Without bothering to sit down again, Harry folded the papers, left the money for his drink and walked out onto the street. The second time he'd seen her in only a few months. The faint knot of regret that usually accompanied thinking of her tightened even further. To think she'd once professed undying love for him, and now to see her like that, unexpectedly, and in such unsatisfactory circumstances. So familiar it was frightening, but a total stranger too. Perhaps this was his comeuppance, payback for being such a fool all those years before. He glanced at his watch. Still nearly an hour before he was due to meet Marcus. Heading towards Covent Garden, he looked for another place to eat, far enough away to rule out a further chance meeting with Jenny, before realizing he no longer felt hungry.

Ten days later, he had done nothing about Julia, nor heard any more from Jenny, but his parents had come to visit, and sat on his sofa, clutching a drink before supper.

'So Julia's not coming over tonight then?' asked Elizabeth, once Harry had made drinks and the three of them had sat down in his large open-plan sitting room.

'No. No – she can't,' he told his mother, then, quickly changing the subject, said, 'So what's this exhibition you're seeing tomorrow?'

'Your mother's been asked to a special preview of the new Portrait of the Year prize,' said Christopher proudly.

'Should be fun,' said Harry.

'Yes, I hope so,' agreed his mother. 'And it's always nice to be asked. Shows they haven't forgotten me.'

'Course they haven't. Anyway, I thought you were still taking the odd commission? What about those children in Norfolk you were painting last summer?'

Christopher joined in: 'You insist you're always winding down, but you can't quite bring yourself to give it up yet, can you, darling?'

Elizabeth smiled. 'I know. I just hate thinking I'm getting old. I always feel if I keep painting I'll somehow stay fit and healthy. Silly really.'

'Course it isn't. Anyway I don't think of you as old,' said Harry, 'not like Pa.'

Christopher chuckled. Although seventy, he looked and seemed younger, Harry thought, despite his white hair, especially as he always dressed so well; he approved of his father wearing chinos, moleskins and the sort of shirts he'd happily wear himself. 'You're only as old as you feel' was a dogma Christopher rigorously adhered to.

Elizabeth sat beside her son on the long sofa, elegant as ever. She was quite tall and slim, her greying hair neatly bobbed. They'd just come back from a trip to Jordan and both looked tanned and healthy.

'You look like a sophisticated ex-pat, Ma,' said Harry. It was a warm summer's evening and she wore baggy linen slacks and a white cotton shirt over an equally white T-shirt.

'Thank you, darling.' She patted his thigh, then looking around said, 'Have you done something else to the flat? It looks different somehow.'

'I painted it. I suddenly went off yellow. Too bloody hearty somehow.'

'I like it – a sort of *boney* colour.'

Harry grinned. 'Grey's the new yellow, Ma.' He loved his home, and was well aware it was the envy of most of his friends. When he'd moved in, it had been a simple, two-storey, two-bed flat, the second and third floors of what had once been a largish Victorian mid-terrace house. But with his artistic flair and architectural training, Harry had relished the opportunity to create something all of his own. Walls had been pulled down and the roof of the house opened up, so that apart from the kitchen and bathroom, the flat was made into one large room, with stairs leading to a gallery running round three sides of the large open-plan room below. It was up on this gallery that he'd decided to keep his desk, computer, easels and bed, with skylights into the roof providing extra light across the whole, enlarged room. The flat had exhausted the vast majority of his savings, so its contents were a mixture of modern minimalist and old, battered and antique, plundered from his parents' Suffolk home. In what he half jokingly called the atrium, Harry had arranged two sofas (one Habitat sale, the other from his grandmother's house) at right angles around an old military trunk, rejuvenated in its role as coffee table and foot-rest. The sleek television and music system in the corner added to the picture of precise order he liked to convey. At the other end of the room stood an unusual square table he'd found in a junk shop in Rotherhithe. Having been stripped down and rewaxed by himself, it now made a formidable-looking dining table, despite being surrounded by a set of incompatible chairs discovered festering in the Hartwell garage back home. He was pleased with it though – a bargain he'd managed to make look stylish. The pictures were similarly eclectic. A couple of small nineteenth-century landscapes held company with two large framed vintage posters of old Cary Grant films, also picked up from an unlikely-looking junk shop, as well as a few of his own efforts. Harry thought of the flat as his den, his own place, and everything about it and in it was his taste and there because he'd wanted it. And it was so light during the day, although much cooler and calmer now he'd painted over the yellow. That had been too sickly, too cloying – Lucie had been right about that. He loved the mix of old and new: the old Victorian house given a modern overhaul inside; the old furniture and paintings that reassured him and reminded him of home, but side by side with his own personal taste and style.

Although he liked cooking anyway, Harry always made an extra effort whenever his parents came to see him. Less inclined to bother much when on his own, he had also enjoyed cooking meals for Julia in recent months, and was even trying to grow his own window-box of herbs. Now, for his parents, he'd concocted a large salad of rocket, basil, mozzarella, anchovies and sun-dried tomatoes, glistening in olive oil and served with fresh cod fillets picked up from the Brixton market.

'This looks wonderful,' said Christopher.

'Good,' said Harry, pouring them both some more wine.

'So why isn't Julia here?' Elizabeth asked after they'd all taken their first mouthfuls.

'Working late,' said Harry, turning to his father as if about to say something.

'Really? Will she be coming along later?' Elizabeth persisted.

'No.'

'That's a shame. I was rather hoping to see her again.'

Harry smiled at her, trying not to rise to the bait. He knew this tactic of his mother's.

'How's it going with Julia then? All well?' asked Christopher, bluntly sweeping over Elizabeth's more indirect questioning.

'Good, thanks,' he lied.

'Ah, because Elizabeth and I got the impression things were slightly rocky.'

'Christopher!' said Elizabeth.

'What?' replied Christopher. 'We were. No point beating about the bush.'

Elizabeth sighed. 'Really, it's none of our business. If you don't want to talk about it, Harry, that's fine.'

Harry put down his fork and drank a mouthful of his wine. 'Well, since you're obviously not going to stop going on about it, I suppose I'm going to have to tell you.' Elizabeth looked slightly sheepish. 'Things aren't that good between us,' he continued. 'In fact, I'm feeling awful about it.'

'Why, what have you done?' asked Elizabeth, stopping eating to look her son in the eye.

'Nothing,' said Harry, 'yet,' then told them about Jenny, and how he'd seen her twice recently, and that he couldn't stop thinking about her. He even told them about his nightmare weekend with Julia's father and how if anything, she'd started to depend upon him even more since that time.

'I think she's great, and we *do* have a lot of fun together, but I just can't see myself ever wanting to marry her,' he explained.

'You've got to finish it with her,' Elizabeth told him earnestly. 'Do you remember that chap who was desperately in love with Charlotte? She knew it was never going to work out, but it was a terrible wrench for her splitting up with him. But she did, and now look – she's happily married to Steve.'

'You're right,' said Harry, remembering his sister's traumatic early romances.

'And you must do it straight away. Julia is clearly very serious about you and so you must end it before it's too late. You're not being fair to her.'

'What does Ben say about all this?' asked Christopher.

'Ben's got his own worries at the moment. What with Thomas, and Lucie being a bit down, I haven't really talked to him about it too much. But I think he thinks I've lost the plot a bit, to be honest.'

'Talk to Julia, darling. And soon,' said his mother gently, putting a hand reassuringly on his arm.

His mother was right. Of course she was. Harry knew that, but even so, it was going to be terrible ending it with Julia. They'd had a good time together and he had no desire to hurt or upset her. And he would miss her – he loved her in a way, but just not to the level she demanded or could rightly expect. All the next day, he fretted while he tried to work, hardly able to concentrate on the job in the subterranean restaurant. Marcus had wanted a circus scene, and Harry had elaborated this basic brief with pierrots and harlequins dancing between masked elephants and tigers, or performing handstands on plumed and dappled ponies. Only the master of ceremonies was without a mask, standing proudly to one side with a top hat and voluminous moustaches. Beyond and surrounding the ring the performers were shrouded by stripy canvas, pulled back at the edges in great folds. Harry had enjoyed getting carried away, and Marcus loved it, but right now he found it hard to concentrate on the finishing touches.

By the time he packed up his paints and left for the day, it was nearly seven o'clock. Harry jumped into his Citroën and headed over to Kensington, a sickening feeling building in his stomach; the time had come.

'Hi, darling,' Julia called out, opening the door to the flat as he strode up the stairs. Then, pausing to give him a lingering kiss on his lips, she said, 'Hmm, it's good to see you. I've missed you these past couple of days.'

The familiar waft of her scent settled over him as he followed her into the kitchen.

'Glass of wine?' she asked, opening the fridge.

'Great,' said Harry, kneading his hands together. As her shirt was half undone, Harry clearly saw the curve of a breast neatly tucked into her pure white lace bra as she peered into the fridge. Momentarily his resolve wavered.

'There you go,' she said, handing him a large balloon of a glass and kissing him once more as she passed into the drawing room. Why did she have to look so particularly alluring? He sat down next to her on the sofa and tried to compose himself.

Tucking her legs beneath her, she smiled mischievously at him. 'So what shall we do this weekend? Perhaps we could take the Citroën to Sussex or something. Stay in a pub. What d'you think?'

'Julia,' Harry began slowly, 'we have to talk.'

Her face suddenly lost its twinkle, and he noticed her fingers tighten around her glass. He took a deep breath and turned to face her.

'I can't ever marry you.'

A pause and then she carefully put her glass down.

'I'm sorry, but I felt it was better to say this now,' Harry continued, desperately hoping she would say something in return; but instead she just looked down, an expression of incredible sadness etched across her face.

'I know you've been beginning to think of that, but I just don't love you enough. I'm so sorry.' His turn to look down. 'And so I think we should probably end it now.'

At last Julia looked up at him, a tear running down her cheek. 'Oh, Harry,' she said quietly, 'I love you so much, and I thought we were having such a good time. I thought we were *right* for each other.'

'I love you too, Julia,' said Harry, 'but not like that. Not in the way you want me to. Of course we've had a good time but I can't ever give you what you want. You deserve better.'

'Don't say that!' she said, anger entering her voice. 'I know you're right for me, and I'm right for you. I can't believe you're suggesting we should throw it all away.'

'You're not the right one for *me*,' said Harry, turning to her once more and seeing her tear-stained face, mascara running down the porcelain features. He felt terrible, cruel and heartless.

'Harry, you're a fool,' choked Julia. 'You have this idealized view of what marriages are like, that two people can be absolutely perfect for ever. But don't you see? That just doesn't happen in the real world. We could be so happy together, but you can't see it. Because I've got a bully of a father or because we don't agree on absolutely everything, you think we're incompatible.'

'It's got nothing to do with your father,' Harry mumbled.

'Please, Harry,' said Julia, softening once more, 'don't throw this away. We've got something really good. It doesn't have to be perfect. We just have to be happy, that's all.'

'But we're not,' said Harry, confusion, guilt and anger filling his mind, 'you're not, I'm not. Not really.'

'Is there someone else?' Julia suddenly asked accusingly.

'No, of course not!' Harry answered quickly. More lying.

'Then don't leave,' she implored. 'Stay. Give us a chance. Even if you don't feel you love me enough yet, I can wait. I'm sure you will with time. We're right for each other and I *know* you'll come to realize it too.'

Harry stood up and started pacing. 'No, Julia, you're wrong. I'm sorry, I'm desperately sorry, but it's over. Completely, irrevocably. I wish it would work out, I really do. But it won't. Ever. And so that's why I'm ending it now, before it's too late.' He leant down to kiss her, but she grabbed his hand.

'Please, Harry.'

'I've got to go,' he said, pulling his hand away. She looked destroyed, completely different, hardly the Julia he knew at all. The colour had drained from her cheeks, the shine gone from her eyes, and her mouth quivered in an unrecognizable downturn of misery. When she'd run from her father there had been anger in her face. Now there was just a sadness; somehow, it was perplexingly familiar.

'I'm sorry,' he said calmly, then turned and walked out of the flat.

For the next couple of days, a confusion of emotions plagued Harry. His final image of Julia persisted in his mind. In no way proud of himself, he felt terrible about what he'd done, and also sad. He was going to miss her, particularly because he knew he would probably never see her again. That wouldn't be fair. They would never become just friends, even after an appropriate period of readjustment. Ben and Lucie sounded sorry – they'd liked Julia. Lucie even told him he'd been brave to break it off when it would have been easy to string it out.

'Well, thanks, Luce, I appreciate you saying that,' he told her.

'That's OK,' she sighed, before ringing off to go and tend to Thomas, whom Harry heard yelling in the background.

Next he rang Flin. His friend had only been gone a couple of weeks, but already Harry was missing him. With Ben not around so much, the two of them had spent increasing amounts of time together. That was what he wanted now: a few quiet jars in the pub with a good mate. But Flin was over three hundred miles away, and for the moment, a phone call would have to do.

'Poor you. Doesn't make it any easier being the dumper rather than the dumped. If anything, it's worse,' Flin told Harry, then added, 'or so I've heard.'

'Yeah, I know what you mean.'

There was a slight pause, then Flin said a bit more brightly, 'Why don't you come up here and see us? Take your mind off things. You can try out our new pub.'

'D'you know what? That's a great idea. When can I come? I'd love to see you guys.'

'Love to see you too. Come whenever you like. Any time but the weekend after next. We're not quite so busy up here. What are you doing this weekend?'

'Nothing. Well, nothing now. I could come up on Friday, couldn't I?'

'Great. The day after tomorrow. Nothing like a bit of spontaneity.'

Harry felt considerably cheered at the prospect. It would be great to see them, and their new house. Much better to have some fun with his friends than mope about London feeling sorry for himself.

For the next two days, he worked hard and late, throwing all his energy and powers of concentration into his circus scene; in doing so, he managed to keep thoughts of Julia, Jenny and the missing ingredient in his life to a bare minimum. By the time he boarded the train at King's Cross, found his seat and opened a new paperback, a sense of calm had settled over him. Between plastic cups of tea and the pages of his novel, the English countryside rushed past. At Durham he stared out at the magnificent cathedral and castle; it was high summer and still perfectly light, and the ancient buildings, high on their perch, appeared so solid and constant. Centuries of change and different lives and yet they remained the same. Beneath these looming edifices, countless friendships had been won and lost, innumerable love affairs grown and fallen apart. He was no different from hundreds and thousands and millions of people before him, from time immemorial.

CHAPTER NINE

Ben begins to feel frustrated (in more ways than one)

As soon as Ben banged the front door shut, he realized his mistake. Sure enough, after a moment's pause a small splutter came from upstairs, followed by another, and another and then the unmistakable full-on wail of a very angry baby.

'Shit, shit,' cursed Ben as quietly as he could, involuntarily tiptoeing down the hallway in recognition of the sound level he should have adopted.

Silently staring at the opposite wall from her position on the sofa sat Lucie, hugging her knees. She was wearing tracksuit bottoms and one of Ben's old T-shirts.

'Congratulations,' she said flatly. 'Once again you've managed to slam the door, and lo and behold Thomas is screaming his head off.'

'Yes, sorry,' said Ben, standing in the doorway still clutching his briefcase. 'I'll go and get him back to sleep, shall I?'

Lucie didn't answer. Instead she snatched the remote control and, pointing it aggressively at the television, switched on to the end-tune of *EastEnders*.

Upstairs, Ben looked down at Thomas's vividly red face and

wondered how such a small being could possibly look quite so incensed. Gently picking him up, Ben clasped his son to his shoulder, patting his back and walking him round the room.

'It's all right, it's all right, go back to sleep,' he said in as soothing a tone as he could muster, 'I know Daddy's a great big clumsy oaf sometimes, but try to ignore it.'

Slowly but surely Thomas began to calm down until Ben felt his son's arm and heavy head go limp with sleep. This, Ben had discovered, was the crucial moment. With bated breath, he carefully rested one of his large hands behind Thomas's head, and lowered him back onto the soft mattress, paused a moment, then slowly raised himself back to full height and tiptoed back out of the room. Leaving the door ajar he clenched his fist in triumph. Mission completed! Two months down the line, and he was just beginning to come to terms with handling Thomas: holding him and talking to him in a ridiculous voice no longer made him feel self-conscious; he could now quite happily coo and wibble along with the best of them.

Undoing his top button and loosening his tie, he went back downstairs and sat on the sofa opposite Lucie.

'Sorry about that, but he seems to have gone back off OK, so no real harm done.'

'This time,' snapped Lucie, 'but really, Ben, I don't know why you can't get it into your head to just be a bit bloody quiet for a change instead of charging about the place like a bloody elephant.'

'Don't exaggerate, Luce,' retorted Ben, a bit hurt.

'Well, just be a bit more careful about the front door then.' Lucie ran her hand through her hair and, avoiding looking at Ben, continued to stare glassily at the television.

'OK,' replied Ben tetchily. He watched her. She looked exhausted, purpling shadows under her eyes. After a short silence she turned to him.

'Sorry, darling. I don't mean to snap. It's just I've had a

hard day with him, and I'd only just sat down when you came back.'

'No, *I'm* sorry,' said Ben, his annoyance fading rapidly, 'I will try to be more careful. It's just that after a long day at work I'm not always thinking properly.'

She switched off the television and came over and sat against him on the sofa, clutching his arm. 'I'm afraid I haven't really got round to supper. Sorry,' she said again, looking up at him sadly.

Again, thought Ben to himself, but instead he said, 'Don't worry about it. I can order something easily enough. What d'you fancy? Curry? Pizza? A bit of sweet and sour maybe?'

'Curry,' said Lucie, not letting go of his arm. Ben's eyes led him round the room. Vast amounts of baby gear as well as the as yet unused three-wheeled buggy Lucie had insisted on, gave their once immaculate sitting room an air of cluttered disorder. The cushions, which the Lucie of old would religiously wander around puffing up, were now wedged into the sides and backs of the sofas and chair. Half-finished cups of tea, which once would have been whisked away before they'd had a chance to grow cold, littered the coffee table. Lucie had vowed the baby would never alter her exacting standards, and Ben had believed her. But in the couple of months since Thomas had been born, the change had been extraordinary. Far from coming home to a spotless house with savoury smells wafting from the kitchen, he was confronted with a place looking like a battleground. He kissed her head. Nor would the old Lucie ever, ever have spent her days in jogger bottoms and T-shirts. He'd loved the care she took about her appearance and the fact that she always looked more chic and glamorous than any of his other friends. Incomprehensibly, she hadn't even opened the latest edition of *Vogue*, even though it had arrived nearly a week before.

'Well,' he said, realizing neither of them had spoken for several minutes, 'I'll order this curry then.' But looking down, he saw his wife was fast asleep.

*   *   *

The following day was Saturday, and by eight o'clock in the morning Thomas had been fed and was back asleep in his cot. Ben and Lucie were just drifting off to sleep themselves when the phone by Ben's side of the bed rang. It was Vanessa, saying she was about to 'pop' round.

'I'm sure that'd be great,' said Ben, then noticed Lucie frantically gesticulating behind him. 'Oh, hold on a minute, Lucie's saying something.' Covering the receiver with his hand he turned to her. 'What?'

'I don't want her round here this morning. She's really getting on my tits. You've got to put her off.'

'I can't – I've just said yes.'

'Well un-yes her then. I don't want her coming round, OK?'

Ben sighed and took his hand away. 'Sorry about that, Vanessa. Sorry, but actually I forgot. We've got to go out this morning. To get some things, you know.'

'Oh. Then why don't I come over later then?' suggested Vanessa.

'No, that won't work,' said Ben feebly, 'as we're supposed to be taking Thomas to see some friends.'

'What friends? Why don't they come to you?'

'It's Harry – Thomas's godfather – and I think he's arranged something at his flat. But we'll see you next week at some point though, won't we?'

'That was a terrible excuse,' said Lucie, once he'd replaced the receiver. She reluctantly smiled. 'Can't trust you with anything these days.'

'I'm glad you made me put her off though,' Ben admitted. 'I know she's been brilliant, but she does sometimes get on my nerves. I think you can have too much of your mother.'

'She's only trying to help out,' said Lucie, her improved humour vanishing.

'I know, but sometimes it's nice to be on our own, that's all.'

'Well, she cares about her grandson.'

'I *know*,' said Ben wearily, 'and that's great, but I don't want her here all the time and nor do you, otherwise you wouldn't have made me put her off, would you?'

'OK, but I just don't like hearing my mother slagged off.'

'But, darling, you're perpetually slagging her off. And anyway, I wasn't slagging her off, I was just saying I was glad she wasn't coming around on this particular occasion, so don't get in another strop with me.'

'Well, it sounded like you were to me. At least she shows she cares, unlike your mother, who still doesn't even bloody know Thomas exists.'

Ben glared at her, then silently got out of bed and left the room. Sometimes Lucie went too far. He tried to be patient, and understanding about the strains and stresses of motherhood, but in mentioning his mother in that fashion, she had aimed to hurt his feelings. Why was she so angry with him? What had he done to warrant this treatment? He wished she would suddenly wake up one morning his old, funny, smart and gorgeous Lucie, who adored him as much as he adored her. He wanted to help her and although he realized slamming doors thoughtlessly didn't help, really, he gave her everything he could. It wasn't his fault he had to work such long hours; that was the nature of the job, and the profession that enabled Lucie to give up work and for them to be comfortably fed and clothed. She knew his mother was a taboo subject. Not since they'd first known each other had he ever discussed her, and that was not about to change. Even after all this time, Ben still keenly felt the devastating pain his mother's betrayal had caused him and the rest of his family. None of them had ever received an explanation or an apology. Nothing. He'd never before been able to understand how a mother could abandon her family – it seemed an act so unnatural, so incomprehensible, a grotesque rejection of all that any normal mother would happily give her life to protect. And yet now, with Lucie almost at her wits' end . . . well, it just worried him a bit, that was all. He couldn't help it.

Not that Lucie would suddenly up stumps and leave them too, but it did sometimes occur to him that this recent antagonism of hers might be connected, as though the problem was somehow with him. Standing by the sink, fishing the tea-bag out of his tea, he realized he was shaking. Deep down a knot of worry and fear had begun to worm its way in.

'I'm sorry, darling. It's not you, it's me,' said Lucie, silently coming up behind him. She placed her thin little arms around him and buried her face in the towelling on his back. 'I'm so, so sorry about what I said. It was unforgivable. I just don't know what's the matter with me at the moment. It's just . . . just that looking after Thomas isn't what I imagined. I feel so tired *all the time*. And I'm clearly such a crap mother. I think he responds better to you than me.'

Ben turned round to face her. 'I love you so much,' he told her, 'but you've got to let me help you. This constant sniping and irritability isn't fair, you know?'

'I know, I'm sorry. I'll always love you, Ben. I promise, even if I don't always show it.'

She hadn't said that in weeks.

The day started to improve. London was in the middle of a dry, sunny spell and so later they drove out to Richmond Park to go for a long walk. Pushing the buggy along the gravelly paths, it pleased Ben to think they were at last acting like a proper family. Lucie was laughing and talking more than at any other point since the birth. He hoped she'd perhaps managed to get past her baby blues.

Sitting down by a large oak for a short while, Lucie once again fell almost instantly asleep. Because she'd always been such a strong character, he supposed he never really appreciated how small she was; clearly giving birth had taken more out of her than he could ever appreciate. She'd been so laid-back and blasé during her pregnancy, assuming she would take to motherhood with the calm efficiency with which she managed everything else in life. But babies didn't respond in the same way adults did, and clearly in Thomas – pumped full of her genes after all – she'd more than met her match. These first months must have been a terrible shock to her, Ben thought. He looked at Thomas, also mercifully asleep in the buggy. To think he'd come out of her such a short time before. He was growing fast, and when he wasn't crying, looked so wide-eyed and gentle with his little tuft of dark, dark hair, it seemed impossible to believe he could wail so angrily only seconds later. Still, lying there, gently stroking Lucie's hair with the sun bearing down on the three of them, Ben experienced a glimpse of his vision of family life. It was just a question of adjustment. How ridiculous he was to make comparisons with his own mother. Such thoughts were damaging and unhealthy and he must try hard to keep them at bay. He closed his eyes too, feeling the heat of the sun on his face. They would be all right, he was sure.

But later that night, it became clear that Ben was still going to have to tread very carefully with Lucie, as another by-product of childbirth emerged. By ten o'clock that night they were in bed. Lucie had yawned, stretched and staggered upstairs just after nine, and Ben, not really wanting to sit on his own downstairs, had followed soon after.

'I'm just so tired all the time,' Lucie told him again. 'It's all this waking up every few hours in the night. I wish I had more energy.'

'We could always get a nanny to help out,' suggested Ben.

'Why, do you think I can't cope?' That snappy tone of voice once more.

'No, of course you can. Don't be all touchy with me, Luce. I just meant, if you wanted some help, we could get you some. That's all. But if you don't want it, fine.'

'Sorry,' she said again, 'sorry I snapped.' She looked at him miserably. 'I'm feeling so insecure about my abilities as a mother at the moment. Why didn't anyone warn me?' She moved over to him and rubbed his chest gently. 'Thanks for the offer, but for the moment I really want to try to do this on my own. I've got to get to grips with it.' Then she reached up and kissed him, softly at first, then more urgently. Ben, keenly aware they hadn't had sex since before Thomas was born, responded happily to her sudden ardour. At last! Slowly, he started kissing her neck, shoulders and breasts, feeling instantly aroused. It had seemed like a long time in waiting, and at times Ben had wondered whether Lucie would ever want to make love again, but this, now, felt so good: intense pleasure mixed with relief.

'No. I'm sorry, darling, but I'm just not ready for this,' said Lucie, suddenly pushing him away.

'What? Why not?' said Ben, disappointment and irritation rising within him.

'Just look at me!' said Lucie, pointing to her stomach. 'I'm so fat. It's disgusting. How can I feel sexy when I know you're about to start kissing rolls and folds of horrible loose flesh?'

'I don't give a shit about that,' said Ben, 'it'll go down eventually, I'm sure.'

'What are you saying? That you *do* think I'm fat?'

'No, no, of course not.'

'Well, I do.' Tears welled up in her eyes. 'I feel my life has been taken away from me, Ben. It's as though this new body isn't mine. I don't feel myself, I don't look myself, I feel moody and tetchy all the time – and what thanks do I get for it? Just a baby that wails all day because I can't look after it properly.' She burst into tears. Ben didn't want to say the wrong thing but felt there was a strong probability that he might. So he just held her tight and said nothing. Bugger, he said to himself sadly, realizing they weren't through the woods yet.

A couple of nights later, since Vanessa was over to keep Lucie company, he went out for a drink with Harry. He hadn't seen his friend much in recent weeks, since he'd been working hard, and then tended to go straight home and help Lucie. But now that Harry had just finished with Julia, he felt a couple of pints were more than justified.

Harry seemed more interested in hearing about Ben, than dwelling on Julia.

'So close yet so far,' commiserated Harry.

'Exactly. It was so frustrating. I mean, I don't care if her stomach's not quite as much of a dishboard as it might normally be. I just want my conjugal rights.'

Harry drank his beer and looked thoughtfully at Ben.

'It's a tricky one, mate. Maybe you should encourage her to do some exercise – it'll probably make her feel less tired and better about herself.'

'Nice idea, Harry, but Lucie's at a low ebb at the moment. Ever since Thomas was born she just hasn't been the same. Honestly, I have to tread so carefully these days.'

Harry gave Ben a sympathetic look, and took another sip of his beer.

'To be honest,' Ben continued, 'it's not quite panning out as I'd hoped.'

'What isn't?'

'Fatherhood. Family life. It never occurred to me that Lucie might struggle with the job. Thomas is fantastic, of course, but it certainly isn't all rosy cheeks.'

'Lucie'll pull through. You've just got to give her a bit of slack and be there for her.'

'Be patient.'

'Exactly.'

'Yeah, well, I suppose you're right.' Ben took a draught of his beer. 'I mean, don't get me wrong, now that we have Thomas, I wouldn't have it any other way – I absolutely adore him and everything – but I didn't really expect my life would change quite so much.'

'It was always going to, Ben, to be fair.'

'Was it? I thought that with Lucie at home, I'd still be able to play football on Tuesday nights, get people over for supper, go out for drinks with mates. Other people do. I know quite a few kids who sleep through the first part of the night, and whose parents are still able to see people. It's just that we've drawn the short straw and have a baby who seems to have colic or something, and can't ever seem to sleep for more than two bloody minutes at a time.'

'Ben, the football's not going to go away. You can always come back to it. And I'm not going anywhere. Just relax about it, and be there for Lucie.'

'Yeah, you're right. I don't know. It's just different to how I imagined it.' He paused thoughtfully, then said, 'When we were first married it didn't feel *such* a big deal. Really, it was as though we were still just going out with each other, but living together. But now Thomas has arrived on the scene, I do feel properly married. It seems very final, somehow.' He paused, then said, 'Harry, do you ever think about old girlfriends?'

'All the time. Wondering why I went out them, most of the time.'

'But do you ever think of missed opportunities?'

'Definitely.'

'It's weird, you know, thinking I will never sleep with any-one else again. I can't help wishing I'd slept with an Orien-tal girl. Just once. I've always quite fancied the Oriental look. And the thing is, *you* still can. There are no restrictions on you.'

Harry laughed. 'Personally, I'd sacrifice that right any day for what you've got. A happy strong marriage has got be worth so much more than a few hours of pleasure.'

'Course it is, but it doesn't mean you can't ever think about it, and sometimes I do envy you all the same.'

'And I envy you. Let's swap. You can have my bachelor pad, the insecurity of being self-employed, having to face splitting up with girlfriends, and I'll move in with Luce and earn a shed-load working in the City.'

'All right, point made. But I also keep thinking I should have gone out with that peroxide blonde girl from John's I met at the end of the first term at Cambridge.'

'Don't think I remember her.'

'She was gorgeous. Sam. From Liverpool. Dyed blonde hair and lovely breasts. And a great kisser. Fantastic kisser, in fact.'

'So why didn't you then? Honestly, I don't remember her at all, so she can't have been that amazing.'

'I dunno. I think we spoke to each other once during the Christmas vac and then we came back the next term, and nothing really happened.'

'Well, I can't stop thinking about this girl I was going out with when I first got to Cambridge.'

'Really? I don't think I remember her.'

'No, you wouldn't have done. It all ended before I'd even met you.'

'So who finished with who?'

'I finished with her, but I was a prat to do so. She was probably the love of my life, but it's a bit late now.'

'What's suddenly brought this on? I mean, I don't want to alarm you, but I don't think I've ever heard you mention her before, and it was quite a long time ago.'

'Just because I haven't mentioned her, doesn't mean I haven't thought about her. Honestly, Ben, she was so lovely. We were perfect together. That summer before Cambridge started, we were really, really in love. Despite what you may say, I've always known in my heart of hearts that I was more in love with her than with anyone else before or since. Anyway, now I know for sure that it was more than that.'

'So why on earth did you ever finish it?'

'God knows. Because everything seemed different somehow once I got to Cambridge. And because I slept with someone else.'

'You did *what*? You can't have been *that* in love with her.'

'I was. But I was too young to handle it. I stupidly thought that if I carried on going out with her then, and throughout university, I'd miss out somehow.'

'Wow.' Ben took a drink from his pint. 'And is she why you finished with Julia?'

'Partly,' Harry confessed. Then, after a slight pause, he added, 'But I do also wish I'd slept with Katherine Tomlinson. I'd never have wanted to go out with her – that would have been a nightmare – but she was lovely.'

'I did.'

'Yeah, sure you did.'

'No, I did, honestly. After the May Ball.'

'Then why didn't I ever know that?'

'Thought you did.'

'Are you being serious?'

'I promise. Admittedly, we were both quite drunk, and it was just the once, but you were right, she was great, as I remember.'

'Bastard,' said Harry, 'and you call me a dark horse.' He stood up to go and buy more drinks.

'Good times, though,' said Ben, as Harry returned a few minutes later.

'Yeah, they were.'

'Lots of sleeping around, getting drunk.'

Harry nodded.

'To be honest, though, Harry,' Ben continued, 'I *am* beginning to feel frustrated. You know, with Luce. We haven't had any nookie for ages.'

'Why don't you get some visual stimulation then?' Ben looked blank, so Harry leant in and said in a slightly lowered tone, 'You know – get yourself a top-shelf mag.'

'Porn?' said Ben a little bit too loudly, so that the girls at the end of their table gave him a scornful look.

'Yes, Ben, porn.' Harry smiled. 'Go to a newsagent and get yourself a *Mayfair* or something.'

'And keep it under the mattress? You must be joking. I'm not doing that. I'm married.'

'OK, suit yourself. But you were saying Lucie isn't interested and you're feeling frustrated. Seems to me the perfect solution for the time being. It's not as if looking at a girlie mag makes you unfaithful, does it?'

'I suppose not. But it'd be so embarrassing. What if I bumped into someone I knew when I was buying it?'

'Ben, don't be ridiculous. Just pick any old corner shop, go in, pluck off a magazine, pay, walk out. Simple. Then you've got yourself hours of fun, *and* you'll feel more inclined to be patient with Lucie. Really, I should be some sort of counsellor.'

As he walked home later, Ben wondered whether Harry hadn't made quite a good point after all: ogling a few photographs of naked women hardly constituted infidelity. Naturally, he'd been scathing of the plan in the pub, but that was more because he didn't want Harry thinking he was going to become some rampant masturbator. But really, if he could just overcome his embarrassment and actually purchase a top-shelfer, his feelings of frustration might be – at least to a degree – lessened.

The next day, while Ben was at work, Harry sent him two pornographic e-mails, the second of which he opened just as Tara walked into his office.

'Feeling the strain are we?' she asked him, a smirk edging her lips.

'Ha, ha,' said Ben irritably, deleting it immediately. 'Actually, a friend sent it to me. The caption just said "Beard" so I didn't know what it was.'

'If you say so,' said Tara, raising an eyebrow as she left.

Stop sending me this stuff, Harry, you pervert, Ben typed back, *Tara just walked in on Beard, not good for boss/secretary relations.*

That Tara had come into his office just as he was opening one of Harry's pictures struck him as a bad omen. What did that augur for when he tried to go to a newsagent? Someone he knew would be bound to walk in just as he was reaching for a copy of *Penthouse*.

But that evening, after glancing either side of him as he walked out through Clapham Junction, he headed off up Lavender Hill in search of a really out-of-the-way newsagent. With all those quiet Victorian terraced streets round about he felt sure there must be a number of corner shops that filled the basic grocery and pornography requirements of the residents. Eventually, having walked down a side street off the Wandsworth Road, he found the perfect place. Even from the outside he could see a stunning array of magazines. Then a BMW shot past – and didn't Julia have a BMW? And wasn't it the same shade of metallic dark blue? He walked on past the newsagent, his head down – just in case it was Julia and she'd seen him and decided to turn around. Then after a couple of minutes he turned back and, without glancing up, stepped into the shop. A young mother with her daughter stood paying at the till, so he loitered by the rack of shelves, flicking as casually as he could through a car magazine. A few agonizing moments later, the woman gave him a dubious look as she and the girl brushed past him. With the shop now empty, Ben seized his moment. Stretching up his arm, he plucked the first magazine he could get his hands on. Grateful to see he'd inadvertently picked up something as innocuous as *Playboy*, he steadfastly approached the counter. The ageing shopkeeper blinked, looked at the top, then picked it up, examining it closely.

'Can't see the price anywhere,' he muttered, as three teenage girls walked in.

Ben snatched it from him, made a quick scan, then handed it back, pointing to the UK price printed in small type. 'There,' he said impatiently, handing over a five-pound note.

'Urgh! That's disgusting,' said one of the girls, 'look, he's buying porn.'

'Keep the change,' said Ben hurriedly, rigid with embarrassment. Snatching back the magazine once more, and avoiding any eye contact with the girls, he resolutely marched back out of the shop, stuffing the magazine in his briefcase. Looking about him one final time, he set off at a brisk pace, anxious to make good his escape. He hoped he wouldn't be attacked or run over – then they'd discover his guilty secret. All so he could alleviate his sexual frustrations over a few pictures of nude American college girls. He doubted it could really be worth it.

CHAPTER TEN

rural realities

From the outset, rural life refused to pan out precisely as Flin had imagined. The first blow came when Iain, Tiffany's new boss, phoned to say the programmes had been put on hold, so he wouldn't be able to honour his offer for the moment. It would be fine, he assured her, in the long run, but Tyne Tees had pulled out and they needed another backer. Channel 4 were more than interested, and he felt sure all would be well before Christmas. In the meantime, if anything came up, he'd be in touch.

'We'll be fine,' said Flin as cheerily as he could manage. 'Just have to tighten our belts a bit.'

'I could temp or something in Newcastle for a while,' suggested Tiffany.

'Oh, we'll manage,' said Flin airily. But it wasn't just the money; Tiffany had been looking forward to working on a fascinating project. However, they had moved in and it was too late to do anything more about it. And as Flin pointed out, they were going to be saving lots of money by growing their own food.

They both gave each other two weeks off to settle into their new house and lifestyle before Flin started work and Tiffany thought about temping. There was all the unpacking to be done, and the local area to discover properly. Flin, especially, was eager to start hunting down local farmer types who might be able to help him with chickens, geese and maybe even the pig. He also needed to make adjustments to the various outbuildings, which were due to house the poultry and swine. There seemed to be so much to do, neither of them knew where to begin, so Tiffany suggested they pay a call on their new neighbour.

'Good idea,' agreed Flin, 'we don't want to seem uppity or unfriendly.'

The house was a hundred yards further on down the road, big-stoned with a slate roof, and half the size of Standing Stone Farmhouse.

'This is so much better than London,' said Flin cheerfully as, hand-in-hand, they wandered towards the house. 'I don't think I even spoke to any of our neighbours when we lived there. There's so much more of a community spirit in the country.'

A radio burbled clearly from within.

'Sounds like they're in,' whispered Tiffany as Flin knocked on the door. Just then they heard heavy footsteps followed by a muffled yell.

'*You bloody bastard!*' Then a pause.

Flin and Tiffany looked at each other. 'Maybe not quite the right time, hey?' said Tiffany. But as they were about to turn, they heard more dampened footsteps, this time running down stairs. Then the door opened.

A lean man, wearing a couple of days' worth of beard, and with piercing eyes and brown hair swept back from his forehead, stood in the doorway, eyebrow raised expectantly. Flin guessed he must be in his mid-thirties.

'Hi,' said Tiffany, 'um, sorry to disturb you, but we just wanted to come round and say hello.' The man nodded, a faint hint of a smirk on his face.

'We've just moved in up the road,' added Flin.

'Right,' he said slowly. 'How you doing?' Flin watched him transfer his gaze to Tiffany, or rather, up and down Tiffany.

'I'm Flin,' he said, thrusting out a hand.

'Callum,' murmured the man, briefly turning to him and offering his hand in turn.

'And I'm Tiffany,' said Tiffany, holding out her hand too.

'Tiffany. Great,' replied Callum, leaning himself casually against the door and staring at her breasts.

'CALLUM? Callum, who's that?' screeched a voice from deep within the house.

'New neighbours,' yelled Callum back.

'If this is a bad time . . .' offered Flin, aware Callum was still leaning against the door and hadn't yet asked them in.

'Don't worry about her. She's always like fucking yelling her bloody head off,' he told them. The accent was thick Geordie but, unusually, he spoke slowly, and for the most part softly too. A plump woman joined Callum in the doorway. She had bright ginger hair pulled back into a clip and very pale skin spattered with an abundance of freckles.

'Oh, hiya,' she said, cheerfully enough, 'we was wondering who was moving in up there. Thought you'd be a bit older living in such a grand place.'

'Ha,' laughed Flin uncertainly, before introducing himself and Tiffany once more.

'Hiya,' she said again, 'I'm Wendy.'

'So anyway,' said Flin, putting his hands on his hips, and wondering whether he and Tiffany should leave.

'You hunt then?' asked Callum, turning to Flin and staring him in the eye.

'Me? God no,' said Flin hastily.

'I used to ride as a kid,' said Tiffany. 'And I'd love to again, although I've never hunted.'

Callum nodded. 'There's quite a lot of hunting round here. And generally they come right past us.'

'Lots of foxes round here,' added Wendy from behind Callum.

'Oh,' said Flin, 'I see.' He sensed this was some kind of test, but couldn't figure out which way he was supposed to respond. Was hunting a good or a bad thing? He certainly didn't want to seem like some horse-riding toff, but otherwise wasn't sure whether he was supposed to be for or against.

'Do you?' he asked, hoping to encourage a clue as to the right response.

'What? Me on a horse! What do you think, mate?'

Flin laughed again uncertainly, totally at a loss as to how to answer. Callum once again began staring admiringly at Tiffany.

'Callum. Stop it, for fuck's sake!' said Wendy suddenly, slapping him on the arm.

'Stop what?'

'Staring at her tits!' snapped Wendy angrily, before turning to the stunned Tiffany and adding, 'Look, I'm really sorry, but he thinks he's Casa-fucking-nova. Just ignore it.'

'I fucking wasn't, you daft bitch,' said Callum, more quietly, but just as angrily.

'Well, don't worry about it,' said Tiffany. 'Nice to meet you anyway.'

'Yes, see you soon I expect,' said Flin, smiling awkwardly and walking backwards away from the house.

'No doubt,' smiled Callum. Wendy had already gone.

'They're insane!' said Flin incredulously as soon as they were a safe distance from the house. 'Christ, the less we see of them the better. I mean, bloody hell, can you believe that? Clearly you're going to have to wear more than a tight T-shirt whenever you see *him*.'

Tiffany laughed. 'Obviously he's a bit of a naughty boy, but, Flin, I don't think you need to worry on my account. He's not my type at all. Anyway, you should have seen what the Australian men were like. It was a national pastime looking at a girl's tits.'

'Yeah, well, this is Northumberland. No going round to borrow milk, OK?'

'OK, I think I can just about promise that.'

'And what was all that hunting crap about? Jesus. Do you think we've come to a village full of nutters?'

'Having doubts already, are we?' teased Tiffany.

'No, of course not. How could I when you look at the place we've moved to?' They stood outside the front of their house. The sun shone warmly, gently, with barely a breath of wind in the air. Ahead lay their empty field, wild flowers growing between the lush, thick grass; and beyond just more fields, dry-stone walls and dark green hedgerows separating each one. Hardly a sound to be heard, just occasional birdsong and crows cawing in the tall beeches along the road away to the right.

The unpacking of their belongings into the bare, unfurnished house proved just about the least time-consuming of all their weekly tasks. Neither had huge amounts of clothes or endless masses of knick-knacks. Until they'd moved in together a couple of years before, Flin had been able to fit most of his belongings into an old trunk, a battered suitcase and a few cardboard boxes. Admittedly they now had a TV and video, a sofa, a few chairs and some kitchenware, but really, there wasn't a huge amount more. Their crockery and cutlery (they had six of everything) filled the drawers and a couple of the cupboards, but even so, once they'd fully unpacked, the house looked pitifully empty.

'We've got to get some more stuff, hon,' said Tiffany, as they began walking the three-quarters of a mile to the nearest pub.

'I know, but we always knew that. Can't we just gradually build up? It doesn't matter if we rattle around for a bit, does it? We just haven't got that much spare cash.'

'I know, but I do think we ought to try to get a few more bits and pieces. There're two whole bedrooms without a stitch in them. And we don't even have a kitchen table. It's not as if we need to spend any expensive weekends heading out of town any more, is it?'

'OK. So we'll try to get a table. What else?'

'Another sofa? Or a couple of armchairs? Preferably a dining-room table too.'

Flin sighed. 'That's going to cost a bit though, isn't it? I suppose we'll just have to put it on a card or something.'

'What about scouring local papers for personal ads? And second-hand furniture shops have got to be cheaper round here, haven't they?' suggested Tiffany.

'I'd have thought so. Let's have a look in Hexham.'

'Come on, it'll be fun.'

'I know. But it's all eating into our funds for self-sufficiency.'

Tiffany laughed. 'Bit of a contradiction in terms, isn't it?'

They reached the pub. When they'd come to see the house, they had stopped for lunch at the Compasses. It had been quiet then – midweek and hardly a soul in the place, just a bored young girl of barely legal age standing dolefully behind the bar. As country pubs went, Flin and Tiffany thought it all right. It might not have been cosy, dark and flagstoned, but nor was it particularly flash and overtly chintzy either. There were beaten copper goods around the fireplace, a flashing jukebox that played no music and a pool table in a part of the pub that stretched away round the other side of the bar. To walk, flick cigarette ash, and spill beer on, there was a deep red and dark blue carpet, much stained. But the dark beams seemed genuine enough, and both left feeling that, as a local, it could have been a lot worse.

But when they walked in on a Sunday night in high summer, the place seemed transformed. Firstly, there were a lot more people. The jukebox was playing an old Jon Bon Jovi number and there was a heavy air of smoke and beer. As Flin and Tiffany made their entrance, they were greeted by a suspicious pause in activity: the pool player momentarily checked his shot, looking up in their direction; the regulars, leaning at the bar or perched on high stools, deliberately turned to eye them up and down, conversations left hanging in a slowly-exhaled cloud of cigarette smoke.

The barmaid lifted her chin as if to say 'What can I get you?' without actually bothering to speak, when Flin and Tiffany made for a gap at the bar.

'Hi,' said Flin, smiling in the hope of prompting an audible response, but the girl just stared back implacably. 'Pint of lager and a pint of best, please,' he asked.

They stood towards one end of the bar, a lone drinker sitting between them and the wall. The man, with neatly coiffed hair and a long, thin moustache, appeared to be staring at some distant horizon above the liquor bottles opposite him. In front of him stood a half-pint of lager in a narrow glass with a gold-rimmed lip. He too, was smoking: Lambert and Butler 100s.

'Evening,' said Flin, daringly.

The man slowly turned, eyed both him and Tiffany, then nodded.

'Thanks, Flin,' said Tiffany as their pints arrived and Flin handed over the money.

'What accent's that then?' asked the coiffed man, still staring ahead rather than at them.

'Australian,' Tiffany told him. Her tone was friendly, wanting to please.

'Jesus,' said the man, 'that's some distance you've travelled for a pint of lager.' He laughed wheezily, and looked at the other regulars who joined in with supportive chuckling.

'Yeah, I guess so.' She smiled. 'Sixteen thousand miles for a pint that's probably Australian anyway. Just my luck.'

'So now you're back in the motherland,' the man continued. 'Were your family convicts or what?'

'No, actually,' said Tiffany, a touch of indignation entering her voice, 'they were Irish and forced out because of tyrannical English rule, if you really want to know.'

The man, his cigarette held just inches away from his mouth, turned to the regulars, an amused, lopsided smirk across his face.

'Ah, well,' he said at length, 'I'm sure you'll be very happy up at Standing Stone.'

'How do you know we've moved in there?' asked Flin.

The man shrugged. 'Heard it was some southerners. You're southern and I haven't seen you before and it's a Sunday night. Hardly like what you'd call rocket science, is it?'

'No, I suppose not,' admitted Flin, and introduced himself and Tiffany for the second time that day. The man, having taken a tiny yet thoughtful sip of lager, admitted he was called Keith.

'So,' said Flin, eager to find out more about village life, 'I suppose you don't have that many people moving in and out around here.'

'More than you'd think in recent years,' said Keith, still looking more or less constantly ahead. 'It's people like you moving up wanting a bit of fresh air and country life and having more money than sense that pushes the house prices up. People can't afford to live here any more.'

'We're only renting though,' put in Tiffany. Flin could tell she was beginning to feel irritated.

'Our work's brought us here,' added Flin, 'and we've got to live somewhere. Anyway, the landlord should be pleased. All that new custom.'

'Oh yeah?' said Keith, sliding off his stool and heading in the direction of the gents.

'He's a bit bloody chippy, isn't he?' said Flin to Tiffany in a hushed voice.

'Yeah, and rude too.'

Flin turned and caught the eye of an older man sitting at the bar to his left silently drinking his pint. He knew the row of them perched there had been quietly eavesdropping on their conversation with Keith.

'All right?' he said genially.

'Bloody foxes,' said the man, then looked at Flin, waiting for a response.

'Quite a problem you seem to have up here,' Flin suggested.

'They're vermin.' He spat out the words so that Flin could see he was missing many of his teeth. 'Get in everywhere. Eat the chickens, eat the geese. They've been known to take lambs too.'

'Really? Whole lambs?'

'Oh yes. They'll take a lamb if they can all right. You don't hunt then?'

'Me?' said Flin, less incredulously this time. 'No, no I don't.'

'I don't either,' added Tiffany, 'but we'll definitely shoot a fox if we see it, won't we, Flin?'

'Yes, absolutely,' agreed Flin nervously.

'That's the job,' said the old man, then added, 'So what're you going to do with those barns then?'

Flin cleared his throat. 'Going to put chickens in them, and geese.' He looked at the man uncertainly, conscious the two next to him were listening as well. 'And a couple of pigs.'

'Pigs, eh? You'd best talk to Melvyn then. He knows a thing or two about pigs.'

'Melvyn's always had pigs,' said the next man along.

'Always,' said the other. 'Not much Melvyn don't know about pigs.'

Flin nodded thoughtfully, then the man next to him said, 'So you've met Keith then?'

'Yes,' admitted Flin. 'He's a regular, is he?'

'Could say that. He's the landlord.'

As they ambled back to their house, Flin couldn't help feeling just the tiniest bit dispirited. So far he'd discovered they had an ogling neighbour with an argumentative wife, and chippy – not to say downright rude – pub regulars and landlord. On top of that, there was this strange obsession with foxes. He supposed it was bound to take a little while to settle in to such a completely new area, but none the less, he'd hoped there might be more genial rosy-cheeked types and fewer antagonistic, whingeing gits.

*   *   *

The following day dawned equally bright, fresh and sunny, and Flin's enthusiasm and good humour had returned in full. As he wandered around the outbuildings with Tiffany, they tried to decide how they could successfully house animals and poultry there. Both had agreed it was pointless even bothering to look for chickens and geese until a suitable coop or hide had been sorted, but really, what with the front paddock as well as the yard, they had more than landed on their feet.

Willie had been very casual about the land and extras that came with the house. 'Can you make use of any of this?' he'd said as Flin and he had ambled through the empty yard and back paddock. 'Shame not to use it, but simply don't need it myself.' Flin had jumped at the chance. 'Great,' added Willie jovially, 'that gets it off my hands then.'

The row of sties was behind the garages opposite the back of the house. As he and Tiffany peered in every pen, they agreed they looked to be in fairly good shape, although a couple of the wooden gates were rather past their prime, hanging limply on rusted hinges. Ancient mulched dung and straw clung to the far recesses of each of the sites, but otherwise they gave the impression of years of wistful vacancy. At right angles to them was a long, narrow barn, with weather-beaten double doors in the middle, and a slate roof missing a few tiles. As Tiffany pushed the doors open with a grinding creak, sunlight hungrily revealed the dust and cobwebs that hung in the air. The barn, long kept in the dark, seemed to squint at this sudden onslaught of light.

'Wow,' said Tiffany, open-mouthed, 'how come I never saw this when we looked around?'

Flin smiled at her. The barn was largely empty, but at one end an old cart, covered in inch-thick dust and riddled with woodworm, stood long forgotten. Several wooden wheels, one badly smashed, leant against the wall. Tiny shafts of light from the roof lit up small patches of the floor at the far end, dust-filled spotlights on an empty stage. In one corner lay a stash of fertilizer bags, once bright blue but now dulled with age and grime, while rope and bits of rusted old agricultural machinery hung on the walls, broken and useless. It reminded Flin of the old barns he used to play in as a boy, with that distinct musty smell of old straw and wood.

Tiffany walked over to him, and put an arm round him, resting her head against his chest. 'You could put the chooks and geese in here, couldn't you? It's not as if we need all this space for anything else. Then they can potter about the yard during the day and be shut up at night,' she suggested. The yard, concreted close to the outbuildings, but with tufts of weeds randomly sprouting, gradually merged into grass before being walled off along a line of trees marking the edge of Cotherwick Wood. It was this wood that separated Standing Stone Farmhouse from the rest of the village.

'What if they fly out through the roof, though? Or underneath those rickety-looking doors?'

'Get their wings clipped and reinforce the door.'

'OK.' Flin scratched his chin thoughtfully. 'How do I do that then?'

'How do you think? You go and buy some wood, a big padlock, and a hammer and nails. Easy.'

'And what about the gate?' Flin pointed at the old metal gate between the wall and garages. It was solid enough despite the rust prickling its way through the dulled black paint.

'Put chicken wire on it.'

'Chicken wire. Fine. Good idea.'

Flin knew absolutely nothing about DIY. He couldn't remember having even used a hammer before. But, undaunted, he headed off towards B&Q, relishing the challenge before him. If they were going to live in the country they would have to have the basics, and Flin filled his trolley with everything from screws to spirit-levels. At the wood section he was completely stumped by the massive variety, but on the advice of a gangly-looking youth with wet hair and a bright red B&Q apron, he ended up buying several strips of sturdy looking pine planks, hoping he'd bought the right size. The Black and Decker multi-purpose drill-cum-saw-cum-everything struck him as a particularly pertinent purchase, and he left with an enormous sense of achievement as though the job were already half done.

'Flin, how much did all that cost?' said a horrified-looking Tiffany as he unloaded the car they'd hired until he took possession of his company one.

'But, darling, we're going to have to have all this stuff. It's essential kit, I'm afraid.'

'Oh yeah? So when are we going to be using a thirty-two-piece socket set?'

'On lots of occasions. Any time we need to tighten something.'

'So how much?'

'It wasn't that bad.'

'How much, Flin?'

'Nearly two hundred quid, but I put it on the card. Honestly, that's how much this stuff costs.'

Tiffany held up her hands with exasperation. 'Flin, we can't afford that. You said we were going to have to tighten our belts. I don't have a job, remember. I can't believe you just spent that amount of money on all this crap.'

'Look, it's an initial outlay we have to make.'

'It just seems there're quite a lot of initial outlays, that's all.' She sat down and looked him sternly in the eye.

'It'll be worth it, and stop scowling.'

'I'm not. I just don't want us to rack up loads of debts before we've even been here a week, you know? Don't forget you told me it'd be cheaper up here.'

'And it is. I had change from four quid for those drinks last night. That would never happen in London, would it?'

Tiffany stood up and gave him a begrudging kiss. 'Well, you'd better get on with it and start using all this stuff. I'm off out for a bit.'

'Are you? Where to?'

'While you were out, Claire, Willie's wife, popped round. To see if we were OK. She's invited me riding.'

'Oh. That was nice of her.'

'Yeah, that's what I thought. And I don't want to look a gift horse in the mouth. Just don't go spending any more money while I'm gone, all right?'

Flin hoped his attempts at making the barn chicken proof would be effective, even if not very beautiful. To begin with, he nailed in the planks so low to the ground he couldn't then open the doors, but the second time around he felt he'd judged it about right. Nor had it taken him too long: nailing the wood haphazardly took far less time than carefully lining up and screwing the planks to the old door.

He stood back, hammer loose in his hand, wiped his brow, and admired his handiwork. Something made him turn, but he still visibly jolted as he saw the old man leaning on the gate.

'Christ, you gave me a fright,' he admitted, clutching his chest. 'I never heard you.'

'No,' said the man flatly. He wore an old dark jacket, flat cap and strong-looking boots. His face, neck and hands were dark and weather-beaten, giving the impression of long years spent outside. The collie sitting patiently at his feet completed the picture. At last, Flin thought, here was someone more like the James Herriot prototype he'd been expecting.

'So, you're the new people then,' said the man. He spoke softly, with a strong accent, so that Flin could barely understand him.

'Yes, moved in a couple of days ago,' said Flin, glad about his own out-of-doors appearance.

'Jus' you and the missus, is it?' He looked thoughtfully about him.

'Yes, just the two of us. You live nearby?' asked Flin.

'Aye, next house down the way. Bluebell Farm.'

'You farm then?'

'Sheep. Mus' be about the last, mind. Can just about scrape together the rates, but that's because I have a special dispensation like.'

'Oh,' said Flin, 'so how long's this been empty?'

The man pushed back his cap, scratched his head, then looked away, so that Flin wondered whether he'd heard him or not.

'Mus' be about fifteen year,' he said eventually. 'No. Hold on.' Flin watched him begin counting on his fingers. 'Yes, about fifteen or sixteen year. People like you coming in's what puts the rates up, you see. They can't afford to keep farming and have to move on. Used to be quite a lively little farm, this one. Stretched right up to the Wall.'

Flin didn't know what to say. He felt guilty, the city yuppie full of selfish ideals about a fulfilling rural existence. 'Well, I'm intending to farm a bit. You know, a few chickens, some sheep, maybe a pig. It'd be good to make use of these buildings again.'

The old man grinned at him, and lifted and replaced his cap, before thoughtfully rubbing his chin. 'Watch out for foxes then. No room for your sentimental city view of them up here. Not if you're keeping chickens and the like.'

'That's why I'm reinforcing the doors,' said Flin, glad to be one step ahead.

'I see,' said the man, and chuckled. 'If I were you, I'd be hoping the hunt gets 'em. You'll get a grand view of the hunt from here. You don't hunt, I suppose?'

'No,' said Flin firmly, 'but I'm all for it. Nothing I like more than watching a good hunt.'

'Ah well,' said the man. 'Come on, Major, back home, the pair of us.' He gave a brief whistle and the dog immediately stood up, looking keenly at his master.

'What's your name, by the way?' asked Flin as the man turned to go.

'Melvyn,' he said. 'I'll be seeing you, no doubt.'

'Melvyn?' Then Flin remembered. 'I heard you know a bit about pigs.'

Melvyn stopped and slowly turned.

'Only I wondered whether you might have any tips,' Flin continued. 'For looking after them.'

'Fattening or farrowing?'

'I was thinking fattening.'

'Sturdy enclosure and plenty of food.' Melvyn turned to go, clicking his fingers at his dog, then muttered, 'Jesus wept,' as he ambled away from the yard.

Flin went inside, crestfallen. There'd been a distinct twinkle in Melvyn's eye. He'd been laughing at him. It made him feel gauche and inadequate, and he cringed as he thought about it. The old salt watching the young upstart about to fail.

'At least we now know for sure that we're supposed to be pro-foxhunting. Blood sports are definitely a good thing round here,' he told Tiffany later.

'And I met another normal person in the village,' said Tiffany.

'Really?' said Flin, his mood brightening.

'Yes. She's about our age. Her parents live in the next village and she's visiting them for a while. She seemed really nice actually.'

'Great. Why don't we meet up for a drink?' Flin realized how already he felt starved of like-minded company. When in London would he ever have suggested a drink with someone they'd casually met on the street?

'Actually, I said I'd call.'

'Great, and how was Claire?'

'Lovely. I think she could become quite a mate. She said I could ride pretty much any time I liked.'

'At least *you're* making friends then,' said Flin.

'Flin, honey, this place isn't like London. It's going to take a while to settle in. I can't bear you getting gloomy already. Get the pigs if you want them, and the chickens and the geese. Who cares what this Melvyn guy thinks anyway? Or anyone else for that matter?'

'You're right. Sorry, Tiff, I'm being over-sensitive. You're right, as ever.'

But the next time they ventured into the Compasses, they were once again met with wary indifference. Keith made a few snide comments about 'wannabe farmers', while the others grunted over their pints. Then Melvyn walked in, saw them and nodded, then headed to the bar and began talking to a couple of the regulars. A few moments later, they all laughed and one of them looked over in their direction.

'Come on, let's go,' said Flin immediately.

'Don't be so ridiculous,' Tiffany told him, placing a hand firmly on his leg. 'You're getting paranoid.'

'It's hard not to be around here.'

'They were probably laughing at something completely different. Just relax, stop feeling everyone's out to get you, and enjoy your drink.'

But Flin still insisted they head home after the one drink.

'We've got to tighten our belts, remember,' he told her.

'OK, you win this time, but don't think you're fooling anyone,' Tiffany said. Then, with a cursory nod towards Keith at the bar, they left the pub and began the walk home.

Willie invited them to drinks before lunch on Sunday. He was sorry about the short notice, but hoped they could come. Sort of a welcome drink, he told them, by way of explanation. Neither knew what they should wear, but having been so over-dressed for their first meeting with him, decided they should err on the side of casual. Tiffany wore a light skirt and T-shirt, Flin an open shirt and everyday trousers. Willie opened the front door wearing a suit and led them into a large drawing room where a dozen people stood in twos and threes drinking champagne. They, too, wore suits and best dresses.

'Sorry, got the dress code wrong again,' said Flin apologetically.

Willie laughed. 'Don't worry about that. You look fine. Everyone else is over-dressed.' Then, ushering them forward, he insisted he introduce them to a few people.

But despite doing his best to say something of interest or worth, Flin found it impossible to force an entry into the conversations around him. After politely pausing to shake hands, each of the people he hovered by returned to their half-finished discussions. Tiffany quickly found Claire and siphoned herself off. Within moments, Flin watched her animatedly recounting some story to their host and two other elegantly bejewelled ladies, before they all threw their heads back in laughter. He turned back to the two men he stood beside. One looked about Willie's age, the other much older, and they were having a heated debate about whether some strange name was really going to be selling off some land with an even stranger name.

'Is it a lot?' asked Flin tentatively.

'Is what a lot?' said the older man.

'The land this chap might be selling.'

'About two-fifty, I think it is,' said the younger man, then, turning back to the other once more, added, 'But what I really want to know is . . .' And they were off again, Flin's attempt at inclusion failing at the first fence.

Willie rescued him, introducing him to an older couple, who were, he said, neighbours of his.

'Oh really? So where do you live then?' Flin asked. Willie's house was situated at the end of a long drive and surrounded by a large, bountiful garden and fields. Flin hadn't noticed another house within eyeshot.

'Just the far side of Hexham,' the man said.

'Pretty close, only about ten miles away,' added the woman. 'What about you?' Her greying hair was immaculately coiffed into a large arc of a headpiece, protecting the small, sharp features of her face. Heavily ringed fingers clutched a glass of champagne.

Flin told them, and they nodded disinterestedly. Sensing this was the moment to maintain the initiative, or lose it for ever, he said: 'Have you lived there long?' It turned out they had, or at least his family had – for several hundred years.

'. . . in 1849 my great-grandfather bought land that neighboured on Willie's great-great-grandfather's land,' the man told him some while later, 'and the boundary, in places marked by the Tyne, and in others by the Wall, still stands today.' Flin tried to listen, to be interested and stifle his yawns, but struggled desperately. The man's somniferous tone didn't help.

'. . . said to Willie why don't you rent out some of your estate properties? That's what we did. Makes a lot of sense. Paid dividends. Bet you're rather glad I suggested it, aren't you?'

Flin was staring at the burst capillaries across the man's nose and the little tufts of whiskers high on his cheekbones.

'Oh, yes, very,' he managed to say after a slight pause.

They began the drive back to Standing Stone Farmhouse in silence, until Tiffany said, 'That was OK, wasn't it?'

'No, it was completely bloody awful. The people I met either talked a different language or bored for Britain. Either way, I couldn't get a word in edgeways. Apart from asking which house we lived in, they weren't in the slightest bit interested in me or anything I had to say.'

'Claire's great though. You liked her, didn't you?'

'Sure, but I only got to chat to her right at the end. I don't know whether you noticed, but mostly the men talked to the men and the women talked to the women. It was just so archaic and feudal.'

'I suppose it was a bit.'

They continued in silence once more, until they turned off the road towards their house. Tiffany said, 'Come on, Flin, it was funny, wasn't it? Why are you so gloomy?'

'I don't know. Nothing. I'm being silly.' He leant over and kissed her. 'Sorry.'

But Flin could not help believing he had arrived in some alien country. Despite mass globalization, uniform fast-food bars and easy travel, here, in a quiet corner of Northumberland, people still followed an older code. Its upper order, born of a long lineage that had survived revolutions and world wars, remained intact, but perilously threatened. Its core, desperately clutching onto an earlier age, demonstrated a wary mistrust towards anyone who threatened this way of life. This was what Flin had come into. It was what the southern villages of his parents' generation must have felt when, thirty years before, the middle-class professionals swept into the thatched cottages as the out-going farm tenants disappeared for ever. But he wasn't there to threaten their existence; he was there to help maintain it. That was why he had escaped London in the first place. He wished he could be more like Tiffany. None of this mattered to her. She took everyone at face value. A gathering like Willie's drinks party would never faze her. He had to try to be more like her. More laid-back. Not take things so personally. Patience, that was all he needed. Patience, and, in time, suspicion was bound to give way to acceptance.

CHAPTER ELEVEN

Harry sees Jenny again but feels tantalized

Flin was waiting for him at Newcastle. Harry saw him, tall and slightly scruffy, peering anxiously at every carriage. Then he waved and bounded over, giving Harry an overly affectionate hug.

'God, it's great to see you,' he said enthusiastically, 'do you realize you're our first visitor?'

Harry grinned. 'But you've only been here a couple of weeks.'

'I know, but it's amazing how cut off I feel from you all already.'

'Regretting it?'

'No, no, no. No, of course not. It's fantastic – the air so fresh, and just wait till you see our pad. But, you know, it's a *big* change, Harry. And having had all my friends more or less around me all the time, it's a bit of a shock to realize there's no one to call up and go to the pub with whenever I feel like it. But honestly, it's great. Really great.'

'Anyway, you'll get to meet people quickly enough.'

'Yeah, of course.' Flin paused as they reached his car. 'I'm sure we will. Although actually, Tiffany met someone last week who sounds quite promising. Her mother's ill or something and so she's up here for a bit looking after her. Anyway, she's our age and might come along to the pub tonight, so you'll be able to see for yourself whether she's potential new-friend material. Jenny, she's called.'

'Jenny?' said Harry quickly. Surely not his Jenny. 'Well, I can't wait. Feel I need a drink or two.'

'Yes. I was going to ask. How are you? No regrets?'

'No, I don't think so. I feel terrible about it, but I knew she wasn't the one for me, you know? So I thought it was best to call a halt now.'

'You're probably right. Still, you're a brave man. How'd she take it?'

'Um, not that great, to be honest.'

'Tears?'

'And the rest. It was awful. Felt like I'd murdered someone or something.'

'Ouch.'

'Exactly.'

'Ah, well.' Flin turned and grinned reassuringly. 'I'm sure you did the right thing. I'm sorry though. She was nice. I liked her, and it gave us all something to talk about, having you go out with someone again.'

Harry smiled and looked out of the window. Newcastle had gone by in a flash. An enormous city, but nothing compared to London. In under fifteen minutes since getting into the car, they had already reached open countryside. Away down to his left lay the Tyne Valley, sheltering the market towns of Corbridge and Hexham. The sun streamed through some clouds, shining beams of light over the valley and hills beyond. Ahead and to their right, stretched gentle undulating uplands of deep greens, the fields bordered by lines of beech and dry stone. Flin sped along the old Military Road; there was barely a car in sight.

'Great countryside, Flin,' said Harry. 'Like a Turner painting. I can just see all those great landscape artists having a field day up here.'

'You should bring your paints up then. I love it already. And damn quiet. That's the Wall over there.' He pointed to a ditch and a grassy mound, running parallel to the road. Occasional houses or hedgerows interrupted the flow, but then determinedly, the mound continued once more.

'I never realized you were so close to it. You'll be able to go on walks along it.'

'That's what I thought. Maybe even this weekend.'

The ground looked damp, as though it had recently rained, and the sky was full of varying shades of cloud. But in between was plenty of blue, and the air was clear, so that Harry could see for miles and miles. 'It's stunning, Flin. Absolutely stunning. What a place to live.'

Flin beamed happily. 'So you approve?'

'How could I not?'

Flin turned off right onto what seemed like a private road. Two stone gateposts stood guard beneath an archway of trees.

'Is this your private drive then?' asked Harry.

'I like to think so. But no, I suppose it must be the old estate boundary or something.' Flin shot him a glance. 'Almost there now.'

A few hundred yards later he said with great excitement, 'There it is! Isn't that great?' Across the field Harry saw the house, a few lights on now, glowing beneath the castellated roof.

'You live in that?' said Harry incredulously.

Flin nodded happily. 'I can't tell you how good it is to have someone to show it off to.'

As they pulled into the drive behind the house, Tiffany opened the back door and stood on the steps jumping up and down happily.

'You've made it! Hooray! How brilliant to see you, Harry!' She flung her arms around him.

'Is this what happens when you move to the country? You become far more tactile and affectionate?' He grinned, hugging her tightly. Tiffany laughed.

'Come on in and let me show you around,' said Flin eagerly. The house, as he'd promised, was wonderful – roomy but cosy, elegant yet solidly aged in equal measures, although still somewhat sparse.

'As you can see, we're slightly struggling to fill it up,' smiled Flin.

'Most of our stuff fitted into the kitchen,' added Tiffany, 'so there's a bit of room left over.'

'You can buy things gradually though,' said Harry.

'Loads of antique shops in Hexham,' put in Flin.

Harry nodded appreciatively and interjected with appropriate superlatives as Flin and Tiffany took him on a guided tour of the house.

'Amazing. You make me feel very envious,' he told them as they returned to the kitchen.

'Yeah, I'm almost jealous of myself,' said Flin, hugging Tiffany happily. Then, looking at his watch, he added, 'we should get cracking. It's nearly ten o'clock – time to go to the pub.'

Harry laughed. It was odd seeing Flin and Tiffany, whom he'd always associated with living in a shoe-box in Hammersmith, transported to this large house in an outcrop of the English countryside. Still, as long as Flin had a good pub to go to, he was fairly sure his friend would make the necessary adjustment.

Flin opened the door of the Queen's Head at Great Whittington, and the three of them entered the warm, smoky air of the pub. And there, at a table near the bar, sat Jenny. It *was* her. Harry saw her first and, an instant later, while he stood dumbstruck with shock, he watched her raise her eyes and fix them on his. For a moment her expression remained one of blank amazement, then, slowly, her mouth widened into the most beautiful smile he'd ever seen.

'Hello, Harry,' she said, making no attempt to stand up, or greet him with a shake of hand or kiss of cheek. This saddened him immediately; his was a reduced status.

'Jenny,' he said, then felt stumped. Of all the crazy bars and gin-joints in the entire world, she had to be in the same one as him. Or however that line went. But this proved it: someone somewhere was smiling down on him. Had to be. It was too much of a coincidence otherwise.

'No way! You two *know* each other?' said Tiffany, open-mouthed.

Jenny smiled. 'Yes, yes we do.'

'Quite a coincidence,' said Harry, unable to think of anything less obvious.

'Great. I always knew England was a small place. Now I only have to make one introduction. Jenny, this is Flin.'

They said hello, and then Flin rubbed his hands together and asked who wanted a drink.

'No, let me get these,' Harry interjected immediately. 'What can I get you all?'

'Oh, OK, if you insist, thanks, Harry,' said Flin, sitting himself down. 'Jenny?'

'I'd love a dry Martini and lemonade, thank you,' she said. So some things hadn't changed. Harry shot her a spontaneous yet knowing smile, which she returned, acknowledging his appreciation of an old habit. Harry quickly turned to Flin and Tiffany.

'Mine's a pint, please, Harry,' said Flin.

'Same for me please,' added Tiffany.

Harry nodded and went to the bar. This had thrown him completely. How absolutely amazing that she should be here. Brilliant news, or at least it should be, as long as he could just be himself and not freeze up. This had caught him on the hop even more than that meeting in the café. Still, might be fantastic. He quickly glanced back. She was still there, chatting to Flin and Tiffany. Real, not some apparition. She looked up and saw him stare at her, so he quickly turned away, pretending to be surveying the entire bar. Cosy; almost quaint. One of the walls was covered with a large mural of a hunting scene. Scarlet-jacketed riders on their horses were loitering outside a pub, taking drinks before the hunt began, the hounds waiting at their feet with eager anticipation.

'Painted in 1922,' said the landlord, 'just outside here. Hasn't changed much.'

'It's good,' said Harry, meaning it. It was amateur, with a slightly naïve feel to it, but, crucially, the artist had managed to capture a sense of atmosphere. Harry looked at it intently, hoping that one day he might have a reason for wishing to remember.

As he held out the exact amount needed, his hand began to shake slightly. As he caught the landlord's eye, a brief moment of understanding passed between them before Harry slammed the money on the counter instead, looking away as he did so. Come on, relax, relax. But he could sense the natural rhythms of easy conversation ebbing away from him.

He walked back to the table, clutching all four drinks together. 'Beer, beer, Martini, Guinness,' he said as he put the glasses down on the table, hoping he sounded more hearty than he felt.

'Thanks, Harry. Cheers,' said Flin happily.

They all chinked their glasses and this time Harry momentarily caught Jenny's eye. He'd been right in the café: she hadn't really changed at all. Her skin still had that smooth, healthy glow, her lips the same fullness, and the long eyelashes suggested a lurking vulnerability. Perhaps there was a faint line either side of her mouth, but that hardly constituted advancing middle age.

'So how have you been, Harry? What're you up to?' Jenny asked, looking him straight in the eye.

'Hang on a minute,' said Tiffany, 'rewind a moment. We want to know how you two know each other.'

'Haven't you told them yet, Jenny?' asked Harry.

'Too busy introducing myself to Flin, actually.' She took a sip from her drink.

'So?' said Flin.

Harry coughed unnecessarily, then said, 'We knew each other a long time ago.'

'We used to go out together.' Jenny put down her glass, then looked up and smiled. Harry wondered whether she was finding this as difficult as he was. Perhaps she didn't want to see him. After all, she had never called him after he gave her his number in the café. Perhaps she still thought him beneath contempt. He felt blood drain from his face. His stomach hurt.

'Really? No way!' said Flin. 'I thought I knew about all your girlfriends, Harry.'

Harry looked down and tried to laugh.

'So: who binned who?' asked Tiffany, eyeing the pair of them.

Harry looked up at Jenny. For a moment, she just stared intently back at him, then, breaking into a smile once more, said, 'I can't really remember, can you, Harry?'

'We were a lot younger then,' he said, turning to Flin and Tiffany. 'Before university. Anyway.' He lifted his pint, suddenly wishing he were back in London.

'*Anyway*,' said Jenny, 'to get back to my original question, how have you been?'

'Um, fine. You know. Trundling along.'

'Harry! Don't be so modest. It doesn't suit you,' chided Flin. 'He's an artist, and he's brilliant. Murals are your big thing now though, aren't they?'

'An artist? Good for you.' She paused, her brow furrowing. 'Wasn't your mother one too?'

'Yes,' said Harry. 'Yes, she was. Still is. Just. You know, she, um, does the odd commission still. At least I think she did one last year. And, um.' Looking apprehensively around, he added, 'So what about you? You're not in London, you said.'

'I'm a teacher. In France,' said Jenny. 'Although it's only playing at teaching really. You know, English to businessmen. Not especially rewarding, I'm afraid.'

'Oh. Whereabouts?'

'Tours. Although I live in Chenonceaux, a village not far away.'

'Great,' said Harry lamely. He'd been to Chenonceaux before, but said nothing, aware of both Tiffany and Flin watching his pitiful performance with bewildered amazement. He wanted to stab himself. What was his problem? Why couldn't he just lighten up and speak normally, converse freely as he did ninety-nine point nine per cent of the time?

'So how long d'you think you'll be up here, Jenny?' asked Flin hopefully.

'I'm going to head back next week, I think. Mum's been ill but seems a lot better now. I've got to earn some money. Still, it's been good fun spending some proper time up here.'

'When did your parents move then?' muttered Harry.

'About four years ago, when Dad retired from the RAF. They both agreed they wanted a bit of peace and quiet, and they like being this close to the coast. Also Dad was posted in Scotland on various occasions. This way he can still go back quite easily. But I'd already left home by the time they shipped out of Suffolk, so coming to stay really does feel like I'm on holiday in a new area. How about your parents, Harry? Still in Suffolk?'

He nodded. 'Yes. Still there.' Then he stumbled more visibly. Having taken an embarrassed glug of his beer, he was so busy silently cursing himself, he managed to put the pint only half on the table. The glass, still two-thirds full, lurched towards him. His heart, in turn, seemed to lurch into his stomach, but with reflexes that impressed even himself, he managed to prevent the pint from completely tipping over. Even so, a good amount of thick, dark stout sloshed over his crotch.

'Watch it!' laughed Flin, a bit too jovially.

'Bollocks,' said Harry, standing up and dabbing himself down with his handkerchief. He felt utterly miserable. It was not meant to be like this.

'Are you OK?' asked Tiffany, looking genuinely concerned, then offering to get him a towel.

'No, I'm fine, really. Soon dry off. Honestly, I don't know what's the matter with me.'

'Well, at least no one will notice you smelling of beer in here.' Jenny smiled at him once more, a warm, lovely smile.

'No, no, I suppose not. Not until I go to the bog and someone beats me up for having pissed myself.' He'd meant to raise a laugh, but unfortunately his delivery had been all wrong; so he ended up just sounding sour instead.

There was a slight pause until Flin said, 'God it's good to be in the pub with normal people, having a few drinks and watching an old friend pour beer over himself.' That time everyone laughed; even Harry allowed himself a slight smirk.

'Flin's upset because the locals haven't overwhelmed us with rural charm,' said Tiffany. 'Everyone's gone on about southerners barging their way in and forcing the house prices to go up. So you're suddenly feeling a bit insecure, aren't you, honey?'

'Honestly, Harry, Tiff does not exaggerate. And they're all obsessed with foxes. Literally everyone I've spoken to so far has brought it up within thirty seconds.'

'How weird,' said Jenny. 'I don't think anyone's ever mentioned it to me.'

'Haven't they? Well, that must be because you're only visiting. You don't really live here, and so you're not a threat. You're not going to ponce up here and push up the rates.'

Jenny raised an amused eyebrow at Harry. He grinned back, only too glad to be exchanging conspiratorial glances across the table. 'What's that got to do with foxes?' she asked.

'Nothing really, except their fox talk is clearly a means of finding out whether we're pussy-footed southern animal rights types or not.'

'Are you?' asked Harry. His turn to glance mischievously at Jenny.

'Are we what?'

'Pussy-footed animal rights types?'

'Not really.' Flin shrugged. 'I certainly won't be if they eat my chickens.'

'You're still planning to do the smallholding thing?' asked Harry incredulously. This was better: a few sly glances towards Jenny and he could also talk to Flin without feeling awkward. His heart-rate had slowed to a more acceptable level.

'You bet we are.'

'Well, Flin is,' Tiffany corrected him. 'Although I'm secretly already quite taken with the chooks, even though they made a total mess of the back of the car when we picked them up last week.'

'And a magnificent cock,' added Flin proudly, laughing at his own joke. 'I'll show him to you tomorrow. They're happily locked up for the night in my new fox-proof barn.'

'Well, if you've already got chickens you must feel well on the way to becoming proper farmers,' said Harry, with just the faintest hint of irony.

'I tell you, Harry,' said Flin animatedly, 'I'm not going to be put off by a bunch of snooty Geordies. They can think what they like, but they'll be laughing the other side of their face when my pig wins the Hexham District Pig of the Year Award.'

'Shh,' said Tiffany, tapping his leg, 'keep your voice down.'

'So you're getting a pig too?' laughed Jenny.

'Definitely. They're quite the most sensible animal to own if you're a smallholder.'

Harry countered, 'But Flin, there're so many breeds. How on earth are you ever going to decide which one?'

'Good question. Any ideas?'

'An old neighbour of mine used to have a Gloucester Old Spot. That was a nice pig.'

'Hm,' said Flin, 'I have to say I'm slightly coming down in favour of a Wessex Saddleback.'

As they argued ferociously about the varying benefits of the one type of pig over another, Harry began to enjoy himself, the earlier tension slowly but surely seeping away.

After another drink Flin suggested they go back to their house for some supper. 'A bit late, but I'm starving. The stew should be more than cooked by now, anyway.'

'You're going to come, aren't you, Jenny?' asked Tiffany. A pang of panic struck Harry. He'd momentarily forgotten she'd only been joining them for a drink and had her own place to return to.

'If that's OK?' she answered. Great, he thought, relieved. Now that he felt just about ready to talk to her properly, he desperately wanted that chance.

Outside, Harry followed Flin and Tiffany towards Flin's new Peugeot, when Jenny said, 'Come and keep me company.'

'Sure,' said Harry, trying to sound nonchalant, and glancing at Tiffany.

'OK, see you back at base in a mo,' said Tiffany.

Moments later, he sat next to Jenny in her car. It felt strange, but exciting. Being so close physically after such a long time apart gave Harry a thrilling kind of happiness. But although pathetically grateful for the moment, he craved more. She looked round, ready to reverse, turning her neck in his direction. Although it was dark outside, the lights from the pub and from Flin's car lit up her face. Her lips, slightly apart, were unblemished by lipstick, but still dark and full. What he would give to kiss them. He wished he still had that right.

'It's lovely to see you again, Jenny,' he said. His confidence with her was growing once more. 'It really is. You haven't changed a bit.'

'Nor have you.' She grinned. 'But you've somehow grown into your face.'

'Really?' He laughed. 'How do you mean?'

'Well, I always used to think you looked so young. You still do, but you don't look fifteen any more.'

'I'll take that as a compliment,' he told her, relieved they were still talking normally. 'What happened to the old Peugeot?'

'It died, I'm afraid. Crashed it. I'll show you the scar one of these days.' She quickly changed the subject. 'Anyway, don't you think it's weird us meeting up like this?'

'Very, although I'm grateful your mother's been unwell. She's going to be all right, is she?'

'You always were a selfish sod, Harry.' A criticism, but lightly said, and he saw she was still smiling. 'But yes, I think she's going to be fine. She's certainly up and about at last, and able to do stuff. I've been here three weeks now, and I'm beginning to get fed up with both her and my dad, so I think I will be heading back early next week.'

Harry nodded. 'That's a shame. Just as I finally see you again, you run off back to Tours.'

'You're the one that ran away, remember.' They had just arrived back at Standing Stone Farmhouse, and Jenny stared ahead for a moment, her hands still clutching the steering wheel. 'Sorry,' she said, slowly turning to him. 'I didn't mean that. Let's go in, shall we?' Harry followed her into the house, his heart racing. It still hurt her. Still, after eleven years. She'd been unable to hide it: a spontaneous reaction from which Harry gleaned just the faintest spark of hope.

Jenny seemed to have forgotten the incident once they sat down at Flin and Tiffany's new kitchen table. New to them, but otherwise old, picked up in Hexham for what Flin happily told them was 'an absolute bargain'. Clearly much used, it none the less looked to be a sturdy piece of pine, stripped and waxed and complete with a drawer at one end that didn't quite shut.

'Flin's certainly been right about one thing,' said Tiffany, 'and that's how much cheaper it is up here compared to London.'

'I noticed that when I paid for the drinks,' agreed Harry.

The conversation moved on. Animals, vegetables; what they

could do with the outbuildings if they had a bit of money; Jenny's life in France, her proximity to all the great châteaux of the Loire and the boulangerie in her village where they sold the world's best bread, and great wine costing next to nothing. She talked of her new friends, people in the village and other English people she'd met through the school. Harry listened intently.

Then the conversation moved to him, and he told them about one of his recent murals: it had been for an ageing and camp actor who wanted his bathroom turned into a Roman ruin. Harry had painted crumbling columns in every corner, as though it were an ancient and overgrown temple. As a backdrop, he'd created a classical Italian landscape with further distant ruins half hidden by rows of cypress trees.

'Wonderful, dear boy, quite wonderful, but where are all the statues?' Harry mimicked, in his very best Noël Coward impersonation. His client, he told them, had then absolutely *insisted* he paint a series of athletic-looking Roman figures, 'Adonis and Narcissus spying on my nightly soak.' His anecdote produced the laughter he'd hoped for, but was it too late? No one had mentioned anything about what they might do over the following two days, and he prayed that this precious time with Jenny would not be over almost as soon as it had begun. Now he'd stumbled over the first nervous hurdle, he wanted – no, needed – to see more of her, and make her see there was still something there between them.

It was well past midnight when Jenny stretched and said she really ought to be going.

'Yes, I suppose it is getting late,' admitted Tiffany. Please say something about tomorrow, Harry thought, wondering whether he should boldly speak out and invite her anyway.

'What are you all doing tomorrow?' Jenny suddenly asked. She said it in an easy-come, easy-go kind of manner, but Harry visibly relaxed.

'Good question,' said Flin, standing next to her, thought-fully rubbing his chin. 'I don't know. Sea or Wall? That is the question.'

'I know,' said Jenny brightly. 'Why don't we go up the coast to Craster, have crab sandwiches in the pub, then walk along the coast to Dunstanburgh Castle?'

'Fantastic,' said Tiffany. 'I want to do that.'

'Fancy that, Harry?' asked Flin.

'Great,' he said eagerly, then remembering himself added, 'whatever.' He wanted to whoop for joy and punch the air. He was going to spend a whole day with her – and at her instigation too.

The three of them headed to bed soon after Jenny left. It had been a long day, and Harry felt suddenly tired. Not only was it late, he'd also spent the evening running the full gamut of emotions. As he helped Flin and Tiffany quickly clear up, both quizzed him a little more about Jenny, but then the conversation quickly moved on to their friends back in London. All the same, as he said goodnight and shut the door to his room, he hoped his embarrassment and awkwardness in the pub had not been too transparent.

Once in bed, he read a bit more of his novel, hoping it might distract him into sleep, but soon gave up, his thoughts too full. Switching off the light, he stared up into the inky darkness, wondering whether there was someone waiting for Jenny back in France. If so, she was keeping very quiet about him. There had been no mention of anyone, no male name dropped into the conversation, unless one of her new French friends was also a lover. Her hands were free of jewellery. No tell-tale rings, just a silver bangle on her right wrist and a single locket around her neck. And would a boyfriend be happy about her spending three weeks away from him in Northumberland? It seemed unlikely; he knew *he* wouldn't like it. Perhaps he should just ask her. Perhaps not. Just in case she said the wrong thing.

*   *   *

The next morning, the weather continued bright and clear. A few white puffs of cloud floated happily across the summer sky, but otherwise Harry saw nothing but blue: smooth, deep and endless. Flin was giving him a tour of the outbuildings, going over his plans and showing him where the Wessex Saddleback (it had been eventually agreed that Flin should maintain some link with the county of his birth, however tenuous) would live and grow. Birdsong, busy, varied, and largely invisible, surrounded them. Harry breathed in deeply, enjoying the smell of the grass and dried hay, sheep and dust; it was sharp but gentle somehow.

Harry watched Flin, like a child showing off his new toy, open up the big double doors to the barn. The chickens clucked about the dusty floor and rafters with mild contentment.

'Those over there are Sussex, that there's a Pekin, and the rest are New England Reds,' Flin told him proudly. 'I think my favourites are the Sussexes though.'

'Mine too,' said Harry.

'Really? Oh, great,' said Flin, ambling towards a large bag of feed propped up in one corner.

Harry felt a pang of envy, not of Flin's attempt to discover the pastoral existence – he still enjoyed London life too much for that – but because his friend had discovered what he wanted from life and, with Tiffany, had found someone to share that vision.

They left for their day-trip soon after, picking up Jenny on the way. Harry hoped he could sit in the back with her, but Tiffany insisted he take the front seat, telling him she didn't mind at all, she didn't need as much leg-room as he did. It was only a couple of miles down the road to Jenny's parents' house in Great Whittington. While Harry and Flin sat in the idling car, Tiffany nimbly jumped out, opened the bright white wooden gate and walked up the path through the neat front garden. Harry watched Jenny's father open the door, shocked to see how much he'd aged. White had replaced the dark head of hair of eleven years before. In those years, Mr Albright had gone from being an agile man of fifty to over sixty and retired. In the same time, Harry had transformed from a boy barely needing to shave his chin to a directionless nearly-thirty-year-old. He saw Tiffany say something, then point in the direction of the car, and Jenny's father looked up and waved benignly. Then, as Flin waved back, Jenny appeared. Wearing long, dark linen baggy trousers, tight T-shirt and white cotton shirt, she looked so lovely, Harry wanted to melt. Her sunglasses rested on the top of her head, keeping her hair out of her face. She kissed her father briskly on the cheek, then happily wandered towards the car, laughing with Tiffany.

Watching her share some joke with Tiffany prompted a small wave of irritation. Why wasn't he in on it? And why didn't he have her all to himself, so that her laughter could be prompted by him, and him alone? He felt selfish, greedy, then remembered his relationship with Jenny was nothing more than casual and platonic, like her new friendship with Tiffany and now Flin. Who was he trying to kid, reading something into the conversation they'd shared in the car the previous evening? He wasn't anything special, not any more. And this was entirely his fault. It was he who had trodden on their love, sneering and full of self-righteousness. If only he'd known there was no one else out there. He might even have been married to her by now. *Might* even have had children. But he'd ruined everything. How humiliated she must have felt that time she came to Cambridge, and how badly he'd behaved towards her. Just thinking about it made him cringe. Well, he was paying for it now, watching her, this vision of perfect femininity approaching the car. She'd always been pretty, but in those eleven years she'd become more sophisticated somehow, a grown, mature woman. She might be shorter, and less obviously striking than Julia, but a warmth exuded from her, unpretentious, natural and instinctive. What he would give to be able to turn back the clock.

*   *   *

166

It wasn't until they were walking away from the pub towards the distant outline of Dunstanburgh Castle that Harry finally managed to talk to her on his own. During their time in the car Jenny had spent much of her time talking to Tiffany in the back seat, and over crab sandwiches in the pub at Craster the conversation was once again general rather than specific. But Harry had also worked himself up into such a state of self-loathing at what he believed to be his past treachery, he'd become, once again, somewhat taciturn, and felt unable to converse as freely and heartily as he'd hoped.

Flin, sensing Harry's growing unease, took Tiffany's hand and slowed their pace, so that very soon a healthy gap stretched between them and Harry and Jenny up ahead.

Harry, relieved to have re-established the intimacy of the previous evening's car ride, toyed with apologizing for his behaviour eleven years before, but wasn't sure whether the moment was quite right. So instead he asked her about France.

'So you're definitely going to go back next week, are you?'

'Monday morning. It's odd to think I'll be home in France by the evening,' she told him. 'I've been back three weeks now and I've rather got used to English country life and not doing a lot.'

'Why don't you stay then?'

'I've got to earn some money, Harry. And I think if I spend any more time with my parents, I'll go mad. They're lovely, of course, but they're getting older and I'm grown-up now. I'm thirty, for God's sake. But I envy Flin and Tiffany and their new life up here. Don't you?'

'I envy what they've got, but I'm not sure I want to keep pigs. And I do love London and my flat. Come and see it next time you're in London.' Immediately, he regretted the remark. He no longer wanted to seem casual or indifferent; it suggested he was happy with this new, platonic relationship.

'So who do you live with then?' she asked. As soon as she said it, Harry realized with alarm that there was now no avoiding the conversation that was to come. The moment of truth had arrived.

'No one,' he told her simply. 'I got to the stage a couple of years ago when I simply couldn't face house-sharing any more. Most of the friends I used to live with had got married or, like Flin, were living with partners, and so I thought it was time to find my own place. I think a point comes when you finally become fed up with other people's mismatching taste, and bored with finding someone else's hair in the bath, or opening a fridge with nothing in it other than a pot of mayonnaise and a rapidly browning iceberg lettuce.'

Jenny laughed. 'So you bought your own pad?'

'Yeah. And just at the right time too, before house prices went really mad. I was doubly lucky because I was left a bit of money by an old second cousin and that paid for a minimum deposit and some alterations I wanted to do. And it's great because it's all my own taste. Virtually every little thing in it.'

'But don't you get lonely living on your own? Or is there a glamorous girlfriend to keep you company? I can't imagine you're ever single for long.'

Harry turned to her to see whether the expression on her face revealed anything. But it didn't. She just looked at him and smiled, then said, 'Well?'

'No, it's just me. Actually, I haven't really been properly out with someone for ages. I had a brief fling recently, but that's over now. Anyway, why do you say that?'

She looked away from him, towards a group of seagulls hovering over the sea. 'Sorry, I didn't mean anything by it. I suppose I just assumed you must be going out with someone. Most people seem to these days.'

Harry laughed nervously and said, 'Not everyone. Why, do you?' But already, he instinctively knew what her response would be. There might only have been a macro-second before she gave her answer, but for Harry it seemed like a long-drawn-out sickening standstill in time, the moment when he realized his fate was sealed.

'Yes. Yes, I do. He's called Phil. We've been together ages. Actually, Harry, we're engaged.'

Those words, softly spoken, stunned Harry so completely, they might just as well have been a huge invisible fist belting him in the stomach.

After an agonized pause, he somehow managed to say, 'Engaged? Wow. Congratulations,' and continue walking forwards. But all he really wanted to do was crumple to the ground and lie spreadeagled until he could make sense of this devastating announcement. His brain whirred, but Jenny talked on: she and Phil had been going out since university, had started living together and then when he'd taken a job working for a French wine company, she had followed him out to France. It had been quite a big decision, she supposed, but then again, she was sick of teaching in run-down schools in London and thought it would be a good opportunity to learn French. Phil had proposed on New Year's Eve. He'd already bought the ring, and everyone was watching. So she'd said yes.

Harry heard all of this, but struggled to take in the magnitude of what she was telling him so calmly. His feet moved forward, step after step, and outwardly he knew his face remained calm and largely expressionless. But inside, his body screamed and burst like an exploding firework factory. He'd persuaded himself after long thought the previous evening that there was no boyfriend after all. Now she was telling him there was, that they lived together, and even bloody worse, she was *engaged* to him. It was a crushing blow, his growing conviction that Jenny was his perfect companion dashed in a trice. For a few moments, life seemed very bleak. There was now nothing to look forward to, nothing but the dreary monotonous daily grind of getting up and leading a pointless existence devoid of love.

'So when's the big day?' he said after a short moment.

'Oh, I don't know. We haven't set one yet. Phil wants to wait a year because then he'll have a better idea of whether he'll want to stay on in France or not.'

'Oh,' said Harry, then glanced at her hand. She wasn't wearing a ring. 'Where's the ring then? I thought you said he gave you a ring.'

Jenny looked at him strangely and then he noticed her cheeks flush. 'To be honest, I don't really like it. Isn't that awful of me? It's a shame as he was terribly proud of himself, having worked out precisely the right size and everything. But I just don't like sapphires, so what's a girl to do?'

'Why don't you tell him?'

'I couldn't. He'd be really hurt. Anyway, I can't say I mind that much. When he's around I wear it.'

Harry was silent for a moment. Ahead, the towering castle loomed, strong, resilient and defiantly perched on cliffs overlooking the dark northern sea stretching away to an ill-defined horizon.

'Harry?' Jenny asked him, suddenly stopping and turning to look at him. Then, slightly nervously, she carefully tucked away an errant lock of hair and said, 'I'm glad we've seen each other again. We did love each other once, however young we may have been, but it all ended so horribly. I do understand what happened, you know, but . . .' She stopped. Harry's throat thickened. He couldn't say anything; if he tried, he thought he'd probably cry. Jenny turned away again, and sat down by the edge of the cliff. 'Anyway, I just wanted you to know it's meant a lot to me, being able to see you again.'

'Me too,' said Harry, sitting down beside her, 'I –'

'Aren't we going to make the castle?' shouted Flin from twenty yards away.

Harry and Jenny turned towards him.

'Of course, just pausing a moment, that's all,' Harry called back, standing up once more. He held out a hand to Jenny, the cool soft skin of her fingers tightening around his.

'Come on, let's catch up with the others,' he said.

Of course it had been the most terrible shock, but in a funny way, Harry very quickly found Jenny's bombshell strangely liberating too, as though a huge weight had been lifted off his shoulders. The unbearable tension he had created between them evaporated once her true circumstances were revealed.

As they approached the castle, he barely said a word. But then, as the four of them clambered over the medieval walls, Harry paused high up on one of the remaining towers. Gulls circled, crying above the breakers below. The day was so bright: the sky vivid blue, the sea dark with stark white peaks; away to one side stretched a long narrow strip of yellow beach, whilst behind lay fresh and succulent fields of green. A breeze was blowing up, making his eyes smart, but Harry felt invigorated by the air, the wind, the colour.

At least now he knew. The what-ifs that had been repeatedly running through his mind had finally been resolved, even if the answer had so emphatically dashed his hopes. Jenny was no longer a fantasy figure of his imagination, but real again, living out her life. As he stood there at the top of the castle, a peculiar sense of calm settled over him. What the future held in store seemed suddenly irrelevant. What was important was the present, here and now: the beautiful countryside on a glorious English summer's day, the company of two of his closest friends, and the girl he loved. Even if she could never be his, that was surely worth making the most of.

For the remainder of the weekend, Harry hardly stopped talking. No longer were there any taboo subjects between them, and once more he could be himself, free from the constraints he'd been imposing. To his delight he and Jenny got on as well as they ever had. They laughed, a lot. All four of them did, but it seemed to Harry that he and Jenny laughed especially. They also discovered they still had much in common. Likes and dislikes were fervently discussed and analysed. Later that evening, he and Jenny were sitting on deck chairs in the garden. They were having a drink on their own, since Tiffany was inside and Flin feeding the chickens. The topic: food and drink.

'Olive oil, sun-dried tomatoes, and anti pasto – I could eat that all day,' said Jenny, her face in paroxysms of rapture. 'Actually, I just love food. Food and wine. They're just the greatest pleasures in life.'

'I completely and utterly agree,' laughed Harry, 'something my parents passed on to me. I'm eternally grateful. But you're so right – Mediterranean food is just the best in the world. Sometimes I think of moving there, just so I can have all that food on tap, and then I could paint vast murals in Tuscan villas.'

'Now *that* would be fun. I think I love Italy even more than France.'

'Do you? God, so do I! Now that would be a place to go on honeymoon.'

'Wouldn't it?'

'Definitely. First of all it's close to England, so there wouldn't be a huge journey involved in order to get there. Also, it's fairly safe. You're not going to catch any terrible tropical diseases nor are there any crocodiles, or particularly unpleasant insects.'

Jenny laughed. 'And think of all that wonderful food,' she added.

'And the drink. Lots of delicious wine, and beautiful cities with plenty to do. It would be perfect! You could lounge by the pool surrounded by vines and embraced by a warm sun, or go sightseeing. All in all, a blissful holiday. And it's important to be surrounded by beauty when you're very much in love.'

'Definitely,' agreed Jenny. 'There's a time for long-distance hauls and intrepid adventure holidays, but a honeymoon is not one of them. Food for thought.'

The next day, all four were walking along Hadrian's Wall, earnestly discussing the most beautiful film stars of all time. Harry favoured Grace Kelly, while Flin argued heavily that it had to be Ingrid Bergman.

'What about Marilyn?' suggested Tiffany.

'No,' said Flin firmly, 'great to sleep with, and obviously very sexy, but for sheer, pure, ridiculous beauty, it's got to be Ingrid. Just watch her in *Casablanca* or *Notorious.* She's unbelievable.'

'I'm with Harry, I'm afraid,' put in Jenny, 'Cary Grant and Grace Kelly in *To Catch a Thief.* The most beautiful coupling ever in the history of cinema.'

'That's such a brilliant film,' said Harry.

'Isn't it?' agreed Jenny. 'One of my all-time favourites.'

'Really? Mine too. I've got an original poster of it in my flat.'

Flin laughed and said, 'Is there anything you two don't agree on?' They both looked at each other and shrugged.

Jenny smiled. 'Not a lot, it would seem.' Harry spotted Flin and Tiffany exchange a knowing look. He was rather pleased about it.

Harry said goodbye to her at the station on the Sunday afternoon, along with Flin and Tiffany. The three of them had decided to go on and see a film in Newcastle afterwards, but even so, Harry was grateful she was there to see him off as well. Was it significant that she was the last to say her farewells? Harry liked to think so. Kissing him on both cheeks, she then hugged him tightly for just a bit longer than he'd expected.

'Bye, Harry. It's been so lovely to see you again. Really, really lovely.'

'Look after yourself, won't you?' he said, breathing in deeply the smell of her hair. He hadn't dared to ask her if he would see her again.

From his seat he saw the three of them waving him goodbye, then they were gone, disappearing from view. He'd been so close to her just minutes before, but now there was possibly a lifetime between them. He would soon be back in London, she in France, never the twain to meet. It left him with a sad and empty feeling.

Back in London, the full impact of Jenny's circumstances soon depressed him once more. Now that she was no longer with him, it was less easy to feel relaxed and magnanimous about her forthcoming nuptials. It had been wonderful spending two whole days with her, but now he felt like an addict deprived of his fix. It wasn't fair for her to reappear in his life and then disappear so completely. France might as well be on the other side of the world, so complete was the severance. Such a waste. He knew, just *knew*, they could have been so good together. Surely she must have felt something too.

This belief slowly began to take root. The more he thought about it, the more he began to feel his position wasn't perhaps quite as hopeless as at first it had seemed. Of course, she might just have been being sensitive towards him, but there had hardly been much enthusiasm in her voice when she spoke of Phil. She'd made out the engagement was a rather unexciting yet obvious extension to her relationship with Phil, and that she'd accepted because lots of people were watching and he'd already bought the ring. And the ring – she didn't even like it! Everything they did together seemed to be because Phil wanted them to, as though Jenny found it easier just to go along with everything rather than kick up a fuss. So where was the passion? Where was the reckless love? Perhaps she was deliberately playing down her relationship with Phil in front of him; but if not, it sounded like theirs was a tired coupling, continuing because nothing better had come along. Perhaps he might be that something better.

In the week following his trip to Northumberland, he inevitably thought about Jenny a great deal. And the more he did so, the more he began to like the idea that she was desperate to be rescued. Phil, he felt certain, must be a boring, misogynistic creep. It was up to him to save her.

The phone rang as he walked back into his flat the Thursday after. He'd worked late, so that he might finish Marcus's mural by the end of the week. A new job had come in, a large drawing-room mural, but it had to be started as soon as possible so that he could finish it in time for a big house-warming party the clients were holding in a month's time. Exhausted, Harry ignored the ringing as he ambled past his kitchen and slumped down on the sofa, listening to the familiar click and bleep as the answer machine switched on. But as the caller began leaving a message, Harry's mouth ran dry and his nerve-ends tingled right down his spine. Then he leapt up. Jenny. It was Jenny. Jenny calling him! His flat resonated with the sound of her voice as he hurled himself towards the phone.

CHAPTER TWELVE

client dinner

Ben was about to stand up and go back to his office when Carl suddenly said, 'You look tired. Kept up by the kid, heh?'

'No, no, he's fine really.' He felt slightly taken aback, having never noticed Carl show such personal concern before. 'But he woke me at four and for some reason I couldn't get back to sleep. I feel fine, though.'

'Just wait till you've got three of them. Now that *is* a full-time job.' Ben smiled. Carl leant back in his chair, hands behind his head, half swivelled towards the great panorama that lay stretched out beyond the glass windows of his office.

'And your wife, um, Lucie?' He raised his eyebrows until Ben nodded confirmation that he'd got the name right. 'She's OK?'

'Great thanks, yes. She's on good form.'

'Excellent,' smiled Carl, both he and his chair suddenly lurching forward. He clutched his hands together, fingers inter-locked and framed by perfectly tailored cuffs. 'Because I want you to ask her to come to a dinner I'm fixing.'

'Great.' Ben smiled too, but his heart sank.

'Yeah, with the Prospero guys. It's about time we all went out, checked they're happy with News Associated. I told you at the time they'd be after more, so I think it's extremely important we keep in with them. You know, Ben,' Carl continued, rubbing his tanned and smooth chin, 'they were impressed with the work you did for them, so I definitely need you to be there. You and, um, Lucie. I want it to be casual. More schmooze, less talking shop, if you know what I mean.'

'Of course. Thanks, Carl. I'm sure Lucie would be delighted.'

Back in his office, Ben sat at his desk, pensively twiddling a pen and wondering what he should do. Lucie was *not* on good form, and furthermore, he was pretty sure she'd be anything but delighted to go out to dinner with his boss and clients. They hadn't even been out to dinner on their own since Thomas had been born, and that was nearly three months ago now. What's more, he wasn't sure he could trust her to behave herself. She was still so up and down, fine one minute, irritable and short-fused the next, and these were important clients. He stood up and leant against the window. The great dome of St Paul's stood proudly ahead of him. Beyond, the curling river, buildings cramming every side. And there was the London Eye, a white, giant fair-ground attraction, already a motif for the city. A view that never failed to impress him, the icing on the cake of a job that was rewarding in every way. Really, he was so lucky: he had a job he loved, a healthy son, enough money, friends. And yet he couldn't help feeling low. Not so long ago, he'd have thought of Lucie as a positive asset at such a dinner. But he could hardly go back to Carl and say, actually, he'd forgotten, but Lucie wasn't in brilliant health at the moment and would he mind terribly if she passed on the invite?

'I think you're proba— —acting,' said Harry. He was still painting the subterranean restaurant, and the reception on his mobile wasn't very good.

'What?' said Ben.

'Probably —ting,' Harry repeated. 'I mean, Lucie'll be —ne. It's not as if she's— —is it?'

'No, I suppose not,' said Ben, not sure what he was agreeing to.

'Look, Ben, I've got to —o. I'll sp— to —ter.'

Ben put the phone down. Why did he always ring Harry about everything anyway? He never used to. They'd always seen a lot of each other, but he hadn't thought of his friend as his own personal confidant. That was Lucie's job. Ben sighed. It *used* to be Lucie's job. He looked at the photo of her on his desk, taken on a beach in Zanzibar during their honeymoon. He wished she would laugh again like she had that day. Neither of them had stopped. It probably wouldn't seem funny now, but at the time – well, it had been very funny.

He thought Harry had been trying to say: stop worrying about it, get Lucie to come, and she'll be fine. And if that *was* his advice, he was probably right.

'OK, I'll come,' said Lucie. She was giving Thomas his bath, cooing and sluicing him down with water. Ben watched, perched on the loo, still in his suit.

'Really?' he said, brightening.

'Yes, really.'

'You don't mind?'

'No, Ben, I don't.' She gave him an exasperated look, then turned smiling and chirruping back to Thomas.

'Well, that's great. Phew, what a relief.'

'What do you mean? "Phew what a relief"?'

'Nothing really. I just didn't think you'd want to come, and Carl really wanted you to, and I was wondering what I was going to do if you put your foot down.'

Lucie nodded suspiciously. 'I'll need a new dress though. None of my old stuff fits any more.'

'Fine. We'll get you one on Saturday.'

Ben had a sneaking suspicion at the time that he'd live to regret accepting Lucie's line of bargaining. By the time they'd got into the car the following Saturday, he was sure of it. Thomas had started wailing as soon as they'd strapped him into his seat.

'I've forgotten Lion,' said Lucie, unfastening her seatbelt.

'I'll go,' said Ben resignedly, and strode back to the house, fumbled for his keys, unlocked the door, then disconnected the burglar alarm.

'Shit, his milk!' said Lucie, turning to him again once he'd got back into the car and was fastening his safety belt for the second time.

'OK. Where is it?' asked Ben, desperately trying to control his irritation.

'Thanks, darling. Sorry. It's by the sink in the kitchen,' Lucie told him as he got out of the car once more. 'In the little blue bag with Thomas the Tank Engine on,' she called out after him.

'Now, are you sure that's everything?' he said, getting back into the car for the third time.

'Yes. Pretty sure. You checked the oven?'

'Lucie, we're only going to the King's Road, not two weeks' holiday in Uzbekistan. I didn't check the oven, nor am I going to.' He turned the ignition and slammed the car into gear.

'OK, fine. But don't blame me if the house burns down.'

Ben ignored the comment, instead focusing his ire on the traffic jam already building on Battersea Rise.

After taking half an hour to travel three miles, Ben spent a further twenty minutes trying to find somewhere to park, driving round and round Cadogan Gardens in the hope of finding a vacant meter. Eventually, and closer to the Fulham Road than the King's Road, they found a space, only to discover neither had any change.

'OK, you wait here with Thomas, and I'll get some coins,' Ben told her, struggling to maintain a calm tone of voice.

'You are a fool though, Ben. Fancy coming without any change,' Lucie told him, turning to look at Thomas.

'What about you? You could have thought of it.'

'You're the bread-winner round here. Money's your job. I've got enough to do as it is having to think about Thomas.'

The King's Road was heaving, making it impossible to walk without having to stop the buggy every few yards to dodge other people's ankles. Ben went in with Lucie to the first shop but, even without a pushchair, there wasn't much room. So, having knocked several shirts off their rail, Ben made a flustered retreat to the street.

'This is such fun,' said Lucie cheerily, joining him back on the street. 'I haven't been shopping for ages. Oh, I *must* just pop in here.'

Lucie disappeared for at least ten minutes every time she 'popped' into a different shop, and Ben stood outside wondering what he'd done to deserve this particular form of torture. *Why* did she always have to take so damned long to buy clothes? Really, what was so difficult about it? Thomas, who'd been asleep, suddenly woke up as Lucie appeared in the doorway holding up a black suit.

'What d'you think?' she asked him, holding it away from herself and scrutinizing it thoughtfully.

'Looks great,' said Ben hopefully.

'No, I don't think so actually,' she said, then disappeared once more. Thomas, looking helplessly in the direction of his vanished mother, was distraught. The tell-tale reddening of his face warned Ben that tears were imminent. They were.

'Sh, sh, ssh,' whispered Ben, crouching in front of his child. Thomas was deaf to his delicate pleas. His mother had gone and he wanted her back, and nothing his father could say would make the slightest bit of difference.

'Please be quiet, Thomas,' pleaded Ben, 'be quiet for Daddy.' Passers-by were beginning to stare, scowling at Ben with obvious contempt. 'If you can't control your child, don't bring him *here*,' they seemed to be saying, and Ben even apologized to one couple who tutted when their path was blocked by the buggy.

'What about this?' said Lucie, reappearing at last and holding up a charcoal skirt and jacket with a velvet collar.

'Oh, yes, definitely. I *really* like that very much,' said Ben emphatically.

Thomas, calmed by the sudden appearance of his mother, looked up wide-eyed.

'All right. I'll take it. Can you go and pay for it then?'

'Sure. I'm afraid Thomas has been making a bit of a scene, though.'

'Are you, poor darling? Have you been missing your mummy?' Ben heard her say as he entered the shop.

Of course, by the time he came out again, having just parted company with over three hundred pounds, Thomas was gurgling happily, a model child. Ben wistfully thought of all the happy visions he'd had of future family life before Thomas had been born. This was not one of them.

Lucie later confessed to Ben that she'd agreed to go to his client dinner primarily for two reasons. Firstly, she didn't want to put Ben in an awkward position at work and secondly, she hadn't been out to a proper posh London restaurant for what seemed like an age. She'd thought it would be fun to dress up, look smart once more, and proudly told Ben she'd also gone out with her mother and bought new lacy underwear to go with her suit. She wanted to feel feminine and attractive again, she told him, and not just some baby producer. Ben was delighted, especially when she admitted she was rather looking forward to it. Vanessa had agreed to babysit and she had her new clothes; and Ben wondered why he'd ever been so apprehensive.

But when the day arrived, Lucie phoned him sounding less confident. 'I feel nervous,' she told him bluntly.

'Honestly, Luce, there's nothing to feel nervous about. It'll be very chilled, I promise.'

'I won't be able to add anything to the conversation. They'll all think I'm boring.'

'That's ridiculous. You, of all people, can talk to anyone,' Ben told her, his early concerns resurfacing.

'And even in my new clothes I'm going to look frumpy and unattractive. Wearing posh underwear isn't going to fool anyone.'

'Luce, you're going to look gorgeous. Now just relax. It'll be absolutely fine. I'll see you at Circus at seven, OK?' Silence. 'Come on, Luce, you used to do this sort of thing in your sleep.'

'OK. Bye.'

Just after seven, he watched her walk into the bar. The place was already busy, full of the media darlings of Soho, but he'd managed to save a square suede leather seat at the far end for them both. Ben waved. She looked as lovely as he'd known she would. He felt proud of her. She saw him wave and made her way towards him. A man with razor-short hair and rectangular horn-rimmed glasses was laughing so much he stepped back and almost knocked her over.

'God's sake,' cursed Lucie, as she reached Ben.

'Wow, you look fantastic,' said Ben. He'd already bought her a gin.

'No, I don't. I look like my hips have dropped about two feet.'

'That's ridiculous. Honestly, you look fantastic. Really gorgeous.'

'Why's everyone wearing black, and why is everyone so thin? Just wait till they have kids, then they won't be quite so eager to wear figure-hugging micro-outfits.'

Ben didn't reply. Lucie smiled at him uncertainly, then

said: 'So, talk me through these people we're having dinner with.'

'They're the Prospero team. Newspaper people. Adam is the managing director. He was brought in only about eighteen months ago, especially to sort out the takeover of News Associated. He's young, slick, fancies himself like mad, but is quite definitely going places. Don't know what his wife's like, I'm afraid, but she's bound to be gorgeous. He's far too smooth to be married to some old frump.'

'Great,' said Lucie despondently.

'He's all right really. I'm sure he'll be very charming to you.'

Lucie sighed. 'And the other guy?'

'John, the finance director. He's a lot older. Mid-fifties probably. A man fattened by years of good lunching and too much wine. But sharp as hell. Never met his wife either.'

'Adam MD, John FD,' said Lucie, 'and the purpose of this is what?'

'Carl reckons they'll be buying other newspapers or media groups and obviously wants to make sure we're involved when they do. So this is just a social gathering really. Honestly, there shouldn't be too much talking shop. You'll be fine.'

His eyes followed Lucie's hands as she went to pick up her glass. He saw they were shaking slightly. 'Are you all right, darling?'

'Fine,' she smiled. 'You know, it's just that I've got used to not going out much. This seems a bigger deal than it probably is.'

'Well, you look drop-dead gorgeous,' said Ben, chinking her glass with his.

When they arrived at the restaurant, Ben turned to his wife as they walked through the door. 'OK?' he said.

'Fine,' she told him, 'but look at the mannequins in the windows.' Most were dressed in old suits that once belonged

183

to the Duke of Windsor. 'Even he was tiny,' she sighed wearily.

Carl and his wife Lori were already there, sitting at a round table by the bar, and sipping Martinis.

'How many kids did you say they'd got?' whispered Lucie as they handed in their bags. 'Three? Jesus, she's *so* skinny. And far too brown.'

'Just relax, darling, OK?' whispered Ben in turn, and led her over.

Carl stood up, as manicured and smooth as his wife.

'Lucie, right?' He grinned, then said, 'What can I get you to drink?' and waved a hand towards a waiter.

'A gin and tonic, please, Carl. Thanks.'

'I *love* that jacket,' oozed Lori. 'My God, where *did* you find it?'

'Thank you – on the King's Road actually, in a –' Lucie began to say, but Lori's attention was gone already, diverted by the sudden arrival of the Prospero team. Ben noticed the slight to his wife, and winced.

'John, Adam, good to see you,' said Carl effusively, prompting the start of fervent hand-shaking and introductions.

As Ben saw, he'd been right about Adam's wife – Sophia *was* stunning: tall, dark and expensive-looking, while John's wife Jane was almost as tall and certainly as refined, even though substantially older. Perfect at any social function, he thought to himself. He looked at Lucie, so small compared to these women. He worried about her. Since Lori had cut her off, she hadn't said a word. But this sort of thing never used to daunt her. After all, it was only a casual work do, not dinner with the Queen. She used to have supreme confidence in her ability to talk intelligently about just about anything. If she'd met someone like Sophia a year ago, she'd have laughed at her glitziness, her almost plastic beauty, but here she was, scowling through her gin and tonic.

Adam came up to her. One side of his mouth was slightly upturned, so it looked like he spoke with a kind of a lop-sided smirk.

'Champagne for you,' he said.

'I suppose a glass won't do any harm. Thank you.'

'Course not. Now will you let me escort you to the table?' Having mechanically taken the frail, narrow glass, Lucie allowed herself to be led.

Ben, only half listening to Jane, just managed to catch Lucie's eye for a moment, before forcing a laugh as an anecdote came to an end. He hoped she was going to manage, and followed the others to their table. Perhaps with a couple more drinks inside her, she'd relax a bit, find her old natural charm once more.

As the meal progressed, Ben stopped worrying so much about Lucie. Despite being sat between Adam and Carl, she appeared to be all right, even if she wasn't exactly the chattiest he'd ever seen her. But halfway through the main course, things started to go wrong.

All the men had taken off their jackets. Adam had been the first, declaring the restaurant was too warm for being formal. After all, he pointed out, it *was* summer. If no one objected? No one did; this was a sociable, casual dinner, after all, and Farman Gore had never been ones to stand on ceremony. Ben had felt the heat too. Lori and Sophia were wearing dresses anyway, so were cooler with their arms already bare; and Jane was wearing a navy blue jacket but declared she felt just right as she was. But Lucie, who Ben noticed had drunk several glasses of wine in addition to the two gins and the glass of champagne, had followed the men, and placed her new jacket on the back of her chair.

Then, out of the corner of his eye, Ben spotted John staring at Lucie's chest. Glancing at his wife, he saw why. An increasingly large damp patch had appeared on her shirt, roughly over the centre of her right breast. She was leaking milk.

This was a potential disaster. It could happen to any breastfeeding mother, and was natural enough, but he knew Lucie would be mortified. She repeatedly complained about her body letting her down since the birth, and really this was a most public betrayal. But how could he get her attention without everyone else noticing? All he had to do was to get her to put her jacket back on. Carl was talking to Jane, with Lucie listening to their conversation, unaware of this uncontrolled excretion. Next to her, Adam and Lori were deep in discussion, which left himself, Sophia and John currently pausing between topics. He needed to get them chatting in a way that would then leave him free to distract Lucie.

'So where is it you both live?' he asked them. It was the first thing he could think of. 'Are you both in town?' Perhaps he could provoke a town versus country debate.

'We are,' admitted Sophia, a trace of Italian in her accent, 'Adam just loves it in Hampstead. I don't think he'd ever want to leave London.'

'Sussex for us,' admitted John.

'And you don't find the commute too much?' Ben continued. He desperately wanted to steal a glance at Lucie.

'Yes, how do you manage it every day like that?' added Sophia. It was a good job she was so attractive: given the choice of directing the conversation towards a thick-set thirty-year-old or a striking Italian beauty, it was obvious John would opt for the latter. Ben took his chance. Glancing briefly round the table, and seeing everyone still locked in discussion, he stared hard at Lucie, hoping the force of his eyes trained onto her, boring into her very soul, would distract her.

But her eyes were heavy. Clearly her thoughts weren't with Carl and Jane; they were somewhere else entirely, perhaps on Thomas, or even her own bed. Ben continued to stare hard, but it was no use. Lucie wouldn't catch his eye.

'Lucie?' he said quietly, hoping no one else would really hear him.

'Lucie, Ben's trying to catch your attention,' said Adam, tapping her on the shoulder. Everyone else at the table simultaneously stopped their conversations and looked at Ben.

'What?' said Lucie, then suddenly froze as damp cotton brushed her skin. Ben saw the moment of realization only too clearly, wishing there was something he could do. Then she made a fatal mistake: she looked down, only briefly, but it was movement enough; as she did so, all eyes round the table followed her gaze, so that they all understood too. She looked back up, her face puce with embarrassment, and then her eyes locked with Ben's, pleading, beseeching him to help. He wanted to, desperately, and all his natural instincts to protect her welled up within him. But what could he do? Helplessly, he stared back. How cruel it was that someone as fiercely proud as his Lucie should suffer such an indignity. Most might have been able to laugh this off, but not her.

'Excuse me, please,' she said falteringly, grabbing her jacket and leaving the table. Ben didn't know what to do. Would it make matters worse if he followed? Or would she want his comfort and reassurance? Incapable of finding the right answer, he stayed put, rigid in his chair, unable to move.

No one else knew what to say either. Had Lucie's embarrassment not been quite so acute, it would have mattered hardly at all. Eventually Lori said, 'Don't worry, Ben, I'll go and get her. It's an occupational hazard, I'm afraid. It was always happening to me.'

Ben smiled weakly.

'Anyway,' said Carl, suddenly brightening, 'who's going to be brave and go for dessert?'

The others all picked up their menus and earnestly and very volubly discussed the various pudding options. It wasn't the greatest ice-breaker, but Ben was grateful to his boss all the same, and equally appreciative of the verve with which everyone else was prepared to go along with it.

Lori returned with Lucie a few minutes later. Ben looked up at his wife anxiously and she smiled at him nervously. He desperately wanted to hug her, kiss her, take her away from the dinner, the restaurant and back to the safety of their home. But again, he just stayed put, glossing over the incident like the others.

'Bloody kids,' she muttered. Everyone managed a laugh.

'What you need is a good drink,' said Lori.

'Absolutely,' agreed Adam, pouring her a large glass of wine.

Lucie glanced briefly at Ben, then said, 'Thanks, Adam, I think you're right.'

Slowly, the slightly stilted general chat broke down into more comfortable groups of conversation. Because she was still breastfeeding, Lucie had drunk very little since Thomas had been born, and so Ben was alarmed to see her alcohol consumption steadily increasing. He wished Adam would stop refilling her glass with wine and try water instead. In the old days, Lucie would regularly drink a bottle of wine over the course of an evening, even if they were staying in and just watching television. Nor did she ever seem any the worse for wear as a result. But that was then; she was certainly making up for lost time now. If she could just hold it together through coffee . . .

'You may not think it, Adam,' said Lucie suddenly, a slight slur creeping into her voice, 'but I used to be a highly confident businesswoman myself once.'

'I bet you were,' he said.

'Used to pretty much run the show at the company I worked for.'

'She worked for a company of conference organizers,' said Ben, alarm bells ringing.

'Could organize anything,' said Lucie, 'and to be honest, I thought organizing a child would be a piece of piss. But, oh no, I was wrong about that all right.'

'Tell me about it,' added Lori.

Ben shifted in his seat. 'How are your kids getting on then?' he asked Lori, but before she had a chance to reply, Lucie butted in.

'Did they make your life a misery when they were first born?'

'Oh yes, but I loved them all the same.'

'You should get some help – a nanny or something,' said Carl.

'Couldn't have done it without a nanny,' smiled Lori.

'Well,' said Ben, smiling awkwardly round the table, 'perhaps we will.'

'No,' said Lucie, 'I'm not beaten yet. I simply refuse to give in. I'm going to crack this motherhood lark if it's the last thing I do.'

'Good for you,' said John. Ben squirmed. It was plain to all Lucie was drunk. She was making a fool of herself – making a fool of him. An awkward tension had developed around the table, and it was up to him to resolve it. He caught Carl's icy glare. Please God, he prayed, make Lucie shut the fuck up. His protective instincts began to turn towards himself, rather than his wife.

'Sorry, everyone,' said Lucie, 'but in the good old days I used to be able to hold my drink. That's something else that's gone out of the window.' Her elbow, with her chin resting in her hand, slipped off the edge of the table.

'Adam,' Lori chided, 'you naughty man, to keep filling her glass like that.'

'Sorry,' said Adam, holding up his hands, 'I plead guilty.' He grinned, and the others laughed, but Ben felt the ground rising around him and swallowing him whole.

'Why don't you take her back home now, Ben?' suggested Lori. Ben looked at Carl, who fixed him with a steely glare.

'Good idea,' he said, pushing back his chair. 'Will you all excuse us?' Lucie had grown suddenly quiet, exhausted by her rant, and sleepily allowed Ben to help her from her chair. Silence reigned around the table as the remaining six pairs of eyes watched him stand up, walk round the table and help Lucie up. His stomach churned, nauseated with despair.

'Night then, everyone,' he said, 'and, er, sorry.' Ben could see Carl was furious and, unfortunately, he was the one who counted. He wished he were dead. Never, as long as he lived, would he forget the feeling of utter humiliation and ignominy his wife had caused him.

Outside, Ben bundled Lucie into a cab. In moments, she was snoring quietly, her chin resting on her chest. Could there be a worse evening? A total, mind-blowing disaster. Christ, how *was* he going to face Carl the following day? Humiliation of any kind was bad enough, but in front of important clients *and* his boss – Jesus, he just couldn't believe what had happened. Carl would never forget it. How incredibly, totally, awfully, *fucking* embarrassing. A huge, silent anger welled up within him. Just how long was this going to go on? The mood swings, the unpredictability, the stroppiness? When was he ever going to get his old Lucie back?

It was late, the traffic for once quiet. Glumly resting his chin on his hand, he watched the city streak past. But more than anger, he felt a terrible disappointment. Disappointment that his view of family life had been so wide of the mark. It was as though he'd been striving all his life for something that could never exist.

Carl called him into his office first thing in the morning.

'Ben, I know it was awkward for you last night, and I think you've been punished enough. But honestly, don't ever do that to me again. If your wife's a touch depressed or whatever, say so. I'd much rather you were honest with me.'

'OK, Carl,' said Ben miserably.

'Well, as it happens the others thought it quite funny, and I think Adam played his part too, so no harm done, luckily for you.'

Ben nodded.

'So just write a note to John and Adam – and Lori for that matter – and then, as far as I'm concerned, the matter's closed. A good wife can really help a man's career, you know, Ben. But it works both ways.'

'Thank you, Carl. I appreciate it. And I'm, um, really sorry.'

Carl held up a hand, then turned back to his computer. Ben was dismissed.

Really, he supposed, he'd got off lightly. And he knew Carl would never mention it again. He was like that; he might not forget it, but Ben knew he could count on his total discretion. Lucie had been contrite that morning, very, very contrite, but of course it was too late for apologies. He hadn't bothered having a go at her. It would have done no good, not helped in any way. So he told her not to worry, to drink lots of water, and to pray that he wasn't home again in two hours' time. He sat down at his desk. At least he had a lot to do. Keep his mind off things.

He looked up as someone knocked lightly on his door, then saw Kate step into his office. The new girl, working with Jon. Ben smiled. Really, she was absolutely lovely. Those pale, pale eyes, framed by dark hair and perfectly arched eyebrows. And her lips! So luscious and full! If he weren't married to Lucie, he would certainly be lusting after her.

'Hi, Ben, not disturbing you, am I?' she asked.

'No. Not at all, not at all,' he replied cheerfully.

'I was just wondering whether you fancied getting something

to eat at lunchtime? Or a drink after work? I mean, I just thought we should. Well, I thought it would be nice.'

'Great. Either. What about a drink later?'

'OK, you're on. I'll come by.'

Ben sat back and stretched, then wrote 'drink with Kate' on his electronic diary. Why did the prospect make his heart quicken with excitement?

CHAPTER THIRTEEN

cold comfort

Flin supposed there were both pros and cons to working in regional PR, rather than the glitzy, glamorous world of film publicity. Driving to work, with a journey time of no more than twenty minutes, was definitely a plus. Compared with London, traffic in the city centre of Newcastle was almost non-existent, and he enjoyed beginning and ending his journey in the calm serenity of deep countryside. Really, when he remembered how long it used to take him just to get out of London! As it was, this new journey saved him twenty minutes a day or, as he pointed out to Tiffany, one hour and forty minutes a week. Over an hour and a half extra that he could spend being a smallholder.

But despite his talk in London of being fed up with all the egos involved in the film world, he did miss it. He missed going to all the screenings, the chat about what good films were coming up, the gossip and the satisfaction of seeing the fruits of his labour plastered all over the nation's magazines and newspapers. Getting national coverage for anything Scarlet Media Relations were working on was a major event, a cause for huge excitement; a couple of inches in the *Journal* or an interview on *Look North* was the normal level of expectations. Still, early on, Flin managed to justify Doug's great faith in him by scoring some spectacular results for a new Roman museum opening up along Hadrian's Wall. By pulling a few strings with some contacts in London, he managed to get a lot of national coverage on the back of a new Roman epic that was promising to be the biggest blockbuster of the summer. More than that, he persuaded *Country Life* to interview the curator and run a feature on 'Wildlife Along the Wall'. Getting positive coverage for a new initiative to make the Tyne greener and more eco-friendly proved a bit harder, but on the whole, Flin found the variety of campaigns he was expected to work on was one of the better aspects of the job. On the other hand, constantly having to write up reports and time-sheets for clients came as a complete shock. Having always worked in-house in the past, such humdrum admin was something totally new, and he very soon began to resent it. He also hated the process of learning his way around the new office. This was something that came with all new jobs, but because he was working in a new field of PR, Scarlet's day-to-day systems were especially different from the ones he was used to, and it took him a while to acclimatize.

But the greatest difference of all lay in the people he worked with. The assistants weren't like the assistants he'd been used to. They weren't smart-arse graduates itching to climb the ladder, but rather career secretaries. This made life a lot easier in one respect, but in another meant Flin had to do every bit of creative work on a campaign himself, with no scope for palming off the tedious bits. His assistant, Jackie, would type out press releases for him and stuff envelopes, but little more.

Flin liked Doug, though, every bit as much as he had when he'd come up for the interview. Perhaps his boss was a bit earnest, but Flin liked his enthusiasm and appreciated the tremendous backing he gave him; and so it gave him even more satisfaction when something went well, and Flin felt able to justify Doug's support.

He liked his office too, with its shot-blasted brick walls, floorboards and views over the Tyne, and soon became a great advocate of Newcastle. This sprawling north-east city had become a more sophisticated place since he'd been at university. He remembered it as being lively but rather run down. But the recent redevelopment, both along the river front and in the centre, had transformed it. Instead of insalubrious-looking tattoo parlours there were now cosmopolitan coffee bars and French pâtisseries. Sleek ultra-modern restaurants selling continental food had sprung up from nowhere, much to Flin's delight. He'd thought the cultural richness and cosmopolitan diversity of London would be one of the sacrifices they'd have to make when they moved up, but nothing could be further from the truth. Modern European had hit the north-east too.

But despite all the good things about his new job, there was one aspect of it that caused him great anxiety. This was the animosity directed towards him by one of his colleagues. Katrina was a couple of years older than him, had worked at Scarlet for nearly eight years, and had been passed over in favour of him when the job had come up. Flin had come up against personality clashes in the office before, but this was worse because of his feeling that he was unpopular within the village too, and he wasn't at all used to being disliked; he'd never even been bullied at school. In London, if there was someone he didn't get on with at work, he always had a bevy of friends to fall back on. But at Scarlet, from his very first day, Katrina had shown her colours very clearly. Every meeting became a battleground, where instead of just getting on with the business in hand, Flin had to watch like a hawk to make sure he wasn't tripped up or caught out by her petty scheming and one-upmanship.

'Have we handed in our weekly reports?' asked Doug at one of their regular Monday morning meetings.

'They're all done apart from one,' replied Katrina, before shooting a glare at Flin.

'Oh, great. Which one's missing then?'

'The Wall Museum account,' said Katrina triumphantly, 'again.'

'Flin? Can you get that done immediately, please? Really they should be done before the weekend in future.'

Flin nodded. He could have told Doug that no one had explained to him these needed to be done before the Monday meeting; and he might have complained that Katrina had deliberately shown him what to do in as unhelpful a manner as possible. But at a meeting with the rest of the department watching, it was not the time or place; it was something he should be able to resolve himself, without bringing Doug into it.

'I'm sure I'll be able to sort out Katrina eventually,' he confessed to Tiffany one night as they sat in the Compasses, 'but it *is* a real pain.'

Tiffany tried to show sympathy. 'The trouble is, honey, you tend to like most people, and expect them to like you too, which is why you get more upset when someone holds a grudge. It's rather contrary to your nature.'

Flin shrugged. 'I mean, in many ways I can understand her resentment, but she'd make life easier for everyone if she accepted me, rather than spent her time trying to catch me out. After all, I'm never horrible to her or anything.' He sighed.

'Maybe she'll leave. Or maybe in time she'll warm to you. Don't take it so personally.'

'I know, Tiff, but it's easy to say that. Look at you: while I'm snubbed and sneered at, you've become great mates with Claire. *And* you've got a relaxed job at the heart of the village.'

It was at Willie's 'welcoming' drinks party that Claire had first mentioned to Tiffany that her husband could do with some more help at the estate office. His estate manager needed a secretary and someone to help out with a few other administrative bits and pieces. It was completely beneath her, of course, but it just might be a mutually beneficial arrangement. What did she think? Would she like her to suggest it to Willie? Tiffany had nodded enthusiastically, but had assumed nothing more would come of it. But the very next day, Willie called by with Peter, his estate manager, and put it to her more form-ally.

'Any good with computers?' Willie asked her casually.

'Sure,' said Tiffany.

'Good, because we've got to get some in. Update a bit, and we could do with someone who knows what's going on about the place. Peter here doesn't know one end of a computer from the other.'

'Nor do you,' said Peter indignantly.

Willie chuckled. 'I hold my hands up. So, really, you could be invaluable to us.'

The pay Willie offered was not high, but as Tiffany told Flin, it was better than nothing, and would be a good way of getting to know the area and the people about the place a bit better.

Flin had agreed whole-heartedly, but now he envied her. The estate office was an old tenant's cottage in the centre of the village, behind the church, and Tiffany very quickly met many of the villagers. Through the churchyard was the shop where Tiffany bought her daily pint of milk. Mrs Mullins, the owner, was initially frosty towards her, but then, clearly recognizing a regular customer when she saw one (and there were precious few of those these days), took a more relaxed tone. Within a short while, Tiffany was able to report back to Flin various pieces of village gossip she had picked up from her visits. People constantly called into the office: Willie and Claire, farm workers, outside con-tractors – fencers, builders, painters and the like. Tiffany met them all, and while some grunted and nodded, others paused to chat.

Peter and Willie were clearly impressed by the proficiency with which she dealt with the installation of the computers, and her cheerful patience when it came to showing Peter, in particular, the basics of how to use it.

'Don't know how we'd have managed without her,' Willie told Flin one night when they bumped into each other on a walk. 'You're a lucky man.'

Within a couple of weeks, Tiffany had won friends and admiration from the very hub of village life. Flin had always assumed it would be she who would find it harder to acclimatize to village life, rather than he, who'd had the English country upbringing. But, as she told him, Outback life was the perfect preparation, so that she took to their new life like a duck to water, while he was left floundering on the edge of the pond. He kept telling himself that all he needed was patience, and that in time, all would be well, but his confidence was being chipped away. He missed his friends too, although several had made it up to see them. And although there was always the telephone, or e-mail, it wasn't the same as seeing people on a regular basis. At least, as far as he could tell from Ben's e-mails, there appeared to be little he was missing out on. *Thomas crying* (Ben wrote one day), *and I feel like shit. Haven't seen Harry for a bit. Can't come up to stay just at the moment – imagine being three hours on a train with Thomas carrying on! – but why don't you venture back down here? Feel all my friends have deserted me.*

As he was unable to afford expensive train journeys to London, these messages cheered Flin considerably: the thought of everyone having a good time back down in London without him made him feel worse, but clearly life was changing for all of them. Of course, it had to. They were all thirty now; things were moving on. They couldn't stay as they had for evermore. And Flin had wanted this change of direction he'd made for himself. It was he who'd been so adamant about it, and he was damn well going to make a success of it.

Unfortunately, though, there were a couple of particular incidents that were to further Flin's growing disillusionment with the perfect world he was supposed to be creating.

In the six weeks since they'd been there, Flin and Tiffany had bought twelve chickens (six Sussex, three Pekins, three New England Reds), one cockerel (Sussex), six white geese, two Wessex

Saddleback piglets and most recently a brown Labrador puppy. A dog had always been a high priority but, with both of them away at work all day, this would have been impossible: animals, fine; pets, no. They would never have a chance to train it properly or provide the necessary companionship required at the outset of its life. But with Tiffany working for Willie and Peter, this was less of a problem. If anything, owning a dog was actively encouraged. Willie's dogs seemed to accompany him everywhere, as did Peter's old Springer Spaniel. So Flin and Tiffany bought Addy, short for Adelaide, Tiffany's closest city back home in Australia, who became the only animal in their household with a name.

By constantly referring to John Seymour's *Self Sufficiency*, Flin increased his confidence in his farming ability. Both the geese and chickens were laying eggs, and the pigs were greedily scoffing every spare bit of food he and Tiffany discarded. Being a smallholder didn't seem to be so very difficult, and Flin rather enjoyed the daily feeding rituals, and locking the animals up for the night, like some kindly guardian.

But one Saturday, with the rain pouring down, he opened the gate of the pig sty and caught his hand on a splinter. Immediately, he let out a short yell of pain, then paused to examine the wound. A fairly large shard of wood had stuck in the side of his hand, and with a grimace he began slowly pulling it out. Distracted, he failed to spot one of the pigs use this opportunity for escape until too late.

'Oi, come back here!' he yelled pointlessly, as the happy piglet careered round the yard, upsetting the chickens and geese. Clucking and quacking with righteous indignation, they flapped about, adding to the mounting pandemonium.

'Tiffany, help, quick!' he shouted, slamming the gate shut. The pig stopped its gleeful jig and stood calmly at the far side of the yard, snuffling and grunting with satisfaction at its new surroundings. Although Flin wore a coat, the rain poured down his face, dripping from his nose and chin.

'Flin? What's the matter? Are you all right, darling?' called Tiffany from the back door.

'Piglet Number Two's got out. At the moment he's still in the yard, but I think I might need a hand.'

'OK, hold on, I'll be right there,' Tiffany yelled back.

Crouching low, his hands ready, Flin inched his way slowly towards Number Two. The piglet looked up, eyeing him suspiciously, then grunted with disdain. Flin stared back, aware that a showdown was imminent.

'Careful, Flin,' said Tiffany, walking up slowly behind him.

'Just another couple of feet and I should be able to catch him,' Flin told her, keeping up the staring match with Number Two.

'I think we should be trying to round him up like a sheepdog would. I'm sure that's the way to do it.'

'Let me just try this way first. Any second now I'm going to be able to get him.' With only a couple of yards separating him from the pig, Flin leapt. Number Two, quick as a flash, ran off, squealing delightedly, leaving Flin lying flat on his front, soaking wet and covered in diluted goose and chicken dung.

'Damn!' he cried, frantically getting back to his feet. Goose droppings covered his hands, while the rain lubricated the runny dung down the front of his coat. Bird shit actually dripped off him.

'Oh my God, just look at you!' exclaimed Tiffany.

'Never mind that,' snapped Flin, wiping his hands on the cold rain-sodden back of his coat, 'where the hell's the pig?'

Number Two had wriggled under the gate, making for the road. Flin, frantically glancing round, caught sight of him just before he disappeared by the front of the house.

'The road! He's heading for the road!' he shouted, and began running to the gate, only to slip up again on more goose dung. By the time he had recovered and made it to the front of the house, the pig was skipping happily in the front field.

'Now what do we do?' he asked Tiffany helplessly.

'God knows. Go in the field and try to herd him back, I suppose. I really don't know. What does John Seymour say about it?'

'Nothing. He assumes you'd never be stupid enough to let it out in the first place.' He wiped the rain from his face with the back of his hand and clambered over the gate. 'Come on. This could take ages. He would have to pick the wettest day of the month to make his escape.'

Half an hour later, they were no closer to getting the piglet back. He clearly thought it the best game in the world. Flin and Tiffany, crouching down, would approach him slowly, but when they were only yards away, he would squeal and run off again.

'He's laughing at us. We're never, ever going to get him, are we?' said Flin, beginning to despair.

'Well, we are closer to the gate again,' said Tiffany. They'd already been twice round all corners of the field.

A whistle suddenly caught their ears, and both turned instinctively. There, at the far end of the field, was Melvyn, buttoned up in a long coat, cap pushed forward. Either side of them, two sheepdogs circled the piglet.

'Thank God,' said Flin, 'Melvyn to the rescue.' The dogs, low and keen, trotted briskly, then kept still, watching their quarry, their ears alert to the commands of their master. In a matter of moments the pig was backing into a corner of the field.

'Walk on towards him then,' shouted Melvyn, 'steady now.' He came alongside them as the two dogs, crouching with far greater efficiency than either Flin or Tiffany had been able to manage, began to converge on the cornered pig.

'Now follow me, and we should have him covered,' Melvyn told them. He blew a couple more commands on his whistle, until the dogs were merely a few yards from the terrified piglet. Calmly, Melvyn stepped forward and neatly scooped the frightened animal up in his arms.

'Got you, you little terror. Been having the time of your life, haven't you?' Melvyn said soothingly.

'I don't know how to thank you,' said Flin. 'Really, I . . .'

'Yes, thank you ever so much, Melvyn,' added Tiffany.

He fixed them both with a distrustful glare. 'I watched you two prancin' about this field. After a while I thought I'd better sort you out, as you'd still be here tomorrow morning the way you was carryin' on.'

'Well, thank you,' said Flin again as they walked back around the house. 'I got a splinter on the gate, you see, and he scrambled out while I was caught off guard.' He sounded feeble, he knew.

Melvyn stared at him. 'Oh aye, got a splinter, did you?'

'Yes, and, well, I'm afraid it distracted me for a moment.'

'There you go,' said Melvyn, putting Number Two back in his sty.

'Would you like some tea or anything?' asked Tiffany. All three were standing in the yard, the rain pouring down on them. Flin, in particular, looked a mess. His hair was plastered to his head, and large droplets of water hung shakily from his ears, nose and chin. White and dark green bird dung streaked the front of his coat and knees.

'No, thanks, I'd better be getting back.' Melvyn turned to Flin. 'Still enjoying playing at farming then?' he asked witheringly.

Flin smiled uncertainly. 'Thank you again, Melvyn. I don't know what we'd have done without you turning up like that.'

'Well, I've certainly seen it all now,' said Melvyn, shaking his head. He called his two dogs, who were sitting patiently at his feet. 'Until the next time then.' Flin saw him smirking underneath his cap.

Flin and Tiffany went back into the house in silence, took off their coats and boots and automatically made for the kitchen and the kettle.

'Thank God for Melvyn,' said Tiffany at length.

'He was smirking again,' said Flin sullenly.

'Well, it must have looked pretty funny.'

'He thinks we're playing at farming – poncy southern yuppies struggling with the realities of owning animals.'

'He's probably right. So what? You'll learn. *We'll* learn. We can't expect to do everything right straight off, can we?'

Flin remained quiet, standing with his arms crossed defiantly, and waiting for the kettle to boil.

'I suppose you're right,' he said eventually, 'but that was bloody humiliating. Perhaps *he's* right. Perhaps we have bitten off more than we can chew. I mean, what would we have done if he hadn't come to our rescue?'

'I don't know. But he did. You know, perhaps you should stop worrying about what everyone else thinks. What does it matter? We're doing all right, aren't we? Really? You can't expect everything to run smoothly and perfectly all the time. I bet even Melvyn's made some mistakes in his life. Don't forget, *you* wanted to do this, Flin. It was your idea to have animals and chickens and things. You've got to be prepared to take the rough with the smooth.'

Flin nodded. 'You're right. I know you're right. I just hate people laughing at me, that's all.' The puppy sat at his feet, and he leant down and picked her up. 'You don't laugh at me, do you, Addy? You love me, even if I do let the odd pig get out.'

'Of course she does, and so do I,' said Tiffany, walking over and putting her arms around him. 'You're such an idealist, darling. Want everything to be perfect all the time. That's lovely, but it does mean you're going to be disappointed every so often.'

Flin kissed the top of her head. She was probably right. She usually was.

But a far bigger disappointment was waiting for him just around the corner.

No one he'd met in the village had ever mentioned anything about the cricket team, but one day he'd spotted the ground, lying prettily in the middle of a large field just to the north of Cotherwick. Flin had always quite liked cricket. He still played for an old university scratch side, but when he'd been a boy he'd played occasionally for his village side back in Wiltshire. Certainly, spending lazy summer Sundays listening to the gentle thwack of leather on willow at picturesque Northumbrian village pitches had been very much a part of his rural vision. Quite apart from the enjoyment he'd gain from playing the odd game, it struck him as the perfect way for both him and Tiffany to get to know a few more of the villagers. So when they were next in the Compasses, he made sure he asked Keith about it.

'They're quite a good side actually. And this year there's a chance they could win their league division.'

'Really?' said Flin. 'So do you think I could get involved? Could they use another bowler?'

'I expect so. They have nets, you know. On Thursdays, down at the ground. Go along and see.'

'All right,' said Flin, 'I will.'

'Ask Callum about it. He plays every weekend. But they play hard up here – none of that southern softness you're probably used to.'

'Whatever you say,' said Flin, 'but we're talking about cricket here, not rugby league.'

'Just telling you, that's all,' Keith told him testily. Flin sighed and rejoined Tiffany.

'Grumpy bastard,' Flin said as he sat down. 'Can't say anything without some gibe about us being southern. Reckons they play their cricket "hard" up here. What nonsense. How can you play cricket harder just because it's up north?'

'You shouldn't ever listen to what Keith says. Ignore him, and go and play cricket and take lots of wickets. That'll show them.'

Callum, showing little enthusiasm at his enquiry, told him nets usually started about six-thirty, so the following Thursday, having arrived back home and checked on the animals, he dug out his kit and headed over to the ground. There were half a dozen people there when he arrived, some of whom he recognized from the pub. Most of them looked at him suspiciously as he approached, an outsider trying to infiltrate the pack. Taking a deep breath, he resolutely put down his kit bag and walked over.

'Hi, I'm Flin,' he said with as much cheer as he could muster. 'Just moved into the village, and hoped I could maybe play a bit of cricket.'

A burly, ginger-haired giant, with a ruddy complexion and enormous forearms, held out his hand. 'Nigel,' he told Flin. 'I'm the club captain. Bat or bowl?' He had a strong, gravelly voice, and dark little eyes.

'Bowl, mainly,' Flin told him.

'Let's see you then,' he said, handing him a worn, loose-stitched old ball.

Having marked out his run, he began with a couple of looseners, then steamed in at full pace. Nigel and the others seemed to be suitably impressed, as Flin sent down a series of quick, swinging deliveries, clean bowling two of the other players.

'Not bad,' said Nigel, 'not bad at all.' Was that just a hint of warmth Flin detected? 'Could you play this Saturday? It's a big game. Win it, and we've got a really good chance of coming top of the division this year.'

'Love to,' said Flin eagerly. 'Where is it?'

'Here, this weekend. You're up at Standing Stone, aren't you,' Nigel continued, 'so you could come with Callum to the away games. He's probably our best bat, to be honest. Already got a couple of hundreds this season.'

Flin drove home greatly cheered. He could tell they'd been impressed by his bowling. Perhaps being part of the cricket team would be just the thing he needed to make a few friends in the village. He hoped he would take lots of wickets and help them win the divisional title.

*   *   *

The day of the game started slightly damp and overcast, but Flin wasn't worried, as he knew such conditions were perfect for his kind of bowling. None the less, as he walked into the pavilion, his stomach tightened with a few nerves. It was rather a shabby old hut. Cotherwick teams from the past lopsidedly lined the walls, in faded photos with tiny insects trapped underneath the glass. The wooden floor, shredded by years of sharp metal studs scraping over it, was littered with dust and the odd cigarette butt. The familiar smell of dried grass and whitewash hit Flin as soon as he entered. Such a distinct smell, with its associations of school and summer and playing for his village back home. Comforting, really.

'Can't sit there, mate,' said a short, crop-haired man with a thick gold chain round his neck.

'Oh, sorry,' said Flin, immediately removing his bag from the old leather chair in the corner.

'That's Callum's seat. Next to him is Nigel's, and then Terry's. You could go over there if you like,' he said, pointing to a short, rickety-looking stool at the far end.

'Oh, OK, thanks,' said Flin. Other players arrived, some with wives and families, obvious regulars armed with chairs, rugs, and games for the kids; all part of the normal Saturday summer routine.

Then Callum appeared. Casually slouching through the doorway, he slung his kit bag on the leather armchair and pulled out a cigarette. He had the beginnings of a black eye developing, something immediately picked up on.

'Wendy give you that?' asked one. Callum smiled ruefully.

'Or was it the girl down the road when you told her you were married?' laughed another.

'Who've you been knocking off this time?' said Keith as he appeared in the doorway.

'Silly cow punched me, didn't she?' admitted Callum as he pulled off his T-shirt, revealing a lean, hirsute body. 'I swear that woman gets more vicious the older she gets.'

'And it's got nothing to do with your wandering eye, has it?' added Keith, patting down his hair. Flin listened with great interest. Both he and Tiffany had assumed Callum must be something of a Lothario, but here was the proof. No wonder they heard Wendy shouting at him so frequently.

Flin kept to himself in the corner while he changed. The other players all grunted at him by way of acknowledgement, but were more interested in talking to each other than having to make an effort with a stranger, especially one who wasn't even from Northumberland. Then he ambled outside, and to his delight saw Willie striding purposefully towards the pavilion, clutching an old and battered leather kit bag.

'Ah-ha!' He beamed. 'So they've roped you in, have they? Excellent. How's the house? Settled in all right?' Already changed into his whites, he put down his bag and sunk his hands deep into his pockets.

'Very well, thanks,' said Flin.

'Good stuff. Must get you both over soon.'

'So what's the opposition like?' Flin asked, glad to find someone to talk to at last.

'Slayley? Not bad, but should beat 'em. They're a few places below us in the division. Sixth, I think. Nice little spot this though, isn't it? Best soil for miles. My old man used to grow wheat here when I was a kid, but much better to play cricket on it, don't you think? Really, it's not a bad little square. Can be a bit dodgy the far end by this time of year, but on the whole I don't think anyone can really complain. What's more they get it at a bloody good rate – nought pence a year, and a groundsman thrown in for free.' He chuckled, his shoulders shaking up and down as he did so.

Flin smiled. 'That's very decent of you.'

'Well, you know, I can't really go about charging them. Not rich men round here. And our gardener quite likes doing it, and he does a good job. Makes all the difference playing on a decent bit of turf.'

They were fielding first, which pleased Flin, and to begin with everything went as well as he'd hoped. The two normal opening bowlers began, but Nigel threw the ball to Flin after ten overs. Carefully he marked out his run, loosened his arms and began striding to the wicket. His first ball clearly startled both the batsman and the wicket keeper with its pace, and Flin smiled to himself as the keeper mumbled something to one of the other fielders and took a few steps backwards. His second ball was wider, but again, the batsman was miles away. With the third, the middle stump very satisfactorily uprooted itself with a clatter as he clean bowled the bewildered batsman. Flin clenched his fist in triumph, delighted his career with Cotherwick Cricket Club had got off to such an ideal start. The players all gathered round, suddenly a bit more interested in him. He felt his back being slapped and heard someone say, 'Bit of a nippy wanker, aren't you?'

'Bloody well bowled,' said Willie enthusiastically, 'marvellous stuff.'

By tea, Slayley were all out for 121, and Flin had five of the wickets. As they ate their sandwiches and fluffy Swiss rolls, the rest of the team seemed suitably impressed by his efforts, and were considerably more forthcoming. Even Keith patted him on the back and begrudgingly said, 'Well done. Not bad for a southerner.' Nigel and Terry, the wicket keeper, sat next to him, now more interested in the new player. Where had he played cricket before? Would he playing for them regularly? How were they finding the village? Flin happily answered everything they asked, pleased at their interest.

'Keith's a bit chippy, isn't he?' he confided, grabbing another slice of walnut cake. 'Not quite sure what I've done to offend him, but there you go.'

'Oh, you don't want to worry about him,' Nigel told him, 'he's chippy with everyone.'

'They reckon he's the grumpiest landlord in Northumberland,' added Terry.

Flin grinned. 'As long it's not just me then.'

'God no. No, he's a right miserable git. Quite likeable once you get used to it, mind. You've got to give him back as good as he gives. That's the way to deal with Keith,' Nigel told him, leaning in and making sure Keith was still out of earshot.

'Right,' said Flin emphatically, 'I'll do that.'

'Make sure you do. But first we've a match to win. Callum'll see us home. He's right good bat, is Callum.'

'Right good,' echoed Terry.

As Willie and the other opening batsmen put on their pads, Flin sat outside, contented and pleased that his job was almost done. He'd told Nigel he wasn't much of a batsman, and so knew they weren't expecting much. Bowling was his strength and, in that department, he'd more than done his share. Then he heard Nigel asking for umpires and, so wanting to further this new feeling of goodwill towards him, immediately offered.

The score was ticking along and Cotherwick had scored twenty-two, when one of the opening batsmen was caught out. With supreme confidence, Callum slowly swaggered to the crease. Flin gave him his guard, then watched him look around the ground, eyeing the fielders, like a panther spying his prey. After a few moments, he settled, his head and eyes level, coolly waiting for the bowler to begin his run.

Then the unthinkable happened. The ball pitched short, but kept low, catching Callum on the back pad and up against the stumps. Flin saw it all, long before the bowler turned, his face puce, the veins bulging and throbbing on his neck and temples, and screamed his appeal. Flin's mouth ran dry with horror. Callum was out. Leg before wicket, as clear-cut a decision as any that could be given. Flin knew that, Callum knew that, and the whole of Slayley knew that.

Flin closed his eyes for a split second, then slowly raised his finger.

'Fucking hell!' yelled Callum, slamming his bat into the ground and storming off the pitch.

'Oh, dear,' said Willie, who as the non-striker was standing next to Flin.

'Shit,' said Flin, clutching his head with his hand. 'What else could I do, Willie? He was about as plumb as it gets.'

'Hm,' said Willie thoughtfully, 'let's just hope we still win.'

But they didn't. Flin returned to the pavilion to get ready to bat when the score stood at eighty-three for seven. No one spoke to him. Instead they just glowered. Callum slumped in his armchair, smoking moodily, a proud beast wounded and angry.

'Look, I'm really sorry, but it kept low. You were really unlucky.'

'There was nothing unlucky about it,' growled Callum, 'except that you had to be fucking umpire.' The exchange ended there as shouts rang around the ground. Another Cotherwick wicket had fallen and it was Flin's turn to bat.

He never even faced a ball. The final wicket went with the score on 115, leaving Cotherwick seven runs short, and Flin nought not out.

'You stupid prat,' Nigel said to him. 'What the hell did you think you were doing out there?'

'It was absolutely plumb,' pleaded Flin, 'about as out as you could possibly be. Callum knows that, everyone knows that. What was I supposed to do, cheat?'

'You don't give out anyone leg before, least of all the bloody star batsman. Jesus wept, that decision of yours lost us the match. Might even have lost us the fucking divisional title. We don't go around giving our own people out round here.

You might do that down in the fucking poncy south, but not round here, got it?'

Flin, humiliation, hurt and anger surging through him, packed up his kit, silently and as quickly as possible.

'Told you we played hard, didn't I?' said Keith, sucking on another Lambert and Butler next to him.

'Oh, fuck off, Keith,' said Flin, and walked out.

'Don't worry too much,' said Willie as Flin reached his car. 'They'll all have forgotten it by next week. Get some more wickets, and keep your finger in your pocket in future, and that'll be the end of it. I'm afraid they play by slightly different rules up here.'

Flin nodded sadly. He'd been really looking forward to going to the pub, happy in the knowledge that he'd contributed to a famous victory. It should have been a chance to bond with some of the team, an opportunity to feel he'd begun to contribute to the community. Instead, he'd been cast out, vilified as the architect of defeat. He paused by his car and looked out around the ground. Another beautiful evening. The earlier cloud had gone, leaving a clear sky, aglow in the west with the deep orange of the dying sun. If only he hadn't been so eager to please, he'd never have offered to umpire. He wished he could rewind the clock. Sighing, he rubbed his forehead. This was not how he'd imagined it would be, not how he'd imagined it at all.

Flin sat at their kitchen table, miserable in his grass-stained whites, and told Tiffany about his disastrous afternoon.

'I mean, what's the bloody point?' he told her, having finished his account. 'How are we ever going to be able to live here, if no one gives us a bloody chance? We're not bad people, are we? We haven't been anything other than friendly towards them. Why can't people just be decent and kind?'

Tiffany sat next to him and stroked his head gently. 'Darling Flin, it's just that this is a small community. People can be a bit wary of newcomers. It's the same the world over. Certainly the same in Australia. It'll be fine though. They're not bad people. You just have to give it time.'

'Tiff, honestly, you should have seen them. They were so angry – shouting and swearing at me, really viciously. And the point was, he was out. You know, he didn't deserve to carry on batting, and so we didn't deserve to win. If you can't play fair and square, what's the point of playing at all? And that on top of everything else. Bloody Melvyn with that smirk of his, always taking the bloody piss. What's so bloody funny about what we're trying to do here? We're just trying to use this place as it should be used. What's to mock about that?'

'Flin, sshh, come on. Everything will work out, you'll see.'

'Yeah, s'pose so,' said Flin sullenly, opening a can of lager. If he couldn't have a pint in the pub, then he'd just have to have a beer at home instead. 'At least you're making friends.' He knew he sounded resentful.

'Flin? Honey?'

Flin looked up and smiled sadly.

'Look at you,' she said, 'sweaty and horrible and a red nose from too much sun.' He smiled at her again, this time more genuinely.

'A bit sunburnt am I?' he asked.

'A bit.' She kissed him. 'It'll be all right, you know. Try to be a bit thicker-skinned. They're decent people really.'

He sighed once more. 'Yeah, I'm sure you're right.'

CHAPTER FOURTEEN

a breath of French air

On the Monday morning, Harry was just getting his paints together for his next job, when the phone rang. It was Caroline Parker, and she was terribly sorry, but they had just discovered some damp in the drawing room and would have to have it seen to before he began painting. It was an absolute bore, a complete bind, not to say expensive, but everything was now on hold – mural, house-warming party, the lot.

How long was it likely to take? Harry asked her. Probably about three weeks: one week until someone could fix it, another week to do the work, and another week until the plaster could be repainted. Could she ring him in a week or so to update him on the situation?

Harry soothingly assured her not to worry. Of course that would be fine, completely understandable. Really though, it was bloody annoying. He'd just spent the whole weekend working on the designs for the Parkers' mural and had even turned down tickets from Ben for the Saturday of the Test Match, knowing he would be working to a tight deadline. Caroline Parker was quite right to assume the wall repairs would be expensive. He'd seen enough of builders to know how much such work could cost. His murals didn't come cheap either. Chances were, they'd decide they couldn't do both. To add to his frustration, he'd postponed a couple of jobs to make way for the Parkers. Even if he managed to bring one of the other jobs forward, he was still likely to be twiddling his thumbs for a few days at the very least. It was very galling. Jobs like the Parkers' mural paid good money, and being private meant he was paid straight away. With businesses, he had to supply proper invoices, which then frequently took aeons to be paid, and left him stranded. For the time being he would be able to survive, but he was counting on Marcus's cheque for the circus mural arriving sooner rather than later.

After a couple of calls, it was clear the earliest he could start on the next commission was the following Monday, leaving him a week of no work, unless something came up in between. It wasn't an unusual situation, and during these lulls he tended either to take some holiday, or use the time to research and make sketches of places and buildings he might be able to use later. Earlier on in the year, he'd made a trip to Ireland; the previous summer he'd gone to Austria and North Italy sketching and painting buildings in Vienna and Venice. On other shorter breaks in work, he had stayed with his parents and gone off sketching with his mother. He knew he always had something more to learn.

As he sat on his sofa, listening to music and wondering what he should do for the next few days, a seed of an idea developed, which, however crazy, rapidly took hold. It was several days since Jenny's phone call, and he'd thought of little else. They'd talked for nearly an hour. Phil had apparently gone to some work party, and so, sitting alone in their house, she'd found herself thinking of Harry and decided to give him a ring. They'd joked and giggled and talked of nothing in particular just as new lovers do. Harry had finally put the phone down and sat staring at the ceiling for nearly as long again, partly from contentment and partly from extreme frustration. It had seemed a heady mix. *She'd been thinking of him and so she'd called.* That's what she'd said. Surely she *must* be feeling the same way as him. But unless he told her how he really felt, and soon, she really *would* be lost to him for ever. This renewed intimacy would pass and she would marry this Phil McSchmuck character, and that would be it.

Very quickly the seed germinated and Harry had made up his mind. He would go to France. The châteaux of the Loire would provide perfect research work, and while he was there he could seek out Jenny and tell her how he really felt, how he'd been feeling for years. Because, as he saw it, he really had very little to lose. His immediate cash situation was a bit tight, but he had one empty credit card left and the promise of a large cheque in the not-too-distant future.

He decided to tell no one where he was going, apart from his mother, but that was only because she spoke French and even with her, he decided to keep his plans vague.

'Yeah, I fancy going to France for a few days. A gap has developed and so I thought I'd take my stuff and do a bit of sketching.'

'Good idea,' said Elizabeth, 'and are you going on your own?'

'Absolutely,' said Harry firmly. He could almost hear his mother's mind ticking over, wondering what was really going on. Well, she could keep wondering, because he wasn't going to tell. Not yet, at any rate. 'Anyway, I was wondering if you could book me into this little hotel I've found at Chenonceaux.'

'Well, all right, if you give me the number. How many nights do you want? And what if they're full up?'

'A week please, Ma, and I'm sure they won't be.' He was right, they weren't, although they only had one room left. Another piece of luck.

Then that afternoon Ben rang, wondering whether he was around.

'No, sorry, Ben, I'm, um, out of action for a few days.'

'Really? Why, what're you doing?'

'Nothing. Just busy.'

'Knock it off, Harry. What d'you mean "busy"? Busy doing what?'

'I'm going to France for a few days. Research.'

'Oh, yeah. And the rest.'

'I am. A job fell through, so I thought I'd go to the Loire and look at the châteaux.'

'And that wouldn't by any chance be where your ex-girlfriend lives?'

'How the hell d'you know that?'

'Flin told me. Come on, Harry, if you weren't so bloody mysterious in the first place, I wouldn't have been suspicious.'

So Harry came clean, and told him all, adding that he knew he was crazy, and that, of course, nothing would come of it.

'Well, happy hunting anyway.'

Harry replaced the receiver, knowing that he'd just started a chain reaction of telephone calls zig-zagging up and down the country. Whoever said only women gossiped was a liar.

The following morning, undeterred by his call from Ben, or the one he received later from Flin and Tiffany, he drove his car to John the Citroën specialist on the Old Kent Road. With so much of the garage's business coming from big, time-consuming restorations, Harry knew he could always persuade them to carry out a service at short notice; it meant instant payment, after all. The car had been working well in recent months, and after an oil-change and a few other minor adjustments, Harry was ready to head off. His bags were already in the back, he had some emergency spare parts, credit card and his passport in his pocket. For a brief moment, he wavered, then, with renewed determination, breathed in deeply and pulled the starter knob, beginning his long journey to the Loire.

Via the Kent motorway, a ferry from Dover to Calais, and the long uncluttered road down through France, he finally reached

Chenonceaux by early evening. It had been a long drive, without incident, and he was glad he'd finally installed a stereo. It meant he'd been able to sing half the way, and listen to the radio for the rest. The combination had gone some small way to keeping his mind off his quest.

He didn't want to see her that night, but decided to scout out her house. He was pretty sure she would have to leave before Phil in the morning, because he worked at local vineyards, while she had to drive all the way to Tours, some twenty kilometres away. All he had to do was watch her leave, then follow at a discreet distance.

He'd been to Chenonceaux before. With a school friend one summer holiday. They'd gone cycling along the Loire Valley, visiting the châteaux, getting drunk on tiny bottles of French beer and camping out. What a laugh that had been. He remembered it as a time of riotous irresponsibility, two friends larking about on a summer holiday without any cares in the world. Well, perhaps he'd been a bit worried about his Art A-level result, which he'd taken a year early, and whether he would keep his place in the school rugby team the following term, but that hardly counted. Certainly nothing compared with the agonies he was going through at the moment.

The Hôtel du Roy was perfect for his needs. The room was quite small, walls decorated with an outdated florid pattern, but the bed was big enough, and there was a window from which he could see the château peeking through the dense trees. By the time he'd showered and unpacked, it was getting dark, perfect for conducting his scouting mission. Then, if for some reason he saw her on the street, it would be easier to duck out of the way. She wouldn't be expecting to see him, so there was no reason why she would ever spot him.

Having had a little supper in the bar downstairs, he put on his baseball cap and a jumper, and headed out. He knew their house was not on the main street, but a little way off, towards the river.

She'd said it was only a couple of houses away from a bar, and he'd wondered whether it was the same one he'd been to with his friend Simon all those years ago. That place, he remembered, was not far from the campsite. They'd spent a hilarious evening there, believing the barmen were really famous people who had secretly given up being famous and were now working as waiters in rural France. He smiled to himself. Well, it had been funny at the time. Now, thirteen years later, he was here in Chenonceaux again, but for a very different purpose. He hadn't seen Simon for years, and slightly regretted it. They'd been mates then, really good friends, but now he didn't know whether his old camping partner was married, doing well in his work, or what he was up to. If they met again now, Harry wondered, could they still be friends? Had they changed too much, or were they still more or less the same, different only in age and experience? He didn't really feel that different himself. The same interests, the same things made him laugh. And then there was Jenny; after eleven years, she'd been just as he remembered.

Although it was the height of the tourist season, the streets of Chenonceaux were almost empty. Occasionally a car drove by, or a couple hastily walked past, but otherwise, the air was still and quiet. Harry found the street and turned right, his heart beating quicker again. He passed underneath the railway bridge. Her house had to be down here somewhere. Then he saw the bar, the one he and Simon had got drunk in, and knew he must be close. Apprehension made his skin tingle. There it was – number twenty-one. A cream-plastered front, slate roof, and four windows with shutters either side: a standard French two-up, two-down. Gingerly, he stepped closer. The lights were on downstairs, and there, in what must be their sitting room, sat Jenny, and presumably Phil. They were watching television together on the sofa, but at different ends, not closely together. Jenny had her feet tucked under her legs, while Phil sat with one leg over the other. With blond hair brushed back and a clean-cut square jaw, Phil demonstrated prime-of-life good looks. His skin, browned by long hours under a more consistent sun, oozed healthy vitality. Harry swatted angrily at a moth fluttering about his face. Phil was hardly the ugly dwarf he'd been picturing in his mind's eye. He peered at him again. Actually, maybe that wavy hair was thinning a little.

Then he turned quickly and began to stride back, hoping he would never actually have to speak to Phil. The operation would definitely have to be covert. There could be no pretending to be a long-lost friend in front of him. Not after seeing Jenny like that, a picture of domesticity on the sofa next to him. If only they'd been rowing or showing obvious signs of discontent, as they had in his imagination. Harry clenched his fists and felt the jealousy boil up within him. Even worse, the seediness of the way in which he'd stood outside, looking in at their private world, had left him feeling slightly ashamed of himself, as though he were a hidden camera, violating people's privacy. He picked up a stone and hurled it at the railway bridge and, for a moment, considered getting into his car and simply driving away. But back at the hotel, with a drink in his hand, he began to calm down. Tomorrow would be the day: having come this far, he *had* to deliver his message, for better or worse.

It was just after three the following afternoon that Harry finally stood outside Jenny's front door and lifted his hand to ring the bell. He'd tried following her to work, but was hopeless at playing detective and lost her as they reached the outskirts of Tours. But, sitting in the bar just down from Jenny's house, he had a clear view of the comings and goings of her street; much to his relief, she appeared much earlier than he'd expected.

Harry had been waiting for this moment ever since making his decision to come to France. But now he found himself faltering. He stretched, yawned, then went to pay at the bar. Checking the time, he glanced about him, then, with small, tentative steps, walked the seventy yards to Jenny's house. He almost sidled up to the front door, terrified she might spot his approach before he was ready to confront her.

His hand rose to the doorbell several times before he actually pressed his finger onto the round little knob. His hands were clammy and his whole body tense as he struggled to control an attack of the shakes. It was all very well being full of determination and good intentions from afar, but now that the moment of truth was upon him, the situation seemed very different. A very great sense of impending doom hovered over him. He just knew, with a sickness of heart, that within the hour he would be packing up his car again and heading back to England.

He breathed in and out several times in quick succession, closed his eyes and rang the bell.

First of all, there was nothing, then, after a few moments, footsteps on the stairs. He held his breath. The door opened and there, in front of him, stood Jenny.

Her expressions were curious: at first she looked stunned, her mouth dropping open, her eyes wide; then she broke into an enormous grin and flung her arms around him. 'Harry, my God! What on earth are you doing here?' Then she suddenly pulled away and, eyeing him suspiciously, began chewing her bottom lip. 'Why are you here?'

'Jenny, I'm sorry to spring on you like this, but –' He breathed deeply once more and held out his hands as though he needed steadying. 'I know it must seem a completely mad, insane thing to do, turning up like this out of the blue, but I just have to say something to you. Something very important. Something worth travelling to France to tell you to your face.'

He saw Jenny's complete confusion.

'The thing is,' he continued, 'I think you're the one for me. I love you, you see. I think I've always loved you, but I certainly love you more than ever now. I can't stop thinking about you and, and I know, I just *know* you and I are supposed to be together, and I thought – well, I suppose I just felt I should tell you, just in you *did* feel the same way. Travelling all this way would be more than worth it if you did . . . er, love me . . . too . . .' He paused, searching her face frantically for some clue or indication of her intent. The blood drained from her face, and she turned her head to one side, raising an arm to steady herself on the door frame.

'I just had to tell you before it was too late,' he continued. 'Before you married Phil.'

'What do you mean?' Her voice was shocked, angry, bewildered. 'I mean, how can you say that? How can you be saying this?'

'It's true. I've haven't stopped thinking about you for years. I –'

'Stop it, Harry, please, stop it!' She turned back to face him, her eyes brimming with tears. 'Just go,' she said, quite calmly.

'But, Jenny, please, let me –'

'Go, Harry. Leave me alone.' With tears running down her cheeks, she turned back inside and began to shut the door. And as she did so, Harry saw his dream rapidly fading. Panicking, he grabbed the door with his hand.

'Please, Jenny, think about it. Don't throw this chance away.'

'Harry, leave me, please!'

'I'll be down by the river, the other side, by the château,' he said frantically as she gently but firmly shut the door on him. She was gone.

Like a drunken man, Harry staggered back down the road, barely able to comprehend what had happened. Disaster! What an idiot he'd been. And what arrogance! To think he could just barge into her house, tell her he loved her and expect her to be happy about it. How could he ever have thought it would work? He'd been blind: blind and stupid and an insensitive bear, crashing about trying to break up people's lives. But Jenny had put him in his place, and quite right too; he was a menace to himself and those about him. Slowly he stumbled towards the river, knowing she wouldn't follow. But he needed time to calm down. A chance to collect his thoughts before starting the journey home.

Stunned by this inconceivable set-back, Harry sat under the trees that lined the Cher, and began sketching furiously. The château, stretching across the river, its image reflected perfectly in the dark water, was perfect subject matter for his sketch-book. With his legs dangling over the river bank, and his eyes protected by the shade of the trees above, he thought bitterly about the beauty of the setting. Why wasn't there someone to share this with? Everything was wrong, topsy-turvy, gone mad. His pencil lead broke and he cursed and flung it into the river.

'Harry?' The voice made him turn. Jenny. She had come. She had come after all. Silently he lifted himself up from the river bank, the shadows from the great elms dappling her with shadow. Standing before her, he saw something in the way she looked at him, and suddenly knew his moment had come. Taking her hand in his, and meeting no resistance, he closed his eyes and kissed her.

How long they stood there, kissing, Harry never knew. It was the most delicious kiss he had ever experienced. The sun fell slanting, glinting through the foliage; and the sweet scent of the summer river bank merged with the clean freshness of her skin. His ears were filled with birdsong and the gentle sweeping of the leaves above as the breeze ruffled them. The moment was so perfect Harry almost believed he must be floating with happiness.

'Harry, why are you doing this to me?' Jenny said eventually, as they lay down on the grass, leaning on their elbows and gazing at each other, their faces just inches apart.

'I've told you. I love you.' He looked intently at her healthy, glowing face, the sun highlighting the tiny fair hairs on her cheek.

'I just don't know what to think. I was going to tell you we had to be friends, you know. That's why I came down. I had no intention of kissing you at all.'

'You didn't. I kissed you.'

'I suppose you did.' She grinned slowly. 'You didn't hear me coming up behind you – you were too busy hurling pencils.'

'With good reason. I thought I'd ruined everything. But you came down. I can't believe it. If I'm dreaming, please don't wake me up.' He kissed her again, then rolled over onto his back, so that he lay supine with his eyes closed momentarily against the brightness of the sun.

'I can't believe it either. What am I doing? I must be mad.' Jenny sat up. 'Harry, let's walk along the river. I just need to walk a moment, if that's OK.' She rubbed her forehead. 'Jesus,' she muttered. 'What am I playing at? Half an hour ago, I had just arrived back from work, thinking of nothing in particular, and now here I am with you, betraying Phil.' Harry saw the turmoil in her eyes, could hear the panic in her voice.

'OK, of course,' he said, getting up. 'Look, Jenny, I know this must seem mad. But the only mad thing I ever did was lose you in the first place. I've regretted it ever since, and especially lately. That weekend in Northumberland just confirmed what I already knew. We're perfect for each other. I just *know* we are. In the same way people say they know they can fall in love with someone at first sight. It's instinctive, a deep-down feeling that can't be explained.'

Jenny was silent, but looped her arm through his.

'I saw you, you know,' said Harry, 'before that time in the café. I know it was you.'

'Where? Why didn't you say anything?'

'I couldn't, you were too far away. It was at the theatre. The Albery. You were in the bar during the interval, laughing, and although I was with someone at the time, I found myself physically yearning for you.'

'You're right, I was there. With Millie. She's a friend of mine from university. I remember that night.'

'Anyway, I realized that you had always been the right person for me, but that you'd come along at the wrong time. I thought I'd never have a chance to see you again and that I was destined to be sad and lonely for the rest of my life. That's what I was thinking this afternoon too, when you shut the door on me.'

They reached the bridge, but instead of walking back to the village, continued along the far bank of the river.

'I don't think you have any idea how much I loved you back then, Harry,' Jenny told him. 'When I left you that time in Cambridge, I sobbed all the way back to Bristol. You tore my life apart. I became a recluse, didn't eat, scarcely spoke to anyone. It was awful, just awful. I could never go through that again.' She looked at him, biting her lip. 'Oh, my God, what *am* I doing?' she said suddenly, tears filling her eyes.

Harry, alarmed, turned to her, taking both her hands in his. 'Jenny, I love you. You know, I was eighteen then, just a kid. But I'm nearly thirty now. Things are very different. I *know* you and I are meant for each other.'

'Are we, Harry? Are you *sure*? I think I've always loved you, but ...' She wiped her eyes with the back of her hand. 'Look, I've got to get back. Phil, he's ...' Tears flowed down her cheeks once more. 'This is madness,' she said, clutching her hands to her face, 'I must be going crazy.'

'No, it's not. It's meant to be. You must go back to Phil now, I know, but I'll wait for you. I'm staying at the Hôtel du Roy. I'll be there.'

Jenny nodded, her face stained by tears. 'God, I look a wreck,' she said. Harry kissed her again, and she smiled, almost laughing through her tears.

'Go now,' he told her, 'and come and find me tomorrow.' She looked down, sniffed, then gently let her hands slide out of his. Giving him a final worried glance, she turned and walked back along the river, towards the bridge.

The next day, they began by taking a step backwards. Jenny had a further half-day of classes and so, already showered and changed, she met Harry at his hotel just after three in the afternoon. Immediately, he sensed the mood between them had altered perceptibly. She looked anxious, uncertain.

'Darling Harry, I know this may seem odd to you, but I just want to talk today. I need time to think. I do love you, but I still love Phil too. You're asking me to throw away a future marriage, a job and a life over here, and that's a big thing to do. I'm scared. I can't help it. You must allow me some time.'

Harry held her tightly. 'Of course,' he told her, 'let's go somewhere, out of Chenonceaux.'

They went to Amboise in his shiny black Citroën, and as he thundered up the hill out of the village, along the quiet windy road with its scorched grass banks, he smiled. Sitting next to him Jenny looked lovely in her light cotton dress, her brown legs occasionally rubbing against his. With the windows open, her hair blew about her face until she clasped it back with a band from her wrist. Warm wind buffeted them and the sunlight glowed against his arm. In front, reflected on the sleek bonnet, white puffs of high cloud danced and streamed as he weaved past fields and trees, until there below lay Amboise and the snaking Loire, silvery in the sunlight.

The little town bustled with the market. Stalls full of brightly coloured fruit and vegetables lined the streets, alongside the shops open for everyday trade. Market sellers tried to out-shout each other. Spices, meats and earthy crops left tantalizing smells along the way, their variety adding to the general air of busyness. Jenny led Harry by the hand through the hordes of people ambling along or pausing by the stalls until, beneath the imposing castle walls, they found a café and an empty table, a peaceful spot amid the surrounding clamour.

'Talk to me,' said Harry. They faced each other, waiting for the wine to arrive. Jenny smiled at him.

'Oh, Harry, I'm sorry,' she said, taking his hand and tracing circles around his palm. 'I want to be with you so much, but leaving Phil after all these years, after everything he's done for me – it's not easy. There's so much of that life I love too. To be with you and to betray Phil is such an enormous decision. And the humiliation of ending our engagement – God, it'll be horrendous. I know that's no reason to get married, but it's bloody scary.'

'I know, I do understand. Honestly, it's OK.'

'You see, I've been going out with him for nearly ten years. After you . . . well, he was there for me, a friend at first but then we sort of fell into a relationship. I trusted him and knew he'd look after me. He wasn't going to turn me out because drinking with his friends was more fun. And he's good-looking too.'

'Jenny, I'm sorry, really –'

'And we *were* really good friends, so it was easy. I suppose I thought that was better, a more solid foundation for a long-lasting relationship. So I stayed with him and, after university, we moved to London and began living together. We had the same friends, so our social life was uncomplicated and, you know, we had a good time. Everyone seemed to have moved up to London too, and most of us lived in the same part of town. It was almost as though we were still students, but in London not Bristol.'

'This sounds very familiar,' said Harry.

'I'm sure it's the same for lots of people. We still went round to friends' houses for dinner parties, still got drunk as much as we always had. Nothing really changed. And by the time it had, and Phil was offered his job in France, I went with him without really even thinking about it. I was used to him, and he was used to me. We were best of friends and everyone knows passion never lasts for ever. I thought what we had was what most couples had: safe, stable companionship, with a bit of sex thrown in.'

'But didn't you ever think there was more to it than that? I was never able to hold down a relationship precisely because of that. I didn't want safe and dependable, I wanted to be madly, passionately in love. And you, I realized, were the only person I'd felt that way about. I kept hoping the next girl I met would make me feel the same way I'd felt about you, but it never happened. Never. Eventually, I gave up.'

Jenny laughed.

'What?' said Harry, feigning indignation. 'I thought I was being very noble.'

'How priggish of you!'

'Not at all. Just practical, like you with Phil.'

Jenny stopped laughing at this, looking away as she drank from her glass. Tears were building up in her eyes once more, wobbling above her eyelashes, shiny under the bright glare of the sun. 'Sorry, here I am off again, snivelling like a pathetic little girl.'

Harry held out his handkerchief. She took it.

'Jenny, tell me honestly, do you think you and Phil would have lasted? Do you think you would have been happy? In five, ten, fifteen years' time?'

'I don't know, Harry. How can anyone know? Probably.'

'Do you know what made me drive down here? What made me think that I might just have the slightest chance?'

Jenny shook her head miserably.

'It was what you said in Northumberland. You told me you got engaged because it was New Year's Eve, there were lots of people there, and he already had a ring, and it struck me later that it was a pretty poor reason to marry someone. You get married because you adore that person, can't live without them, and because they light up your life every time you see them. You think they're sexy and you fancy them like mad. They make you laugh, and you *have* to marry because that person is more important to you than anything else on earth. They make waking up each day worth while and give you more joy than you ever thought imaginable. That's why people marry.'

'And is that what I mean to you?'

'Yes, Jenny, it is.' He leant back on his chair and stared at her. 'Is that how you felt for Phil, when he asked you in front of all those people? You know, Jenny, when we were in Northumberland, you weren't even wearing his ring. Now admittedly you might have been hiding what you really felt from us all, but everything you said made me doubt it.'

She chewed her lip again, silent for a moment. Then she looked up. 'I love you, Harry. I've never stopped loving you, but if you were to leave me again, I don't know how I could cope.'

'I never would. You and I are meant to be and I want to look after you for ever, I promise. *I'd* marry you tomorrow, if you'd let me.'

'I want to believe you, Harry, I really do. But how do I know this isn't just some wild romantic notion and that next week, next month, or even next year, you'll change your mind and leave me again? I don't think I could go through that again.'

'I'm different now. I've grown up. I *know* you and I are meant to be. Jenny, I'm not going to leave you again, you have to believe me.'

Jenny smiled through her tears.

Eventually, she said, 'You should go back to London now. I'm sorry, Harry, but I just can't promise you here and now. I need time to think about this. Wait for me though. I promise I'll tell you what I've decided in a week.'

'OK, Jenny. I'll wait. I understand, I really do.'

She fingered her locket. 'Eternal happiness or a life of torment. I can't quite tell.'

Harry decided to say nothing more. He took her hand and squeezed gently, hoping the gesture would reassure her. Around him the market and the life of the town continued as always, bustling and busy, the crowds of people unaware of the great events occurring in his life.

Harry left Chenonceaux convinced that all would be well, euphoric that his mission had succeeded and that he and Jenny would soon be back together. But as the kilometres ticked by, and the distance between them increased, so his spirits began to fall, so that by the time he turned into his street back in London he was convinced nothing other than disappointment and disaster awaited him.

Opening the front door, he turned on the light switch for the stairwell, but nothing happened. The bulb must have gone. He bent over and picked up three days' post, stumbled up the darkened stairs to the kitchen, and turned on the answer machine. But that didn't work either. Nor did the kitchen light. Nor any other light. Nor was the trip switch in the wrong position and, for a moment, Harry stood by his phone, wondering what on earth the problem might be. Then he glanced down at the array of letters. One was a red-topped phone bill. With horror, he remembered he'd been given seven days to pay his electricity bill from some time the previous week. In the excitement of going to France, it had been left unpaid. He rapidly shuffled through the remaining letters. An update about the family he was sponsoring in West Africa (something he always forgot he contributed to until the biannual progress report came through); a reminder from the dentist that it was fast approaching check-up time; an alumni letter from his old Cambridge college; and a few pizza delivery fliers. But no cheque from Marcus.

After racking another £154 onto his swollen credit card, and a short wait, his electricity was restored. But his funds were rapidly running out. He would have to go round to Marcus and physically demand the money. And he hated doing that; it was so humiliating.

The answer-machine light had resumed flashing, so he turned up the volume and pressed Play for his messages. One from Caroline Parker, just asking him to ring her. Tone of voice ominous. Then one from Julia, asking if they could meet. They needed to talk, she said – and he owed her that. Did he? Harry didn't really see why. Then a wrong number – someone called Alan asking whether Chris was still all right for Saturday. But nothing from Jenny.

On an impulse, he rang Flin, who had heard about his mission to France from Ben, and was agog to hear what had happened. Harry, grateful for his interest, told him all.

'Well, it sounds like a great success,' Flin told him.

'I thought so too to start with, but now I'm not so sure. I have a sinking feeling that I probably won't see her again.'

'You're only feeling like that because you've just got back. It'll be fine.'

'Maybe,' said Harry doubtfully.

'Harry, you can hardly expect her to drop everything just like that. She's been with this guy for years. And, you know, she is living with him, not to say engaged too. I know we all thought it sounded a bit loveless, but even so, she was never going to walk out on him just at the click of your fingers. You've got to give her a chance to sort herself out in her own time.'

'Yeah, I suppose so,' said Harry grudgingly. He sighed, pausing for a moment. 'I've also got another message from Julia, still wanting to meet up. I don't know whether I should.'

'Tough one, Harry. You're probably going to have to ring her and be firm. Or maybe meet her on neutral territory. You can't just ignore it though.'

'No, I guess not. Well, that's another fun thing for me to do this week.'

'This is what comes of being a heartbreaker.'

'Very funny.'

'Actually, Harry – and I feel a bit awkward about this – but I think Julia's coming to see us next weekend. Apparently she's got a wedding in the area – one of Willie's relations – and so asked if she could call by.'

'Why on earth did you agree?' said Harry, his voice rising.

'What were we supposed to say?'

'What about that you weren't going to be around?'

'Well, I didn't think of that at the time, did I? She caught me off guard. Sorry. I don't want her to come. I barely know the girl.'

Harry sighed once more. 'Look, it doesn't matter. Honestly.'

They talked on, until Harry finally put the receiver down and slammed a fist onto the work-surface in front of him. Harangued by someone he didn't want to be with and stony silence from the one he did. And bills. Bills and no cash.

As the evening progressed, Harry's mood darkened. Caroline Parker wondered whether he'd mind postponing a bit longer. They were getting several quotes for the plastering and the whole process was taking longer than she had anticipated. Harry interpreted that as a ploy to let him down gently. Then his phone was cut off too – for the rest of the night – prompting renewed waves of panic. He became convinced Jenny would phone that very night, and then, getting no answer, would assume everything had changed and not leave Phil after all. Ben assured him he was being ridiculous, but such platitudes did little to allay his fears.

He plucked up courage to call Julia in the morning, and they met at a café on the King's Road, surrounded by other people. But after talking reasonably sensibly for ten minutes, she began crying again, then resorting to insults. In the end he just stood up and walked away. But it did make him wonder why Jenny would ever actually *want* to come back to him. He didn't like himself very much that day: he upset ex-girlfriends, couldn't be depended on to pay bills, and was struggling to keep the operations of his business in order. *He* wouldn't want to be giving up everything for someone like that.

Too many little things were going wrong. He vowed to pay all bills immediately from henceforth, but he'd promised that to himself before and not kicked the habit. The Sunday after he came back, he stayed in his flat all day. He wanted to save money, but also simply couldn't be bothered to do anything. Couldn't be bothered to talk to anyone, couldn't bothered to get in his car, or sit on the Tube, and couldn't be bothered to watch lots of other people walking around, hand-in-hand, arm-in-arm, looking happy and lucky in love. And when he wasn't watching television, he sat at his desk, sketching and drawing designs, and noticing how very silent his flat could be.

Then on Friday, a day after Jenny's deadline, his fortunes began to change. Firstly Marcus's cheque arrived in the post. Then, as he was half-heartedly toying with his cereal, Caroline Parker rang to say work was finally beginning on her wall, and she definitely still wanted him to do the mural after it had been completed. But it wasn't until thirty-three minutes past six that evening, after a day spent in a state of alternating gloom and panic, that Harry's mood changed. At that precise moment, not long after he'd arrived back from work, Jenny finally called. As he listened to what she had to say, Harry felt a whole new system of nerves alive in him, and his heart began to thump in his chest. She would be arriving at Waterloo the following morning. Coming back to him after all.

part three – *autumn*

CHAPTER FIFTEEN

Ben confused

Ben had always felt in two minds about the end of summer. He didn't like deep winter and the dark, but autumn was fine with its dazzling array of colours and the onset of the football season; and that slightly damp, mulchy air when the days were overcast, and the crisp, biting freshness of cold, clear weather made him feel fresh and vibrant after the sluggishness of summer.

He should have been playing football that afternoon. It had been planned for ages, agreed to by Lucie, the one match he hadn't missed in years. Of all the games in the season, the Old Boys game was the one he enjoyed the most. They all travelled to Cambridge together, spent a night on the town reliving their golden days of undergraduate life, then, jaded but content, drove back the following day. He had promised the captain he wouldn't let him down, assured Harry he'd drive up with him, as usual. Then Lucie had decided she had flu. She was simply too ill to get up, and Ben would have to look after Thomas instead.

'Can't your mum lend a hand?' Ben had pleaded.

'No, she's away for a romantic weekend with Terrence.'

'Well, what about someone else? What about a nanny just for the day?'

'Ben, he's our son. You have to take responsibility, you know.

You can't just switch off parenthood like a tap whenever you want to.'

Ben paced up and down the bedroom, desperately trying to contain his anger. 'I know that,' he said, 'but I haven't played football yet this season, and this is the one match in the year I really love playing. It was all agreed. Please, darling.'

'Ben, I'm not doing this on purpose, you know. I can't help being ill, can I? It's not very good for Thomas if I'm spluttering germs all over him. If I rest up now, there's every chance that by Monday I'll be much better. I'm sorry about your football, I really am, but what about all the sacrifices I've had to make? It's not just you that has to lose out, you know.'

'Well, what if I come back, and don't stay over?'

'For God's sake, Ben, stop being so fucking selfish. It's today that's the problem.'

'But it's not fair on the others suddenly dropping out like this.'

'Ben, I didn't decide to be ill today. For God's sake. Look, he's sixteen weeks old and at this age it's absolutely essential we protect him from any bugs flying about.' Then she began an elaborate display of coughing and hacking from her sick-bed.

And so he'd cancelled. Harry took the news philosophically.

'Don't worry about it. There'll be other years,' he told him. 'Get some games in later on in the season.'

'Yeah,' said Ben miserably. Had he truly believed Lucie was ill, he would have accepted the situation with better grace. But to him, it seemed as though she had little more than a bad cold.

So instead of playing football, Ben took Thomas to Battersea Park, leaves turning and falling about him. His son gurgled happily enough, but it did little to cheer him. He kept thinking about the game he was missing out on. Two o'clock: the whistle would be blown for the start of the game. Two-forty-five: would they have scored yet? Or would they, like last year, already be a goal down?

If only he could sort things out with Lucie. He knew if he wasn't careful their relationship was in danger of totally deteriorating. It worried and upset him desperately, but he felt so helpless to do anything about it. Nothing he did or said seemed to be the right thing. The Prospero dinner had never been mentioned again, but then, since that fateful night, they hadn't talked about anything much of any consequence. And he missed his friends. Every time he suggested they have some people over for supper, she dismissed the idea out of hand. How long was it going to go on like this? When would life return to normal?

As he ambled through Battersea Park, pushing Thomas round the edge of the lake, he thought bitterly about the similar patterns of so many of their conversations, prompted by the baby crying, needing his nappy changed or, now that Lucie had stopped breastfeeding, requiring a new bottle.

'Oh dear, you stink, Little Man,' he might say.

'Needs his nappy changed,' Lucie would reply. 'Give him to me.'

'No, honestly, I'll do it. I don't mind.'

'I'll do it.'

'No, Lucie, please, you sit still.'

'Well, thanks.'

He'd then remove the nappy, clean up and unpack another from the Pampers box. Then would come the instruction or criticism. 'Don't wipe too hard, you don't want to hurt him,' Lucie would call out. Ben always waited for it, hoping she'd be able to resist the urge for once, but she never could. This habit of hers came to annoy him more than just about anything else.

Harry and other friends he talked to about it urged him to patience. He should just give her time. It was a big shock, having a baby, and a massive change both physically and emotionally, and some people were bound to take longer than others to settle down, let their hormones recover, and return to some kind of normality. What was making Lucie behave so differently was nothing to do with him, not personal in any way; he should just be there for her and all would be fine. With this in mind, Ben believed he'd developed the patience of a saint. He resisted snapping back at her, and helped as much as he could with Thomas whenever he was at home, and it seemed to be getting him nowhere. Would Harry and the others really be giving him the same advice if they were in his position? Somehow, he doubted it. Perhaps the time had come to get counselling. Or maybe that would make things worse. Ben kicked a large stone in his path, then noticed he'd almost reached the far end of the park.

But life was better at the office. True to his word, Carl had never again mentioned Lucie's performance, and in between that time had praised Ben in front of the rest of the team for his work on a completely different merger. Not long after, he began to become good friends with Kate. Although normally she tended to work with Jon, as the deal gradually began to hot up, she was brought in to work with him. Ever since she'd first suggested they go for a drink, Ben had known they'd get on. She was married herself, but from the outset, as she sipped her wine and he his pint, they seemed to talk about everything but their home lives. That first evening they had chatted and gossiped about work and the office, and Jon and Carl, then moved on to their past histories and university. It turned out she'd been at Cambridge at the same time, but in a completely different college and doing a completely different degree. She was sure she'd met Harry, though.

'Wasn't he an artist?' she'd asked. 'Painted amazing sets for various plays at the ADC.'

'That's him all right,' Ben assured her. It turned out there were numerous people they vaguely knew in common.

Ben had been enjoying this light relief so much, he drank four pints and stayed far longer than he'd intended. Noticing his watch said the time was nearly eleven o'clock, he panicked, finished his drink and dashed off, racked with guilt. Lucie, of course, had smelt the beer on his breath and demanded an explanation, accusing him of having an affair. Ben laughed at the suggestion, but still had to swear on everything he held dear.

'We were working late and then Carl wanted to go for a drink. I haven't done that for ages. I'm always making excuses to him, and I just thought that for once I should take him up on the offer.'

'You might have phoned,' Lucie complained.

'I could have done, you're right. I'm sorry.' Lucie had eyed him suspiciously, but then dropped the matter. But lying in bed that night, trying to read a book while Lucie's back rose up and down gently with sleep, he realized it was the first time he'd ever properly lied to her. How stupid he'd been. He should have phoned Lucie in the first place and told her he was going for a drink with Kate. It wasn't as though there was anything wrong with that. Such behaviour was perfectly normal, that's what work colleagues did. Perhaps he felt so guilty because he'd actually had a good time. Kate knew nothing of his domestic trials and Ben hadn't wanted to talk about them. The lightness of the conversation had made a refreshing change.

As the deal went hot, they were spending most of the day as well as the evening together. One day she would dash out and grab the sandwiches, the next it would be his turn. In a very short space of time, they knew precisely which was each's favourite type of Prêt à Manger sandwich and why. It was silly, he knew, but as they sat in one or the other's office, pausing for a few minutes to eat their late lunch, Ben became increasingly conscious of an intimacy growing between them that he hadn't felt with anyone since courting Lucie. He supposed they were a bit flirtatious, but what if they were? There was nothing in it. They were both married, after all. No harm in a bit of platonic lust.

The deal suddenly went off the boil. One of the parties pulled out at the last minute, so unless another bid emerged within a week, the motor company would be sold off to asset strippers. Ben's concerns were more for the thousands of workers whose jobs now looked to be at risk, rather than the months of work down the pan, but both Carl and Jon seemed to be confident another venture capitalist group would enter the fray.

'So go home, have the weekend off and come back on Monday expecting serious work to be done,' Carl told him. 'Spend some time with that kid of yours.'

That was something Ben was certainly looking forward to.

He arrived home early enough to help Lucie give Thomas his bath. This was the first time in nearly two weeks, as he'd had to work throughout the previous weekend. In that time, he'd only ever seen his son first thing in the morning. There was nothing he could do about it, but it didn't stop him feeling he was missing out on important moments of Thomas's development.

'I'll wash him, darling,' he told Lucie, as she felt the temperature of the water.

'OK,' she said flatly, retreating to sit on the loo seat. But Thomas wasn't happy about this. Ben watched his face break into a terrified bawl when he began to lather soap onto the pudgy little body.

'It's all right, Thomas, I'm not going to hurt you,' Ben told him gently, 'Daddy's just getting you clean.'

'Do you want me to do it?' asked Lucie, moving to the edge of the loo.

'No, I'm OK.' But Thomas wasn't. The wailing continued, long pitiful sobs of distress. Out of the corner of his eye, Ben saw Lucie preparing to pounce and take over. He had just moments in which to calm his child and earn his trust. Desperately, he tried to soothe him, making inane noises and continuing to work soap over his arms and back, until Thomas managed to put his soap-covered arm to his eyes. A cry of pure pain rang out and with lightning pace Lucie pushed Ben aside and came to her son's aid. Rinsing him with the shower head and dabbing his face with a clean flannel, she then scooped him out of the water and into a large towel, cradling him gently in her arms and repeatedly kissing the top of his head.

'Poor fellow,' said Ben, upset to think he'd hurt his son, 'are you all right?'

Lucie glared at him.

'Sorry,' he said miserably, looking at her, 'I didn't mean it.'

'I know, but try not to be so bloody oafish around him. It scares him.' So his son was frightened of him, thought Ben sadly.

The following morning, Ben tried to improve the father/son relationship by jiggling bleating toys in front of Thomas and then giving him his bottle of milk, while Lucie talked on the phone for twenty minutes to her mother. What they could possibly have to talk about, he had no idea, especially since Vanessa seemed to spend increasing amounts of time at their house during the week. Before Thomas had been born, Lucie tended to end any phone conversation to Vanessa with a sigh and a phrase such as 'She is *so* infuriating', and pre-empt any call from her by saying, 'If it's Mum, I'm not in.' But now they were thick as thieves. If only she would talk as much to him.

'She's coming over in a bit to talk about the christening,' said Lucie in a tone that was deliberately nonchalant but was clearly expected to provoke a challenge; which it did.

'Tell me you're joking.' Ben's heart sank, not just at the thought of Vanessa sticking her nose in, but also because of the argument that was inevitably about to occur. Another one.

'Well, you don't seem to have any time these days to help.'

'I know I'm busy, darling, but really, do we *have* to have your mum running the show?'

'Yes, we do. She's brilliant at organizing things. I can assure you, you'll thank me for this in the long run.'

'Lucie, just remember the wedding. Remember how much she annoyed you. Remember how many arguments you had over it. The number of guests, the colour of the flowers, the font type for the invitations, the food, the drink, your dress. You argued about absolutely everything! And you swore you'd never, ever let her organize anything for you again. Your words, not mine.'

Lucie shrugged indifferently. 'I was probably just as much to blame. Honestly, Ben, don't make a big deal out of this. Thomas needs to be christened, you're working all the bloody time, I don't have the energy and Mum's prepared to sort everything out at no extra cost to you. So stop being so obstreperous.'

'I'm not. I just don't want our quiet and intimate christening being hijacked and turned into the social event of the autumn.'

'It won't be. No one's suggesting this will be anything other than what we want. You know, Mum *is* his grandmother, and it's nice for her to be involved.' She smiled at him with something like tenderness. 'Come on, you must see it makes good sense really.'

'All right,' agreed Ben begrudgingly, 'but I want to be in on the discussions, and not totally frozen out, OK?'

'Whatever you say, darling,' said Lucie, looking back down at her magazine.

Thomas not only recognized Vanessa, but also made it fairly clear how delighted he was at her arrival, waving his arms up and down and giggling happily.

'Who's my most gorgeous boy then?' she said, taking him in her arms as easily and naturally as if he'd been her own. Once she'd said her hellos and put away her coat, she passed Thomas back to Ben and sat down. Immediately Thomas looked frantically in her direction and held out his arms, pleading with her to take him back and away from the large, hairier person now cradling him.

'He's determined to be with his grandmother,' said Ben, his grin belying the irritation he felt.

'Are you, darling?' cooed Vanessa. 'But be a good boy and stay with Daddy.'

'Yes, just entertain him for a while, can you, Ben, while Mum and I sort out a few things.'

'I want to listen in too, though,' protested Ben as Thomas wriggled about in his arms, still desperate to make good his escape.

'Ben, someone's got to look after Thomas and if he's being a

242

nuisance we'll never get anything resolved. Please, just take him upstairs or something.' Lucie gave him a withering look, then turned back to Vanessa.

'No way,' Ben retorted, 'you're not organizing the christening without me being here.' He could see Lucie about to unleash another scathing attack, when Vanessa intervened.

'Look, give him to me then.' She sighed wearily. 'You'll just have to make the notes, Lucie. I suppose I have been seeing so much of him recently, he's bound to get a bit clingy occasionally. It is lovely though, to see how much he loves me already.' She looked up and smiled triumphantly, firstly at Lucie and then, for a fraction longer, at Ben. Ben struggled hard to bite his tongue, aware of how fatal succumbing to Vanessa's goading could be. He decided to press on with the christening plans.

'We really don't want it to be a big occasion,' he began, 'just for immediate family and the godparents, and then we thought we could have a few drinks back here and call it a day. Didn't we, darling?'

'That sort of thing,' agreed Lucie, although Ben thought her tone was hardly emphatic.

'That's fine,' said Vanessa, looking straight at her daughter, 'but we have to invite Susie and Bill, obviously, and your grandparents, Lucie, and I was rather hoping you might allow me to invite Terence.' She raised her eyebrows, smiling with practised coyness. Ben nodded, and watched Lucie add his name to the list. 'And I think it's only fair that you invite your own godparents,' Vanessa continued quickly.

To Ben's horror, Lucie nodded.

'Come on, Luce, surely you don't need to invite them?' he said. 'I mean, when did you last see them? At our wedding?'

'Yes,' Lucie said quietly, 'perhaps we should leave them out, Mum.'

'But, darling, they'll be terribly hurt. And they were so good to you when your father died.' Ben cursed silently; Vanessa always used that trick when she didn't get her own way. He distinctly remembered how infuriated Lucie had become when Vanessa had used the ploy to get more of her friends invited to the wedding. 'They really were. And remember how sweet Michael was to you at your wedding. He'd be mortified if he found out he hadn't been invited.'

'I suppose you're right,' agreed Lucie.

'Lucie!' exclaimed Ben.

'Well, Mum's right. He has always been good to me and his speech was really sweet, wasn't it?'

'OK, well, invite him, but surely you don't need to invite the other two.'

'Ben, darling, you can't possibly invite Michael and not Jane and Rosie.' This time Vanessa's voice had a hard *fait accompli* edge to it.

'Oh, fine,' said Ben sarcastically, 'next you'll be telling me I have to invite all my family too.'

'Well, of course you must. Family is very important at such occasions.'

'I'll invite my dad, but that's it,' Ben told them.

'Come on, Ben,' said Lucie, 'we should ask your brothers too. Don't you think?'

'What, and have all their kids running around the place banging into everything being complete pains in the arse? You must be joking. Anyway, they'd hate it. I always did when I was forced to go to weddings and stuff as a kid.'

'You're not honestly proposing we hold it here, are you?' said Vanessa, incredulity etched over her entire face.

'I'm not proposing, Vanessa, I'm saying. Quiet and intimate, remember? I'm not hiring some private venue and that's final.'

'It might be fun though, don't you think?' Lucie smiled, clearly excited by the thought. 'Come on, darling, don't be tight.'

'I'm not being tight!' Ben said, clenching his hands together. 'I thought we agreed to keep this small.'

'*You* agreed,' muttered Lucie, and then Ben saw her catch Vanessa's eye, and the look of understanding that passed between them.

'Oh, I get it,' he said slowly, 'this was all planned, wasn't it? United front against Ben. Bulldoze him into agreeing. Well, I'm not falling for it. We're having it here, in our house, and that's final.' He stood up and began to pace about the room.

'All right, if you insist,' said Vanessa, 'but don't blame me if things get broken. And, of course, the house will be chaotic, with drink and food all over the place. You have to think of your carpets, you know.'

'Come on, Ben, Mum's got a point.'

'If we just have white wine and a bit of champagne, and don't invite all my family and their brats, it won't be an issue,' said Ben, his anger rising.

'Well, I think you're being really selfish. It's just as much up to me what we do, and I agree with Mum.' Lucie gave up any pretence of humouring him. 'You know,' she continued, 'it's our son's christening and you're trying to turn it into nothing more than a pre-lunch sherry. You might dislike your family, but I happen to think mine is important and I want them to be there and share it with us.'

Ben looked at them both, and their steely eyes defiantly glaring at him. 'Oh, do what you fucking like,' he said after realizing the game was up, 'you always do. I'm going to take Thomas to the park, so that maybe he can get to know his father almost as well as his grandmother.'

Pretty soon after, as he strode down towards the Northcote Road with the buggy, he regretted making that last comment. Now they'd think his rampant jealousy of Vanessa was the real reason for his reaction against her plans. He pictured the two of them gossiping together about him and how unreasonable he was. He cringed. Maybe he did resent the bond that was building between grandmother and grandson; even now, Thomas wailed at being parted from his beloved women. This was inevitable, he supposed, considering the hours he had to work, but made it no less upsetting. That was the price he paid to keep Lucie at home and them in the style to which they'd become accustomed. None the less, this sacrifice would be far easier to bear if Lucie would only show him something of the person he'd married. Eventually, Thomas's crying turned to sleep, and Ben's anger cooled. He paused to sit on a bench. If someone would only tell him how he could get things back to normal, he'd gladly do it. Anything. He looked at Thomas, peaceful in his sleep. This little being was supposed to bring so much joy, the ultimate representation of a contented and happy family. Yet ever since he'd been born, Ben felt his life had a taken a dramatic downturn. He wondered how he could have got it so wrong.

On Monday, as Carl had predicted, new venture capitalists had emerged and the deal was back on with a vengeance. For two frantic weeks, Ben was forced to work all hours of the day to resolve the necessary refinements before the deadline passed and the owners offered the company to the asset strippers. But they managed it and, with just hours to spare, all the necessary signatures were on the table. Just after eleven o'clock, the champagne corks burst up to the ceiling of the Farman Gore offices to celebrate the success of their biggest-ever UK deal.

Kate, who'd once more been working closely with Ben, hugged him tightly and said, 'We did it! We did it!' Laughing, Ben poured them both some champagne.

'We don't make a bad team, do we?' he grinned.

'The very best,' agreed Kate. He could see the excitement in her face and the glint of triumph in her pale eyes.

'Yes, I agree,' interrupted Carl, 'I think we should get you two working on other projects in future.' He raised his glass. 'Here's to you guys. Good work.'

Ben was already feeling quite drunk when, a while later, Kate suggested they leave and share a taxi home. She lived in South Kensington, which was just about on Ben's way home. Certainly, it was an arrangement they'd been carrying out with increasing frequency in recent weeks. It had become as much a ritual as the sandwich buying. In many ways, Ben believed he knew Kate as well as he knew many of his good friends, but apart from the colour of her front door, he still knew nothing about the inside of her flat or much more about her home life. Theirs was a work friendship, and the boundaries, however unwritten, were well defined.

But sitting together in the back of the taxi, something happened that changed those rules. Kate took his hand in hers. Nothing changed in her tone of voice, nor did she say anything that might suggest something more. Had it not been such a surprise, Ben would have thought it the most natural thing in the world. Her fingers, longer than Lucie's, were cool but soft. Ben's heart began thumping, and he felt himself get an instant erection. He crossed his legs and smiled at her, unable to let go. She was so beautiful, so *sexy*. Her grey eyes twinkled at him, full lips smiling happily. And her legs, folded towards him, shimmered with the nylon, emphasizing their slender elegance. Her husband was a lucky, lucky man. He couldn't imagine they had much to argue about.

'Come in for a coffee,' she said suddenly as the taxi drew up outside her flat.

'Why not?' said Ben, a little too quickly. Lucie would already be asleep anyway, so another half-hour wouldn't hurt. And Kate's husband would be there, so it wasn't as if anything was going to happen.

None the less, as Kate unlocked the front door and led him into the entrance hall and up the stairs, Ben felt keenly aware that another boundary between them had been knocked down. And with it, his excitement grew. The flat was clearly a family property, passed down either to Kate or her husband, and as such it was filled with old furniture and heavy curtains. The carpet, once elegant, now appeared a little tired. A silver vase and a minuscule music system were the only obvious hints of modernity.

'What can I get you?' asked Kate, flinging down her coat on an armchair. 'Coffee, or something stronger?'

'Coffee would be great,' said Ben following her into the kitchen. Kate talked on, but Ben found it harder to feel quite so relaxed. The holding of his hand and now being in her flat – it confused him. Just what was going on? Was he reading too much into it, or was he missing something more? He shifted edgily from one foot to the other, and kept his hand surreptitiously in his pocket.

'So where's your husband then?' said Ben as they sat down on the sofa.

'Oh, he's away at the moment. In Frankfurt. So you see, we have the flat to ourselves.'

Ben froze, an inane smile glued to his face. Her shirt buttons were undone at the top, revealing a tantalizing glimpse of her breasts. She inched closer towards him and carefully put her cup down. Ben stared at her, still unable to move. Her lips were slightly parted, her eyes locked onto his. She could be all his. In moments, they could be naked, his hands on her breasts and running over every inch of her body, feeling the smoothness of her skin and the willingness of her sex. This temptress leaning towards him could satisfy all the sexual frustrations of the previous months. Pure, carnal pleasure awaited him.

'Ben?' she said softly, her lips just inches from his. She placed a hand on his erection. The moment had arrived.

'No!' said Ben, suddenly standing up. 'No, I must go. Sorry, Kate.' He barely looked at her, just grabbed his bag and ran out of the flat, down the stairs and into the entrance hall, then out into the cold autumn night, not thinking how Kate must be feeling. He walked, his head whirring, still a little drunk.

But the shadows began to close in around him. The long dark lines of the streetlights seemed to be following him, so that he began walking faster and faster in an effort to escape them. Down over the Fulham Road, and across the King's Road towards Albert Bridge, still lit up like a Christmas tree.

Every way he turned, lights glared at him accusingly. The streetlights, the lights from the cars, now the bridge. Spotlights homing in on him like interrogation lamps. 'You'd sleep with her, would you?' they seemed to be saying. 'Betray your family, would you?' Images of Kate's face, her bee-stung lips parted seductively and her eyes twinkling, filled his mind. 'Succumb to temptation would you? *Just like your mother.*'

No! He wasn't like her, never could be. He stopped, rubbing his hands across his face. Despite the cold, his face felt hot, and sweat trickled down his back and from his forehead. *He wasn't like his mother.* Those genes went elsewhere. He was a good man, a family man, not a traitor, not a Judas. Above, the hundreds of individual lightbulbs bore down on him. Below, the water, with mesmerizing swiftness, rushed past, occasionally carrying pieces of flotsam and driftwood with it. Lights above, water below, trapping him in between. His head swum and then there in his mind's eye was Kate, leaning towards him, her tongue glistening between her parted lips.

He turned and leant against the edge of the bridge, trying to rid himself of the image of Kate. The effects of the drink were still with him, dulling his senses. But more than that, he was very, very tired, and suddenly desperate for bed. His bed with Lucie. He took some deep breaths. He had to get home, and as quickly as possible. Delving into his bag, he pulled out his phone and called for a cab and then began walking. He desperately wanted to be with Lucie and Thomas. He had to make it work, *had* to rekindle the old relationship between Lucie and himself. Stumbling down Albert Bridge Road, he knew he'd come close to throwing everything away. He, who had all a man could possibly want, very nearly had nothing. His throat tightened and his mouth dried, and he knew there was nothing he could do to prevent the tears that were about to flow. Whether they were from relief, sadness, or gratitude, he wasn't sure. Maybe they were from a combination of all three.

CHAPTER SIXTEEN

town and country

In Northumberland, summer turned to a long, rusty autumn, and as the temperature fell with the leaves, so Flin began to worry about the pigs. They seemed perfectly happy, but he didn't want to wake up one frosty morning and find one of them frozen to death. Perhaps, if he was feeling plucky, he would ask Melvyn about them when he next saw him. He was less worried about the geese and chickens, who had the barn to protect them. The up-ended wooden boxes stuffed with straw had proved a great success, and he was able to collect fresh eggs every day, more than they needed themselves. This cheered him enormously. Tiffany had even taken some down to the village shop, for which she was given five pence an egg.

'Now we're even making money out of this,' Flin told her.

'Um, sort of,' said Tiffany, slapping three twenty-pence pieces on the kitchen table.

His first crops from the vegetable patch had also sprouted from the soil: two rows of physically handicapped carrots and a few contorted French beans. But Flin cared neither about the size nor quantity. He had planted and they had grown, one small personal victory among the disappointments. And both he and Tiffany admitted, as they tucked into their roast chicken, that the carrots, in particular, were a triumph of taste and freshness.

Flin still struggled to feel accepted within the community, however. Keith continued with his snide remarks whenever they went to the pub, and Callum and Wendy avoided them. Others would nod and grunt, if he was lucky, and Melvyn might pause and mumble about the weather if Flin happened to bump into him, but it did little to assuage his growing feeling that while he might live in the village, he would never be a part of it.

Then Willie invited him shooting. He rang one night and Flin, completely caught on the hop, accepted without pausing for thought.

'Damn, damn, damn,' he said, moments later, as he paced up and down the kitchen. 'What am I going to do?'

'What's the big deal? It'll be fun, won't it? All my brothers used to love going out and shooting things.'

'No offence, darling, but it's probably slightly different in Australia.'

'I don't see why.'

'For starters, do your brothers have to dress up for it?'

'No.'

'And are there hundreds of codes of practice that have to be observed at all times?'

'Don't think so.'

'Exactly. I've shot clays a couple of times, but that was at an outdoor activity park in Wales. Somehow, I don't think Willie's private shoot is going to be quite the same thing. I'm going to be horribly exposed, and then Willie won't talk to me ever again either.'

'Don't be ridiculous. Willie's about as laid-back as they come. You'll be fine. It'll be fun.'

The next day in Newcastle, Flin paused at the magazine stand in W. H. Smith and flicked through a copy of *The Field*. All the guns pictured wore thick tweed plus-fours, flat caps and tweed coats. At least he had the coat, had done for years. He'd bought it to make himself feel more countrified on weekends out of London. Although it was quite old now, he was sure he could get it cleaned and smartened up. But what about the plus-fours and the cap?

Harry knew the form.

'Get some moleskin jeans and a pair of thick woollen socks and tuck your trousers into the socks, then wear wellingtons over the top of that. You'll be fine.'

'Are you sure?'

'Honestly. I did it once, and no one cut me dead. It was awful though. You're going to find the whole thing very pompous and feudal.'

The next anxiety for Flin was his lack of a gun. He'd thought Willie would assume he didn't own one, then realized how presumptuous this was.

'This whole thing is turning into such a palaver and there's still two days to go,' he told Tiffany despairingly.

'Just phone and tell him. Make up some excuse.'

'It's so embarrassing.'

'Just do it, Flin. It'll be more embarrassing turning up on Saturday without one.'

So, reluctantly, Flin phoned Willie, explaining he'd left his gun in the safe with his father down south. Stupid of him, he knew, but he'd completely forgotten about it.

'No problem at all,' Willie assured him. 'Silly me, should have thought to ask.'

The day arrived. A blanket of grey cloud covered the sky, accompanied by a light breeze. Peter, the estate manager, was already at the Hall when Flin arrived, as was Willie's 'neighbour', who reintroduced himself as Hugh. Soon the others arrived until there were eight of them. Flin reckoned he was the youngest, although there was a man with a large baggy flat cap and a raffish cut of tweed who must have still been in his thirties. He jauntily introduced himself as 'Teddy'. Flin earmarked him as the crack shot. The others were two generations on, garrulous, white-haired men with ruddy noses, the latest in a long line of Northumbrian warlords and landowners, stalwarts of the *ancien régime*, so obviously grand that Flin did not know what to say to them. At least no one passed comment on his lack of plus-fours.

To begin with, the conversation focused on the weather. Rain was forecast, which would keep the birds low, but maybe, with the bit of wind there was at the moment, they would get a couple of decent early drives. Flin quietly nodded agreement, then they drew numbers – Flin plucking the sliver of ivory with the number seven – and ambled outside to the waiting Land-Rovers.

Despite the apparently good shooting conditions, not a single pheasant came anywhere near Flin during the first drive. Standing towards the far end of an arc in the middle of a ploughed field, he watched several fly down the hedgerow only to be systematically blasted from the sky by Teddy. Then a whistle blew and everyone put their guns away again.

He was walking back towards the parked Land-Rover when, to his horror, he saw Melvyn and Callum, both covered head-to-toe in waterproofs, striding towards him with the other beaters.

'Hi,' he said as they approached him.

'Moving with the nobs then,' said Melvyn.

Flin laughed weakly. 'Haven't a clue what I'm doing though. First time.'

'It's easy,' muttered Callum. 'You see a pheasant, point the gun and shoot.' Then they were gone. Silently, Flin clambered into the back of Willie's Land-Rover, and wished Willie had never asked him in the first place.

On the second drive he fired one shot and missed, but, to his relief, so did Hugh, who was next in the line. On the third, he stood in the corner of a field by a copse. He was still thinking with irritation about Melvyn and Callum, when a flurry of birds rattled out the trees in front of him. Swinging his gun into his shoulder he squeezed the trigger and, to his amazement, one of the pheasants, a magnificently tailed cock, dropped dead from the sky, landing with a solid thump at his feet. Frantically reloading, his fingers shaking as he fumbled with the cartridges, he snapped the barrel shut as another bird whirred clumsily from the trees. As he swung the gun into line and fired, his second pheasant abruptly ceased flapping, crash-landing the other side of the fence. His relief was stronger than the sense of guilt he felt at killing two birds for sport; and the sense of exhilaration surprised him.

Picking up the bird at his feet, he walked triumphantly back towards Willie and the others. Everyone had done well that drive but, as Willie began ladling soup from flasks in the back of his Land-Rover, no one mentioned Flin's two.

'Thanks ever so much for this, Willie,' said Flin as he waited his turn for soup.

'Pleasure, pleasure. Come and have another crack, only, Flin, watch it a bit, eh? Think that last one might have been just a tad low.'

Flin felt his heart stop and the colour drain from his face. Even he knew shooting low was considered the ultimate in bad form.

'Really? Willie, I am so sorry,' he stammered. 'Honestly I –'

Willie held up a hand to stop him. Any form of scene would only make matters worse. 'Anyway, glad there've been a few birds about. Can be a temperamental lot sometimes.'

Then one of the older guns came over and asked Willie whether he'd managed to get any fishing up in Scotland that summer. Flin listened, unable to add to the conversation, his mind racing with shame and a degree of humiliation he did not know were possible.

After lunch, Flin declined the offer of a 'spot of duck shooting' and, having thanked Willie profusely, left. Nothing more had been said about his *faux pas*; none of the others mentioned it. Perhaps the heavy, cold rain that had started to fall soon after the fourth drive had distracted them. Flin had thrust his hands deep into his pockets, felt the raindrops run down his face, and trudged between drives, only going for anything that meant raising his gun to almost perpendicular levels. After the last drive, Teddy said cheerily, 'Bag a few then?' while over lunch the others chatted with a polite lack of interest whenever they were caught with no one else to talk to. But it was with a sense of enormous relief that Flin got into his car and drove home. Perhaps he was over-reacting. Perhaps it wasn't such a big deal. But the thought of earning the disapproval of the one person who had treated him with kindness and affability was bitterly disappointing.

The following day, Flin wiped the condensation away from the window and peered out towards the yard. The sky was still an even all-over grey with no let-up in the rain.

'Still raining,' he said loudly.

'Oh,' said Tiffany. She was reading a Battle of Britain memoir on the sofa in the sitting room. Iain had phoned, and the making of the documentary was back on, and could she start work at the end of November? Flin and Tiffany were delighted. The money would be a godsend. Country living *was* much cheaper, but even so, Flin's two credit cards were fast approaching critical levels of debt. The animals, buying furniture, not to mention smart new caps and cartridges, had taken their toll. And Willie had been in no position to kick up a fuss, as working for him had always been a temporary arrangement.

'D'you want some tea?' he shouted from the kitchen. No reply. 'Tiff? Tea?'

'No, thanks.'

Addy stood behind him, as bored as he was with the rain. 'When's it going to stop, eh?' Flin asked her, stooping to tickle her behind the ear. 'What's it been? Four days now almost without let-up.' Addy began to gently chew on his hands. 'Ow,' said Flin, as one of her incisors dug too hard into his thumb, 'go and chew your slipper, not me.' Tiffany suddenly had a lot of research work to do, and there was no one else to chat with. The rain made him feel even more isolated. Nor was there was much excitement to be gained from sliding about the slippery courtyard to feed the pigs and birds, or squelching down the lane for Addy's daily walk.

'Sometimes this place is like a bloody desert island,' said Flin, stomping into the sitting room and plonking himself down next to Tiffany. Addy followed and sat balefully at his feet.

'I thought it didn't rain on desert islands,' said Tiffany, without looking up from her book.

'OK, well, sometimes this place feels like a *wet* desert island then.'

'Why don't you read a book if you're bored?'

'I suppose I could.'

'Or you could go for a long walk and just accept you're going to get wet.'

'Maybe,' said Flin doubtfully. He picked up the latest copy of *Country Smallholding Monthly* from the coffee table, flicked through it, then put it back down again. Going to his nearest newsagent in town and getting this and his weekly edition of *Farmers Weekly* no longer caused quite the same tingle of excitement it had when they'd first arrived.

'I'd go to the pub if it was open,' he sighed, 'but they don't have all day opening hours up here.'

'Come on, Flin, don't be so feeble. Surely you can think of something to do,' Tiffany said sternly, putting down her book and frowning at him.

'I'm just hacked off, that's all. I feel as though I can't be bothered to do anything.' He paused for a moment, staring out of the window. 'Perhaps I will go for a walk. Along the Wall. Zip up and brave the elements. Don't suppose you want to come?'

Tiffany kissed him. 'I'm going to stay and read this. But go and get rid of your grump, OK?' She pulled a long face, then grinned at him.

The wind bit hard across Win Sill, so that the rain stung his face.

Digging his hands into his pockets, he turned to Addy, skulking behind him. 'Come on, Addy, don't be a wimp,' he told her, 'it's bracing and good for us.'

It wasn't just the rain that was bothering him. It was lots of things. Everything. Perhaps he *had* been too blinkered. He always let himself do this: throughout his life, he knew he tended to rush at new ideas or crazes with enormous enthusiasm and then be disappointed. It had never occurred to him that people were basically the same the country over: suspicious of strangers, wary of anything new. Generally bigoted and small-minded. Being unpopular had been his biggest shock. He'd always thought it was easy to make friends. But maybe that was because, up till now, he had surrounded himself with people of a similar age and interests. Up here, though, it was different. The truth of it was, he realized, Willie and his landed friends existed in a world in which he did not belong. But nor was he a part of Melvyn's or Callum's world either. He wished they hadn't seen him shooting with the 'nobs', as Melvyn had called them. Cavorting with the other side. No, he was stuck in the middle. It wasn't something he'd ever paused to consider during his former dreams of rural bliss.

At least his friends could always come and stay, as several already had. And he did now have Addy. He looked at her tenderly. She was only little, but was bravely walking on through the rain, her normally large brown eyes squinting in the wind. At least she adored him. Or, at least, he thought she did. And obviously so did Tiffany. Where would he be without her? She was so brilliant, far more consistent and level-headed than him. If she was feeling as disappointed as he was, she never showed it. Perhaps growing up in the Outback had been better training. His feet squelched beneath him, syrupy mud spattering his boots and trousers.

The Katrina problem at work was another cause for anxiety. It was as though he always had to be on his guard, watching out for her attempts to sabotage him. Only the week before, he'd walked in on her very obviously talking about him to two of the assistants. Their conversation suddenly stopped, the assistants looking down with reddening faces, embarrassed to be so obviously caught out.

'Well, *some* of us have a lot of work to do,' she'd said, a false end to their little chat, and marched past him, her long hair sashaying from side to side as she disappeared down the corridor. What had that been all about? And why was she implying he didn't pull his weight? He knew it was ridiculous to get so upset about it, but he'd hoped by being nice to everyone and not adopting her own Machiavellian tactics he would win the day. Maybe he still would, but it seemed to be taking a lot longer than he'd hoped.

A couple of hikers appeared up ahead. Otherwise he hadn't seen anyone from the moment he'd parked the car. He walked towards them, a middle-aged couple who beamed as they drew near.

'Nice weather you have here,' grinned the man. He had an American accent.

'Yes, sorry about that,' apologized Flin. 'I hope it improves for you.'

They acknowledged with a wave and strode past. The man had been wearing a baseball cap with 'NYC' written on the front. New York. That was where his old friend Jessica was. Still, not for much longer. Next week she was coming back for a few days and he and Tiffany were going to go down to London to see her. He couldn't wait. She was one of his oldest friends and he hadn't seen her since the previous New Year's Eve. They spoke quite a lot, and e-mailed each other regularly, but it would be great to see her again. He also felt excited about going back to London and seeing everyone else. Lucie was organizing a big supper party on the Saturday night. He hadn't seen her or Ben since he'd left London, and it would be good to catch up with them too. And Harry and Jenny. A big dinner party, just like the old times. Lots of people who liked him and whom he liked back. It would be the first time he'd been back to town since leaving the previous July. Now it was October. Four months. He turned and looked out across the windswept uplands of Northumbria. Faint outlines of raincloud hurried across the grey-green landscape, the rain almost horizontal. So bleak and unforgiving. Thank God he hadn't been born a Roman soldier, he thought to himself. But this was his home now, this under-populated tract of land at the top of England.

Perhaps he had over-romanticized his childhood. Certainly, when he thought of the valley in Wiltshire where he grew up, of the long avenue of beeches leading down the hill and the church at the bottom, the trees were always in full leaf, the sun always shining. Would he think the same way of Northumbria in ten years' time? Would the image in his mind's eye be of the amazing colours of high summer, and the skylarks twittering in the field in front of Standing Stone Farmhouse? Or would it be one of grey driving rain over the uplands? He looked down at Addy. She had stopped, her tail low, and was looking up at him pleadingly, her body and legs shivering silently.

'Come on then, let's go home,' he told her, patting her sodden head.

'Do you think the animals will be all right?' Flin asked Tiffany as he chewed at his fingernails.

'I'm sure they will. Stop worrying about it,' she told him, linking her arm through his and resting her head on his shoulder. Outside, Yorkshire then Lincolnshire whistled past as the train hurried them further towards London. Tiffany had come up with the brilliant idea of asking Jenny's mother, Mrs Albright, whether she would mind looking in on the pigs and birds and giving them their feed. Originally, they'd planned to take Addy with them, but Mrs Albright had agreed to look after her too. She had lived on a farm herself, she explained, when she'd been a girl, so it would be fun to have this little reminder of her youth. Flin, in addition to detailed typed notes, had laid out the various feeds in carefully arranged and marked bags in one of the sheds, and then painstakingly talked her through everything.

'That should be straightforward enough,' said Mrs Albright simply.

'And if there're any problems – any problems at all – here's a list of contact numbers,' he said, handing over a further list.

Tiffany laughed. 'I'm sorry, Mrs Albright. Ignore him. He's just over-anxious about going away.'

'You never know though,' said Flin, 'it's far better to plan for everything.'

'But, darling, we're going away for one night, not two months.'

'Sorry,' said Flin, looking sheepish, 'it's just this is the first time we've left them.'

'Don't worry – I promise I'll follow your directions very carefully.' Mrs Albright winked at Tiffany. Then she added, 'And I want a full report on my daughter in return.'

'Fair deal,' Flin had laughed. He and Tiffany were as keen to hear all about Jenny and Harry's reunion as Jenny's mother. Up in Northumberland, they both felt somewhat out of the loop. The train thundered on southwards, so far on time. Flin continued to stare out of the train window, the book on his lap unread. Of course they were kept up to date with most of the gossip, but there was no substitute for actually discussing the minutiae over a beer in the pub, or sitting round a dinner table and arguing over a six-way analysis of why such-and-such should never marry so-and-so. Telephone gossip always tended to be diluted. Seeing everyone together again was going to be really good fun.

Flin and Tiffany had arranged to stay with Harry and Jenny, so, having met up with them first and dropped off their bags, they all headed off to Clapham together. Ben had said they should come early so they could see Thomas before he went to bed, and so by half past six, the four of them were outside the house in Bennerley Road.

The door opened. There was Ben. Flin gave him a huge bear-hug.

'It's *so* damn good to see you again!' he told him. 'But where's Lucie? And Jessica?'

'I'm here,' said Lucie, joining them in the hallway, a grubby-faced Thomas in her arms, 'but Jessica's in the bathroom getting ready. She's already been there nearly an hour, so it's good to see some things never change.'

'I'll go and chivvy her along,' Flin laughed, and bounded up the stairs. 'Jessica?' he called outside the bathroom. Dense wafts of lotions and scent oozed from underneath the door.

'Flin? Hello, darling!'

'Hurry up, will you?'

'All right, all right, give me a chance. I'll just be two minutes.'

'She says she'll be down in a couple of minutes,' Flin told the rest of the gathering downstairs. Ben was busily fixing drinks, while Lucie tried to wipe Thomas's face.

'Britain could be invaded tomorrow, but nothing, not anything, gets in the way of Jessica and her me-time, especially something as insignificant as old friends coming to see her,' said Lucie. They all laughed. Lucie was right, Flin thought to himself, but Jessica's apparent inability to change in any way was one of her most endearing qualities. The same could hardly be said for the rest of them. Flin felt quite shocked by how pale and drawn Lucie looked. She had always been something of a rival for Jessica when it came to style and glamour, but since he'd last seen her, she seemed to have somewhat let herself go. Her hair had grown unkempt and her face, so naturally pretty, looked blotchy and tired. More startling were the clothes she was wearing: old leggings and one of Ben's over-sized shirts. The contrast was even greater once Jessica appeared.

'Sorry, darlings, but you know me. I just can't bear being rushed in the bathroom,' she told them as she swept into the room.

'Hello, darling,' Flin grinned, standing up and hugging her tightly.

'Careful,' she told him, 'I don't want you to crush my new jacket.'

'Of course not, how stupid of me.' Flin laughed. 'Great new hair-do.'

'Yes, well, I thought I'd go short for a change.'

After the kisses and welcomes, Flin sat back on the sofa next to Tiffany, his mood light and contented. Ben passed round more drinks, while Tiffany, Jenny and Harry took it in turns to hold Thomas, under the watchful gaze of Lucie.

'Here's to Ben and Lucie,' said Flin, raising his glass, 'and to everyone being together.'

'Yes, it's so lovely to see everyone,' said Jessica. Turning to Flin and Tiffany, she added, 'You two look just the same. I was expecting you to be wearing checked shirts, with straw in your hair and deep ruddy complexions.'

'It's been raining virtually non-stop for the last couple of weeks,' said Tiffany, 'so not much opportunity to be outdoors and hearty.'

'It's positively tropical down here at the moment compared to Northumberland,' added Flin.

'Poor Flin's been bored witless,' Tiffany continued.

'Surely not,' put in Ben, 'I thought you could never be bored in the country, Flin.'

'It can be boring wherever you are when it's raining all the time,' replied Flin defensively.

Jessica came to his rescue. 'Well, you should try a New York winter. Honestly, I don't think I've ever been so cold in all my life. I was practically a permanent ice-block from January to March, I felt so frozen.'

Lucie, still preoccupied with Thomas, said, 'Well, if you will insist on living away from all your friends in a country with a stupid climate, what can you expect? I think you should come back immediately.' Without waiting for a reply, she stood up. 'Time to put the babe to bed, I think. Wave goodnight to everyone, Thomas.' She lifted her son's hand and moved it up and down. Thomas looked nonplussed. 'Are you going to say goodnight to him, Jessica?'

'Of course, as long as he doesn't dribble all over me.'

'Such a tender godmother,' sighed Lucie.

'I'll be brilliant when he's older. I'm just not very good with babies. You can't complain – I've never hidden the fact. But I'll be fine once he's learnt to eat properly.'

Ben looked anxiously at Lucie, clearly expecting her to react, but she said nothing.

'I'd like to say goodnight to him,' said Harry, suddenly standing up and taking him from Lucie.

'What a natural,' said Ben, clearly pleased his friend was showing so much interest. Flin noticed Jenny smile happily too.

At supper Flin sat next to Jessica and Lucie, who both peppered him with questions about his move up north.

'It seems just such a big move,' said Jessica, 'bigger in many ways than me going to New York. I mean, at least that's another big cosmopolitan city.'

'Exactly,' added Lucie. 'I just don't know how you manage without twenty-four-hour shops and decent coffee.'

'Yes, but coming back here, I found myself wondering how you managed with all the grime and filth and ludicrous number of people,' said Flin. 'I know it's only been four months, but honestly, it was quite a shock. Getting to Harry's on the Tube was a bloody nightmare. No escalators working, and everything hot and sticky. I forget how clean the air is up where we are. I reached Harry's and immediately had to wash my face and hands, I felt so grimy.'

'But all that mud,' said Jessica, 'I don't know how you can put up with it.'

'I know. Dreadful stuff that mucks up your Versace jeans,' said Flin. 'How we can stand it, I just don't know.'

'Seriously though, Flin,' said Lucie, 'don't you get bored with mud and puddles?'

'Not at all, it's not as though there isn't any paving or tarmac up there. It is possible to avoid it, and anyway, it's only been in the past few weeks that there's been any mud. It was really dry all summer. And I'd rather walk in mud than be surrounded by endless amounts of litter and graffiti.'

'And you're not in any way bored up there? Not missing your long-lost friends in London?' teased Lucie.

'Well, yes, I do miss everyone. But you know, people come up to stay. Harry's been up, so have Geordie and Molly. You two and Ben are just about the only people we haven't seen. But I promise, there's so much to do – loads of walking, things to see, animals to look after. It's great. There's even a local cricket team.'

'Hm, I'm not convinced, I'm afraid,' said Lucie.

'You don't have to be,' Flin pointed out, 'which is why you still live here.'

A cry from upstairs interrupted the conversation.

'I'll go,' said Lucie, looking at Ben and pushing back her chair.

As soon as Lucie was out of earshot, Flin said to Jessica quietly, 'You've got to sort her out.'

'Darling, I'm as shocked as you are. My God, she's let herself go!' Jessica leant in towards him. 'And poor Ben – he's so edgy!'

Flin glanced at Ben, who was deep in conversation with Harry and Jenny at the other end of the table. 'I know, it's amazing. What are you going to say then?'

'I'm not sure yet, but she needs to pull her socks up. Ben told me she's even cancelled some of her magazine subscriptions.'

Flin grinned. 'Things must be bad.'

'Seriously though, darling, are you sure you're all right all that way up north? We're all a bit worried about you too.'

'Are you?' Flin was touched.

'Of course we are. We know how you love to get all excited about things without always thinking them through. Lucie and I wondered whether you'd just over-reacted to your mugging.'

'Well, that did play a big part, I suppose, but no, we've definitely made the right decision. Obviously it's not all sweetness and light, but then what is? There're flip-sides to everything. The way of life up there is much more how I want to live. And a much better place to bring up kids. I wish you could come up, see the house and the pigs and everything. It's a great set-up.'

'Kids? Something you're not telling me?'

'Not at all, but you know, at some point I think we'll want to try.'

'And marriage?'

'No. I can't see us getting round to it. I think we both like it the way it is.'

'Fair enough. Just think, I could have been like you, living in the country, but I'd probably have kids already. That was what Titus wanted – for me to move straight up to his farm in Norfolk and start breeding.'

'Do you ever regret turning him down?'

'I don't know. Sometimes. I do miss him. A lot, even now.'

'But you wanted different things then. You weren't ready to be all grown up and settled at that point in your life. And it would have been much harder to always wear designer clothes if you lived on a farm.'

'It would, wouldn't it? Just imagine, what a nightmare! How would I ever have survived?' She laughed.

'Do you think you will come back soon, though?'

'In the spring actually. Don't tell anyone, because it's not confirmed, but it does look that way. So you see, I'll see you again before you know where you are. And then I promise I'll come up. You know, darling, I do miss everyone, but to be honest, being the other side of the Atlantic hasn't affected any of my good friendships. By our age, you should know who are going to be your friends for life. I mean, you and I still speak on the phone, we still communicate regularly. I may not have seen you since New Year, but do you feel out of touch? Of course not. We've carried on tonight as though we only saw each other last Thursday. In many ways, being in the States has just helped me ditch all those friends I used to feel I ought to keep in touch with but could never really be bothered with. You might miss us by being in Northumberland, but you'll never lose touch. At least, not with the friends that count.'

The following day, on the train heading back to Newcastle, Flin thought about the previous evening. Jessica had been right about friendships. The important ones would always remain. As she'd pointed out, they *were* still as close as ever, despite her being in New York. And he was still very much in touch with Josh, even though he really was on the other side of the world in Sydney. And as Tiffany was continually pointing out, it was always going to take time to be properly accepted in a small community such as Cotherwick. Perhaps he didn't need to slot into some particular group of people. Perhaps he just needed to stop worrying about everything, and take the rough with the smooth a bit more.

The fields and trees rushing past him outside comforted him. London had seemed a horribly unnatural environment in which to live. No matter how despondent he might feel at times, he realized he could never again live in the capital. Despite the rain, and sneering neighbours, the countryside was the place for him.

'Good to be back, isn't?' said Tiffany, as the train pulled into Durham.

'Isn't it? Home again,' agreed Flin. 'I can't wait to see Addy and all the animals again. I've missed not hearing the cock crowing and the geese burbling away. So much nicer than listening to traffic and police sirens.'

'I agree,' said Tiffany. 'It's not until you leave some things that you realize how fond you've become of them. I love our geese.'

They finally reached Newcastle, and walked over to their car, still parked where they'd left it, and still smelling of dog. Slinging their bags in the back, Flin kissed Tiffany and drove them out past the Vickers factory, away from the city and onto the Military Road. The familiarity soothed him. This was home, this was where they now belonged.

As soon as they stopped the car, a couple of feathers, gently blown by the breeze, landed on the windscreen. Tiffany, worry etched across her face, looked at Flin.

'Something's happened,' he said, momentarily unable to move.

'Come on,' said Tiffany, 'let's go and look.' They'd already collected Addy, who bounded out of the car and into the narrow strip between the house and the barns.

Pushing open the gate and turning into the yard, Flin nearly tripped over the remains of one of their geese, entrails strewn across the mud. Feathers were everywhere. A half-eaten chicken lay across the other side by the paddock. Crows, just disturbed, cawed angrily and took to flight.

'Jesus,' he said, marching towards the big barn. The doors were still padlocked, but along one of the walls disturbed soil and a small, newly created tunnel provided clear evidence of the break-in. Inside, carnage reigned. Two more chickens lay dead on the ground. Feathers covered the floor.

'Oh no!' cried Tiffany, following Flin and clasping her hands to her face. Four of the geese emerged from the shadows and a further seven chickens cowered in the corner, but it had still been a considerable massacre.

Flin looked about him, then stooped to pick up a long, dark green tail feather.

'Bastards even got the Sussex cock,' he said bitterly, 'plus two geese and five chickens.' Addy, sensing the air of gloom, sat humbly at his feet.

'How could this be?' said Tiffany incredulously. 'Mrs A. said they were all fine when she came round this morning.'

'Fuck knows,' said Flin, 'but we need to get that hole filled in straight away, or they'll be back for the others.'

With a mixture of soil, rubble from one of the old sheds, and boards, they stopped the hole, and with a shovel, Flin scraped up the remains of the birds in the yard and in the barn. One by one, he watched them slide off the steel and into a black bin-liner, heavy and stiff. Tying the top tightly, he then buried it at the far end of their garden. Nothing since they'd moved had made him feel more depressed. Not the cricket, nor Number Two's escape, nor the neighbours. They were nothing compared to the anger he felt at this desecration.

The next evening, as Flin took Addy for a walk, he met Melvyn coming up the track towards him.

'Sorry to hear about your break-in,' he muttered.

'Thanks,' said Flin, waiting for the snide remark to follow.

'Them foxes are blighters. Sometimes it doesn't matter how much you make a place like Fort Knox, they still seem to get through.'

Flin nodded.

'It's one thing putting a goose into your own pot, but quite another seeing them bloody and strewn all over the place,' Melvyn continued, leaning on his stick and eyeing Flin.

'Well, you did say foxes were a problem round here, so I was warned, I suppose.'

Melvyn chuckled hoarsely. 'Aye, they've had quite a few of mine down the years. Still, at least your pigs seem to be under control. No more tearing off into the fields.'

'Yes, I suppose that's something,' agreed Flin.

There was a pause, but not an awkward one, then Melvyn said, 'So, enjoy your shooting last weekend?'

'Sort of,' said Flin. 'They're a snooty lot though. Not really my cup of tea, I'm afraid. I'm sure I broke every rule in the book.'

Melvyn chuckled. 'Different world, isn't it? Ah, well.' He laid a hand on Flin's shoulder, then ambled off, his bow-legs carrying him down the lane, his dog at his heels. Flin called Addy, and headed back home, his step suddenly lighter.

CHAPTER SEVENTEEN

Harry in Arcadia

Late summer and autumn that year were one of the happiest times of Harry's life, as day followed day of cocooned bliss. Quickly reverting to the climate of their first romance, his and Jenny's togetherness was one that excluded all others. Harry barely saw his old friends, ignoring the messages left for him. He needed to devote his time to Jenny only, and to spend it with an intensity that made up for the years without her.

They'd adopted this exclusivity from the outset. She'd arrived in London on the Saturday, nine days after he'd left Chenonceaux. Her train was late, and Harry had waited with mounting anxiety as floods of arrivals swept past him and out onto the open concourse of Waterloo. She'd been imprecise about her arrival time – there was no two o'clock train, the closest being one that came in at one-fifty-six. That had to be it, and that was the one that was late, but as the minutes ticked by, doubts began to creep in. Had he definitely got the right train? What if she'd managed to catch an earlier one and he'd missed her? Further arrivals appeared, from Lille, from Brussels, the corresponding information vanishing from the overhead screens. More people swarmed down the concourse. It wasn't until Harry's jangled nerves were at breaking point that he finally spotted her, laden with cases and bags. Just one of thousands passing through that day, a nobody; but not to him. He rushed towards her, kissing and holding her, breathing in her scent deeply until he truly believed it was her, returning for him, his nagging three days of doubt finally dispelled.

Eventually he pulled away.

'Are you OK?' he asked.

Jenny nodded.

'You sure?'

'Yes, just about.' She forced a smile.

'And Phil, he . . . ?'

'I think he'll be OK. Really. I'll tell you everything later. It's been a horrible week though. Telling him it was over was the hardest thing I've ever had to do in my life. And then the packing up.' She raised a hand to the corner of her eye.

'I'm sorry,' said Harry.

Jenny kissed him again, then, brightening, said, 'I can't believe I'm here. That I've really done it. I feel quite shaky.'

'Come on, let's go.'

There was so much to do, so much to show her and catch up on. Driving away from Waterloo, he kept glancing at her, still unable to accept his enormous good fortune.

'Thank you,' he'd told her, 'thank you for doing this, for coming back.'

Her eyes seemed to twinkle at him. 'I feel so light-headed, almost giddy,' she told him. 'Now I'm here, I know we've done the right thing. It's madness, but the right kind of madness. I love you so much, Harry, I really do.'

Harry beamed, so deliriously happy he found it hard to concentrate on the road. She'd sacrificed everything for him. As they drew nearer his road, he began worrying about what she'd think of his flat. He desperately wanted to impress her and for her to love it as much as he did.

'Here we are,' he said, struggling to slot the key into the lock, until he steadied his right hand with the other. He led her up the stairs, carrying most of her bags, pausing only once they were in the main sitting-room area.

'It's amazing, Harry,' she said, putting down her bags and looking about her with an open-mouthed smile. 'Will you give me a proper tour? Now?'

He kissed her. 'Of course. Follow me.' At various points she paused to inspect something more closely – usually his pictures – uttering superlatives at regular intervals.

'Can't wait to try a bath in here,' she said of the bathroom, 'these murals are *wonderful*.' Or the gallery: 'How fantastic. I love it!' And then gazing up at the overhead skylight: 'This is amazing. I can't believe you did this yourself.'

Bursting with pride, Harry said, 'Well, I may not have become an architect, but at least those years at Cambridge were good for something.'

'I love it, Harry. I really love it. Lucky old me, being able to stay in such a stylish place.'

They were now standing on opposite sides of the bed, and Harry paused, desperate to make love to her, to see every inch of her body, and feel her wrapped around him. But at the same time, he was struck by momentary panic. He wanted it to be perfect, for *her* to think it was perfect. He'd never felt these kinds of doubts before. It just suddenly seemed such a big deal. He gazed across at her. She was looking around, an arm on the iron bedpost. The sun shining through the skylight bathed her in light, and Harry wondered whether this was done for his benefit only, a wondrous gift from above. Beneath her skirt lay the outline of her legs, while the shadows across her T-shirt accentuated the curves of her body and the soft lines of her face.

'Nice bed,' she said coyly.

Harry, rapt by the vision of loveliness before him, still stared, speechless. Slowly, she moved around until she stood next to him. Putting her hand on his face, Jenny leant up and kissed him, her lips soft and moist on his. Harry closed his eyes. At that moment he believed himself very close to heaven.

They barely ventured out of the flat that first weekend. A dizzying day-and-a half of hedonism. On the Sunday afternoon, they lay together in the bath, a light breeze fluttering across them from the half-open window. His hands gently, almost absent-mindedly, rubbed soap over her belly and breasts.

'My tummy's bigger than the last time you saw it,' she said.

'Hardly,' Harry replied.

'It is. Look, it's got a little curve to it.'

'Well, I like it. I can't bear just skin and bones. That curve is both soft and feminine.'

Jenny said nothing for a moment, then she said, 'I don't think Phil fancied me. Not really.'

'Course he did. You're gorgeous.'

She clutched his hand. 'I don't think he did. I think I properly realized that just after you turned up. When I saw you on the doorstep like that, I felt so confused. I cursed you, actually. I cursed you and slumped to the floor, wondering what the hell you were thinking of, springing on me like that. I thought about the life I was making with Phil, and how I was really quite happy, and then you suddenly turned up and upset everything. I can't believe that was only two weeks ago. Seems ages ago, doesn't it? Another lifetime.'

'And one I never want to go back to.'

'Anyway, eventually I picked myself up and went upstairs to have a shower. I thought it might help. Relax me, make me see things more clearly. That's when I realized Phil and I weren't right. In fact I'd probably been thinking that since Northumberland, but had put it out of my mind. I can remember feeling the hot water pounding and soothing my head, and streaming all down my face and body. That was one good thing about that house – it did have a great shower.'

'But now you've got a great bath.'

'That's true.' She laughed lightly. 'I was in the shower, soaping myself, remembering when my belly had once been flat. Then I worked the soap up to my breasts. I hadn't thought about them for years. They were just there. Hardly huge, rather boring really. And that got me thinking about my legs. They were all right, but I suddenly wished they were longer. I hadn't thought much about any part of my body for ages, because I had no reason to. Phil never mentioned it, never said whether I looked good or bad. And then I thought about you, and all your passion and energy, when my life had so clearly become passionless. I wondered whether you'd meant what you said. You were always a romantic – it was one of the things that attracted me to you in the first place.'

'Really? I don't know that I am particularly.' Harry was genuinely surprised.

'Course you are. The only person I've ever met who is so unashamedly.'

'I'll take that as a compliment. So when did you decide to come down to the river?'

'I don't know. I think I'd just convinced myself that this was nonsense, that I was engaged to Phil and that was that. But then I felt guilty. I suppose I wanted to see you in the same way that I'd wanted to phone you the week before. I did that when Phil was out. How I'd ever have explained the phone bill, I don't know. But I must have still been in denial, because what I told myself was that it was a very long way for you to come just to be shown the door. As I dried myself, I began hoping you *had* gone to the river, and not jumped straight into your car and driven off again. I did feel calmer, and I wanted the chance to just talk to you. After all, it wasn't often there were friendly faces in Chenonceaux. I thought I'd persuade you that your mad declaration was just romantic nonsense, and that you couldn't possibly really love me. Especially since this Julia person sounded so amazing. A stunning blonde with big tits and great legs.'

'Who on earth told you that?'

'Willie.'

'Who's he?'

'A cousin of Julia's who owns Flin and Tiffany's house.'

'Believe me, she's got nothing on you.'

'Well, that's what I thought then. So I decided I'd go down to the river and talk to you sensibly, and then hopefully we could move on, and become really good friends instead. But as I walked along the river, I found myself yearning for you still to be there.'

'Thank God I was. Clearly, it was meant to be.'

'Anyway, I was obviously right about Phil, because really he took my decision surprisingly well. Annoyingly well, actually. I think he felt a bit hurt and humiliated, but he was definitely rather relieved too. And I'm not just saying that to make myself feel better. I think we both knew we weren't head over heels in love with each other. It was awful, though, packing up and going. I really hope, one day, Phil and I will be friends again. Because he was a good friend to me.'

'Will he stay in France?'

'I think so. For the moment. The worst bit was giving him back the ring. Neither of us knew what to say. So he just held it clenched in his fist for a moment, then walked out of the room. But already the idea of being married to him for forty years seems totally incomprehensible.'

Jenny was silent for a moment. 'I think I've just admitted all my deepest thoughts and secrets to you. But I want you to know, to understand why I'm here. I suppose I've never stopped loving you, you see.'

Only much later, as they lay in each other's arms, the faint neon glow of London night the only light, did they talk about what they were actually going to do.

'You don't need to worry about that,' Harry told Jenny when

she brought the subject up. 'I've just got a huge cheque from the restaurant mural, which will last us several months, and another commission in the West Country for a couple of weeks' time, which will be well paid. Can't we have a short sabbatical?'

'But, Harry, I have to work. I can't just live here for the rest of my life, however nice that might be.'

'Why not?'

'Seriously, Harry. We haven't thought this through at all.'

'OK, this is the plan: we have a holiday now. We could go somewhere for a week. Scotland, or one of those last-minute holidays abroad. I've just got a very small job to finish, which will take a day or so, but we could be out of here on Wednesday.'

'Not France, if that's OK with you.'

'Not France, certainly. Then the week after that I've got this smallish job in Cornwall painting some murals. I haven't finished the plans yet, but I could do some of it on holiday. I've already got a room booked in a pub down there. You could come too. Then after that you can get some supply work until you find a proper teaching job. Or you can do something entirely different. Whatever you want. In the meantime, we live in perfect harmony here.'

'You want me to stay here then? With you?'

'Of course. No one else lives here. It's the perfect set-up, isn't it?' They lay facing each other, their heads very close together, Harry running his fingers slowly through her hair.

'Well, if you're sure,' said Jenny eventually. 'I mean, I did think I'd like to go back to teaching properly. I'm supposed to be a fully qualified primary-school teacher. Teaching English as a foreign language was a complete waste of my time, to be honest.'

'Brilliant,' said Harry brightly, 'because then you'll get lots of holidays and since I'm self-employed I can take time off and we can do lots of wonderful things together. Now, doesn't the future look damn bright?'

Jenny laughed. 'I suppose it does, when you put it like that.

And I have got a little bit of money saved away, so I don't need to be dependent on you.'

'Jenny, honestly, I've just had a big pay-out. You don't need to worry at all for the moment. I was fantastically broke when I got back from France, but that's all changed. When I get short, I'll let you know.'

Jenny kissed him. 'Perfect,' she said. 'Were you always so strong and masterful?'

'Always, baby.' He grinned and kissed her back, then, pulling her towards him, added, 'But I just want it to be the two of us for a little while. Do you think we could be selfish and not really see anyone else for a few weeks? I feel we've a lot of catching up to do and I need you all to myself to do that properly.'

'All right. Just you and me it is.' She smiled at him. 'Harry, you've made me very happy. Very happy indeed.'

Harry closed his eyes, wondering what he'd done to deserve such incredible good fortune.

They went to Greece. The following evening the two of them sat side by side at his computer and looked up the very best dot com deals. In the end it became a toss-up between a week on a Greek island and a tiny cottage on the west coast of Ireland.

'Ireland could be good,' said Jenny. 'Lots of rugged coastal walking and fresh air.'

'And Guinness,' added Harry.

'But it would be much hotter in Greece. Could get a bit of a tan, drink lots of wine, feel lazy.'

'And feel romantic in the clear-blue Mediterranean sea.'

'Exactly,' agreed Jenny.

'Corfu then?'

'I think so.'

They went two days later.

And they did drink plenty of wine, and spent a great deal of time frolicking in the sea. The sun shone down, turning their skin a healthy dun, and making each even more attractive to the other. Harry particularly liked the way the sun brought out the slight freckles on Jenny's face and shoulders. During the day, when they weren't eating, sunbathing, or swimming in the sea, they hired a moped and toured the island, visiting the mountain villages with their bleached white houses. In the evenings they ate at cheap restaurants, then returned to their hotel to sleep and make love. Invariably, Harry would wake first, and spend ages gazing at Jenny, learning every inch of her body, from the tiny mole behind her ear to the pale scar above her knee.

They came back and almost immediately left for Cornwall. If Jenny resented not being with Harry all the time, she never said so. He made quite sure he allowed plenty of time to spend with her, and they both agreed about how right they'd been to go to Corfu, when they now had as much cliff-top fresh air as they could possibly want.

One evening, late in August, Harry finished his day's work and announced to Jenny that he wanted to take her somewhere special.

'Where?' she asked. 'What is it?'

'Somewhere that's important to me. Come on. Grab a jumper and let's go.'

'Give me a clue.'

'No. It's just a place, but a very beautiful one. You'll see.'

It was quite a drive from Helford, where he was working, but Port Quin, on the north coast, was somewhere he'd always meant to revisit and, with Jenny beside him, Harry couldn't think of better circumstances in which to do so. As they turned off the main road, he became silent. He vividly remembered that long, windy road leading to the village. They turned a corner and there, perched high on the cliffs, with the Atlantic stretching away beneath, was the Regency folly of Doyden Castle, guarding the narrow inlet. Harry smiled to himself, then slowly descended the steep hill down to the tiny harbour. A couple of small fishing boats bobbed on the sea in the cove, just as he remembered. The sun, beginning to set over the hill to their right, lit up the mouth of the harbour with sparkling brightness, whilst sheathing the cliffs and the harbour with long shadows and a warm amber glow.

'Well?' said Harry, parking the car. 'What do you think?'

'It's stunning. What is this place?'

'Port Quin. It's where we went on holiday once when we were younger. I must have been eight or nine I suppose. Charlotte was suddenly growing up a bit, and it was one of the last of our proper childhood holidays together. But Mum and Dad always believed in British holidays. They said we lived on a great island with lots to see and do and there was no point going abroad until we knew a bit about the place we lived in. I remember being jealous of friends who disappeared abroad every summer, but now I'm very grateful to Ma and Pa. We had fantastic times, but the one here was definitely the best.'

Jenny took his hand and leant against him, absorbing the view. A few birds sang in the hedgerows behind them, and a lone gull called out over the cliffs rising in front, but otherwise an early evening stillness seemed to have settled over the place. Nothing stirred. Harry led Jenny towards the path that ran up along the cliff over-looking the edge of the inlet, the heat of the day now growing softer.

'I don't want this honeymoon ever to end,' he said wistfully. 'I'm getting used to spending most of my time with you and no one else.'

'I know. But we've done what you suggested and now I've got to find some work. I suppose I'm not really the most ambitious person in the world, but I don't want to waste my time, or my qualifications. When we get back to London, I've really got to get my head down and look hard for a job, you know?'

'Yes, but we should remember this moment. Now. Everything's so perfect: the quiet, the peace, the sea, the rocks. Not a cloud in the sky. Just me sitting next to you. No matter what happens, I always want to think back to *this* moment and feel happy.'

It was in this giddy mood of high romance that they returned to London.

With the sort of good fortune that was becoming a feature of their new life, Jenny managed to get a job in an Islington primary school for a whole term, just a week before the new academic year began. Out of working hours, Jenny and Harry remained inseparable. At weekends they rediscovered London or disappeared for romantic breaks in the country; and during the week they spent their evenings going to films or staying in and eating and playing games. They simply didn't need anyone else when each satisfied the other so completely. By the autumn, they'd still seen almost no one apart from themselves. They rarely phoned anyone and ignored most of the messages on Harry's answer machine. Ben complained vociferously, but it made little difference; although neither Harry nor Jenny articulated as much, somehow friends and family presented an intrusion that threatened to break their spell. By the time Jessica was over, Ben had seen his friend only twice in as many months. In the end he gave up trying. Harry would return to earth eventually; his relationship with Jenny couldn't continue at the same intensity for ever.

Although he hated to think about it, this same thought nagged at Harry too. He'd predicted as much on the cliffs at Port Quin. But as the autumn leaves tumbled from their branches and the days became short and dark, Harry could have been forgiven for not noticing the dark clouds gathering on the horizon. So when the storm finally came, he and Jenny were ill prepared for the swiftness and violence of its arrival.

part four – *winter*

CHAPTER EIGHTEEN

Ben

Ben believed his night on the bridge had been his Road to Damascus; his salvation. Gradually, during the days that followed, a change came about him; not in personality, but in his whole outlook.

By the time he'd finally staggered home that night, it had been nearly four in the morning. Lucie had been fast asleep. The following morning he'd avoided her and slipped back off to work, too ashamed and scared of revealing his guilty secret to really talk to her. Only months before he'd been vowing to love her and look after her until his dying day, and then, after just a few difficult times, he'd nearly betrayed her and everything he'd promised. Nearly thrown away everything he held dear. His behaviour had been contemptible. That morning he'd felt sick at heart.

But that had been his nadir. After lunch, Kate had knocked on his door. At first, his heart had sunk when he saw her, but she'd come to apologize, and beg his forgiveness. She didn't know what had come over her, but if her hangover was anything to go by, she must have been very drunk indeed. Could they still be friends and not let this error of judgement come between them? Ben, recognizing how hard it must have been for her to come and say that, forgave her instantly. Anyway, he wasn't one to bear grudges, and knew he was just as much at fault as her. Their friendship was certainly a bit strained from then on – no more taking it in turn to buy the sandwiches – but it was a great relief to Ben that in such a small office there was no one he had to steer clear of.

But in that simple gesture, Kate taught Ben an important lesson: instead of running away from a predicament, she'd confronted it head on and tried to resolve it. It was not something he'd done with Lucie. Since Thomas's birth, he'd responded to Lucie's mood swings and depressed state by tiptoeing round her and doing his level best to avoid an argument. Burying his head in the sand. No wonder Lucie tried to provoke him. Pretending there was nothing wrong was never going to help her. It wasn't Lucie's problem, it was *their* problem, for them to resolve together, and by him being there for her. Strong and unwavering.

He was surprised that this revelation cheered him up so much. But, at last, he felt he had worked out a strategy that was at least constructive. He'd been in the dark, but just by recognizing how wrong he'd been, he believed he was taking a step in the right direction. For his old Lucie, he'd have done absolutely anything – *anything* – at all; surely he should be prepared to do anything to get his old Lucie back.

He began simply, concentrating on the small things once habitual, lately forgotten. Phoning her a bit more often during the day and not using a heavy workload as an excuse not to ring; then asking her more about how she felt, and taking more obvious interest in everything she and Thomas had been doing. Once a week he made sure he brought flowers home with him, one of his former regular rituals that had been abandoned without him even realizing it. Nor did he just bring her any old bunch. Finding himself a quality city florist, he made sure he ordered her favourites – large tulips, sweet-smelling lilies, or sometimes roses – immaculately wrapped for him to pick up on his way home. He also made a point of trying to notice anything she did about the house, even if it was something as small as tidying the sitting room or changing the sheets on their bed.

Initially, Ben had wondered about buying her something like a necklace too, or some such piece of jewellery as a way of marking this new resolution, but then decided against it. That could come later – for her birthday perhaps, or at Thomas's christening. No, what was needed was something more subtle. That was when he rang Jessica, Lucie's oldest and greatest friend, and pleaded with her to visit from New York. Could she phone Lucie and invite herself over? If she did that, he'd suggest to Lucie they get Flin and Tiffany down, and Harry and Jenny, and a few others. All her old friends.

Jessica played her part perfectly. Ben could see how excited Lucie was at the prospect, although persuading her to invite the others was harder.

'I'm not sure, Ben. It's such an effort and I've become used to not seeing too many people. And then there's Thomas.'

'Look,' Ben had said firmly, 'I'll do all the cooking. Even better, I'll get someone to do it for me, then just before they arrive I'll put it in the oven and no one will know. Flin and Tiffany can stay with Harry, and you won't have to lift a finger, just look like the gorgeous mother you are.'

Lucie had smirked at this. 'Well, I suppose Flin *is* Thomas's godfather, and so is Harry, so it would be good for them to see him, wouldn't it?'

'Exactly. So come on, what do you say?'

'All right, but I must lose some more weight.'

'Fine – we'll both go on a diet.'

Lucie had smiled again. 'You're a very persuasive man, but why are you being so nice at the moment?'

'Isn't a husband allowed to be nice to his wife?'

'Hm, I'm just a bit suspicious, that's all.' But Ben knew she was pleased.

*   *   *

The weekend was a success. Ben had been careful to allow Lucie and Jessica plenty of time on their own, and at the dinner everyone had laughed and drunk and it had seemed just like old times. Jessica's stories of New York and Flin's tales of pigs and locals and their new rural life entertained them all, not least Lucie. Flin, in particular, had made light of his various calamities, but Ben could tell things hadn't quite worked out as his friend had planned. It made him realize he'd been so wrapped up in his problems, he'd forgotten everyone else had difficulties too. No one's life was perfect.

But the following day, with everyone gone and Jessica back in New York, Ben worried that Lucie might retreat once more. What if he'd been wrong? What if it had been the thought of Jessica coming back that had been cheering her up? Now that she was gone, Lucie had nothing to look forward to, just the same old daily routine. Perhaps he might still yearn for her and their old togetherness, but maybe she had already fallen out of love with him.

The seed of this idea took root. The more he thought about it, the more it seemed to make sense: the lack of interest in the bedroom, the stroppiness and now her apparent intention to avoid him as much as possible. She wasn't suffering from any form of post-natal depression; she'd gone off him, as simple as that. This sudden and terrible sense of doom and despair rose with alarming speed, so that by the Monday afternoon, when he phoned and phoned and got no answer, he became convinced she'd left him. By six o'clock that night, mounting paranoia left him reeling. As he walked home from the station, with increasing briskness, he could actually feel the quickening pulse in his neck and the sweat forming on his temples. With utter dread, he slotted the key into the lock and stepped into the hall.

Sweet smells of baking and cooking flooded his nostrils, and then he saw the trail of clothes and silk underwear leading up the staircase. Dumbstruck, Ben called out.

'Lucie? Are you there?' No answer. Tentatively, he began walking up the stairs, confused, not daring to believe what he hoped would be true. At the door of their bedroom, he paused, his mouth hanging open in shocked wonderment.

Silk sheets covered their bed, and half beneath them, half out, lay Lucie, wearing nothing but a flimsy camisole. In her hand she held a glass of wine.

'Hi, baby,' she said.

'Wow,' said Ben, dropping his bag.

'Well, are you going to stand there looking like a startled rabbit, or are you going to come to bed and ravish me?' She'd cut her hair, added a hint of make-up. In fact, she no longer looked like the permanently exhausted brow-beaten mother she'd become, but the gorgeous, seductive Lucie he'd fallen in love with.

'I'm going to come to bed and ravish you,' said Ben, his face breaking into an enormous grin, 'this must be my lucky day.'

They made love with an intensity and passion Ben had almost forgotten.

Afterwards they showered – together – then Lucie, dressed only in her camisole and dressing gown, led Ben downstairs for the supper she'd been preparing all afternoon. Their table was already beautifully laid out.

'Where's Thomas?' said Ben suddenly.

'My mother's looking after him tonight,' she told him, then added, 'and next weekend.'

She disappeared for a moment, then returned with an envelope. 'Here,' she said, handing it to him.

Silently, Ben took it and opened it. Plane tickets, and a hotel voucher. For Venice. Next Friday night.

'My God,' said Ben, unable to stop grinning. 'Thank you. I ... I'm just – well, I ... I can't believe it. I thought you'd left me.'

A tear ran down Lucie's cheek.

'How could I ever do that? I love you, Ben.'

'You don't know how good it is to hear that. I thought you'd fallen out of love with me. Convinced myself. I couldn't get hold of you this afternoon.'

'I *was* here. I wanted to surprise you.'

'You did. It's wonderful, just, just wonderful.'

'I'm sorry, Ben. I'm sorry for everything. For being so awful the last few months.'

'No, I'm sorry. I was thoughtless. The changes, in you, in us, I ran away from them, rather than trying to help. I was wrong.' He looked down, but Lucie, from the other side of the table, took his hand.

'I need to tell you something. To try to explain.'

Ben started to interrupt, to say there was no need.

'No, listen, Ben, it's important. Important that I tell you what I've been feeling. Being a mother is so completely different from what I'd expected. I've always managed my life and other people without any problems and I thought a baby would be the same. Ben, you simply can't have any idea how inadequate I felt those first few weeks. After the initial elation, I think they were the worst days of my life. I couldn't do anything without this baby – it was totally dependent on me for everything and I was crap at looking after it. No one had warned me. No one told me about just how massive the responsibility is, or how a baby totally runs and controls your life. Nor was I ready for the shock of seeing my body change, physically and psychologically. I knew my glands were shooting off all over the place, knew they were affecting my moods and desires, but I was helpless to do anything about it. It was as though I was being force-fed drugs I didn't want to take. And seeing great big flabby folds of flesh was deeply, deeply traumatic. For me, who has been obsessed with style and looking good and been proud of my flat stomach for most of my life, the change was just disgusting – it was so drastic – and I hated myself for it. And on top of that, I just felt so tired. Exhausted all the time. You thought I was letting myself go – well, I was, but because I simply didn't have the energy to tidy things, put everything away, and make delicious dinners. It wasn't just being up all night, it was the constant attention Thomas needed, and the concentration that required. I've never felt real exhaustion like that. It was debilitating, boring and utterly depressing. I didn't make an effort with myself because there was no point. My body looked disgusting and anything nice I put on was immediately covered in baby-gunk. And all that crying, darling. It drove me nuts. You were away at work, you missed out on the worst of it. Honestly, I can see how mothers sometimes lose it and put pillows over their babies' heads. It's a terrible thing to say, I know, but on occasions the noise just became too much. Even when he wasn't crying I felt on edge, wondering when he'd start again. And all the time, this made me feel even more useless and inadequate.' She wiped away a tear.

'And now?' said Ben gently. 'How do you feel now?'

She tried to smile. 'Better. Much better. I feel something like my old self again physically. I think I'm better with Thomas now. And my hormones seem to have settled again. I mean, that night in the restaurant. Leaking milk might not have mattered to anyone else there, but for me it was just about the most humiliating thing that could have happened. I just couldn't believe my body had let me down so badly. And I hadn't really drunk for ages and, well . . . I'm sorry, you know?'

'Forget it, it doesn't matter.' Ben paused a moment. 'We should have talked more. I never really understood what was wrong. I'm sorry I wasn't there for you.'

'I love him now though. Thomas, that is. He's gorgeous and I couldn't imagine life without him. He's got your smile.' She laughed. 'When he smiles or makes funny little faces, it makes everything worth while. We're lucky, very, very lucky.'

'I know,' said Ben simply.

'But let's always be there for each other in the future. I never want to be without you, and I want us to work things out together.'

Ben raised his glass. 'I agree,' he said, 'I'll always love you.'

'Good. That's settled then. Let's eat.'

They made love again that night. Then, later, lay in bed talking in a way they hadn't since before Thomas had been born.

'In a way, I suppose we should be thanking Jessica, you know.'

'Why, what did she say?'

'That I looked a mess, that she was shocked and that you were gorgeous and I ought to pull my finger out.'

Ben laughed. 'What a sensible person she is.'

'And she also told me it was you who really invited her over. That was so sweet of you. I cried when she told me that.' Ben stroked her hair gently. 'And there's one other thing.'

'What?' said Ben.

'It's about the christening. I've postponed it.'

'You've what? How come?'

'You were right. Mum was being annoying about it. She was getting carried away. I want a small affair in our house, just as you suggested. So I thought we could do it in the spring instead.'

Ben rolled over and lay on his back. 'Thank God for that. You can't know how much I was dreading it.'

'So godparents and immediate family only, OK?' said Lucie.

'Very definitely,' said Ben.

By the end of their weekend in Venice, Ben felt his relationship with his wife was closer than it had ever been. They'd come through the difficult times and that had made them stronger. But there was still something else that bothered him. It wasn't just the problems with Lucie he'd run away from. His burying his head in the sand was something he'd developed as a child.

'Luce, I'd like to take Thomas down to see Dad,' he said a few days later when they were back in London.

'OK,' said Lucie. 'Do you want me to come, or would you rather go on your own?'

'I think I should go on my own actually. Do you mind?'

'Course not. When were you thinking?'

'This Saturday, if he's around.'

He was, just as Ben had known he would be. On the phone he'd hoped his father might have sounded a bit more pleased. 'See you about lunchtime then,' he'd said and put the phone down before Ben had properly finished what he was going to say.

Driving down a couple of days later, with Thomas asleep in the baby seat in the back, Ben thought about what he might say to his father. There was so much he wanted to tell him. But most of all, he wanted to apologize. His desertion may not have been so cruel or acute as his mother's, but that was what it had been. Ever since setting off to Cambridge, Ben had turned his back on his father and his family. He'd blamed his father for his having to grow up without a mother. He'd blamed him for the oppressive despair that hung over their house. But he'd seen things through blinkered eyes. Parents were supposed to be perfect, like Harry's. Perfect, like advert families. The sun shining, white teeth, mother and father happy and loving, and proud of their bouncing baby boy.

How could he have ever been so naïve? How could he have ever thought family life would, or could, be like that? And yet what he did have was wonderful. Thomas was happy and healthy. He and Lucie, if anything, were closer than ever. He never again wanted to go through what he had that autumn, but in some perverse way, he recognized those experiences had helped him. Helped him understand a bit more about himself, about Lucie and about family; his family. His life *was* perfect; it was just that his view of perfection had been wrong.

His father's house – once his house too – was largely unchanged from when he'd been a boy. The same pictures still hung on the walls, and the same fifties furniture filled the rooms. Everything was so familiar to Ben, yet so alien too, even the slightly foody smell that permeated every room in the house, save the bathroom. There, Ben realized as he went for a pee, the odour was, as it always had been, one of over-sprayed air freshener and bleach.

'So how are you, Dad?' Ben asked as he came back downstairs. His father was jiggling Thomas on his knee.

'Oh, fine. Not too bad really. Andrew came down last week. He's thinking of leaving Bristol and coming back here.'

'Oh, OK,' said Ben, nodding. He hadn't seen Andrew in over two years.

'How's Lucie?' asked his father, after a short pause. 'I thought she might be coming too.'

'No, well, she, um, went to spend the day with her mum. But she's fine, thanks. Anyway, I thought it might be nice to see you on my own.'

His father nodded thoughtfully, then handed Thomas back and stood up. 'I'd better get our lunch ready.'

'Oh, don't worry about that, Dad,' said Ben hastily. 'I thought we could go out somewhere. To a pub or something. My shout.'

'Would you rather?' said his father, pausing by the door. 'Only I've got something ready.'

'No, no, I just thought – well, I hadn't meant for you to go to any bother.'

'It's not. Really.'

'Then that'd be great. Thanks.'

Ben followed his father into the kitchen and saw the table already very precisely laid out. Two places for them and the old high chair, dug out from the attic and cleaned and dusted for Thomas.

'I'm afraid my eating habits haven't got any more sophisticated, but you still eat steak, don't you?' his father muttered, clattering the grill into the old enamel cooker.

'Of course. Dad, this looks great.'

'And I bought in a bottle of wine. I know how you and Lucie

like your wine. Don't really drink it much myself, so I hope it's OK.' He handed Ben the bottle to uncork, which he did using the corkscrew on the can opener. It was a Bulgarian Cabernet Sauvignon.

'I'm not sure what Thomas eats, but I got some tins of baby food too. It said four to six months on the label, so I hope that's all right,' said his father, producing a selection from one of the cupboards. 'Although I suppose they'll keep.'

'They look perfect.' Ben smiled, and strapped a bib around his son.

The rump steaks were delicious, and Ben ate his hungrily. 'Damn good meat, Dad,' he said through a mouthful.

'Good. I thought since it's a bit of a special occasion, I'd splash out.'

Later, they walked along the beach. The day was quite mild, but even so, Ben made sure Thomas was safely wrapped up in the chest sling. Was this the time for him to talk properly to his father? Ever since they'd arrived, he'd been waiting for the right moment. He desperately wanted to articulate his thoughts, but somehow the words failed him. The companionable silence began to stretch into something more awkward.

'Dad?' said Ben at last as they approached the spectre of the West Pier.

His father turned to him.

'You know you're welcome to come up and stay any time you want, don't you?' Ben said. 'I mean, would you like that? We could visit some sights, go to a play or something. You could see a bit more of Thomas.'

'Thank you. Perhaps I'll take you up on that sometime.'

'Why don't you – soon? Any time, really.'

'How's work then?' asked his father, and Ben felt a stab of irritation at how quickly his father had switched topics.

'Fine. Not quite so busy as normal, I'm glad to say. But, Dad?'

'Yes?'

'Are you OK? I mean, shouldn't you be retiring and enjoying yourself now?'

'Oh, don't you worry about me. I'm fine. What would I do if I didn't work?'

'I don't know. Have some fun. Go abroad, join some clubs. Take up bowling. Whatever. But, you know, I'd gladly help you out if you did want to go away on some kind of trip.'

'That's very good of you, but you hang on to your money. You'll need it for Lucie and Thomas here.' He lifted an arm and gently brushed the back of his hand down Thomas's cheek.

Ben picked up a stone and hurled it into the sea, irritated and frustrated, but wishing he felt neither. Then he stopped and turned, facing his father.

'Look, I suppose, Dad, what I'm trying to say is "Sorry", OK? I'm sorry I've been an ungrateful son. I'm sorry I haven't been here for you, and I'm sorry you live all alone in that house and that you still have to work your arse off even though you should be enjoying an easy retirement. And I'm sorry I blamed you for Mum leaving us like she did.' He stopped suddenly, feeling the blood rushing to his face, then picked up a handful of stones and one after the other flung them as hard as he could towards the sea.

His father looked at him. 'Ben, you're being a fool. The best thing you did was get yourself out of here. If you really want to know, you've made me very proud. You've made something of yourself. Stop being so hard on yourself.'

Ben silently passed Thomas to his father and sat down on the cold pebbles. After his outburst, he suddenly felt at a loss as to how to behave or what to say, overwhelmed by what he'd said and by his father's response.

'But thank you for saying that anyway,' added his father. 'Just promise me something, will you?'

'What?' said Ben, turning to him.

'Don't make the same mistakes I made.'

'What do you mean, Dad?'

'Look after Lucie. Look after Thomas.' His father picked up a pebble and flung it awkwardly out to sea. 'We should probably be heading back, shouldn't we?' Then he turned, and began walking back towards the promenade overlooking the beach.

Later that evening, Ben watched Lucie giving Thomas his bath. His son gurgled and laughed and splashed the water, and Lucie laughed with him, the tension gone from her face. His wife, his son: his family. Perfect.

CHAPTER NINETEEN

Flin

Outside, something clanged. Then footsteps to the side of the house.

'What the hell was that?' said Flin.

'Dunno,' said Tiffany, clutching Flin's jumper. Otherwise, neither of them moved, their bodies tense as they waited for the next sound.

The footsteps drew nearer. Outside the sitting-room window now.

'He's right outside!' said Tiffany in a terrified whisper, the grip on Flin's arm tightening further.

'Sh, ssh!' said Flin, praying they weren't both about to be shotgunned to death by a lone Northumbrian maniac.

Whoever it was tapped on the window.

'Who's there?' Flin called out uncertainly, as both he and Tiffany cringed further into the depths of the sofa.

'Callum,' came the muffled reply. They both sighed with relief.

'Callum?' Flin stood up. 'What the hell are you doing?' He walked through to the hall and out of the back door. 'Callum? Where are you?'

His neighbour stumbled round the corner, clutching one hand with the other.

'What are you doing?' said Flin again as Callum, ashen-faced, came into the light. Flin saw his hand was bleeding.

'Sorry, man,' said Callum, 'but it's Wendy. She's locked me out. I was trying to climb the gutter to get back in, but I slipped and cut my hand. Don't have a plaster, do you?'

'Um, sure, probably,' said Flin, 'come on in.'

'Sorry, I couldn't see jack-shite like, so that's why I tapped on the window. It was the only one that was light.'

Tiffany insisted Callum run his hand under the cold tap, before she administered further first aid. The cut was quite deep, but she managed to stop the flow of blood.

'You should take that to the doctor, really,' she told him firmly.

'Ah, well, thanks anyway,' he said, looking suddenly sheepish.

'So what're you going to do now?' asked Flin. 'If Wendy won't let you back in?'

Callum scratched his head. 'Go to the pub?' he said, then, pausing by the back door, added, 'I don't suppose either of you fancy a pint, do you?'

'I won't, thanks, Callum,' said Tiffany quickly, 'but you go if you want, Flin.'

Flin looked at his watch. Just after nine. 'All right,' he said, 'why not?'

Flin drove, and then bought the first drinks, and when Callum said he was just popping round the corner 'to get some fags', feared he might be left high and dry at the bar, with no one to talk to but Keith. But Callum returned, and hoisted himself onto the bar stool next to him.

'Heard the foxes got to your birds,' he said, drawing deeply on his cigarette.

'Yeah,' said Flin. 'When I first got here, everyone kept going on about the foxes. To be honest, I thought they were taking the piss.'

'They probably were,' chuckled Callum, 'but no, seriously, everyone I know has had trouble with the foxes at some time or other.'

'Well, I've reinforced the barn, so hopefully that'll keep them out for a bit.'

They were silent for a moment, and Flin wondered what topic they might turn to next.

'So,' said Callum after both had thoughtfully drunk from their pints, 'reckon you'll be playing any cricket next year?'

Flin smiled. 'Maybe, if I'm asked. I certainly couldn't face playing again this last season.'

'Oh, you'll be asked all right, isn't that so, Keith?'

'What's that?' said Keith, looking up from his half-pint of lager.

'The cricket team – we need good bowlers.'

'Definitely, just so long as he doesn't umpire,' muttered the landlord.

'Ah, bollocks to that,' said Callum, 'you can't talk. This guy, Flin, I tell you, used be the most trigger-happy person around. All it had to do was hit the pad and up would come his finger. Sometimes it didn't even need to do that, did it, Keith?'

Keith gave him a withering look, then silently stared ahead and lit another Lambert and Butler.

'Well, you *were* out when I gave you,' said Flin resolutely.

'Yeah, I know. People get a bit over-excited sometimes. I wouldn't pay any attention.'

'Easy for you to say that,' said Flin feelingly. 'It was my first game for Cotherwick and I was being labelled Public Enemy Number One.'

'Yeah, well,' said Callum, then looked at him keenly. 'You know what?' he said after a moment. 'When you first turned up here, I thought you were a right nonce. But you're all right.'

'You know what?' said Flin in turn. 'When I first got here,

300

I thought you were an anti-social git. But actually you're all right too.'

Callum laughed, then, draining his pint, said, 'Another?'

'Sure,' said Flin, adding, 'Why have you been locked out, by the way?'

'Bloody Wendy,' mumbled Callum. 'She thinks I've been seeing Jane Burroughs again.'

'Have you?'

'Well, yes, but there's no way she could know that. She's accusing me because of something completely different.'

'Oh,' said Flin.

'She'll come round. She always does. Anyway, it's not as if we're actually married or anything.'

'Aren't you? I thought you were.'

'Nah, I don't want to feel tied down. I wouldn't feel so good about seeing all the women I do if I was married.'

'Fair enough,' said Flin, and left it at that.

They drank two more pints, and Callum told him a little more about the people in the village. About Mrs Turner who ran the village shop, and how she still looked the same as she had when he'd been little, but who, it was rumoured, had once had an affair with Willie's father. Flin couldn't wait to tell Tiffany that. Then there was Nigel, the cricket captain, who'd once been inside for a short spell for GBH. Then there was Jim Binyon, who ran the family garage out by the Military Road.

'Their garage opened just after the First World War apparently,' Callum told him. 'Jim's grandfather had been in the Engineers or something in the trenches, then came back and set it up.'

'They still seem to get quite a lot of business,' said Flin.

'I'd never take my car anywhere else. What Jim doesn't know about engines isn't worth knowing.'

'And what about Melvyn?' Flin asked eventually. 'What's the story on him?'

'Melvyn?' said Callum, lighting up once more. 'Melvyn's had it tough. His wife and daughter were killed by a lorry. Not far from Jim Binyon's garage. The girl was learning to drive and was pulling out of the Corbridge Road, and a lorry went smack into them. Both killed instantly.'

'Bloody hell, that's terrible,' said Flin.

'Yeah, it was sad. I can only just remember it. It was when I was little. Least, I remember how shocked everyone was at the time.'

'And he never remarried?'

'No. Just carried on farming and looking after his dogs and sheep and everything.'

'He seems like a good bloke,' said Flin, 'although I don't think he thinks much of us.'

'What, Melvyn? No, he likes you two, he told me. He's pleased you're using the farm again even if you haven't got a clue what you're doing. Actually, I think he likes Tiffany more, though. You should watch him.' They both laughed.

By the time they got back to their houses, Wendy had unlocked the door.

'See?' grinned Callum, pausing in the doorway. 'I told you she always comes round in the end. See you then.'

Flin wandered back to his own house, glad he'd spent the evening with Callum. It was good to know a bit more about the village and to feel he was, at last, beginning to be accepted.

If only his work situation would improve too. Several things had gone wrong recently, starting with a big party he'd been organizing for the launch of a new Tyne Tees documentary series. First of all, the invites had gone out with a glaring typing error. He'd spotted a mistake initially, asked his assistant to get it changed, then failed to notice the reprints had acquired a new one. Unimportant in the scope of things, but embarrassing and unprofessional, as Doug had pointed out to him.

Then the drink hadn't arrived until the very last minute,

prompting pandemonium and frantic uncorking to get everything ready before the first guests arrived. They'd managed it, just, but Doug had said quietly to Flin, 'Couldn't you have sorted this all out a lot earlier?'

'They were massively late delivering everything,' Flin explained.

'All a bit chaotic though, isn't it, especially when added to the invites.'

This would not have mattered had Flin not missed an important meeting two days later. Doug had stormed into his office just after eleven, demanding to know where the hell Flin had been.

'What do you mean?' Flin asked, genuinely perplexed.

'The Northumbrian Wildlife Trust, Flin. The one where you were supposed to be presenting our pitch.'

'But that's tomorrow,' Flin told him, fishing for his diary. But when he opened the right page he saw someone had crossed it out and moved it forward a day. 'No one told me it had changed,' he said. 'I'm really sorry, Doug, but I've had no e-mail about this. And I swear, when I looked at my diary last night, it still said tomorrow.' He knew this sounded unlikely.

Doug, he could see, was furious. 'Jesus, Flin, Katrina said she'd told you in person, as well as putting it in your diary yesterday morning.'

'She said that?' said Flin. 'And you believe her over me?'

'Well, let's go and ask her then,' shouted Doug, storming out of the room.

Flin followed, rage and frustration mounting.

But Katrina was unfazed. 'I told you, Flin, yesterday morning, having changed your diary,' she told him matter-of-factly.

'Come on, Katrina, you know that's not true,' said Flin, desperately trying not to raise his voice.

'I'm sorry, Flin, but it is.' She turned to the fuming Doug. 'Sorry, Doug, I know I should have confirmed by e-mail, but I thought telling Flin and changing his diary would be enough.'

Doug glared at Flin. 'Well, let's hope for your sake we still get this deal,' he said between gritted teeth, then stormed off back to his office.

'You're unbelievable,' said Flin, shaking his head at Katrina.

'You should look at your diary a bit more closely, shouldn't you?' She smiled, then returned to her work.

Ben, responding to a furious e-mail from Flin, suggested he calmly talk through the problem with Doug in a day or so, once his initial anger had subsided. Everyone had work crises at some time or other, he pointed out. He could have come across a Katrina just as easily in London; it was simply unlucky that she was there at his first job in Newcastle.

Tiffany agreed. 'So what happened about the contract?' she asked.

'Luckily, we got it anyway. I got a curt message from Doug later. He's obviously a master at ad-libbing.'

'Things will turn out right, you'll see,' said Tiffany.

'You keep saying that, darling,' said Flin shortly, 'but when? Just when I think nothing else can go wrong, something else does. I'm sick of it.'

But a week later, things did start to improve.

'Ah, Flin,' said Doug, walking into his office one morning. His tone was far friendlier than any he'd used for a while. 'May I have a quick word?'

'Of course,' said Flin.

'I just wanted to apologize really. I know things have been a bit tense recently, but, um, well – I've got a note here from Tyne Tees, thanking us for the "superb work" we did on *Child's Eye View*. And they thought the party a great success too, so it seems I spoke hastily. Good work, Flin.'

Flin nodded. 'Thanks.' Then, after a slight pause, he said, 'Doug, can I ask you about something?'

'Sure. Fire away.'

'It's a slightly delicate matter. About me and Katrina. I didn't really ever want to mention it to you, but we just don't see eye to eye. I've tried to smooth things over but it isn't really working, and I don't know what to do about it. I do see why she should feel a certain amount of resentment, but it's very frustrating.'

Doug rubbed his chin thoughtfully. 'I see.'

'I was thinking of taking her out to lunch,' Flin continued, 'and thrashing out our differences. But I was wondering if you might have a word with her first. Smooth the way.'

'Yes, of course. We don't want you two at loggerheads. You should have mentioned this earlier, Flin.'

'As I said, I wanted to try to sort it out on my own first.'

'Well, yes, I will talk to her. But please, do come to me if anything like this arises again. That's what I'm here for. And, Flin, I want you to know that I think you're doing great work here.'

'Thanks, Doug.' As his boss left the room, Flin felt his confidence soar.

Two days later, he and Katrina sat at a table for two in the Malmaison over-looking the Tyne.

'Look, Katrina, I know you can't stand me, but can't we at least try to work together without me constantly having to look over my shoulder?'

'Course I can stand you,' said Katrina truculently, 'it's not that.'

'So what is it? It's not my fault I came in above you, is it? You should be having it out with Doug, not me.'

'Do you know what it feels like though, to have everyone telling you a job's in the bag, to have your boss saying the same thing in as many words, and then, right at the last minute to be told some hot-shot from London's coming instead? It's bloody humiliating.'

'Yes, I do, actually. Exactly the same thing happened to me once in London. But you know what? When I look back on it now, I'm glad that happened, because otherwise I probably wouldn't have got the jobs I later went on to get. I probably wouldn't be here. And the same will happen to you. You're good at your job, when you're not being a pain in the arse to me, and you will get a promotion or a better job at some point, probably better than this one I've got.'

Katrina looked sheepishly out of the window.

'Come on,' said Flin. 'I'm not that awful. Stop constantly trying to undermine me and we could probably even be friends.'

'All right,' said Katrina eventually. 'You're probably right. And I don't think you're that awful really. But all I saw was some cocky golden boy from London and it pissed me right off.'

'Well, if it's any consolation, I never saw myself in that light. You know, I can help you too. If we work together, properly, we'll get better results, which will then reflect on you.'

Katrina nodded, then held out her hand. 'I still think you're a cocky southerner, but you're right. Let's agree a truce.'

'Thank you,' said Flin, shaking her hand as their food arrived. 'Anyway, Doug wants us working on two big campaigns together, so we're going to have to start getting along.'

'Great. Well, let's really show him then.'

In the weeks that followed, the days grew darker and shorter and noticeably colder, but this didn't bother either Flin or Tiffany. Katrina never actually apologized to him, but her attitude did change, and with it, the atmosphere about the place lightened considerably.

Tiffany was enjoying her job too. Willie and Peter had been distraught to lose her, and although working for them had been no hardship, Flin knew she was relieved to have her career back on track and to be involved with such a stimulating project. Although she had to spend occasional nights away, either interviewing veterans or researching in London and around the country, a lot of the time Iain was happy to allow her to work from home. Even better, Iain had been commissioned to make another history series, this time about soldiers returning from war, and had asked her to stay on in her role as researcher. It meant she would be in work for most of the following year.

Flin usually saw Callum once a week for a drink in the Compasses. After that first drink together, they discovered they had more in common with each other than Flin had supposed. They shared a love of sport and the countryside and that gave them plenty to talk about. Going for a midweek evening pint with a friend had been a ritual from his London days he'd badly missed, and so this new friendship cheered him enormously. Moreover, by becoming friends of sorts with Callum, he began to get to know other villagers better too. Along and around the lanes by their house he also found himself pausing for increasingly lengthy chats with Melvyn whenever they bumped into each other. He liked that too.

Then, just before Christmas, Flin and Tiffany were faced with two big pieces of news that would force them into decisions neither had expected to make. The first came when Flin went down to the estate office to talk about a leak from the roof into one of the spare rooms. He'd been expecting to see Peter, the estate manager, but instead found Willie sitting at a desk with plans of the whole estate stretched out in front of him.

'Ah, Flin, just the fellow,' he said genially, 'how are you, sir?'

'Good, thanks, and you?'

'Pretty damn A-one,' Willie told him. 'Actually got Julia coming up to stay weekend after next. You around?'

'Julia?' said Flin. He hadn't heard from her for a while. 'Think we probably are. It'd be nice to see her.'

'Well, I'll tell her. She's got quite thick with an old mate of mine and the pair of them are coming up. Small world, eh?'

So Julia had found someone new.

'Good for her,' said Flin, meaning it.

Willie turned his attention back to the map. 'Look, here's your fellow,' he said, pointing his finger at Standing Stone Farmhouse. 'Nice little house that. Happy there?'

'Definitely,' said Flin emphatically.

'Good, good. Excellent. Fandabidozey,' said Willie, thoughtfully rubbing his chin.

'So, what are the chances of a white Christmas up here?' said Flin brightly.

'What? Oh yes, I see, very good. Well, it has been known.' He straightened up and his brow creased. 'Look, Flin, how d'you fancy buying the place? The house, barns, fields, the lot.'

'Buy it?' said Flin incredulously.

'Yes. Off me. You see, here's my predicament.' He came round to the front of the desk, folding his arms and propping himself against it. 'A small farm – about two hundred and fifty acres – has come on the market right next door to us. It's pretty good land, to be honest, and I want to buy it. The only thing is, I need to free up a spot of capital to get it. Now, Standing Stone is no good to me from an agricultural point of view. I certainly don't need the sheds and the couple of fields you've got don't make much of a dent. So, if you want it, it's yours, first refusal.'

'First refusal?' repeated Flin, still struggling to come to terms with the shock.

'Yes. It could be your own little island, so to speak. Flinders Island surrounded by the Sea of Powlett.' Willie chuckled at his own joke. 'And because I know I'm putting you in a bit of a tight spot I'll let you have it for one-nine-five if we can shake on it before Christmas. What do you say?'

'Wow,' admitted Flin, 'I mean, I hadn't ever thought –'

'Don't need to tell me now. Obviously you need to talk it through with Tiffany. Big decision and all that. But, you know, think it over and then give me a call and we'll have another little chat. And, Flin?'

'Yes?'

'Must get you over for another day's shooting before the season's out.'

As Flin drove back to the house, his mind raced. They could probably do it if they sold the London flat. They'd bought it nearly three years before for just over a hundred thousand. It was probably worth twice that now. But if they bought now, then they really were committing themselves to staying in Northumberland. Investing in the north would make it harder ever to go back down south. Really, it boiled down to making a decision about their long-term future. It was one thing to plan for the next few years, but this was something much bigger.

He hurried into the house, only to find Tiffany sitting at the table, looking worried.

'What is it?' asked Flin. 'What's the matter, darling?'

'Nothing. Nothing at all,' she said, looking up. 'Um, darling, can we go for a walk somewhere? Take Addy to the Wall or something?'

'Sure, but I've got something to say.'

'What?' she asked.

'This place – the farm, barns and fields. Willie wants to sell it.'

Anger burnt across Tiffany's face. 'What do you mean? He can't! It's our home and we have rights!'

Flin laughed and, sitting down by her, put an arm around her shoulders. 'He wants to sell it to *us*. We could own it ourselves.'

'Us?'

'Yes, us.' He told her everything Willie had said.

'Wow,' said Tiffany.

'That's what I said. But what do you think?'

'I think we need to go on that walk.'

The last time Flin had been on Win Sill, he'd looked out on an inhospitable country, dark and unforgiving. But now, despite it being deep winter, the air was still and clear, and ahead lay uninterrupted views across northern England.

'It's quite a big commitment, isn't it?' said Flin, taking Tiffany's hand. 'But I have to say, I feel much happier here now. We've settled in OK, haven't we? And now you've been offered this job, well, that means –'

'Flin, honey,' said Tiffany, cutting him off, 'before we go any further with this, there's something you need to know.'

Flin stopped, looking her in the eye. 'Tell me.'

'Right.' She sighed. 'Here goes: I'm pregnant.'

Pregnant. She was pregnant. They were going to have a baby. A child. Them. For life.

'Flin?' said Tiffany, her eyes searching his face, pleading with him. Flin clutched his forehead and staggered back a few steps, before leaning over, his hands on his knees.

'Flin?' pleaded Tiffany again. 'Please say something.'

'Just a second,' he gasped. He needed time to adjust himself. Willie's bombshell was one thing, but now this! His life had been so untroubled when he'd woken that morning. He tried to think as calmly as he could. He adored Tiffany, could never think of being with anyone else. That was an important point. Willie was offering the house for sale and they were now about to have a baby. The one, by a strange twist of fate, seemed inextricably linked to the other. He'd always believed fate had brought them to Northumberland in the first place. Wasn't the decision about the house being made for them by the tiny seed of life growing inside Tiffany? He'd never imagined being a father. That was something grown-up people were and he'd never considered himself grown up. But he was thirty now, and it was time he put away such thoughts and accepted he was ready to take the next great step in life.

'Flin, please,' begged Tiffany, 'talk to me!'

Slowly, he looked up. There in front of him stood Tiffany, her tiny body covered by an outsize woollen jumper, her face taut and worried, but lovely. His heart went out to her. In that moment, he knew everything would be all right. Now that his momentary panic attack was over, Flin felt suffused with a deep and dizzying contentment.

'That's wonderful, just wonderful.' He grinned. Tiffany flung her arms around him, laughing and kissing him happily, while Addy joined in the excitement by barking and nibbling at Flin's ankles.

'Tiffany, will you marry me?' asked Flin.

Tiffany laughed. 'If you really want me to. But I thought we'd agreed not to bother.'

'Yes, but you're pregnant now.'

'I love you,' she said, putting her arms around him, 'but let's not worry about getting married just yet.'

'But we'll buy the house then?' Flin said, as Tiffany still clung onto him.

'Yes, please!' said Tiffany.

'And properly make a life for ourselves here?' Flin continued.

'Yes,' said Tiffany, letting go at last, 'I want to, darling. I like it. I like the country, I like the house, I like the job, I like our animals. And I want to stay and bring up our child here.'

'You know,' said Flin as they stood there, arms around each other, 'I had a very unrealistic view about our life up here, didn't I?'

Tiffany laughed into his jumper.

'I thought everything was going to be just perfect right from the word go. But you have to work at it, don't you? Things don't always go exactly to plan.'

Tiffany nodded. 'But that makes things seem even better when they're going right,' she said.

'Very true,' grinned Flin, 'very true indeed.'

CHAPTER TWENTY

Harry

It all began during a weekend in Suffolk. Harry and Jenny had decided to go back for the weekend. They wanted to look around their old haunts, visit a couple of the pubs they used to sit in that summer eleven years before, and find the field with the big oak tree down by the river where they'd once enjoyed a romantic picnic. Jenny also hoped to see her old house and Harry thought it was probably time they visited his parents. Just for one night it might be fun, and at least he'd be able to show Jenny off a bit. He knew his parents would think her wonderful, and anyway, his mother had been itching to meet her again.

Dinner with his parents had been very jolly and Harry felt both glad and proud that his mother and father had so obviously taken to her.

'She's charming,' said Elizabeth as Harry and she took some plates through to the kitchen.

'Isn't she great?' Harry grinned. 'Honestly, Ma, I knew she was the one for me, didn't I?'

'Well, you make sure you hang on to her then,' she told him.

'Of course,' he replied, taken aback, 'I intend to.'

His mother kissed him. 'I'm glad.'

Jenny liked them too. 'They're so lovely, Harry,' she told him

312

later. 'I'd forgotten how laid-back they are. And very sweet together.'

'I know. Do you think we'll be like that when we're their age?'

'I'm sure. Of course, I might be withered and no longer attractive to you by then,' said Jenny, hugging him tightly.

'And you might find me dull and boring,' replied Harry.

'Never, darling,' laughed Jenny. Harry was pleased. He'd wanted his parents to think Jenny as wonderful as he did, and vice versa. Such mutual approval was important.

But the following day, neither of them could help feeling a little disappointed. It was winter, not summer, and the field with the oak by the river was no longer a sweet-smelling meadow, but rather, just a ploughed stretch of land with stodgy furrows of mud replacing the multifarious wild flowers and grasses of their memory. And the oak, which once had provided dappled shade, now stood cold and darkly skeletal against the grey winter sky.

Their favourite pub had changed in the year or so since Harry had last been there. The old landlord had gone and his replacement had irrevocably altered the place from a slightly dark, old-fashioned local drinking hole to a newly refurbished food pub, complete with dried hops and *faux* rural accessories stuck to the walls. Even Jenny's old house seemed much smaller than she remembered. The windows looked tired with cracked and peeling paintwork. The lilac tree to the side had been cut down and the gravel at the front replaced with dark tarmac.

'It doesn't look like my old home at all,' she said despondently. Then the rain began to fall.

Getting back into the Citroën, they looked at each other and decided to head back to London.

'It's even more miserable now the rain's started,' said Harry, starting the car. Neither of them said anything for a short while. The windscreen wipers whirred away, doing their level best to clear the rain.

'Not quite how I remembered,' said Harry at last.

'No,' agreed Jenny. He glanced at her. She looked wistful. For the first time since they'd got back together, an almost palpable black cloud seemed to hover above them.

'Talk to me,' said Harry. 'What's going through your head?'

'Nothing. Sorry,' she said, 'I just found that a bit depressing. Now I don't feel very talkative.'

Harry nodded, and another lengthy silence followed.

'Do we have to have the window open?' said Jenny eventually. 'I'm freezing.'

'Well, if we don't, the windows all steam up and then I can't see anything,' said Harry.

'OK,' sighed Jenny. 'Don't worry.'

'No, I'll put them up, but I might need a bit of help wiping the windscreen.'

The car droned on down the A11 at a steady sixty miles an hour, the light already fading, and with no sign of a let-up in the rain. The car suddenly missed a beat.

'What was that?' said Jenny. 'Didn't sound too good.' It lurched again. Harry said nothing. And again.

'Harry, what's wrong with it?'

'Nothing,' said Harry, irritably.

'Then why is it juddering?'

Harry cursed to himself. The points. It was bound to be the points. This had happened before. The juddering usually grew gradually worse until eventually the car ground to a halt. It was a simple thing really, something he should have learnt how to fix, but he hadn't, and so it would mean calling the AA and either hoping they could fix it, or getting a tow back into town.

'Harry?' said Jenny again. 'What's wrong with it?'

'Um, probably the points,' he told her, wiping the windscreen as the car juddered again.

'Meaning what? Is it serious?'

He told her.

'Great evening for it.'

His annoyance and frustration rising, Harry said in as calm a voice as he could muster, 'We might still make it.'

'Might? What do you mean "might"? Are we going to break down completely?'

'Dunno,' mumbled Harry. Jenny clasped her hand to her head. The juddering grew steadily worse, as did the silence between them. Harry dropped his speed, but two miles from the junction with the M25, he could carry on no further. Switching on the indicator, he pulled onto the hard shoulder and drew to a halt.

'Sorry, Jen,' he said, 'but I'm going to have to call the AA.'

Silently she opened the glove compartment and handed him his mobile.

'How long?' said Jenny, once he'd registered his call.

'An hour, I'm afraid.'

'Fantastic,' said Jenny sarcastically, then added, 'Well, at least I can put the window up now.'

But after an hour there still wasn't any sign of the AA man. Harry phoned again, and was told that, by some bizarre anomaly, his call had never been registered. They were terribly sorry, couldn't understand how it could have happened, but they'd make him a top priority and get someone out to him as soon as they possibly could. Harry cursed, doubly so because he felt edgy about Jenny's mood. Neither said much to the other. Occasionally, as a particularly large lorry roared past, the car would shudder slightly in its wake.

Nearly an hour later, the AA van eventually pulled up behind them. After opening up the bonnet, the man scratched his head and said he didn't think he could help.

'Think it would be best if I organize a tow for you,' he told Harry as they stood by the car getting rained on.

'How long will that take?' asked Harry, exasperation creeping into his voice.

'Not too long. I'll ring through now.'

They sat alone on the hard shoulder for a further three-quarters of an hour, the silence between them deafening.

'Sorry about this, Jen,' said Harry at length. 'Luckily it doesn't happen very often.'

'Let's face it though, Harry, it's not really a winter car, is it? The lights are crap, the windscreen wipers don't work very well, and it's freezing.'

He was about to reply when a huge tow-lorry drew up in front of them, and a large man bounded out of the cab towards them.

'Sorry, been here long?' he asked cheerfully.

'Nearly three hours,' said Harry bitterly.

'One of those days, eh?' The driver grinned. Neither of them replied.

It didn't take long to winch the Citroën onto the lorry. Harry and Jenny sat miserably in the cab while their rescuer tightened the safety straps around the wheels and then at last they were off.

'That's the trouble with these old cars,' said the man as they edged back onto the main road. 'They look very pretty and everything, but are a right bugger when things go wrong.'

'True,' said Harry, 'but fortunately that's not very often. For me, the pros far outweigh the cons.'

The man laughed at this. 'Yes, well, you wouldn't catch me driving a classic. I'll stick with my modern car, I think. May not look too special, but it gets me from A to B every time.'

'Here, here,' said Jenny.

Harry looked at her accusingly, but said nothing. He didn't want to spend the rest of the journey arguing his corner. Right now, he just wanted to be back at home, dry and warm, and to put this little mishap behind them.

But Jenny didn't let the matter go away. Once they eventually made it back, and were sitting down on the sofa with mugs of tea, Harry tried to make light of the situation. 'Ah, well, we're here now. Never mind.'

'I'm sorry, Harry, but that was utterly miserable. Your car may look great, but it's slow, cold and breaks down. I think in future we can use my car for long trips.'

'What do you mean? That was hardly a long trip.'

'Believe me, it was quite long enough. It's no fun driving around in that in mid-winter. And that drive to Cornwall we made. It went on for ever. Can't you sell it and get something a bit more up to date?'

'More up to date?' Harry couldn't believe he was hearing such heresy.

'Yes, you know, something that drives at a decent speed and gets us there too.'

'You don't know what you're suggesting,' he said, standing up.

'Well, really, Harry. I mean, it's not as though you have to prove anything with it. I know cars are a bit of a penis-extension for men, but I love you as you are. If you won't sell it, can we at least use mine a bit more?'

'I think I'm going to go and have a bath,' said Harry, his anger rising.

Lying in the warm water, Harry gazed around at his murals. He'd always found his bathroom relaxing. And it was different, had a little bit of style. Like his car. The Citroën had not been expensive – at least, not really. No more than a half-decent second-hand small Peugeot or Golf. But it *was* unusual, and it did look beautiful. He didn't want to sell it. He didn't *ever* want to sell it. He couldn't understand how Jenny could ask him to do something that she knew would upset him so much. All the time they'd spent whizzing around the country lanes of Cornwall and subsequent weekends in the country, he'd been as happy as could be: in the car he loved, with the girl of his dreams. He'd assumed she'd felt the same. Now it turned out she hadn't. He was over-reacting, he knew, but somehow this revelation affected his memory of those times. He'd thought everything had been

317

perfect. In a way this made him feel a bit foolish, humiliated even. She'd been humouring him, rather than enjoying it too.

'Sorry, Hal,' said Jenny, coming into the bathroom and sitting on the rattan chair in the corner. 'I didn't mean to be horrible about your car. If you want to keep it, then of course you should. It's just that it's been a long day and the breakdown came on top of the disappointments in Suffolk. But I hate the thought of us arguing, so let's be friends again.'

'OK,' said Harry, 'and I'm sorry we've had a bad day. Let's forget it.'

But he couldn't, and, later that evening, he lay in bed wide awake while Jenny slept peacefully next to him, and thought sadly about how the afternoon had signalled a change in their relationship. That had been their first argument; did it mean the first dizzying days of being in love were over?

During the next couple of weeks, further cracks appeared. Jenny was working hard. The school had proved to be tougher and rougher than she'd first thought, and she was having to spend quite a lot of time working late on the next day's classes and keeping up to date with her marking. Initially, she did this at the flat, but then she began staying at school to finish her work.

'I'm going to be late again, I'm afraid, Hal. Sorry, but I'll see you later,' she said one afternoon, catching Harry on his mobile.

'Again? Why don't you do it at home?'

'It's easier at school, that's all,' she told him.

'I don't see why. I've got the computer and desk and everything.'

'Well, if you really want to know, it's because you're too distracting. You play your music too loud and you talk and kiss me and don't let me get on with it. But I won't be too long, I promise.'

Why didn't she say before? And why didn't she just ask him to stop? He would have, happily. Then there were her little habits, which at first he'd never noticed. Like her lateness. Jenny was late for everything. Not hugely so, but he tended to be early, so if they went out together, and she was late, then he'd be late too, which irritated him. Nor was she particularly tidy, whereas his flat had always been immaculate when he'd lived there on his own. Now he would find piles of clothes in the bathroom, or by the bed, and shoes left on the stairs. He could never find the television and video controls, because Jenny had used them and had managed to drop them down the side of the sofa. She always forgot to put the milk back in the fridge, and left half-full mugs wherever she'd last drunk from them.

None of this had mattered one iota at first; he'd been so deliriously head over heels it had been simply impossible to have a care in the world. But now that they were no longer making love every day, and were settling into a calmer day-to-day routine, the sum of these habits began increasingly to annoy him. Worse, it annoyed him that he was annoyed about it.

Then there was the issue of what they would do next. Jenny didn't really want to stay in London, but he did. He liked the capital, and he liked his flat even more.

'But what if we ever have kids? We couldn't bring them up here, could we?' Jenny argued.

'Can't we cross that as and when?' he retorted.

'OK, but I'm just saying I don't want my children growing up in London. I want them to be brought up in the country, and nothing you say will change my mind about that. You know, Harry, I can't help thinking about this, especially now that I've got to apply for a permanent job. I'll stay in London for a bit, but can you at least think about moving to the country?'

Harry dropped the matter, but it bothered him. He'd rather hoped to stay in London for ever. The argument had only been postponed.

His latest job was turning a Chelsea dining room into a glorious striped tent, with hints of sunbathed countryside through gaps in the canvas. But whilst he was painting this new mural, his old tendency to brood began its work once again. Perhaps these differences were irreconcilable. Perhaps his habits were just as annoying to her, in the same way that she disliked his car. Perhaps they'd simply been too busy being in love to have noticed such problems, but now the initial excitement and euphoria had died down, the reality of their situation was becoming apparent. He thought about his parents. Did they have habits that annoyed one another? If they did, he wasn't aware of them.

Harry tried to push these thoughts from his mind and tell himself he was being over-sensitive. So one night he decided he'd cook them a really good supper: a romantic dinner for two. When she rang, she told him she'd probably be home in good time, so he left work a bit early, bought some ingredients on the way, and started creating a three-course feast for them both. Just thinking about it cheered him up no end. Carefully he set the table, agonized over the pastry and shelled the prawns. He needed to feel they were back on track, that was all. A light evening, just the two of them, with lots of laughter and maybe taking her to bed soon after.

By the time Jenny eventually appeared, Harry had long since given up waiting and eaten his meal, his anger and hurt steadily rising with every mouthful.

'Oh Harry, I'm so sorry,' said Jenny, dropping her bag, 'please forgive me. I'm so sorry, I really am. I had no idea this was going to be a special night.' She went over to him and tried to kiss him, but he turned his cheek away.

'Really, it doesn't matter,' he said coldly. 'Anyway, yours is in the kitchen. A bit cold now, I'm afraid.' Then pushing his chair back, he silently left the table and disappeared up to his desk.

After a few minutes, Jenny followed, and stood leaning against the gallery railings behind him.

'Sorry, Harry, I really am. The marking took longer than I thought and then one of the fathers rang and was on the phone for ages. I should have phoned, I know, but I hadn't realized it was so late.' She stopped for a moment, but Harry silently continued sketching. 'Harry, please talk to me. What's happened to us the last couple of weeks?'

'It's simple really,' said Harry. 'We were madly in love, and now we're just settling into the sort of mundane everyday routine all couples do, wherein we argue and get on each other's nerves.'

'What do you mean? What a horrible thing to say,' said Jenny, her voice breaking. 'You think this has all been a terrible mistake, don't you?'

Harry, staring impassively down at his sketch-pad, was still too hurt, confused and upset to know what to say. So he said nothing, just shrugged instead. He heard Jenny quietly walk away without a word.

Neither spoke again that night, or the following morning. Harry deliberately pretended to be asleep while Jenny got up and dressed and didn't venture to the bathroom until he heard the front door shut. A night's sleep hadn't helped his humour, although he wished they'd had a chance to try to make up before they'd gone to bed. But both had been too proud to break the ice. A pile of her clothes lay heaped on the chair in the bathroom. Julia had been neither untidy nor late.

Harry was about to leave for work, his heart still heavy, when the phone rang. For a moment, he thought about leaving it, but then something made him stop by the kitchen and pick it up. Perhaps it would be Jenny.

'Harry?' said the voice. It sounded like his mother, but strangely unlike his mother too.

'Yes?' he said.

'Harry, oh God, your father – Christopher's died. My darling's dead.'

For a moment, Harry remained there, frozen. Life stood still. He still held the handset by his ear, could still hear his mother's grief-stricken sobs. He slid to the floor.

'No, no, it can't be true,' he said. For some reason, he felt out of breath.

'Come, Harry. Come quickly. You've got to help me.'

'I'm coming,' he said. 'I'm coming right now.'

Mechanically, he put down the phone, grabbed a bag of clothes and his wallet and jumped in his car. He felt as though he were drunk, unable to absorb the enormity of this terrible piece of news. His father couldn't really be dead. It simply wasn't possible. Such things didn't happen to his family. They'd been far too happy and perfect all their lives for this to happen now. Tragedy belonged to other people.

He was still in this dazed state of shock when he reached Suffolk. His mother was inconsolable. On seeing him, she simply collapsed in his arms with a terrible outpouring of grief. He'd never seen his mother cry before, let alone gasp in great waves of convulsive sobs. His father had gone to sit down in an armchair after breakfast, and a short while later had died, just like that. His mother had found him sitting there. At first she'd thought he was asleep. But he wasn't. He'd had a heart attack, and was gone. By the time Harry arrived, the ambulance had long since been, leaving his mother broken-hearted and alone in the house.

Not long after he arrived, the doctor called by and gave her a sedative. It would knock her out for while, he told Harry. In the meantime, he should just be with her, try to comfort her as best he could.

Having helped his mother lie down on the sofa, he took up his own position on the armchair opposite. The room had altered so little since he'd been a boy. The wall colours were frequently changed, as were the paintings. As well as his mother being an artist herself, both his parents regularly bought small pieces too. These, plus Elizabeth's own work, were rotated round the house.

The phone rang, but instead of picking it up, he ignored it until the answer machine clicked on and he heard his father's voice on the message tape. Clear, precise, but unreal. Harry could hold back his own tears no longer. The stunned trance that had fuelled him through the day so far suddenly dissolved. He would never hear his father's voice again, never see him sitting at the table in his flat, reading the morning paper. Never again would they go to the local pub together, or sit up long after his mother had gone to bed, drinking a bottle of wine and talking until the early hours. Each day would follow the next, Christmas would come, and a New Year follow, but his father would see none of this. The person he looked up to more than anyone else in the world, the man he loved the most, was dead, gone, for ever. Whatever occurred in his life from now on would have to do so without the guidance of his father.

While his mother continued to sleep, Harry began ringing round his various relations. Most difficult of all was the conversation he had with his sister Charlotte. She was fast asleep when he rang; it was about three in the morning in Sydney. Both broke down, her spontaneous grief reawakening his. So many tears. People sounded so different when they cried. Steve, her husband, called back later. Charlotte would catch a plane back to London later that day. Then his uncle offered to take over the phone duties, and Harry gratefully accepted. He felt exhausted, completely drained. Occasionally, his mind drifted onto other things, before lurching back to the realization that his father was gone. He wandered over the house, the scene of so many good times. Evidence of his father's living being filled every room. Harry found scraps of paper covered in his immaculate handwriting; the latest *Sharpe*, which he'd always so enjoyed, left open on the kitchen table; his wellingtons, still covered in mud from the day before; the answer machine, with the same message repeating itself over and over and over, until Harry could bear it no longer and switched it off. With these reminders, his death seemed even more incomprehensible. How could someone be alive for over seventy years, and then, in one moment, cease to exist? Harry found his grief oppressive, inescapable, a weight that hung around him constantly, shadowing his every thought.

Because of such thoughts, and because he needed to look after his mother once she awoke, he forgot to call Jenny and let her know what had happened. When he did try to ring, it was past nine o'clock at night, and there was no answer at the flat. Panicking, he rang Ben.

'Oh, Harry, I'm sorry, so sorry,' said his friend.

'It's pretty hard, I don't mind telling you,' Harry told him. 'But listen, Ben, has Jenny called?'

'Yeah, about an hour ago. In quite a state, I'm afraid to say. Worried about where you were.'

'Shit,' said Harry, and explained about the argument and forgetting to tell her what had happened.

'I think she might be at her friend Millie's flat,' said Ben.

'Damn. I don't have the number.'

'She'll be all right. She'll have to go back to the flat tomorrow morning even if she doesn't tonight. And Harry? I'm really sorry about your dad. He was a wonderful man. I'll miss him.'

Harry rung off and left another message at the flat. Someone else had been leaving messages there too. Then he put the receiver down, knowing that if he spoke any more, he'd only start crying again. And he didn't want to do that; he wanted to be strong for his mother. Breaking down every two minutes wasn't going to help her.

Harry finally spoke to Jenny first thing the following morning.

'Harry, I'm so sorry. So sorry about your dad, and for our silly argument. I desperately wanted to talk to you last night, but didn't want to disturb you or your mother.'

'I'm sorry too. And for not ringing you earlier, I –'

'Darling, forget it. I understand. I'm here for you, you know.'

'Thanks, Jen. Am I forgiven?'

'Don't be ridiculous. There's nothing to forgive. I can come to you any time you want.'

'It's not good here just at the moment. The shock really. And Ma, you know, she's not good. I'm just so stunned. Can't take it all in.'

'Of course not.'

'I'll call you later. Love you.' He rang off.

That afternoon, the day after his father's death, he and his mother managed to go for a walk. The day was clear, sunny, crisp and fresh.

'Christopher loved days like these,' said his mother. 'He said he always thought winter was earth while as long as there were some cool frosty days in between the grey.'

'Well, he's right,' said Harry, putting an arm round his mother.

'How's Jenny?' she said after a small pause.

'OK.' He told her about the row of two nights before.

'But what on earth were you arguing about?'

'I don't know. Lots of little things evolving into something bigger. I thought she was perfect, the one for me. Lately, I've not been so sure. I certainly love her enough, but there're so many things we differ on. Whenever I look at you and Pa, I always think you have the perfect marriage. You never seemed to argue, you did loads together, had fun, always seemed so happy together. I suppose I think of your marriage as the perfect role model.'

His mother stopped. 'Is that what you really think?' she said, turning to him.

'Yes. I want to be as happy as you two were. Perhaps I'm expecting too much.'

'Harry, sometimes you are a fool,' she said, linking her arm through his. 'Your father and I *were* very happy, of course we were, but if you think we never argued, then you're much mistaken. Especially at the beginning. My God, the rows we had! I should tell you something, something I've never told you before and something I probably never would have. But I do think you should now know. When we were first married I got pregnant, not with Charlotte, but with another baby. I miscarried, but quite late on in my pregnancy. It was horrible. Awful. In those days one didn't have much help or counselling or anything. One was expected just to get on with things. I suppose I became depressed, although I didn't realize it at the time. Reclusive, sullen. Your father found it very difficult – me, the loss of the baby, everything. Harry, he had an affair.'

'Pa? Surely not!' said Harry.

'It's true. It was over almost as soon as it began. I forgave him, and we moved on. Charlotte was born happy and healthy, and then so were you.'

'I can't believe it,' said Harry, 'not Pa, he wasn't like that.'

'I promise you it's true. But the point is, things didn't always go our way. Every marriage, every relationship has its problems. And every person is different. You wouldn't want to marry an exact duplicate of yourself, or at least I hope you wouldn't. If you love Jenny enough, I'm sure she *is* the one for you, regardless of whether she's untidy and sometimes a bit late. Anyway, tastes and habits merge. When we were first married, there were lots of things about your father that used to annoy me, but you change, you evolve together. God knows, Harry, I'm going to miss him more than you will ever know. We *did* have a perfect marriage. I wouldn't change anything, even the lows, because, you see, they made the highs even better. But I think your idea of perfection and mine are a little bit different.'

It surprised him that he didn't feel more upset about his father's infidelity. His mother was having a rest while he made them some supper, and as he chopped and peeled, he thought hard about what she'd said. Certainly, it changed his opinion of how they must have been when they'd been younger. All his life, but especially latterly, he'd put a halo round his parents' marriage, a shining beacon of perfect virtue. Now he saw he'd been wrong. Not only did they have their own problems, they had once suffered a series of catastrophes that would have broken many marriages completely. What a prig he'd been. And naïve too. Thirty years old in a few days' time and he was still trying to live his life according to some false ideals. His mother was right – he *was* a fool. Jenny's tardiness, her messiness – what did that matter? What did that matter *at all*? He chopped harder and harder, faster and faster, then stopped, and banged his head gently against the cupboard in front of him. She'd made him happier than he'd ever been before, but he'd still let himself become sulky and sullen because of the odd disagreement. He'd acted like a spoilt brat. Perversely, it had taken an event as tragic as his father's death for him to realize this.

He desperately wanted to be with her; physically yearned for her. He'd been so blind, but now, finally, everything seemed so clear. She should be with him, the one person he could really, properly talk to. Instead he'd selfishly failed to call her and she'd disappeared. She'd probably assumed he'd walked out. How could she possibly have known what had really happened? Jesus, when he thought about the past couple of days . . . He began to shiver, although it wasn't cold. He held out his hands, watched them shaking in front of his very eyes. Every muscle in his body had tensed. A brief spasm caused him to shudder and drop the knife. He felt very bleak and heavy, as though something, someone, was pushing down on his head and shoulders, pushing him into the ground, to a darkness that excluded all light, a barren wasteland where there was no hope, no joy. He dropped to his knees, overwhelmed with despair.

The ringing brought him to his senses. The telephone. He stood up and staggered into the hall.

'Harry? Sorry, I know you said you'd ring me, but I just wanted to know how you were.' God, it was good to hear her voice.

'Jenny? I love you so much, Jen. Please come here as soon as you can.'

'Of course I will. I'll jump in the car now. Are you sure though? What about your mother?'

'No, I need you here. As soon as possible. I'm sorry I've been so awful the past couple of weeks. I don't know why. I must have been mad.'

'I've been awful too.'

'I just want you to be with me.'

'I'll come now. And Harry? I love you.'

Four days later, with Jenny by his side, Harry watched his father's coffin being lowered into the ground. On his left stood his mother, dignified and brave. Next to her, his sister Charlotte. The wooden casket looked so impersonal somehow and Harry found it impossible to believe his father's body lay within it, soon to be covered by a mountain of loose soil. So this was goodbye. Farewell to a father who'd be in his thoughts for the remainder of his life. The man who had taught him so much, but who still had one lesson to teach him even after he'd gone. Jenny tightened her hand around his arm. He would miss him sorely.

christening

Spring was very definitely in the air. As the little ensemble walked back up the road from the church, Ben looked down at his newly christened son and saw him squinting in the bright sunlight. Lucie, demure in a long dress and jacket, tightened her fingers around his hand.

'Wasn't he well behaved?' she said, grinning at her husband.

'A model child,' agreed Ben. He turned his head and looked back at the rest of the party. His father, talking with Harry and Jenny, Flin and Tiffany further behind with Vanessa and Susie, and then Jessica, now back from New York for good. A small, intimate party, just as they'd originally planned.

Inside the house, their sitting room was full of daffodils. Sunlight poured through the bay window.

'The last Sunday I was here, it poured with rain,' said Flin.

'That was almost exactly a year ago,' said Lucie. 'We watched *Rebecca*.'

'And Flin saw the picture of the house in Northumberland,' said Tiffany. Although five months pregnant, her growing bulge was barely noticeable. 'Just think, if we hadn't come here that day, we might never have ended up there.'

'I seem to remember I made a particularly fine Sunday roast,' said Lucie.

329

'Things have never been quite the same since,' called Ben from the kitchen, grinning. He stood by the fridge, opening a couple of bottles of champagne, and watched his son crawl with fearsome speed towards him.

This was what it was all about, he thought to himself. He felt so proud of Thomas and Lucie. She looked so gorgeous, and so did Thomas, with his flushed little cheeks and dark, soft hair. How rewarding fatherhood could be – far more so than he'd ever imagined. Now that Thomas was crawling and responsive, he felt so much more involved, somehow. And now a second was on the way. He wished he could tell everyone, but Lucie had sworn him to secrecy.

Flin was finding it hard not to worry about the chickens and geese, but had spent all the previous weekend going round reinforcing the barn. He told Tiffany he defied any fox to be able to get through his defences, but even so a nagging doubt tugged at his mind. And it wasn't just Tiffany who was expecting. Number One was pregnant too. Soon they would have little piglets scurrying around the sty. He couldn't wait. Melvyn had promised to come and lend a hand once they were born – show him what to do and what not to do – so he was fairly confident all would be well. He sidled over to Jessica, glad she was back for good at last.

'So when are you going to come up and see us?' he asked her as Ben handed round the glasses of champagne.

'Soon, darling, I promise, although I'd quite like it to be a bit warmer first.'

'Come and see the piglets,' he said, 'and everything bursting with spring. It's lovely.'

'All right. You are funny. Somehow, I thought the whole farming thing would have gone off the boil by now.'

'Absolutely not. Tiff's even got into growing vegetables too. It's all very healthy, so you should be encouraging me.'

'Darling, I'm full of admiration, it's just that I hadn't expected you to stick with it.'

Flin laughed. 'Well, we have.' He put his arm round Tiffany. 'Still, it's great to be down here and to see everyone.'

Harry was proudly showing everyone Jenny's ring. 'And the great thing is, she really likes it this time,' he told Ben.

'Harry, shut up!' said Jenny indignantly. 'Really, Ben, he's so rude sometimes.'

'So the next time we're all together will be your wedding, I suppose,' Ben said.

'Probably will be. Working on your speech yet?' Harry asked him.

'Don't you worry. I've got enough material to keep everyone amused for hours.'

Flin wandered over, and Ben took him out into the garden, clutching a bottle in one hand.

'Did you see Julia's got engaged?' he said.

'I did actually. Harry's quite relieved. Do you ever see her?'

'Occasionally. She's our old landlord's cousin and her fiancé's his oldest friend.'

'Small world,' said Ben.

'That's what her cousin said.' Flin sat down. 'So what's the latest on the promotion, Ben?' he asked.

'I'm not sure. I think it will be fine. Carl's definitely going back to New York, so it's just a question of whether I get his job, or they bring in someone else. He's certainly hinting pretty heavily that it's going to be me, but I'm trying not to get my hopes up too much.'

'Would it be more work?'

'Already is. There's no way round it. It's long hours or don't bother.'

'Rather you than me.'

'Yeah, well. I've thought about this long and hard. I thought I could have everything: a good job and still be back at home every night to tuck my son up in bed. I wish it was the case, but I chose

331

this job, and it does allow us to live well and Lucie to stay at home. At least there's always one of us with Thomas. I'd be stupid to bite off the hand that's feeding us. Anyway, it goes in fits and starts. I probably work longer hours than most, but not all the time.'

'Well, as long as you're happy,' said Flin, patting him on the back.

'That's what I think, and I am. Very.' Ben smiled.

'It takes a while to adjust though, don't you think?' Flin said. 'To work out what it is you really want. It's been quite a shock realizing I'm at the Next Stage In My Life. But now I'm there, and I've acclimatized, I couldn't be happier. In fact, I don't think I've ever been happier.'

Ben grinned, and chinked Flin's glass.

'Good to see you, Flin.'

Later, Harry and Jenny walked back towards home, across Clapham Common, arm-in-arm.

'That was lovely,' said Jenny, 'really good fun.'

'Wasn't it?' agreed Harry. 'Everyone seems to be OK, to have sorted their lives out, haven't they?'

'Including us.'

'Yes,' grinned Harry. 'Including us.'

The sun was beginning to set, but above them the sky was still clear.

'Look,' said Jenny, 'look at the moon. Up already. It's almost full. Almost perfect.'

Harry stopped and looked. 'Yes,' he said, 'an almost perfect moon.'

the end

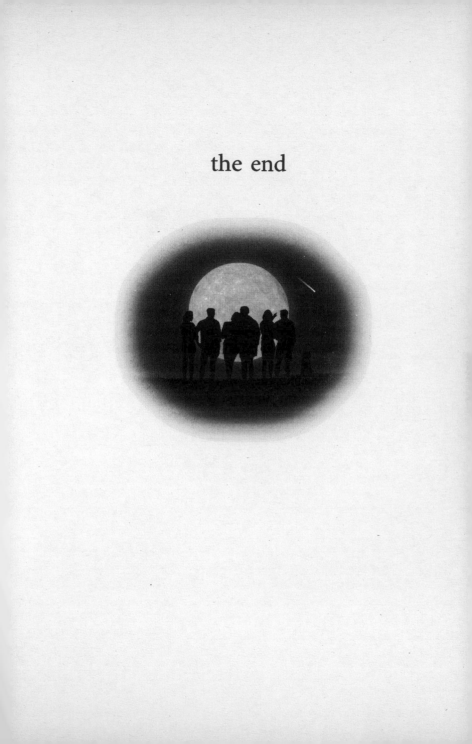

Also by Jamie Holland

One Thing Leads to Another

Flin, Geordie and Jessica, the best of friends, are about to move into their first house. But now in their mid-twenties, has life somehow lost its zest? A few years into their careers, work is no longer quite so interesting. And when are they ever going to have a real relationship?

And so a pact is made. One year on, as the lease on the house runs out, they all have to have moved on in life, with better jobs and love lives blooming. The race is on.

As each season unfolds, the competition has its peaks and troughs – themed parties and office romances (women), rugby matches and stag parties (men), romantic holidays in Italy (disastrous), weekends in Cornwall (even worse), first babies, first weddings, first funeral and a humiliating lost catch.

And the winner is . . .

One Thing Leads to Another is an enchanting story about that time before one quite faces all those serious words like commitment, responsibilities and career. Full of warmth and humour, it is a perfect read for all those lovers of *Four Weddings and a Funeral*.

'Absolutely pukka – how long do we have to wait for seconds?'
Jamie Oliver